IT ENDS IN FIRE

IT ENDS IN FIRE

ANDREW SHVARTS

JIMMY Patterson Books
Little, Brown and Company
New York Boston

JIMMY Patterson Books / Little, Brown and Company
Hachette Book Group
1290 Avenue of the Americas, New York, NY 10104
JamesPatterson.com

Originally published in hardcover and ebook by Little, Brown and Company in July 2021
First Trade Paperback Edition: June 2022

JIMMY Patterson Books is an imprint of Little, Brown and Company, a division of Hachette Book Group, Inc. The Little, Brown name and logo are trademarks of Hachette Book Group, Inc. The JIMMY Patterson Books® name and logo are trademarks of JBP Business, LLC.

The publisher is not responsible for websites (or their content) that are not owned by the publisher.

The Library of Congress has cataloged the hardcover edition as follows:
Names: Shvarts, Andrew, author.
Title: It ends in fire / Andrew Shvarts.
Description: First edition. | New York : Jimmy Patterson Books/Little, Brown and Company, 2021. | Audience: Ages 14 & up. | Summary: Raised by an underground rebel group after the murder of her parents, seventeen-year-old Alka goes undercover at the most prestigious school of magic in an attempt to recruit for the rebellion and win the Great Game, which would give her access to the seat of her enemies' power.
Identifiers: LCCN 2021008999 | ISBN 9781368057950 (hardcover) | ISBN 9780759555990 (ebook)
Subjects: CYAC: Magic—Fiction. | Revolutions—Fiction. | Social classes—Fiction. | Schools—Fiction. | Fantasy.
Classification: LCC PZ7.1.S5185 It 2021 | DDC [Fic]—dc23
LC record available at https://lccn.loc.gov/2021008999

ISBNs: 978-0-316-38144-4 (pbk.), 978-0-7595-5599-0 (ebook)

Printed in the United States of America

LSC-C

Printing 1, 2022

To my parents, Anya and Simon, for raising me to be skeptical of institutions, and to always find my own path

JIMMY Patterson Books for Young Adult Readers

James Patterson Presents

Stalking Jack the Ripper by Kerri Maniscalco
Hunting Prince Dracula by Kerri Maniscalco
Escaping from Houdini by Kerri Maniscalco
Becoming the Dark Prince by Kerri Maniscalco
Capturing the Devil by Kerri Maniscalco
Kingdom of the Wicked by Kerri Maniscalco
Kingdom of the Cursed by Kerri Maniscalco
Gunslinger Girl by Lyndsay Ely
Twelve Steps to Normal by Farrah Penn
Campfire by Shawn Sarles
When We Were Lost by Kevin Wignall
Swipe Right for Murder by Derek Milman
Once & Future by A. R. Capetta and Cory McCarthy
Sword in the Stars by A. R. Capetta and Cory McCarthy
Girls of Paper and Fire by Natasha Ngan
Girls of Storm and Shadow by Natasha Ngan
Girls of Fate and Fury by Natasha Ngan
You're Next by Kylie Schachte
Daughter of Sparta by Claire M. Andrews
Tides of Mutiny by Rebecca Rode
Freewater by Amina Luqman Dawson
Hopepunk by Preston Norton

Confessions

Confessions of a Murder Suspect
Confessions: The Private School Murders
Confessions: The Paris Mysteries
Confessions: The Murder of an Angel

Crazy House

Crazy House
The Fall of Crazy House

Maximum Ride

The Angel Experiment
School's Out—Forever
Saving the World and Other Extreme Sports
The Final Warning
MAX
FANG
ANGEL
Nevermore
Maximum Ride Forever
Hawk
City of the Dead

Witch & Wizard

Witch & Wizard
The Gift
The Fire
The Kiss
The Lost

Cradle and All

First Love

Homeroom Diaries

Med Head

Sophia, Princess Among Beasts

The Injustice

For exclusives, trailers, and other information, visit JamesPatterson.com.

IT ENDS IN FIRE

CHAPTER 1

Now

It's half past noon and there's no sign of the wagon, so the bandits are all starting to get restless. I am, too. For the last two hours we've been sitting crouched in the undergrowth of Dunraven Forest, hidden among the tall ferns just off the dirt highway. It's a nice enough day: sunlight streams through the canopy of the towering oaks, and somewhere nearby a redbird is singing its jaunty tune. But my calves hurt, my back's sore, and if this wagon doesn't show soon, I'm in for a world of trouble.

"Getting late, Alka," Drell says. He's the leader of the bandits, a burly bruiser with a mouthful of gold teeth and a tattoo of a skull on the back of his bald head. I spent a solid week casing the taverns of New Finley, sizing up all the cutthroats and lowlifes, before I settled on him. Drell acts gruff and smells like sour beer, but he's not all that bad for a highwayman. He thinks things through, listens when I talk, and hasn't made even a single advance on me. "You sure your tip was good?"

"I am," I say, even though I very much am not. Whispers said the carriage would pass through in the morning, and here we are edging into the afternoon.

"All right." Drell rests his hairy hand on the pommel of the cutlass sheathed at his hip. "I hope so. I like you plenty, Alka, but the boys aren't going to be happy if you wasted their time."

"The boys" are precisely what I'm worried about. Doing a job like this meant putting together a team. There's Leland, lanky and pale, scowling my way as he holds his crossbow; Phaes, a scarred Sithartic mercenary with a bandolier of knives around his chest; and Griggs, a hulking Velkschen who carries a giant axe.

I could probably kill them all, if it came down to it. But I'd rather not put that to the test.

Leland breaks the tension with a sharp inhale. "It's coming," he growls, and nocks his crossbow. "Positions."

Thank the Gods, he's right. I can hear it now, the clip-clop of hooves, the crunch of wagon wheels on dirt. We all hunker down, holding our breath, drawing our weapons. Well, they draw their weapons. I don't have any, not that they can see. As far as Drell and his boys know, I'm just a traveling grifter with a lead on a job, a tavern flirt looking for a bit of gold.

They have no idea what I'm capable of.

The trees by the roadside rustle as the wagon rolls into view. It's fancy, all right, an ornate wooden carriage with a rounded roof and gilded wheels, pulled by two stocky, spotted horses. A coachman sits at the front of the wagon, his face hidden behind a wide-brimmed hat, and the sword at his side says he doubles as a bodyguard. The windows are shuttered so I can't see inside, but the seal on the wagon's side tells me everything I need: a growling tiger framed against a red sun. The Dewinter family crest. My target.

Drell shoots me a nod. It's time. I take one deep breath, collecting myself, and then I push through the ferns, right into the road. "Help!" I yell, throwing up my hands. "Please, sir! Help!"

The coachman jerks the reins, and his horses rear back as the carriage skids to a hard stop. "Gods!" he snarls. "Who the hell are you?"

"Please," I sob, actual tears running down my cheeks, and it's quite a convincing performance, if I may say so myself. "You have to help me. My family was set upon by outlaws just up the trail. I barely got away. They're all . . . they're all . . ." I collapse to my knees, blocking the wagon's path, and I can see, just barely, my bandits creeping around the wagon, sliding into position. "Oh, Gods! They're all dead."

The coachman cocks a skeptical eyebrow my way. I can practically see the gears in his head whirring as he sizes me up. I'm seventeen, but I look younger, standing a little over five feet. My dark brown hair hangs tousled around my shoulders, and I'm wearing a long rose dress with frilly sleeves, the hem caked in mud and torn along the sides.

It's not enough. "Sorry, girlie," the coachman says with a shrug. "I'm on business. You want a constable, follow the road to New Finley."

"That's at least a day away!" I plead. "Please, sir. I beg you! Have mercy!"

"Mercy doesn't pay for ale," he sneers. "Now move out of the way, before I—" but he never gets to finish the sentence because Phaes leans around the side of the wagon, pressing the edge of a dagger to the underside of the coachman's throat. The coachman startles back, his hand darting toward his sword, but Phaes stops him by pressing the blade up, drawing a trickle of blood as it cuts into the soft stubbly flesh of his neck. "Wouldn't do that," Phaes says. "Not if you value your life."

The other bandits emerge around us: Leland with his crossbow leveled, Griggs with his axe unsheathed, Drell pacing confidently up the road. The coachman's eyes flit around, and he's not looking anywhere near as worried as I'd like. "This is a robbery, friend," Drell calls out. "Play along and no one gets hurt."

I rise to my feet, brushing away my tears with the back of my hand, and the coachman snarls at me with a scowl so deep it could cut stone. "You're making a mistake," he says. "A grave mistake."

Leland tugs on the wagon's door, and it doesn't budge. "Locked."

"Hand over the keys, friend," Drell says. His voice is calm, gentle, even as it's clear he means business. "We want your goods, not your life."

I'd hoped the coachman would make this easy, but he's not budging, which is impressive for a man with blood trickling down his neck. "My goods," he repeats, shaking his head. "You have no idea what's in here, do you?"

Leland jerks the handle again, just as uselessly, and now Drell finally draws his sword. It's an expensive curved cutlass from the Kindrali Isles, its blade shining gold in the wan light. "I know you've got one last chance to open it," he says. "And then it gets ugly."

The coachman's bleary eyes narrow. "Now you listen to me. I am in the employ of General Grayson Dewinter, his line recognized by the Senate. His daughter is in this carriage. His *Wizard* daughter. Do you understand what that means, you pissants? Do you have any idea what'll happen to you if you don't let us go?"

The bandits glance at me uneasily. "What's he talking about?" Leland hisses.

"He's lying," I say, but my voice chokes up for a moment. "It's a bluff. The only thing in that wagon is sacks of gold."

"A bunch of Humbles killing a Wizard? The Senate will never let this go," the coachman continues. "They'll hunt you wherever you hide. They'll flay the skin from your bones. They'll kill your wives, your mothers, your children. This is your last chance."

"No, this is *your* last chance," Drell commands. He understands, even if the other bandits don't. It doesn't matter what's true at this point. We're in too deep to turn back. "Griggs. Break the door down."

Griggs lets out a grunt of approval and steps forward, pushing Leland out of the way. He hefts his axe back, ready to bring it down in a massive chop.

Then I feel it. A chill in the air, unnatural for a midsummer day. A buzzing sound, like a swarm of locusts. And the carriage grows darker, like the light around it is dimming, like it's cloaking itself in shadow. The others don't see it, but I do, and my stomach plunges.

Gathering magic. A coming storm.

Everything goes to hell.

A thunderclap booms from within the carriage and the whole side of it explodes outward, shattering into a wave of jagged shards that tear Griggs into bloody scraps. His axe flies back into the brush, useless, and his body, what's left of it, hits the trees with a wet splat. Dust floods the air, blinding and stinging. The force of the blast knocks me to my knees, hurls Drell into the woods, and sends Leland staggering, fumbling for his crossbow. There's movement from inside the ruined carriage, a glimmer of light, the sound of scraping metal, and a hot black streak cuts through the air impossibly fast. One moment Leland's head is on his shoulders. The next, it's bouncing away into the brush.

"Stand down!" a man shrieks, his voice cracking with fear. It's Phaes, and he's in the middle of the road, holding the coachman in front of him like a shield, his dagger still pressed against the man's throat. "Stand down or your man dies!"

There's a moment of silence, long and tense, and then a figure emerges from the side of the carriage. I can make her out now as the dust clears. Lady Alayne Valencia Dewinter. We've never met. She has no idea who I am. But I know all about her. For the past three years, she's all I've thought about, her name dancing through my head as I've fallen asleep every night. Alayne Dewinter, Alayne Dewinter, Alayne Dewinter.

Alayne is a girl my age in a long blue gown, her long brown hair running down her back in beautifully interwoven braids, a gold necklace with a massive ruby glinting at the base of her neck. She's deep in the Null: her eyes are a sheer black, dark as the night sky, glistening with dozens of dancing points of light like fireflies. Phaes and the coachman are staring at her face, but I'm looking right at her hands, sizing up the Loci in her grips. Wands, matching, one in each hand. Blackwood by the look of them, with sharpened ivory tips and leather grips. Expensive. Professional. Powerful.

My heart is thundering against my ribs, and my breath is caught in my throat. Alayne was supposed to be an untrained novice who's never even held a Loci. And yet here she is, carving battle Glyphs.

"I mean it!" Phaes repeats, shoving the coachman forward. "Drop those wands, or your man here dies!"

"Please, m'lady," the coachman pleads, and now, *now*, he looks scared. "I had your back, didn't I? I did as I was told? I'm on your side!"

Alayne's lips twist up in a cruel smirk, and just like that, the coachman's fate is sealed. He might well be on her side. But in the end, he's just another disposable Humble, and she's a Wizard having a bad day. Her hands fly up, imperceptibly fast, a precise jagged blur as she carves a Glyph into the air in front of her. The coachman barely has time to scream before a lance of cragged stone shoots out from the ground at his feet, plunging into his chest, out his back, and into Phaes behind him. The two men stand there, stunned, gasping, and then the lance explodes, leaving nothing of them but dust and a fine red mist.

Alayne's shimmering nightscape eyes flit to me. I lean back on my hands, pressing them up against my lower back, sliding them under my gown, toward the leather band around my waist, toward its hidden sheaths. My palms find two hilts and close tight. I've got one shot at this, one chance to get out of this alive. Alayne cocks her head to the side, studying me like an insect. And as badly as I want to strike, as badly as my whole body is screaming *fight!*, as badly as my forearm is tingling, pulsing, burning, I know I have to wait and let her move first.

Alayne's left arm jerks up, raising a Loci.

Now.

I let out a roar, lunge to my feet, and whip my hands out, unsheathing two short knives, carved from bone, their edges razor sharp, their handles pulsing with magic. My Loci aren't as fancy as Alayne's, but they'll do the trick.

I slip into the Null.

The world melts away around me, and time slows to a crawl. The bright green of the forest, the blue sky overhead, the crimson blood splattering the trees, all of it fades into a gray haze, like the scene around us has been lost in fog. Black ash flits through the air like falling snow. There is no sound in the Null save the thundering of my heart and the deafening roar of magic. For one moment, one lingering, vital moment, everything else disappears. There's just me and Alayne, facing off.

I see her eyes widen with shock as she realizes what I am, but it's too late. She's already carved the first two lines of her Glyph, and they hover in the air at the end of her left Loci, spectral and elegant and the brightest red. A long line slashed down at a forty-five-degree angle, bisected at the halfway point by a vertical cut. Fire Base. And judging by the way she's raising her right Loci, the turn of her wrist, I'm guessing she's going to circle it for the second form, making it a single blazing blast.

It's a basic attack Glyph. The kind you'd use when slaughtering a defenseless, cowering Humble. Definitely not what you want against another Wizard. But it's too late for Alayne. She's already started cutting that Glyph, and if she stops now, it'll blow up in her face. An expert Wizard could redirect, maybe, find another form off that base, but Alayne's nowhere near that good. So even though she knows it won't work, even though she knows she's doomed, all Alayne can do is lift up her right hand and finish it off.

The Null throbs around us, smoky and dark. I whip up my Loci, and with those two bone knives I carve my own attack Glyph into the air in front of me, my blades sinking deep into the skin of the world. A three-stroke triangle for an Ice Base, and a crosshatched hexagon around it for a solid block second form. It's more complicated than Alayne's, but it doesn't matter, because in the Null time moves slowly and in favor of the defender. Alayne's ball of flame is already forming in front of her, the air around it wavering in the heat, but before it can get to me, I close the hexagon and my Glyph is finished, a perfect shield of blue ice hanging in the air, spinning like a coin.

I blink, pulling back into the Real. Color and sound come back in a flash, as does the rush of time. Alayne's fireball streaks toward me like a meteor, but my ice shield surges to meet it, leaving trails of sparkling frost in the dirt below. Ice meets fire, and ice wins; the fireball dissolves midair into steam. And my shield hurtles past it, a battering ram of glowing blue that can't be stopped. Alayne lets out the tiniest shriek as it hits her, and then it passes through her, into her. Her skin turns blue as her blood freezes in her veins. Frost crackles in her hair. Her terrified expression stays stuck, even as her eyes go glassy and her breath freezes on her lips.

The shield's mostly dissipated on impact, but a few streaks of ice go whistling off into the forest beyond, shattering against trees and freezing through the brush. Alayne stands there for a moment, a statue, and then topples over and lies still, her Loci still trapped in her icy grip.

I let out my breath in a gasp, collapsing onto my knees. My whole body is quivering. My left sleeve's been jerked up, and the Godsmark on my forearm is blazing. It hurts, hurts so much, like my whole arm is full of ice, which I guess in a way it was.

It hits me in a rush. I won. I actually won. Alayne's not the first person I've killed, but she's the first I've killed like this, the first Wizard, head-to-head, Glyph against Glyph. My first real duel with another Wizard, and I won, walking away without a scratch. I let out a wild noise, somewhere between a laugh and a gasp, and I feel the hot glow of pride swell in my chest. Gods be damned, I actually *won*.

Then I hear a metal click from behind me. It's Drell. He's pulled himself out of the brush, a bleeding scratch on his cheek. He's also picked up

Leland's crossbow, which he's aiming right at me. And he is very much not laughing.

"She was a Wizard," he says, staring at Alayne's body. His voice is flat, stunned, and I can see the crossbow just barely trembling. "She was a Wizard. And you killed her."

"Yes. I did. I saved our lives." I try my hardest to sound calm and friendly, even as my eyes fixate on the point of his crossbow's bolt. "Relax, Drell. Put the crossbow down."

"And you... you're a Wizard, too," he says. "What the hell have you gotten me into?"

"Easy, Drell," I say, and even though I don't want to hurt him, my hands are tightening around my Loci. "Listen to me. This is all part of the plan. This is going to be taken care of. No one is going to know you had anything to do with this."

" 'Part of the plan?' " he repeats. "You knew about this all along, didn't you? You set this up!" That flat, stunned affect is gone. There's anger now and a surprising amount of hurt. "You're one of *them*! A Revenant! A godsdamned rebel!"

"Drell, please," I beg, and I really don't want to hurt him. He's a decent man, for a bandit anyway, and it's my fault he's out here at all. "Put the crossbow down, and I'll explain everything. We can both walk away from this."

"No." His face curls into a scowl. "Not you."

He pulls the trigger, and I slip into the Null.

Time slows here, but it doesn't stop. I can see the twang of the string in Drell's crossbow as he fires, can see the bolt leave the shaft and come flying toward me. It's moving ever so slowly, like it's underwater, but it'll still hit me in twenty seconds, thirty at best. I whip my knives up and carve the simplest Glyph I can: four notches for a Wind Base, surrounded by a Circle Form for a push. It throbs a faint white, enough for me to see through the ashy haze and make out the look of utter hatred on Drell's face.

I snap back to the Real. A gust of wind bellows out from me, a forceful, focused blast. It's enough to stop the bolt in midair and send it whistling harmlessly away. It's enough to rip apart the crossbow. And it's enough to lift Drell off his feet and send him hurtling backward into a tree, where his bald head hits the trunk with a loud, awful crack.

Shit.

He lies slumped against the base of the tree, feet twitching, his gray eyes wide and his lip trembling. There's a long streak of blood running down the trunk to the back of his head, which is cracked like a saucer that was slammed down a little too hard. He's still alive, but he won't be for long.

"Oh, Drell," I say, pacing over to him. His eyes flit up to me, practically popping out of his head, and I can see him straining to talk, to will his body to work, to force his lips to move. Is he begging for mercy? Or is he threatening me, insulting me, cursing my name? If his hands could move, would he wrap them around my throat?

Doesn't matter, I suppose. Either way, he deserves better. With a weary sigh, I hunker down next to him and slip into the Null to carve one last Glyph, a circle for life with a crescent around it. Then I snap back to the Real and blow with my lips, just the tiniest bit. The Glyph dissolves into dust, sparkling green dust that dazzles like stars and floats gently across Drell's face, washing over him, sinking into him.

It's a Glyph used to help children fall asleep, to give a moment of tranquility and calm. Drell's chest heaves as he draws a deep breath, and his eyes droop shut. His head slumps sideways onto his shoulder, and he lies there, still, at peace.

A gentle death. It's the least I could do.

With a deep swallow, I rise back to my feet and turn away. I can't afford to feel sad for him, can't afford to feel anything. Not now, not when I'm this close. I shut my eyes, breathe once, twice, three times, and bury all that feeling deep down.

We're at war, Whispers would say. *And all wars have casualties.*

Right, then. Back to the mission. With everyone dead, I have a little more time than I'd planned, but sooner or later someone else will come riding up the trail. I make my way back to the carriage, to Alayne's frozen corpse. It's the first chance I get to take a really good look at her, and I understand why she was the target Whispers picked. We definitely look alike. My skin's a shade darker than hers, a light tan from my Izachi mother, and her eyes were a pale brown while mine are a sharp green. But we've got the same lean features, the same sharp chin, the same smattering of dark freckles. We could pass for sisters, easily. Could have, anyway.

I step over her and lean into the broken hole in the side of the carriage. There's still one thing I need before I burn this whole clearing to the ground. Alayne's suitcase rests on the cushioned seat where she'd been sitting, and I crack it open. There are clothes... books... a few elegant jewels... and...

There it is. On the bottom. A crisp envelope, expensive looking, with elegant script on the front and a glowing wax seal. The seal's already been cracked, of course, so I flip it open and pull the letter out. The paper has an image at the top, a towering castle framed against a full moon, with five symbols around it: a crown, a sword, a quill, a chalice, and a scale. But my eyes flit to the text below.

Lady Alayne Dewinter,

It is my great honor to invite you to attend the Blackwater Academy of Magic for our upcoming term in the Fall of 798. All uniforms and materials will be provided, though you may bring your own Loci. If you wish to attend this term, please meet us on Autumnal 9th at the Lauderdale Docks, and provide this letter to gain admission to the ferry.

Your family has earned a place within our esteemed halls, Lady Dewinter, and I greatly look forward to making your acquaintance.

Yours sincerely,
Headmaster Magnus Aberdeen

My hands are actually shaking. This is what it was all for. Ten years of training. Ten years of blood and sweat and pain. So many lives taken. So much given up, so much lost, all for this moment.

Blackwater Academy is the most elite school of magic in the Republic of Marovia. Any Wizard who's anybody graduated from its halls. Senators, generals, and high clerics, the wisest scholars and the most powerful leaders, the nobles who've made the world such a godsdamned mess. Blackwater Academy is the true seat of power in the Republic, maybe in the world, where entire generations are molded into a powerful, unbending, uncompromising aristocracy. Blackwater Academy is where Wizards are made.

And I'm coming for every last one of them.

Chapter 2

Then

I am seven years old on the last good day of my life.

I'm living with my family in Laroc, a small coastal town on the Republic's western coast. It smells like fish, and the shops don't carry plums, but I like Laroc, at least more than the last few places we've lived; it's better than New Seylem, with its dark, scary slums, and Washburn with its surly miners and sulfur reek. In Laroc, we have a nice first-floor apartment by the town's edge, close enough to the ocean that I can smell the salt in the air when I stand by the window. It's small but snug, and I have a shelf full of carved animals, and I get to sleep on my own little cot by the foot of my parents' bed. It's the best home I've ever had.

Even at seven, I know there are things I'm not supposed to question. There are the protective wards all over the walls, spiderwebs of red string adorned with multicolored crystals. There's my father's job, which requires him to vanish for days at a time, a job of utmost importance that no one will explain to me. There's the heavy wooden chest under the bed, the one with the shifting lock that hurts my eyes to look at. And there's the Mark on my forearm, the Mark just like my father's, the Mark I have to keep hidden, forever, no matter what.

On that day, that last good day, I wake up just a little after sunrise to the smell of breakfast. My mother's still asleep, curled onto her side in her bed, and my little sister, Sera, is sleeping next to her, snoring with her mouth open wide. My father is up, though, standing in the kitchen, and he's laying out all my favorites on our little round table: a wooden bowl of olives, a tin cup of milk, and, best of all, some scones from the bakery down the street, the sugar-glazed kind filled with chopped apples. I run over to eat, still in my nightgown, and my father laughs at the sight of me shoving the entire scone into my mouth.

"You really like that one, Monkey?" he says, grabbing a cup for coffee. He's a south Marovian, with pale skin, messy red hair, and a smattering of freckles across his pointy nose. He's short, like me, a good half a head shorter than most men, and he wears a delicate pair of golden spectacles over his sharp green eyes that instantly mark him as a scholar. "I always preferred the blueberry ones."

"Apple's the best, and everyone knows it," I reply, spitting chunks of scone everywhere. My father just smiles and shakes his head, turning back to the kettle resting on our stovetop. He sets the cup down and picks up his Loci, slim greenwood wands engraved with strands of ivy, wands that I want to play with more badly than anything in the world. I don't see him cut the Glyph, because I can't slip into the Null yet, but I see his hands flit imperceptibly fast, and then the kettle rattles as it's instantly heated.

"Do you *have* to go today?" I ask, even though I already know the truth. He's wearing his suit, the one with the little bowtie and the watch-chain, and he only wears that when he's going to work.

"I do. Duty calls." He finishes making the coffee, then walks over to hunker down by my side. "But I promise I'll be home for dinner." He leans down to kiss my forehead. "Be good. Have fun."

I grin, despite myself. "Can't do both." It's our little joke, and I have no idea when it started, just that we say it whenever we part. "Bye, Monkey," he says, and with a smile so kind and warm, he leaves.

My mother wakes up half an hour later, groggy, rubbing her eyes. She's Izachi, one of the Scattered People, with tan skin and curly black hair, her eyes an endlessly deep brown. She pads over barefoot, because she's always barefoot, and drinks the cup of coffee my father left her like it's the nectar of the Gods. She tries to move quietly, but Sera wakes up anyway, shooting bolt upright in the bed, her eyes instantly on me. "Scones?" she asks. "Did you save me a scone?"

"Nope," I lie, as a joke, but instead of laughing she just looks down, heartbroken. "I mean, yes! Of course! I was kidding!" I rush over, handing her the last one.

"Not a funny joke," she grumbles, even as she takes a delicate bite. Sera just turned six, and if I take after our mother, she takes after our father. She has his pale skin and freckles, his scholar's disposition. But what really stands out is her hair. It's as vibrant red as the sunset and cascades down her back to her waist with beautiful curls like waves in the ocean. Every stranger we meet comments on it, and I'd be lying if I said I wasn't jealous.

I have one thing she doesn't, though. The Mark on my left wrist, the tattoo that glows hot red and gold. Sera's wrists are as bare as my mother's. I'd asked, just once, why I had one and she didn't, and my father's face fell. "Because she's lucky," he'd replied.

"I don't suppose you saved *me* a scone?" my mother asks now, and my sugar-glazed grimace of guilt is the only answer she needs.

The three of us get dressed and head out to run errands. We visit the market square, crowded with dozens of stands, flooded with the din of shouting vendors. We stock up on bread and fruit and salted meat, and my mother buys a book of poems for Sera and a little wooden horse for me. "His name is Boneshanks, and I love him!" I scream, to the bewilderment of everyone there and the great amusement of my mother. We go to the library next. Sera sits quietly reading while I run wildly through the aisles. We grab lunch in the Izachi neighborhood, a spiced beef dish my mother loves that burns my tongue just a little, and spend at least half an hour watching a juggler toss balls and staves and knives. He's all the more impressive because he's just a Humble, no magic involved.

Because we were good girls, we end the day with a walk on the beach, which is my absolute favorite part of Laroc. I dance Boneshanks around in the sand and chase Sera in the crashing waves and bury myself up to the waist and pretend I'm a bog goblin. My mother just sits on the sand, gazing out at the endless blue.

This is how I'll always remember her. Resting by the water's edge on that brittle gray sand, a little smile on her face as I cartwheel around her, her eyes full of kindness and love and, just below, an unbearable aching sadness. This is her, forever.

Our walk back takes us past the docks, which is a mistake. The docks are always unpleasant, packed with angry grunting sailors and reeking of fish. A massive ship has come into port, an enormous galleon with giant fluttering sails and a bronze mermaid on the front, so the docks are even more crowded than usual, crowded enough that I hold tight onto my mother's hand as we shove our way through. But that's not all. There's something in the air, something wrong, a sense of malice and tension, a smell of decay and flame. Everyone's scowling, sweating, staring. The Mark on my arm starts to burn, and I clutch my sleeve tight.

We push forward, into the public square at the dock's edge, and I see what all the commotion's about. A statue of Javellos, the God of Commerce, towers over us, gazing down at the courtyard with his eight glistening eyes. Beneath him, on the dirty cobblestones, three men stand bound to whipping posts, their hands locked in thick metal clamps. Their bare backs are exposed, taut and muscular. Humble sailors. And there are other men around them, too, men who do not seem happy. City watchmen in their leather armor keep the crowd at bay, clubs in hand, shoving anyone who gets too close to the square's edge. A heavyset older Wizard stands on a dais before them, wearing an ill-fitting black suit and tugging at his collar with a ring-covered hand. But all eyes are on the Enforcer, standing silently behind the bound men. She wears a tight black robe, her face is hidden behind a blank silver mask, and in each hand she holds the most sinister-looking Loci I've ever seen, gnarled bone wands with jagged tips and little carved skulls at the hilts.

My mother clenches me tight with one hand and Sera with the other. "We should leave," she says, pulling back, but there's nowhere to go. The crowd is packed dense behind us, and the square's ahead of us. So all we can do is stand and watch.

"As the vice chairman of the Laroc Trading Company, I find these men guilty of sloth, cowardice, and desertion!" the Wizard on the dais bellows. His voice is coarse and phlegmatic, and sweat streaks down his stubbly face even though it's chilly out. "Their mutinous actions at sea not only sank a prize vessel but cost me nearly four thousand valmarcs' worth of cargo! Four thousand! For a price like that, I could well sentence you all to death!"

Two of the sailors stand firm, but the third, the youngest, begins to sob. "Please, sir, have mercy," he begs. "It wasn't our fault! We had to abandon the ship or go down with it in the storm! Please!"

"Mercy." The Wizard chews the word like a bitter herb. "Yes, I suppose I can grant you a drop of that. And you'll serve far better as examples." He waves a hand at the Enforcer. "Give them the thorns."

The Enforcer raises her two Loci, arms crossed, even as the men grit their teeth. "Close your eyes," my mother hisses, and Sera listens, but I don't. I can't. I watch as the Enforcer tenses her arms and sucks in her breath, and then I feel it, feel it for the first time in my life, the call of the Null, a feeling like I'm being pulled toward that woman, toward her Loci. It's like there's something in my body being drawn out through my skin, wrenched out of me, out of reality, into somewhere else. My stomach lurches, my vision spins, and my arm flares with a horrible stinging pain, like there are thousands of needles inside it and they're starting to break through.

I let out a little scream and my mother squeezes her hand tight over my face. I can't quite see what happens next through the cracks between her fingers, but I see enough. I see the air crackle and waver behind the men, see tendrils of hazy green light shoot out of the end of those bone Loci, see the men's backs rip open as they're struck by hundreds of invisible hooked thorns. I smell blood and hear screams and feel that throbbing painful pulse of magic within me, straining to break free, tearing me apart from the inside, like there's a hurricane surging within me and my body's just barely, barely, keeping it in.

Later, as we walk hand in hand back to our apartment, I finally find myself able to speak. "Why?" I ask my mother. "Why did the Wizards do that to those men?"

My mother glances down at me, and I can tell, even at seven, that she really doesn't want to have this conversation. "Because the laws of the Republic allow Wizards to punish Humbles as they see fit," she says, teeth clenched, choosing every word carefully. There's an anger in her expression, dancing behind her eyes, and it scares me.

"But why?" Sera asks. "Why do they *get* to?"

"Because they hold the power," my mother replies. "Because they control the government and the trade companies and the schools and the law. Because they hold in their blood the ability to shape the world, to conjure flame and ice, to bring life and death. Because they're strong, and we're weak."

"But..." I ask, knowing full well I shouldn't. "I'm a Wiza—" and I never get to finish the question because she squeezes my hand so tight it hurts.

My father is waiting for us when we get home, and I sprint over to grab him in a hug so hard he almost falls over. While my mother takes a moment to herself, gazing out at the sunset from our patio, my father sits down with me and Sera in the kitchen to do our schoolwork. By the flickering yellow light of a candle, we read a story about a little sheep who had no friends and do a few pages of arithmetic. Sera follows along diligently, doing every step, while I fidget wildly in my seat and stare out the window. But even I pay attention later, when we huddle up against him as he reads a chapter of *The Sagas of Naeflein*, that heavy, dog-eared book with all the stories about princes and witches and creatures of the deep. I love how he sounds when he reads, so patient and calm, and I love how he wraps an arm around us to hold us close to his chest, and I love how he does silly voices for all the characters.

We eat dinner, a simple stew with some bread and onions. We sit by the fire and talk about the day. My parents nod patiently as I ramble about how Boneshanks is a magical horse who can fly through time. Then they tuck us in and blow out the lights, and both lean in to kiss my forehead as I drift off. "I love you, girls," my father says. "More than you'll ever know."

For the rest of my life, I'll wish I'd stayed awake longer. I'll wish I'd had another day, another hour, another minute with them. One more story from my father. One more hug from my mother. Even if we'd gotten into a fight, even if they'd had to threaten no treats the next day, even if it had ended with me crying and stomping around. I'll spend the rest of my life wishing I could give anything, everything, to just have had more time with them.

But instead, I fall asleep, and I only wake up because all the crystals in our apartment are ringing.

I shoot up in my bed. It's the middle of the night, but our apartment is lit up bright because the wards are all going off, those crisscrossed spiderwebs shaking and shivering, the crystals flaring red and green and blue. I'm still groggy, but I know enough to be scared, so I go rushing into the kitchen, where my parents are both up. Sera's right behind me, crying with fear. "What's happening?" I yell over the din. "What's going on?"

"They found us," my mother replies, and I don't know who *they* are, but I know it's not a good thing. My father waves a Loci through the air, and the crystals all go silent. His face is pale, paler than usual, and sweat streaks down his brow. "How the hell did they find us?"

"I don't know," my father says. He grabs one of the crystals in his hand, holding it tight, and his expression grows even more grave. "Four of them. Coming fast. And *he's* with them."

"Oh, Gods," my mother whispers, and I'm more scared than I think I've ever been in my life. "We have to run. Now."

"We can't," my father replies, unable to meet her gaze. "They've got eyes on us. If we move, they'll strike." He takes a long, deep breath. "They've got us, Kaelyn."

My parents share a heavy look, the kind of look that's an entire conversation, the look where you're making a decision you can't even speak. Then my mother nods, rushing forward to tidy the room, while my father hunkers down next to me and Sera. "Listen, girls," he says, forcing a smile. "We're in a bit of trouble, but it's all going to be okay. Some very serious men are coming here, and they want to talk to your mother and me. The most important thing is that they don't know you're here. Do you understand?"

"No!" I cry. "I'm really scared, Papa..."

"I know, Monkey," he says, squeezing my shoulders, and his eyes are glistening behind his glasses. "And I'm sorry. Sorry we've forced you into this mess. Sorry for the world we brought you into. Sorry for everything.

But right now, if we stay calm, it'll all work out just fine." He leans down and hooks his fingers through a gap in the floorboards, prying up a plank to reveal a tiny crawl space underneath. "I'm going to need you two to hide in there, understand? Hide in there and don't make a single sound. I'm just going to tell these men what they want to hear, and then they'll leave, and we'll come get you."

"But—but—" Sera stammers. "I don't *understand*."

"I know," my father says, and pulls us into a hug so tight I almost can't tell he's trembling. "Someday you will. I promise." He pulls back, clears his throat. "Now listen. I think it's all going to work out. But if it doesn't… if this goes bad… if those crystals start ringing… I need you two to crawl back out through that little tunnel and run as fast as you can." He takes out a folded piece of paper and tucks it into my pants pocket. "There's an address written on that paper. Find your way there. Ask for Whispers, and tell them Petyr Chelrazi sent you. They'll understand."

My mother glances out the window. "I see them coming. We have to get ready. Now."

My father brushes a tear off his cheek and collects himself. "Whatever happens, girls… however this goes down… I need you to know that your mother and I love you more than anything. That it was all worth it, all of it, for the time we've had together. That you are the absolute best thing that ever happened to us." He brushes my hair and leans down to give me one last kiss. "Alka… you're going to have a hard road ahead of you. Fight for those who need it. Be good, my Monkey. Be *good*. And Sera, my little Sera…" Tears streak down his cheeks, too many to stop now. "Look after your sister. Be strong and brave. Be kind." He leans down, gently guiding us into the crawl space. "Now hide."

It's dusty down there, and dark, and probably full of spiders, but I don't say anything because even though I don't understand, I can tell this is all very serious. Sera crawls in first, sliding to the back, and I go after her. I lie flat on my back in that dark little tunnel, barely wide enough for my seven-year-old body, and my father leans down to replace the board. I can still see, sort of, through the cracks between them, enough to see the kitchen and my mother and father. He wraps an arm around her, and she huddles against him, and they just stand there, holding each other, breathing deeply.

There's a knock on the door, a gauntlet pounding on wood. "Petyr Chelrazi! Open up!" a voice booms.

"Come on in," my father says, and his voice has changed; it's lower, more adult and serious, more fake.

The door swings open, and four people enter. Three are Enforcers, armor clad, faces hidden behind blank silver masks. I recognize one as the woman from the docks earlier, the one with the bone Loci, and the other two are men, one short and lean and the other tall and burly. The Enforcers stomp their way into the kitchen, shaking the floorboards and sending dust billowing into my face, and for one awful moment I think I'm going to sneeze. But I hold it in, thank the Gods, even as my parents back away and the Enforcers take up positions along the edges of the room.

The third man is clearly the one in charge. He's a Wizard, and maybe the most impressive one I've ever seen. He's wearing a neatly fitted robe with a plush fur trim that sparkles black and gold in the candlelight. Rings with giant gemstones adorn his pale fingers, and a necklace with a golden moon dangles across his neck. He's Marovian and looks to be about my father's age, with a brown beard that descends to a point and curly dark hair that runs down his back in a neat braid. As he walks in, he smiles, even as his gray eyes sparkle with menace. "Petyr," he says. "It's been some time."

"That it has, old friend," my father slides a chair out. "To what do I owe the pleasure?"

"I think you know exactly why I'm here," the Wizard says, jerking a head at his Enforcers. "Hand over your Loci. Now."

My father glances at my mother with a nod. She reaches onto the counter and hands over my father's greenblossom wands. The female Enforcer grabs them out of her hands and tucks them into a bag at her hip.

"A reasonable precaution. I'm sure you understand," the Wizard says.

"Of course," my father replies. "Can I get you something to drink? Some tea or wine, perhaps?"

"Not at the moment." The Wizard takes a seat at the table opposite my father, steepling his long, narrow fingers. "I do believe there's one member of your family unaccounted for. A girl of seven years?"

Me? He's looking for me? Why? Why would *I* matter? And why doesn't he ask about Sera? But I don't have time to even think about that because my father immediately lies. "She's not here. We sent her to stay with a friend, somewhere far away."

"Really?" the Wizard says. His features are sharp, angular, like he's been cut from a slab of cold stone, and his voice oozes contempt. "So if I have my Enforcers search this house, they won't find her?"

"Afraid not," my father says, then leans forward, his voice almost a whisper. "Look. My wife has nothing to do with this. I'm the one you want. So why don't I leave now, with your Enforcers, and if you just let Kaelyn go, I'll tell you everything."

"Everything," the Wizard repeats. "About what, exactly?"

"About the Revenants," my father says, and all the Enforcers stiffen. "Their plans. Their leadership. All of it."

For the first time, the Wizard's cool facade seems to break. "So it's true. You really have gone rebel."

"Afraid so."

"Damn it, Petyr," the Wizard growls. "I'd hoped this was just personal. That you'd fled your duties to be with your family. That you were merely a coward. But no. You sold us all out to a bunch of Humble terrorists. After everything we went through, everything we've built, you've turned traitor to all the Republic stands for!"

When my father speaks, his voice is ice. "Everything we went through is a lie. Everything we built is an abomination. And the only thing the Republic stands for is injustice and oppression."

The Wizard's nostrils flare, his brow furrowed deep, and it almost seems like he's going to throw a punch... but then all at once, his expression changes, his lips twisting into a cruel smile. "Oh, Petyr," he says, "You almost had me fooled. But it looks like you missed something."

Everyone follows his gaze to the floor, to just a few inches away from where I'm hiding. I see it the same time the others do, and my stomach plunges. It's Boneshanks, my wooden horse. We forgot to hide him.

The Wizard rises from his seat, pacing methodically toward the horse, toward me. "If your daughter's not here... then what's that?" he says, and my mother and father share a worried glance, because if he bends down to pick the horse up he's going to look through the floorboards and see me, and I don't know what that'll mean but I know it'll be very, very bad, and I'm wondering if I should start crawling but I can't make my body move and behind me Sera is starting to cry and my heart's racing and then the Wizard is there, right over me, reaching down...

But he never actually gets to the horse because my mother grabs a knife off the counter and drives it into the small of his back.

There's a pulse through the air, the oppressive wrenching tug of magic, and for the first time in my life, I slip all the way into the Null. The room, the house, the city all vanish, plunging me into that gray, ashy world. There, in the lingering, deafening silence, time moves at a crawl, and I see everyone spring into action. The Enforcers raise their Loci. The Wizard, stabbed and howling, draws his own. My mother jerks back, reaching for another knife. And my father falls back out of his chair, raising his hands, as two hidden Loci, two small jagged blades, slide out of his sleeves.

The air crackles and hums, tempests of power flickering through the room, as lattices of arcane geometry dance and blaze. The world freezes, trembles, and shakes. Glyphs hit counter-Glyphs. Whips of light slash through the dark. I smell earth and taste blood and feel that horrible surge within me, pressing out, as my parents fight their last fight.

The whole thing is over in less than a second.

I'm wrenched back into the Real, trembling, sweating, gasping under the floorboards. Above me, the kitchen is a shattered ruin. The table has been upended, the ceiling scorched, a giant hole knocked through one wall. Leaves of paper, the remains of my father's beloved books, flutter charred in the air around us, and a layer of crackling ice covers the floor.

Two of the Enforcers, the woman and the burly man, are dead, their blackened bodies smoldering at the far end of the room. The third, the small man, isn't in much better shape: he lies out in the street, through that hole, moaning with a lance of rock driven through his chest. Their leader, the Wizard, is still alive, but he's hunched over, his back to me, coughing and gasping and howling with pain.

And my parents...

My mother is already dead. She lies slumped against the far wall, her head down and a gaping hole where her chest should be. A small trickle of blood runs down her lips, and her hands twitch uselessly at her sides. My father lies next to her, not dead but dying; his right arm is missing, slashed off, and spiderwebs of ice push out against the skin of his face, like he's been frozen from the inside. His breath comes in ragged gasps, each shorter than the last.

My eyes sting. My heart beats so hard it feels like it's going to smash out of my chest. I want to scream, to sob, to wail, to fight, but my body won't move, so I'm just stuck there, panting under the floor, paralyzed, trapped. This can't be happening. It can't. It can't it can't it can't.

The Wizard, the one who did all this, moves first, limping over to my father. He kicks him onto his back and kneels down over him, pressing down on his chest with a knee. The Wizard's hair is wild, singed black.

The right half of his face is a scarred, bubbling mess, his eye burned clean out. My mother's knife still juts out of his lower back. But for all that, he's still somehow going, like his sheer hate is pumping through his veins.

"You little bastard," he hisses, spitting blood into my father's face. "You really thought you could do this to me? To *me*?" He jerks my father up by the collar, their faces just inches apart. "You listen here, Petyr, and you listen well. I'm going to find your daughter. I'm going to track her down. And I'm going to make sure she dies the slowest, most painful death you can imagine. I'm going to make her suffer, Petyr. I'm going to make her suffer so much."

My blood is ice, my breath frozen in my throat. I've never been more scared in my life. But my father just smiles, a hard cracking smile that takes every ounce of strength he has. "No, you won't," he tells the Wizard, "because you're already dead." Then he glances down at me, just out of the side of his eye, and I look at him, really look at him, one last time, my father, my hero, my world.

Run, he mouths.

Then it appears above him, glowing into existence like an ember sparking to life. A Glyph, carved into our ceiling, big enough to cover the whole surface, hidden from sight until now. It's intricate beyond words, a half dozen intersecting circles, connected like links in a chain, a snake eating its own tail. The Glyph fades into being… and then it glows brighter and hotter than the sun.

Pure instinct takes over. I still don't understand anything that's happened, can barely begin to fathom it, but my body knows to follow my father's command. I grab Sera by the hand and jerk her forward, and the two of us scramble under the floorboards like a pair of mice, pushing through that narrow dirt tunnel, and I can hear the bells ringing louder and louder, hear the Wizard scream in horror, hear the walls vibrate and whir with the hum of gathering magic. Sera and I burst out through a little opening under the side of the house, onto the dark, cramped street, and then I'm running, dragging Sera behind me, my side hurting, my eyes burning, my whole body driven by nothing more than the desperate need to get away from this house.

I don't see it explode. I don't need to. I hear a thunderous blast louder than the loudest thunderclap, feel a scorching wave of heat pass through me, feel the earth shudder beneath my feet. For one moment, the night is as bright as day, as a column of swirling, howling flame shoots up fifteen stories into the sky. Glass shatters. Brick cracks. The city howls with the voices of hundreds crying out in fear.

I don't stop running. I can't. I have to keep moving, even though my little legs are already flaring, even though I'm barefoot and I'm pretty sure I stepped on some glass, even though I have no idea where I'm going. I have to keep running, because if I stop even for a second then what just happened is real, and it can't be. It can't be. So I run on, through alleys and streets, past noisy taverns and bustling night bazaars, a seven-year-old girl soaked in blood with singed clothes and wild eyes, a seven-year-old girl suddenly responsible for her sister, a seven-year-old girl who's just lost her entire world.

We run out of city. The streets end and we stumble onto a beach, the same beach where we'd sat just hours ago. I sprint to the ocean's edge, and I collapse there in the wet sand, staring out at that endless vast expanse of cold, unknowing darkness. Sera sits next to me, silent, frozen. She doesn't speak, doesn't cry, doesn't move. It's like she's a candle that's been snuffed out.

But I'm a fire raging hotter than the sun. I let it all out, a howling, furious scream that's angry and despondent and lost and scared all at once, a scream that goes on until my voice is gone and my throat is ripped raw. It's a scream of fury and despair, a scream that would kill everyone in the city if it could, a scream I'll never forget.

I die that day, too, alongside my parents. The girl I was, the one who played with a little horse, who felt safe and secure, who thought the worst thing that could happen is her father coming home late, she's gone, burned up with the house.

All that's left of me is that scream.

CHAPTER 3

Now

The ferry to Blackwater Academy leaves at midnight, but I don't want to risk being late so I get there at sundown, which means I'm standing around by myself on the Lauderdale Docks for a good three hours before anyone even arrives. Lauderdale's a nicer town than I'm used to, a small cluster of elegant estates and upscale markets on the southern coast. Being in places this nice makes me uneasy; money and magic always go hand in hand. And I really don't like being this exposed, standing by myself under a streetlight in a stuffy dress. I want nothing more than to scramble up to a rooftop and scout the scene, to crouch in the shadows, Loci in hand, ready to strike. But instead I have to wait around here. All exposed. Like a sap.

The others begin to show up around eleven. They trickle onto the docks slowly, first a few at a time and then a crowd, the rest of Blackwater Academy's incoming class. They look harmless enough, teenagers dressed in crisp suits and sparkling gowns. I can make out features from all over the Republic: southerners with pale skin and reddish-brown hair, Velkschen northerners with icy blue eyes, tall lanky Sithartics with their black hair in beaded braids, a pair of Kindrali Islanders, heads shaved bald and ornate gold jewelry shining against their black skin. Some students walk alone, shy, nervous, while others clearly know one another, chatting as they stroll across the pier. Looking at them, you'd never know that in just a decade, they'd be among the most powerful people in the world. Looking at them, you'd never know how dangerous they all are.

Murderers. Tyrants. Monsters, the lot of them.

I feel a sudden pang of uncertainty. This is the last opportunity I have to turn back, my last chance to run before walking into the lion's den. This is the point of no return.

I wish Sera were here. I wish we were doing this together. Gods, I wish she was with me.

But no. I'm on my own and I haven't come this far just to come this far. So with a deep breath I pull myself together and stroll right into the enemy's ranks.

I blend in with them instantly, slipping right into the crowd. I'd damn well better, because getting myself dolled up had taken the better part of my week, not to mention the last of my coin. I had my hair dyed a dark black, I went to one of those expensive salons where they clean your nails, and I bought myself a long beautiful dress, the kind the rich Wizard girls wear, with the lace trim and the little jade clasps and the embroidered flowers along the sleeves. It's not that I don't like it. I do, especially the way it swishes when I twirl and the way the yellow light of the lanterns catches the purple fabric just right. But it feels wrong to be dressed up so fancy now, on the most important mission of my life. I feel trapped.

The crowd makes its way along the pier, and I lose myself in the bustle of their chatter, their laughter and excitement. My normal posture is hunched, hidden, trying not to draw attention to myself, but here I try to walk like them: head held high, long confident strides, pushing forward like I own the world. The crowd bustles onward, none the wiser, and comes to a massive ferry anchored at the end of a dock. It's the nicest boat I've ever seen, big enough to fit a few hundred, with a fresh coat of bright-red paint and two enormous waterwheels spinning along the sides. Each wheel has a glass orb at its center, and in that orb swirls a column of dancing fire, a bottled tempest of flame. Dozens and dozens of Glyphs line the orb, glowing silver and red and iridescent purple, generating the heat and trapping it inside.

I can't help but gawk. I've heard of Magic Engine Vessels before, of course, but I never imagined I'd see one in person. They're the most ornate and expensive artifacts in the Republic, requiring thousands of hours of labor from the most masterful of Wizards. And they're using one to ferry us to the campus. I know that attending Blackwater is an enormous honor, but it's still hard for me to wrap my mind around.

We board one by one, and as I make my way up, I can see a burly bald man at the edge of the gangway, flanked by a pair of Enforcers, checking each student's paperwork before letting them on. The man wears a rumpled black cloak that hangs on him like a shroud, and a scowl seems permanently etched onto his bearded face. The process looks simple enough, just hand him the invitation, but I can't help worrying: what if there's something I'm missing, something Whispers didn't know about, like a secret password or a special wink? But there's nothing to be done now, not with a student pressing into my back, so I swallow hard and shove out the paper I took from Alayne's carriage.

The man glances down at it, reads it closely, then looks right at me. He's got deep creases in his forehead, a mottled scar along his cheek, and his beady black eyes narrow with disdain. "Alayne of House Dewinter?" he asks, slurring his words just a little.

"Yes. That's me," I reply. Did I sound right? How would Alayne say it?

He turns the paper over, squinting at it like he's looking for a sign of forgery. "Don't recognize your family," he grumbles, and the Enforcers' masks flit toward me. My hand inches down for the hidden sheaths under my dress that strap my Loci to my thighs. I don't know what's going to happen next, but by the Gods, I'm not going out without a fight.

But the man doesn't fight, and the Enforcers don't strike. "Let me see your Godsmark," he says instead.

Of course. Godsmarks are the most precious currency of the Senate, the ultimate source of power, the line that divides the world in two. When a baby is born, its parents may petition the Senate for the child to be given a Godsmark, to be made a Wizard. If both parents are Wizards, the request is usually granted; if only one parent is, it depends on their standing with the Senate. Children of Humble parents are almost never even considered, except in the cases in which one of the parents has distinguished themselves in their service to the Republic. It's the ultimate reward, the great hanging incentive for Humbles. Serve us well, the Wizards say, and you can become one of us.

As a child, I'd always wondered why I had the Mark and Sera didn't; I wondered if I was special somehow, more my father's daughter, destined. Now I know it had nothing to do with me at all. When I was born, my father was still beloved by the Senate; a year later, he was a fugitive on the run.

But that doesn't matter now. What matters is getting onto that ferry. So I roll up my sleeve and shove out my left forearm. There it glows, just above my wrist, the Godsblood tattoo that grants me my magic: two diamonds pulsing a delicate blue, with a serpentine band running through their centers. The Mark of a Wizard.

The bald man squints at it, then nods. "Well, all right then, Alayne Dewinter. Looks like you get to board after all."

"I'm the first Marked of my line," I explain, though why am I talking at all? "The first Dewinter to be a Wizard."

"Ha!" he laughs. "You're not a Wizard yet, missy. Not till you graduate. And looking at you, I wouldn't hold my breath." Then he shoves the letter back into my hands and jerks his head up the gangway. "Move along, then. We don't have all night to gawk."

A few of the students around me chuckle, and I give the man a polite little laugh like I'm in on the joke, even though I'm burning with rage. I know I'm not *actually* Alayne Dewinter, but I also know that I don't like being laughed at, especially not by some drunk old Wizard who pulled ferry duty. And my Loci would make a deeply satisfying crunch if I drove them into his skull.

Another time. I keep my friendly smile and make my way past him, up the gangway, and onto the deck of the ship. This is a fancy vessel, all right. A band plays on a stage, while trays of salted oysters and cubes of cheese rest on a long buffet. The other students loiter around, leaning on railings and sitting on benches, chatting away without a care in the world. I know I just cleared the biggest hurdle and I ought to relax, but my neck's still tight and my heart's still pounding, the hairs on my arms standing on end. I've spent the past decade fearing Wizards, running from them, hiding in the shadows as they hunted me down. How am I supposed to relax when I'm *surrounded* by them?

I make my way across the deck to the most remote spot I can find, an empty patch of railing on the bow, looking out over the endless expanse of starlit ocean. A night breeze blows over me, and I close my eyes and grip the railing, savoring its chill on my skin, the way it runs through my hair like a gentle caress. Somewhere behind me, the bald man yells "All aboard!" and the other students clap and cheer. There's a dull groan as those massive waterwheels spin to life, cutting through the water like giant plows as they push the boat out from the docks, into the water, into the night.

Somewhere out there, Blackwater Academy is waiting.

"Are you really the first of your line to get a Mark?" a girl's voice asks from behind me.

I spin around to see her sitting up on a platform a few feet away. She's another student, with pale skin and narrow black eyes. "I am," I say cautiously. Who the hell is she and what does she want? Is she testing me?

"Wow," she says. She's holding a palmful of nuts in one hand, and she casually pops one into her mouth. There's something odd about her, a scruffiness that makes her stand out among her peers. Her black hair is cut short just below her ears, and she wears a crisp suit with a short red tie, black gloves, and a pair of tall leather boots. She's pretty, pretty in a way that says she's not trying too hard to please. "I thought the Senate stopped handing out Marks to new lines in our parents' generation."

Oh, she's definitely testing me. Good thing I know Alayne's history better than my own. "They still make some exceptions for those who distinguish themselves in service to the Republic," I confidently reply. "My father is a decorated general who helped put down the Sithartic Uprising. The Senate let me have the Mark as a reward for his valor."

"Oh. That's nice of them." The girl finishes off her nuts and hops off the platform, pacing over to me. "All my father ever did was run our family business into the ground." She extends a hand. "Fylmonela Potts. But you can call me Fyl."

I glance down warily. I'm still not sure what's happening here or what her game is. But the last thing I want right now is to make a scene and draw attention to myself, so I reach out and take her hand, a firm shake. "Alayne Dewinter," I say.

"Alayne Dewinter..." she repeats, like she's tasting it. "Where are you from?"

"New Kenshire. It's an island off the coast of Sithar."

The girl—Fyl—lets out a low whistle. "You *are* far from home, aren't you? That's, what, a month's travel away?"

"Two," I reply, going off the script I've memorized. "Wizard ships don't run out to New Kenshire, so we have to sail the old-fashioned way."

"Two months from home." Fyl cocks her head to the side, studying me like I'm a strange specimen. "So, do you not know anyone here?"

"Not a soul," I reply, and it's the first honest thing I've said. "Why? Do you know many of the others?"

"Well, of course." Fyl leans with her back against the railing, gazing out at the bustling crowd of students on the deck. "Most of us grew up together in Arbormont. We went to the same schools, mingled in the same circles, got drunk at the same parties...." She lets out a weary sigh. "I could probably name three-quarters of the people here."

I nod, taking it in. Arbormont is the capital of the Republic, a bustling, prosperous city a few days' ride south of Lauderdale. It's the seat of the wealthiest families in the Republic, home to the High Temple and the Senate. I knew going into this that many of the students at Blackwater were from the Republic's elite, but still, if a solid three-quarters come from Arbormont, that's even more tightly knit than I'd expected. And it doesn't answer the most pressing question I have. "If you know everyone else," I ask Fyl, "why are you talking to me?"

"Maybe I just like meeting new people," she says, but an odd expression flashes across her face for just a second, a hint of vulnerability beneath her confident facade.

She's lying, but why? Is she trying to play me? I'm not buying it. I turn away, facing back out to sea. "I'm fine on my own, thanks."

I hear Fyl sigh and then she's up against the railing next to me. "Look," she says, "I'll be honest with you. From everything my parents told me about Blackwater, we're about to be in for the two most brutally competitive years of our lives. We're going to be tested, we're going to be punished, we're going to be at each other's throats. And before I left, my parents sat me down and told me the first thing I'm going to need to do is make some allies, because there's no way in hell I'm making it through on my own. So... here I am. Making an ally."

"Why me?"

"Because you look smart and capable and on your own?" Fyl says, and her eyes dart down. "And, well... because no one else would *want* to be my ally."

She's being honest now, or she's a great actress, but either way, I'm not going to fight it. "So your parents went to Blackwater?"

"That's right. And their parents before them, and *their* parents before them, and so on, all the way back to the first class. We used to be a pretty important family. We even have a wing of the library named after us." She tilts her head up, staring up into the clear sky above. "The Potts were once one of the Great Families of Marovia. And now we're just a sad joke." Then she sees someone coming, and her expression darkens. "Speaking of Great Families... incoming."

I turn around. Three students are walking toward us across the deck. There's a burly boy with his shirt half untucked and crumbs in his mossy beard, and a tall girl with raven-black hair and intelligent green eyes. But it's the boy leading them who catches my gaze, in part because he's looking right at me. His skin is perfectly tanned, the kind of tan you get when you spend your days luxuriating under the southern sun. His neat brown hair billows elegantly down his shoulders. His eyes are a dazzling blue, his teeth sparkling white, and there's a solid dimple in the middle of his chin. His clothes look like they're worth more than my life, an ornate suit with jeweled buttons and a gold watch clasp, glistening diamond studs in his ears, the shiniest leather boots I've ever seen.

But it's his Loci that really catch my eye. Everyone else has theirs stowed in their bags (or, in my case, on my thighs). As far as I know, Loci aren't permitted yet. But his are out nonetheless, hanging by his hips in brown leather holsters with the tops poking out. I've never even seen Loci like his: long, lean wands made of a material I can't place, a deep black that glistens blue and gold like a dancing flame, with golden carved stags' heads at the tops.

"Fylmonela Potts!" He swaggers our way with a wide smile. "It's been ages! I haven't seen you since..." He snaps his fingers, trying to remember. "The Founders' Day Gala? At my father's estate?"

"Oh, no, I...I wasn't there, actually," Fyl says, and in that moment, it's like she's instantly become a different person, someone so much smaller, shyer. "Not that I wouldn't have wanted to. I just wasn't...well...I never received an invitation...."

"Oh. Must have been an oversight," the boy says gracefully. His smile is warm and his eyes friendly, but there's something off about him, something I can't quite put my finger on, something that sets me deeply on edge. "I'll make sure you're invited next time."

"Yeah," the burly boy with the mossy beard snorts. "I mean, we're going to need someone to pour us drinks, right?"

"Very funny, Dean." Fyl forces a smile, even as her gaze drops to the floor. I know that smile, the smile where you pretend you're in on the joke even though you're the butt. I hate that smile. "Besides. We'll all be celebrating together at Blackwater."

"That's right. I've heard their Founders' Day Gala is amazing," the handsome boy grins, gazing out at the night with a kind of sincere optimism that's infectious. "We're finally getting there. To Blackwater. To the best years of our lives." Then he turns back, and his eyes flit from Fyl to me, and I can feel them roam over me like an unwanted caress, sparkling that bright blue as he sizes me up. "Ah. I don't believe I've had the pleasure of making your acquaintance?"

"She's a new Mark," the raven-haired girl answers. Her voice is flat, affectless, like she's bored out of her mind. "Alayne Dewinter."

Had she been eavesdropping when I'd gotten on board? Or had word about me somehow spread? I press back against the railing, uneasy. "Yes. That's me."

"Where the hell is House Dewinter?" the bearded boy grumbles, but the handsome one cuts him off with a sharply raised hand, a gesture that makes him instantly go quiet. "You're General Grayson Dewinter's daughter," he says, taking a step closer to me. He smells like expensive perfume, flowers, and cinnamon, a smell at once intoxicating and overpowering. "My father spoke highly of him. We all thank him for his service." He nods respectfully, and I force an honored smile. "Listen. I know it can be pretty hard being new. If you'd like, I can show you around this ship. . . ."

"Thank you," I say, and everything about this interaction is unsettling, destabilizing, like I'm standing on cracking ice. I don't know who this boy is, don't know what his intentions are, don't know why he keeps the company of a boor like his bearded friend. I know his lips are smiling, but his eyes aren't. And I decide I'm not going to take the chance. "But I'm all right out here with Fyl."

Something changes in that moment. It's subtle, but there all the same: the way Fyl sucks in her breath, the way the bearded boy's nostrils flare, the way the raven-haired girl looks up, for the first time, with interest. The handsome boy's smile doesn't fade. But something flickers in his eyes, a hint of surprise. This is not someone who's used to hearing the word *no*. "Is that so?"

"Marius," the tall girl says, and she sounds almost amused. "She doesn't know who you *are*."

"Should I?" I ask.

I hadn't meant to be cutting, at least, not *that* cutting. But now the edges of Marius's smile twitch, and I can see the strain to hold it up, the anger inside, the quiet menace, the wounded pride. He reaches out, patting my shoulder a little too forcefully. "Right, then," he says. "Of course.

You do whatever you think is best for you. I'm sure you'll make all the right choices." Then he turns back to the others, gesturing to the opposite end of the ship. "Come on. Let's go see what's going on below deck."

The three of them walk off, with the bearded boy shooting me a particularly livid glare over his shoulder. I turn back to Fyl, and she's staring at me with her jaw hanging wide. "You didn't have to do that," she whispers.

"No, but I wanted to." I shrug. "I didn't like how he was talking. I didn't trust him."

"Yeah, but that was...I mean...he's..." Fyl blinks. "Wait. Do you *genuinely* not know who that was?"

"Should I?"

Fyl stares at me like I just said I've never heard of the moon. "Oh. All right. Wow. So the bearded boy is Dean Veyle, son of Dorothea Veyle. You know...of the Veyle Trading Company? The wealthiest merchant family in the Republic?"

"I've heard of them," I say dismissively, even though I'm almost certain I bought my clothes from one of their stores.

"The tall girl who looks so bored she's going to die? That's Vyctoria Aberdeen. The headmaster's niece." Fyl's voice drops low, conspiratorial. "Rumor has it she's a genius and already a master Wizard. Hope we don't end up in *her* class."

"The fancy one, with the gold-headed wands," I ask. "Who's he?"

"The one you just insulted? That's Marius Madison," Fyl replies. "As in...the son of Deckard Madison? Grandmaster of the Senate? The most powerful man in the Republic?" She must see my expression change, because she nods. "You *do* know Grandmaster Madison, right?"

Oh, I know him, all right. Grandmaster Madison, the leader of the government, the Wizard at the top of the Wizard food chain. The man who wrote the Humble Servitude Act, the man who ordered the raids on Laroc and Hellsum, the architect of the Dissident Labor Camps and the Purge of Sithar. A man with his hands soaked in enough blood to drown an ocean. Just hearing his name makes my ears burn and my heart pound. Grandmaster Madison is the greatest enemy the people of the Republic, of the world, have....

And his son is right there. *Right there.* Walking away from me with his back turned, none the wiser, no one protecting him. I could kill him right now. I could draw my Loci and send a spear of ice through his heart, cleave off his head with a whip of thorns, send a gust of force that'd splatter him against the mast. It would be so easy to do. So easy. And so satisfying.

But I can't. I have to play the long game. I have to remember the mission. So I force myself to turn away, to let Marius Madison walk off, to gaze out at the endless dark ocean. *Keep it together, Alka*, I tell myself. *Think of the mission.*

"Are you all right?" Fyl asks.

"I'm fine," I say, and I hope she can't see how tightly I'm gripping the railing. "Just... ready to get there."

Fyl pops a little watch out of her suit pocket and checks it. "Well, you don't have to wait long. We're almost there."

I blink, because there's nothing but ocean in front of me, and I don't know much about Blackwater, but I know it's on an island. "Where?"

"You really don't know anything, do you?" Fyl grins, leaning up on the railing next to me. "Watch closely. You're going to like this."

There's a rush of wind as the boat accelerates, the giant waterwheels turning faster, the flames in their engine cylinders flaring and crackling. A massive horn at the front lets out a low, mournful wail and then... it's like the world wavers and melts. The stretch of ocean in front of me shimmers like an oil slick on a lake, rippling and distorting. All of it warps, the air, the water, the sky, wavering like a painting drawn on the side of a bubble. It's an illusion, I realize, on a truly massive scale, and I have just enough time to gasp before it vanishes altogether, burning away like a tapestry set to flame.

Then it's right before me, where just a second ago there had only been empty ocean. An entire island, at least fifteen miles long, that had been hidden behind a massive illusion spell. I can see dark beaches and stony crags and a sprawl of ominous, sheer rock. And resting at the center, like a blade driven into the earth, is a towering five-story manor, the largest I've ever seen, lit up by hundreds and hundreds of multicolored lanterns. The walls are made of cool slick stone, the pointed rooftops lined with twisting spires and looming gargoyles. I can see stained-glass windows and elegant balconies, gilded awnings, and marble columns. Dozens of smaller buildings flank it, a whole campus: dormitories and libraries and a round five-spired church.

It's terrifying. It's awe inspiring. And as much as I hate to admit, it's beautiful.

Behind me on the ship, students let out whoops and cheers. With a booming rumble, fireworks blast out from behind the manor and explode above us, dazzling blue flowers and lances of dancing flame, topped off by a shimmering green dragon that screams across the sky. Next to me, Fyl grins, her whole face lit up and tears in her eyes. I suppose I can understand it. For these Wizards, getting to Blackwater is a moment that's been built up their whole lives. But all I can think about is that manor, so massive and ancient, hidden in the dark. What's waiting for me when I get there? What have I gotten myself into?

Fyl must sense my tension, because the smile fades off her face. The other students are all still celebrating, clapping and dancing, raising glasses and laughing. There's no sign of Marius, not now, and no one seems to even notice the two of us at the end of the deck, looking back, lost in thought. "It's funny," Fyl says quietly. "Everyone's so happy now. But the next time we're all back on this boat, two years from now, headed back to the mainland . . . only two-thirds of us will be here."

"What do you mean?"

"Well, there are three hundred students in every incoming class, but just two hundred or so graduate."

I cock my head to the side. "They drop out?"

"Yeah," Fyl replies with a shrug. "Or they die."

CHAPTER 4

Then

I am thirteen years old when I finally learn my purpose.

My company of Revenants is staying in Hellsum. Well, in the fields outside of Hellsum. Whispers found us an abandoned estate, its brick walls rotted and overgrown with vines, the fields around it long fallow, probably since the drought of 723. Whoever lived here is long gone, which makes it the perfect hideout for a bunch of rebels on the run.

The others have taken up rooms in the main manor house, but I've claimed a little wing of the Humbles' quarters. It's quiet up here, and private, and no one can bother me without climbing up a rickety flight of stairs first. I'm sitting there by myself, idly carving my name into the wood with one of my knives, when I hear the tapping of Whispers's cane in the hall. "Alka," she says, from the other side of my door. "We need to talk."

The door creaks open and Whispers steps in. She's a Marovian woman of more than fifty years, her straight shoulder-length hair graying, her face ruddy from the long walk to see me. Her blue eyes meet mine, and

I glance down with an instant discomfort. Even when I'm angry at her, she can't help but command my respect. A lot of that comes down to her look: a tall, angular woman in a frayed soldier's uniform, a sword at her hip, a blackwood cane in her hand, and expressions that range from stern to dour.

"What do you want?" I ask. There's no one else in the rebellion who'd dare talk to her that way, but then again, there's no one else in the rebellion she's raised like a daughter. Not anymore.

"It's time we talked." She paces across my room to rest against a chair. "It's time you learned the truth."

"About what?"

"About you. Your purpose. Your destiny." She swivels the chair around and takes a seat. "Tell me, Alka. What makes a Wizard?"

"A Godsmark."

"Is that all?"

Yes? I think but don't say. After all, the Godsmark is what separates Humbles from Wizards. No one knows how they're made or what they really are; it's kept secret even from most Wizards. Once a baby has been granted the Mark by the Senate, it's brought by its parents to the High Temple in Arbormont at no older than six months. The high cleric takes the baby in, and some kind of ritual happens, and when he comes out, the baby bears the Godsmark. They say that in the ritual the Five Gods themselves descend and bless the baby, marking it with their blood, granting it access to their realm, to their Glyphs, to their power.

They also say that a third of babies who receive the Mark die within a week. That doesn't sound very blessed to me.

Whispers clears her throat sharply. "A Godsmark makes a Wizard, yes. But so does their education. Tell me, Alka. What do you know about Blackwater Academy?"

"Blackwater?" I wrack my memory. "It's some big fancy academy where all the rich Wizard kids go to learn magic, right? And it's really secret and hard to get to, and no one knows what happens there?"

"Yes. That's all correct." She nods. "Blackwater is one of the most important bastions of power in the Republic. It's a repository of knowledge, of secrets, of magic. And above all else, it's an incubator of power."

"I don't follow."

"There are other schools of magic," she explains, "But they are for lesser Houses, for common Wizards, for churning out city Enforcers or weary bureaucrats. The Wizards that matter, the Wizards that lead, the senators and clerics and merchants, the elite? They all go to Blackwater. And it's a place that, until now, has been utterly closed off to us." She pauses, and I feel my stomach knot with tension. "Alka Chelrazi... we need you to infiltrate Blackwater."

My mouth goes dry, and the room suddenly feels very cold. "Why?"

A flicker of annoyance dances across Whispers's face, like it should be obvious. "You'll be a spy in the heart of their empire. You'll learn their secrets. You'll position yourself within their elite. You'll rise through their ranks undetected. You'll learn *everything*." It's rare to see her smile, but now she does. "And when you're done, you can burn that place to the ground."

I shake my head. "I don't know...."

"Think of it this way," she says, and I can tell by the way she leans forward that she's moving to the hard sell. "You'll walk out of there as skilled as any Wizard in the Republic."

I breathe in sharply. I've spent the last three years frustrated in my magic, limited to the basic Glyphs that Pavel could teach me, stuck at the level of a beginner. I've lost hours, days, weeks, months, trying to do more and failing, bursting out of the Null with aching hands and blistered skin and tears in my eyes.

I glance at my knives. Glyphs. Real Glyphs. Advanced Glyphs. As skilled as any Wizard in the Republic.

"How am I supposed to get in there?" I ask at last.

"There is a girl a year older than you, Alayne Dewinter of New Kenshire. She was given a Mark at birth as a reward to her father, the first of her line. Three years from now, she'll be invited to attend Blackwater," she says. "You'll intercept her on the way, kill her, and take her identity. Her letter of admittance and your Mark should be enough to get you into the school. No one there will have met Alayne or will know that you're not her. New Kenshire is half a world away, and she's never even set foot on this continent. As far as everyone at Blackwater will know...*you* will be Alayne Dewinter."

"Won't her parents eventually come visit?"

"Her father is an old man in poor health, his mind and memory clouded. Her mother has been removed from the equation." Something dark and frightening dances across Whispers's eyes. "For all intents and purposes, Alayne Dewinter is on her own."

"Still..." I say. "It seems too easy...."

"That's because you haven't seen the years of work that have gone into this," she says curtly. "This is a plan a decade in the making, Alka. Dozens of our best operatives have given their all...even their lives...to set it in motion. Everything you've been through, everything you've suffered, has been for this." She leans forward and puts her hand on mine, and I jerk back a little because her affection is so rare. "You're the only one who can do it."

She goes, the door creaking gently shut behind her, leaving me alone with the weight of everything she's just laid on me. She knows I'll say yes. I have to. No matter how angry I am, no matter how scared, no matter how badly I just want to curl up into a ball and never get up, I have to now.

For Sera.

I pick up my knives, turn them over in my hands, hold them with a new sense of purpose. "Alayne Dewinter," I whisper, saying her name for what will be the first of a million times, tasting it, trying it, letting it run down my tongue. "You're mine."

CHAPTER 5

Now

The ferry drops us off at the island's southern tip, on a long wooden dock that juts out like a tongue. My mind's whirring with each step as I scan every detail, trying to commit it all to memory. The docks, about forty feet long, lead to a rocky beach. No visible defenses. No cover, either. Plenty of room to land a ship full of Revenants, but nowhere to hide when we do. I know I'm getting ahead of myself, that I ought to be focusing on just getting in without blowing my cover, but I can't help it. Planning an invasion's easy. Fitting in with this lot... that's the hard part.

"Well, we made it to Blackwater," Fyl says as we step onto the docks. "And we managed to make enemies of just three of our class's most powerful students."

I can't help but smile. "It's a start."

The docks give way to a long, windy road leading up the hill to that towering manor. It's even more impressive up close than it was from the boat, as big as a castle and twice as fancy, its polished stone surface shining in the moonlight. The road that leads up to it is lined with lamp-posts, and each lantern burns a different color: flickering crimson and ocean blue and blazing white and even a dark obsidian flame that strikes my eyes as deeply wrong. I can hear music playing from somewhere, a rousing rendition of Marovia's national anthem, and as the wind blows through the trees around us, their leaves sigh and sparkle. Is it always like this? Is this just how they live?

I take a step forward, toward the road, and then I see them. Dozens of young men and women, waiting at the end of the docks. Their features are varied, Marovian, Velkșchen, Sithartic, and Kindrali, but they all wear matching beige uniforms, and they watch us with expressions at once expectant and apprehensive.

Servants.

Humbles.

I suck in my teeth. Of course they'd have a full staff of Humbles here. Wizards this rich can't go to the bathroom without a servant to wipe their ass. Even here, in a place that oozes magic out of every brick and stone, they've still got Humbles to do the dirty work. Why bother going through the effort of using magic when you can just throw a body at it? Why bother doing something yourself when you can force someone else to do it for you?

My vision flares red. I turn to Fyl, but she's actually smiling at the sight. "Finally, some help. I was getting really tired of having to do everything for myself."

I smile again, but this one's forced. It's a harsh reminder. Fyl might be friendly, but when it comes down it, she's still one of *them*.

One of the Humbles spots me, her eyes lighting on my own. A pretty girl, tall and willowy, with pale skin and jet-black hair up in a neat bun. She approaches me slowly, her amber eyes flitting up to meet mine and then back down, her expression guarded, hard to read. A long horizontal scar runs the length of her jaw. There's something off about her, something I can't quite put my finger on, like when you're trying to remember a word but it's just out of reach.

"Welcome to Blackwater, my lady," she says. Her voice is low and husky, not quite what I expected. "May I take your bag?"

"I can carry it myself," I say, before I can think better of it.

She pauses uncertainly. "I don't understand," she says. Her eyes meet mine, cautious and curious. "Have I displeased you? Would you prefer another servant?"

"No," I say, "It's not that... it's... I..."

Fyl cocks a skeptical eyebrow my way. "Do you not have Humbles in New Kenshire?"

"No, we do, I just..." I take a deep breath and collect myself. The mission is what matters. Not my feelings, not what's right. The mission is to be Alayne. And what would Alayne do?

Sera's words echo in my ears, like always. *Find the truth behind the lie.*

"I was just feeling a bit overwhelmed. I wasn't prepared for such a magnificent sight." I shove my bag forward, into the Humble's hands. She hoists it onto her back, straining just a little. "Lead the way."

"Of course, my lady," the girl says, and we walk forward, up the cobblestone road to the manor. Back on the boat, the night air was cold, but here I just feel the soft warmth radiating from all those magical lanterns, like I'm sitting by a crackling fire. Fyl lags behind, chatting with some scrawny red-haired boy who shouted her name, so I keep pace with the Humble girl instead. "Where are we going?" I ask her.

"To the grand hall. The Welcoming Banquet has been set up for the incoming class," she says. "Don't worry. I will make sure your bag gets to your room."

"Thanks. I appreciate it." I glance around to make sure no one else is listening. "What's your name, anyway?"

She arches an eyebrow. "We don't typically share our names."

"Well, I'm from New Kenshire, where we do things differently," I say, because I can just maybe force myself to give this girl orders, but the very least I owe her is learning her name. "I'd like to know who's carrying my bag."

She pauses, and for just one moment, I swear I can see her lips twitch into the tiniest hint of a smile. "Marlena."

"Well, then. I appreciate your service, Marlena. I'll call on you if I need anything else."

She nods. "It would be my honor."

The path winds up the hill, through a tall grove of birch trees. Statues of legendary Wizards watch us from the shadows with blank eyes. Dark chittering birds call at us from the branches. I can make out more of the manor above and the buildings around it. Their architecture's varied, some made of fresh brick and others ancient stone. "Do you live in the dormitories as well?" I ask Marlena.

"Oh, no." She shakes her head, like the idea's unthinkable. "There's a small village on the island's eastern coast, beyond the forest. The servants all stay there."

"A village?" I repeat. "Is that necessary?"

Marlena shrugs, which is impressive, given my bag slung over her shoulder. "Working for the Wizards of Blackwater is an incredible honor, and it carries great responsibility. We've all dedicated our lives to protecting the secrecy of this sacred place."

Gods. A whole village of people, living and dying on this rock, just so the richest Wizards in the world don't have to carry their own bags. I'll help them, I decide. I'll make sure they make it out of this. Marlena especially.

I walk the rest of the way in silence, to the top of the hill, through an ornate iron gate with BLACKWATER ACADEMY etched on top. The main manor stands before me, all five stories of its elegance. Huge marble columns frame the carved blackwood doors of the entryway. Ornate shingles sparkle on the colossal domed roof. I swear, for one moment, a gargoyle's head swivels.

Marlena peels off, walking alongside the other Humbles to carry our bags to the cluster of secondary buildings, the dormitories. I stick with the other Wizards as we pass through the open doors into the manor itself. It's the most beautiful building I've ever been in. Slick marble floors reflect torchlight like the surface of a still lake, golden filigrees line the vaulted ceilings, and the walls are adorned with towering bookshelves and elegantly framed oil paintings.

I give up on mapping the place out, at least for tonight. There are too many doors, too many halls, too many stairways. It feels like a maze, which makes me a trapped rat. But I follow the others, rounding one corner, taking a short flight up, before passing through yet another set of wide doors into the most elegant banquet hall I've ever seen.

The room is huge, with a high domed ceiling decorated with an intricate mural of the Five Gods above. Dozens and dozens of slick wooden tables sit beneath in neat rows, and students have begun taking seats at their benches. A rotating candelabra sits at the center of each table, its light dancing off the silverware and porcelain plates. Glyphs pulse in glass orbs mounted along the walls, some familiar, others arcane and inscrutable.

But it's the food that really catches my eye, not to mention my nose. There's so much of it, and all of it is amazing. Plates of fluffy, buttery rolls. Trays of sizzling peppers stuffed with minced beef. Skewers of grilled onions and seasoned tomatoes and spicy Sithartic chicken. Bowls piled high with ripe pears and fresh berries and juicy melons. And at the center, a tower of creamy frosted cakes taller than me.

My mouth waters and my stomach lurches and my eyes actually burn for one second, because somehow it's this room, this food, that's bringing the conflicting emotions churning within me to a boil. It's more food than I've seen in my life, combined. I want to eat all of it, literally all of it, and I want to *enjoy* eating it, because how could I not? I want it so bad, it actually hurts. But at the same time, as badly, maybe even more, I want to scream at the sight, to grab one of those rotating candelabras and burn this whole place to the ground.

There were months of my life when all I'd had to eat was stale bread and brittle dried meat, months of boiled potatoes and maybe, if I was lucky, a few scraps of cheese. In the forests of Galfori, I'd gotten by on nothing but a stew of stringy rabbit meat for a year. I once went three days without eating. *Three days.* And here, they have so much food in just this one banquet, enough to feed so many hungry mouths, to fill so many stomachs, and they just lay it all out. Would the leftovers even go to the servants' village, to Marlena? Or would they just be thrown away?

No. I push those thoughts down, all the way down. Not tonight. I can be angry tomorrow and the day after that. Tonight, I just need to fit in.

I join Fyl at one of the tables closer to the back. The others are all eating calmly, patiently, normally. A Humble boy comes by, offering wine. I look to Fyl to make sure it's acceptable, but she's already downed her goblet, so I take that as a yes and get one of my own.

The wine hits me instantly, settling into my chest with a soft warmth, and for a moment I relax enough to really take in the room. It's noisy and bright, thrumming with the chatter of three hundred students, some shouting, some laughing, some clinking their glasses together in boisterous toasts. I crane my head back and for the first time notice there's a whole second story, a long balcony along the room's far wall. A few dozen adult Wizards sit there, men and women in elegant robes, stern and scholarly. The professors, I imagine.

Fyl taps my shoulder, jerking my gaze down. "Hey," she says, her cheeks a little flushed. "Check him out."

I follow her eyes to the farthest table at the back of the room. A young man sits there, completely alone, arms folded, not eating. His skin is a rich black, the darkest I've ever seen, and his hair runs down his back in long, thin braids. He's a good head taller than most boys in the room, and he's wearing a style of shirt I've never seen, a flowing black tunic tied together over a series of clasps in the middle. It's cut off at the shoulders, and it's his arms that catch my attention: lean, strong, and covered with intricately drawn lines and swoops that pulse orange like a flickering candle. "Who is that?" I ask.

"Prince Talyn Ravensgale of the Xintari Kingdom," Fyl replies. "I heard a rumor he'd be in our class, but I didn't really believe it…."

I blink. I've never even met a Xintari, much less a prince. "What's he doing here?"

"It was part of that big trade deal Grandmaster Madison signed," Fyl explains. "An exchange of wards. Some of our best and brightest went to stay with their royals, and they sent him here." She pauses, popping a ripe red berry into her mouth. "Can't say he looks happy about it."

She's not wrong. Talyn sits slumped in his seat, his dark-brown eyes scanning the room with a mixture of curiosity and boredom. I know that look. It's the look I'd have if I didn't have to pretend to be one of them. For one single moment, his eyes find mine, and his eyebrow arches just the slightest bit with intrigue, and I glance away.

"So," Fyl says, dragging out the word into at least four syllables. "Do you favor men or women more?"

I don't actually know Alayne's preference, so I decide to just answer honestly for myself. "Both. Equally."

"Mmm. I mostly favor men," Fyl replies. "And I have to say, the prince there is awfully easy on the eyes."

Maybe it's the wine or the conversation, but I feel my cheeks flush. I haven't had much experience with romance. There's not much time for it when you're fighting alongside the Republic's most wanted fugitives. I've only ever kissed two people: Dina, the flirty daughter of an innkeeper who sheltered us, and Grenn, a scrawny mop-haired recruit who'd joined us at Deneros Point, who'd kept me warm through the night during that wicked snowstorm. Poor Grenn.

"Is there much of that here?" I ask Fyl. "Favoring, that is. Romance."

She stares at me. "We're three hundred teenagers cooped up on an island for two years with unlimited wine. Are you really asking if people get together?"

"Fair enough," I reply, downing the rest of my goblet.

"It's half the reason my parents were excited for me to go. 'Maybe you can meet someone,' they said, 'someone nice and wealthy, from one of the proper families.'" Fyl rolls her eyes. "Like that's the best they can hope for."

I'm about to say something when I'm cut off by the sound of a dozen horns playing, and the room goes silent. "All rise for Headmaster Aberdeen!" a voice booms from the professors' row. We all stand, turning to a small platform at the front of the room. A door behind it swings open, and the headmaster steps out, smiling and waving. All the students around me applaud, their faces bright and eager. I've heard of Magnus's reputation and how the Wizards fawn over him: beloved headmaster, brilliant Wizard, advisor to the Senate, famed throughout the Republic for his kindness and wisdom.

Then I see him.

My breath dies in my throat.

He's aged a bit in the past decade. His pointy beard and curly hair are now a dull gray. His stomach bulges out a little more against his ornate sparkling robe. A leather patch covers the place where his right eye would be. But I recognize him all the same.

Magnus Aberdeen, headmaster of Blackwater, is the man who killed my parents.

CHAPTER 6

Now

In that moment, I don't think. I don't choose. My body moves of its own volition, carried in a trance by a lifetime of bottled rage. I rise from my seat, ignore a startled Fyl, and make my way forward, through the banquet hall, past table after table, toward the podium at the front. Toward the man standing there. The man I'm going to kill.

The world around me is a dull roar. The past, the future, my plan, my purpose, all of it has faded into a pounding red throb. I don't care about being Alayne Dewinter anymore. I don't care about Whispers or the Revenants. I don't care about living to tomorrow.

He's alive. The Wizard who killed my parents. The man who took everything from me, who set me on this path. The bastard, the murderer, the monster. I don't know how, but he's alive, and he's right there, just half a room in front of me, smiling warmly as he soaks in applause, not a care in the world.

He's going to die. Now.

My heart slams against my ribs. My blood roars through my veins. My hands flit to a table, grab a serrated knife. I'm not going to use magic on him. No, that'd be too quick, too easy. I'm going to drive the blade right into his chest and watch him bleed out. I'm going to stare into his eyes as he dies and whisper my name in his ear.

Twenty-five feet away now. Twenty. Fifteen. I take stride after stride, drawing closer and closer. No one's noticed me. Every eye is on the front, on him, the murderer. I'm not a person, not then. I am an arrow fired from a bow ten years ago, hurtling toward its inevitable destination. I'm going to die here, I know that. But I'm going to die satisfied.

Headmaster Magnus Aberdeen still hasn't noticed me. He's turned to the side, toward the balcony with the other professors, a hand raised as he beams in their adulation. His eye is twinkling, beard crinkled in a warm smile. He has no idea the shadow that's coming for him, that's about to end him, that's about to drown that smile in a torrent of blood.

Ten feet. This is it. I turn the knife over in my hand, steadying its point. I swallow my breath. Magnus's head turns to me, just a little, his gray eye finally seeing me, widening just a bit in suspicion. I draw back my hand and—

Someone collides with me, hard, from the side, and I tumble down onto the banquet hall's floor. My wrist hits marble, and the knife goes skittering out of my grip, sliding under a table. The room goes silent as every head swivels our way. Something cold, wet, and red pours onto me, soaking into my dress. Blood? No. Wine. I scramble back, instinctively, and see the face of the person who ran into me, staring back in horror. Amber eyes. Jet-black hair. The Humble servant girl, Marlena.

"I am so sorry, my lady!" she says, frantically dabbing at my dress with a cloth. "I—I was merely serving wine—I didn't see you coming."

It's like I've been wrenched out of a dream, like I'm being dragged up above the surface from the depths of the sea. The world comes back in a rush: the smells of the feast, the dancing of the lights above, and the voices, so many voices, chattering, whispering, laughing. I feel the penetrating heat of a thousand eyes as every single person in the room stares at me, and that certainty I'd felt just a second ago curdles into cold dread. I'm exposed. Trapped. Vulnerable.

But the focus isn't on me. "Girl!" Headmaster Aberdeen barks. "Watch where you're going! You've just ruined that young lady's dress!"

"Forgive me, Headmaster!" Marlena begs, terrified. "It won't happen again. I promise."

I don't know what to do. Everything's happening too fast. The knife is still lying there, just a few feet away. I could grab it and still follow through, leap up and plunge it into the headmaster's chest. Even with everyone watching, they couldn't stop me in time. But I can't pull my gaze away from Marlena's, from the terror in her eyes, the way her hands tremble as they dab at my dress, the way her slim collarbone rises and falls with every breath. She's a part of this now. If I strike, everyone will assume she was in on it, a distraction. She'll be tortured. Killed. Probably her whole family, too. And it'll be my fault.

I can't do it.

"Groundskeeper Tyms," the headmaster growls, and the surly bearded man from the ferry, the one who'd demanded to see my Mark, steps forward. "Please see that this Humble is duly punished. Ten lashes."

The man, Groundskeeper Tyms, grins. "My pleasure," he says, striding forward to jerk Marlena up to her feet as she gasps.

No. Not for me. I rise to my feet. "Apologies, Headmaster, but it's my fault, not hers," I say, and I hear an odd murmur run through the room. "I was careless. I ran into her. Go easy on the girl."

Headmaster Aberdeen looks at me, seeing me, really seeing me, for the first time. His beady gray eye meets mine, taking me in, scrutinizing. Could he somehow recognize me?

No. He glances away with a bored shrug. "Fine. Five lashes," he says. "Now can we resume the banquet, please?" He smiles wide, welcoming, and the room is effortlessly his again. "I do believe I have a rousing speech to give!"

Everyone laughs, a booming roar. I can barely breathe. The crowd turns back to Aberdeen as he begins his big welcoming address, but I can still feel some eyes on me: Fyl, flushed with vicarious embarrassment; Marlena, grateful, even as Tyms drags her away; and at the table right next to me, Marius Madison himself, shooting me a knowing "told-you-so" smile.

I don't know what to do. But I know I can't be here anymore, not with these people, not like this. Not if I want to preserve my mission. Not if I want to preserve myself.

I rush away, between the tables, toward a pair of glass doors at the hall's west end. I push through them and out onto a balcony, a curved ledge with an ornate railing overlooking the forests to the east of the school. The cold night air washes over me like a torrent and I gasp, and I think it's the first time I've breathed since I saw Aberdeen's face.

He's alive. How? How is he alive? He was in the house when my father's wards went off. He died screaming, burning, I know it, I *know* it....

But here he is, alive all the same.

He must have shielded himself, somehow. He made it out. He's been alive this whole time, safe within these walls, gaining power, growing stronger. While Sera and I starved and bled and fought, while my parents lay still below the earth, he was *alive*, drinking the finest wines, eating at banquets, giving rousing speeches while basking in praise and adulation. While I lost everything, *everything*, he was alive!

I want to scream, to cry, to snap the railing clean off and hurl it into trees below. I want to tear the bricks out of the walls, to plunge this island into the sea, to set the whole world aflame. I want to—

"Too much to drink?" a voice asks from behind me.

I spin. The boy from before, the prince, is there, leaning back against the doorframe with one knee bent. He holds a small chalice in a broad hand, watching me with amusement. The absolute last thing I want to do right now is talk to a stranger, but I've already made myself suspicious enough, and at this rate it's clear that a moment alone is an impossibility. I pull myself together with a breath. I become Alayne.

"A little." I force a laugh. "I suppose I'm not used to a vintage this strong."

"That's funny. I was just thinking it was surprisingly weak." The boy takes one last sip of his wine, then rests his chalice on the railing as he walks toward me. "I'm Talyn. Talyn Ravensgale IV, technically, but I doubt there are other Talyns here."

"Alayne Dewinter," I lie. He steps forward, bathed in soft moonlight, and I get my first good look at him. He stands a good two heads taller than me, his body the kind of lean that suggests hidden strength. His hair hangs in dozens of neat braids, and the finest hint of a beard decorates his jaw. His cheekbones are angular, his chin sharp, and his dark-brown eyes, flecked with gold, sparkle softly as he sizes me up.

More than anything else, though, I'm drawn to his arms. It's not just that they're nice arms, though they're definitely nice, lean but toned, with wide hands decorated in silver rings and long veins pushing against his forearms. No, it's what's on his arms that I'm fascinated by. Runic symbols, dozens of them, spiral around his biceps, complex and bright. From across the banquet hall, I'd thought they were tattoos, but I can see now they're something else. They're drawn on, I think, in some kind of soft colored dust, a dust that shines gold and blue against his skin, like stars in the night sky.

I strain to remember everything I know about the Xintari Kingdom, which is embarrassingly little. They rule the continent far to the south, across the Everwarm Sea, a land of vast deserts and towering volcanoes. They're rich, I think, richer than Marovia, but also secretive, isolated, negotiating with the Republic through a single ambassador. And they have Wizards, powerful ones, ones the Senate fears. The Republic has never tried to conquer their lands, which speaks to their strength more than anything else.

Talyn notices me staring at his arms. "A Xintari custom." He shrugs. He's as much an outsider here as I am, more even, but he seems completely at ease. No. More than at ease. He seems utterly indifferent. "I wouldn't normally bother, but my father insisted I go formal for my arrival. Representing the royal family and all that."

"So it's true then. You're a prince," I say.

"I am," Talyn admits with a crooked smile. "Though I assure you, it's much less exciting than you'd think. I've got six older brothers and three older sisters. My odds of sitting on the Golden Throne are just barely better than yours."

"Given that I've just heard of the Golden Throne for the first time, I can't imagine that's true."

"It's not really golden. Not all of it anyway," he replies. "That's the downside of being a youngest child. My oldest sister leads the army. My oldest brother, the treasury. And I'm stuck here, halfway across the world, given the honor of representing our kingdom in a school for Marovian brats."

I let out a little laugh, a genuine one, if only because it's such a relief to hear someone on the same page. "So you're a diplomat," I say, and my eyes travel to his bare wrists. No Godsmark. "Not a Wizard?"

"Oh, I'm a Wizard. But Xintari don't tattoo our *wrists*," Talyn replies as if that were an actual answer. "Enough about me, though. I want to know more about you."

"Me?" I ask, and by the Gods, what I would give for just a few moments of solitude, a few moments without pretending. "There's not much to know, I'm afraid. I'm certainly no princess. Just another student here, same as everyone else."

"Oh, I don't know if that's true," he says, eyes flashing to mine. "You're the only student I saw storming through the banquet hall with a knife in her hand."

My blood runs cold. He saw. He *knows.* And he's just standing there with that bemused smile, his eyes drinking me in. "I…I don't…I wasn't…"

Talyn laughs, shaking his head, and his braids sway, tiny silver beads at their tips jingling. "Relax. I'm not judging," he says. "I'm just curious which of those pompous little shits you wanted to stab so badly."

I let out the tiniest breath of relief. So he doesn't know everything. He doesn't know I was going after Aberdeen. He just thinks I'm holding a grudge. That, that I can work with. "Marius Madison." I try out a playful shrug of my own. "And I wasn't going to stab him. Just give him a little scare."

"Marius Madison," Talyn says, and for the first time, his smile vanishes. "He and his father greeted me as I arrived. A pair of preening peacocks, desperate to prove themselves superior. Now I wish you *had* stabbed him."

"So you won't report me?"

Talyn lets out a low chuckle as he turns back to face me. "Never. Your secret is safe with me."

"And why is that?"

"Because I've been on this wretched continent two whole weeks, and you're the first interesting person I've met." He reaches down and takes my hand in his. His palm is soft, warm, and he raises my hand gently to his lips. "It's been an honor to meet you, Lady Dewinter."

I still have no idea what this boy is after, but I know I can't trust a word he says. "And you, Prince Talyn IV."

"Just Talyn," he says, and then with one last smile, he vanishes back through the curtain into the banquet hall, leaving me alone in the night.

Gods. Gods! I practically collapse against the railing. The world spins around me, pulsing at the edges. My knees feel weak, my breath ragged. It's too much, it's all too much. I can't do this. I'm a fighter, not a spy. I can't keep up this front day after day. I can't keep playing games with these schemers, parsing their every word for cunning intent. I can't walk back into the hall, can't force another smile, can't *do this.* Not while my parents' killer draws breath. I just can't. Not by myself. Not without Sera.

I close my eyes and remember Whispers's training. *Let your thoughts go*, she says. *Take in only what you feel.*

The cold metal of the railing against my palms.

The smell of salt on the chill breeze.

The whistling of the wind, the indistinct chatter from the hall.

My breath, rising and falling. Rising and falling. One, two. One, two. One, two.

I open my eyes and see it. The treetops laid out before me, sprawling, beautiful, swaying ever so slightly. The ocean, vast and endless beyond. And at the island's edge, a tiny tinkling of lights, flickering like distant fireflies. The village, the one Marlena told me about. The Humbles.

I can do this. I can finish my mission.

I have to.

I smooth out my dress (which is, of course, utterly ruined by the wine), and push my way into the banquet hall. It's just as I left it: noisy, blinding, a sensory maelstrom. A few heads pivot my way, but most of the students are lost in their own conversations, which is quite the relief. Thankfully, Aberdeen has left the stage, so I don't have to deal with seeing him, not yet.

"Are you all right?" Fyl asks as I slide back down next to her. "What *was* that?"

"Sorry. I just got a little overwhelmed and needed some fresh air. And, apparently, some wine poured on me." I pull on my dress, its deep-purple stain. "What did I miss?"

"Headmaster Aberdeen gave his big speech, the faculty introduced themselves, they served little cakes with coffee liqueur. Nothing interesting. Well, that's not true, the cakes were extremely interesting." She nods her head toward the table. "You're just in time for the important part."

I glance down and notice for the first time that there is a massive scaled egg, black as obsidian and big as a melon, resting in an ornate clawed holder in front of me. Looking around, everyone else has one, too.

"Um," I say.

"Gods, you know nothing!" Fyl laughs. "This is where we learn which Order we've been placed into!"

"I'm going to need more than that."

"All of us are going to get divided among five Orders of Blackwater. One for each of the Gods." Fyl gestures up at the stage, and I see five long banners unfurled. Each one is a distinct color, each adorned with an animal sigil at the top. "The Orders all represent the traits of the Gods," she continues. "Vanguard, the golden stag, for power and dominance. Javellos, the green monkey, for cunning and commerce. Selura, the blue raven, for wisdom and patience. Zartan, the red bear, for bravery and aggression. Nethro, the black kraken, for death and . . . everything else."

"And the egg . . . ?"

Fyl snorts with laughter. "It's a divinity egg. It'll tell you which Order you're supposed to be in by reading your soul. It's *magic*," she says, waggling her fingers. "Not really, though. I mean, there's some neat magic with how the eggs reveal it, but everyone knows they just decide which Order we're in before we get here."

Up ahead, some students whoop while others clap. Marius Madison hops onto a bench, pumping his fist in the air, with his egg cracked open in front of him. "Vanguard! Yes! The strong shall prosper!" Names are appearing on the banners as eggs crack, and I see Marius's fade onto the gold banner in an elegant script.

"Like there was ever any doubt." Fyl rolls her eyes, and I can't help but notice her egg sits uncracked. "I'm going to be in Javellos. I mean, almost certainly. Every Potts ever was. Hooray for merchants, right?" She smiles but her body radiates nervousness. "Go on. Open yours."

Might as well see where this goes. I reach out and press my hand on the top of my egg, and instantly an electric tingle runs through me, lightning in my veins. I let out a little gasp. The grooves between the scales light up with a blinding light, forming a honeycomb of dazzling hexagons, and then the whole thing crumbles into a fine white ash. I feel the pull of the Null and see the aftershock of an illusion Glyph blink in the air, like the colors you see when you press your palms to your eyes. Then it's gone, and there's just a pile of ash with a small black stone lying in it.

"Looks like you're in the Order of Nethro," Fyl says.

I look up at the black banner with the kraken at the top and see my name, well, Alayne's name, appear on it. "Is that bad?"

"No. Not at all. None of the Orders are bad, really. It's just a matter of personality." She takes a quick swig of wine, exhales, then reaches out for her egg. "All right. Let's do this." Her hand touches it and it glows, and when it crumbles, there's a black stone there, just like mine.

Fyl's face falls. "Nethro?" she whispers, lip trembling. "Shit. Really? *Shit.*"

"I thought you said all the Orders were the same?"

"That's when I thought I was getting into Javellos! I was being nice!" She slumps forward, face in her hands. "Wow. The first Potts to not even qualify for Javellos. Nethro. *Nethro.*"

I know it's irrational for me to be offended given that I'm not really Alayne, but I can't help prickling. I take my black stone in my hand, turning it over. It seems ordinary enough. "What's so bad about Nethro?"

Fyl sighs. "The ambitious political kids? They get put in Vanguard. The cunning kids go to Javellos. The bookworms go to Selura. The athletes to Zartan. And Nethro... it's the reject Order. Where they send all misfits and outcasts and, well, new Marks. All the students they expect to fail." She takes another sip from her goblet, realizes it's empty, and angrily tosses it aside. "You know what my father always used to say? Vanguards lead, Javellos greed, Seluras read, and Zartans bleed."

"And what do Nethros do?"

"Absolutely nothing." Fyl angrily shoves her stone aside. "Gods. My parents are going to be devastated."

I lean back, taking it all in. I'd always thought the world was divided into two groups: Humbles and Wizards, the powerful and the oppressed. I'd assumed all Wizards had it easy. But it's clear to me now that I was wrong, that the structure of power is so much more complicated. Hierarchies within hierarchies, ladders within ladders, a never-ending nesting doll of social climbing. Fyl probably has more money than anyone I'd ever met in my first seventeen years, but within these halls, she's treated like a nobody.

It's hard to believe, but it makes so much sense. We've been students here less than an hour, and already we've been sorted and divided, judged arbitrarily and shuffled into factions. It's cruel, unimaginably cruel, but I can see the purpose. Already I find my eyes roaming the room for other black stones, seeking allies. Already, I feel hatred blossoming toward the Vanguards, Marius's faction, for no other reason than he's one of them.

It's the way of Wizards, summed up. Under the table, my hand clenches involuntarily into a fist, and I long for the cold grip of my Loci. This world is wrong. Every part of it.

I need to focus, so I turn back to Fyl. "Do the Orders really matter? What do they get you?"

"Status?" Fyl says, like it's the most obvious thing in the world. "Social worth? The validation of our parents? And, you know, the Great Game. If you care about that."

"The what now?"

"You would've heard it if you'd been here for Headmaster Aberdeen's talk," Fyl teases, not realizing how close I came to making sure Aberdeen never talked again. "The Great Game is a big contest held over the course of our first year. There are three challenges, one every few months, where all the Orders compete for points. And at the end of the year, the Order with the most points is crowned the Order Triumphant. They get a big celebration where the Grandmaster honors them on the floor of the Senate. It's a whole thing." She shakes her head. "Not that it matters, though. Vanguard wins every year."

Fyl turns away, flagging down a Humble for more wine, which is good because she doesn't see the look on my face. The whole world seems to grow quiet and still as the weight of her words, thrown off so casually, wash over me. The Grandmaster honors the winning Order on the floor of the Senate. *The floor of the Senate.*

The Revenants have been around, in one way or another, for a century. We've had our share of victories: a garrison burned, a Wizard assassinated, a labor camp liberated. But the Senate has always been the crown jewel that's eluded us, the conquest we've never even come close to claiming. We've tried, oh, we've definitely tried. But the Senate of Marovia is the most secure building in the world, nestled in the heart of the impenetrable Arbormont, hidden by layers and layers of protective Glyphs, guarded night and day by an army of Enforcers. Whispers long abandoned hope of ever attacking it directly.

She sent me here to learn the secrets of magic. But even she had no idea of the real prize at play. If I can keep up my act, if I can rise through the ranks, if I can win this stupid game, I'd go where no Revenant has ever been. They'd *welcome* me into the Senate itself, past the wards, past the walls, past the Enforcers. They'd bring me onto that floor and surround me with all of the Republic's most important and powerful people. They'd leave themselves wide open.

And I smile. Not the fake smile I've been forcing all night, but a real, genuine smile, because I just can't help myself. I look up at the professors, right at Aberdeen. He's leaning back in his chair, laughing as he sips wine from a jeweled chalice, not a care in the world. A minute ago, that would've made me livid. But now, I see it for the weakness, for the vulnerability, that it is. His guard is down. He has no idea that his destruction, his ruin, is sitting just on the other side of the room.

My calm gives way to resolve, to confidence, even. I'm going to fulfill my mission. I'm going to learn all their secrets. I'm going to be welcomed, *welcomed*, onto the floor of the Senate. And then I'm going to destroy it.

Aberdeen boasted of the order he built before killing my parents? Well, I'm going to make him watch as I burn it down around him. I'm going to set his entire beloved Republic ablaze before his eyes.

And then? Then when I've taken everything from him? When I've made him feel a taste of what he did to me?

Then I'll going to kill him.

Chapter 7

Then

I am seven years old when I find my new home.

After my parents are killed, after I scream and howl at that beach, the next few days are a blur, a daze half remembered through burning eyes. I stagger through the streets with Sera, hiding from patrolling Enforcers. We huddle in dark alleys, drinking water out of puddles, eating discarded scraps from the market. We beg strangers for help and catch only averted gazes and scowls of disgust.

And somehow, somehow, as dawn rises three days later, we find ourselves on the other side of Laroc, in the slums, where wooden shacks grow off one another like barnacles, where the air is hazy with smoke and noisy with the chatter from brothels. I shove the paper my father gave me at a bleary-eyed drunk who points us to our final destination, an old warehouse with a high roof and walls of crumbling red brick. I stagger toward it, my messy hair caked to my head, my clothes tattered, my face blackened with ash and dirt. Sera follows, head down, hidden behind her tangled red curls. She hasn't spoken a single word since the night that our parents died, no matter how much I begged her, no matter how hard I cried.

I'm afraid she'll never speak again.

A massive blond Velkschen man stands guard by the warehouse door, a hand resting on the wide flat blade sheathed at his side. In the years to come, I'll know him as Crixus; I'll learn the art of the blade from him; I'll cry when he dies. But for now, he's just the terrifying man blocking me from the place I need to go.

I approach anyway. What else can I do? "Please, sir," I say. "I...I..."

"No money," he says with a guttural accent, and I can see how awful I must look by the revulsion in his eyes. "No give."

"My name is Alka Chelrazi," I choke out. "This is my sister, Sera. Our father was Petyr Chelrazi. He sent us here. To talk to Whispers." I collapse to my knees, because I can't go any farther, and if this doesn't work, nothing will. "Please."

The man stares at me, alarmed. "Wait," he says at last, then ducks inside. Minutes pass, long minutes in the hot sun, and then he comes out again, looking no more certain. "Whispers not here, but...come. Come!"

He pushes aside the door and ushers me in. Sera and I follow him into the cool shadows of the room, and right away I understand we are somewhere secret, somewhere dangerous and forbidden. The warehouse has been repurposed into a barracks. Dozens of men and women fill the place, sitting on catwalks, poring over maps and papers, chatting softly under rickety awnings. Weapons in racks line the walls, swords and spears and crossbows. At the far end of the room, on a raised platform, a lean woman spars against a shirtless man, circling as their wooden blades strike with resounding clacks. Was this where my father would go during the days? What had he been involved in?

"Wait here," the guard says, gesturing us to a bench. "Whispers back soon." I slump down on the bench, aware that the room has gone silent, that the fighters have stopped fighting and the plotters stopped plotting, that everyone is staring at us. I don't know what I'm doing here, don't know where *here* even is, don't know what happens next. I just know that my parents are dead and my world is shattered. I just know that nothing will ever be right again.

I put my head in my hands and I cry.

"It'll be okay," Sera says.

I stop and slowly look up from my hands. Sera's sitting next to me on the bench, and she's brushed her curls aside so she's looking at me with her big eyes. For days, every time I looked at her they were bleary and bloodshot, but right now, they look clear, focused, determined.

"You talked," I whisper. "I was so scared you wouldn't talk anymore. I was so scared...." I look around this big dark room, at the surly faces watching us, at the jagged weapons and dirty floors. "I'm still so scared...."

"We can't be scared," she says. Her voice is determined, serious, older than it has any right to be. "Papa said we have to be strong and brave. He said if we came here, we'd be safe. So we're going to be safe. Because he said so."

"Papa's dead," I say, for the first time out loud, and putting those words into the air somehow makes them real. "Mama's dead, too. They're both dead!"

"But we're not dead," Sera says, and when she looks at me she's somehow at once incredibly strong and desperately weak. "You're still alive. I'm still alive. We have each other."

Then she lunges forward and throws her arms around me, and I hug her tight and we just hold each other, two sisters, two souls adrift in a dark sea, clutching each other just to stay afloat. I have spent three days alone in a storm, unable to see anything but pain and despair, and here, here at last is an ember of warmth burning in the darkness. I don't know it now, but that hug is one of the most important things that will ever happen. Sera and I have always been close, but from that moment on, we're inseparable.

That hug sets me on the path that will define the next decade of my life, that will send me to Blackwater. Everything that follows, all the fire and blood and pain and love, all of it can be traced back to that hug.

"I love you," I tell her.

"I love you, too," she says, and her little arms hold me so close it hurts. "We'll be all right. We have to be."

Whispers arrives in the late afternoon, limping into the room with the steady thumping of her cane on the wooden floor. The other rebels drop what they're doing as she enters and stand bolt upright, fists pressed to their heart in salute. Without a word, she makes her way to me, her icy blue eyes boring clean through mine. "By the Gods," she says at last. "Petyr Chelrazi's girls. You survived."

"Our papa sent us here," Sera explains, her voice trembling. "He said we'd be safe."

Whispers lets out a long exhale. "I'm sure he said that," she says, carefully measuring each word. "But the reality is . . . is . . ."

Her voice trails off as her eyes widen. She's staring at me. At my arm. At my Godsmark. I pull down my sleeve instinctively, because my parents told me to never let anyone see it, but it's too late. Whispers grabs my wrist and jerks my hand up. "Is this real?" she hisses. "Tell me!"

"Y-yes," I stammer. "It's real! It hurts!"

The silence in the room is so thick it's smothering. She lets go of my hand, and I pull back, clutching it tight. She looks back at the others, then kneels in front of us. In that second, she transforms. The coldness, the stern detachment, it all melts away. She smiles, a gentle, kind smile, and wraps her arms around the two of us. "Oh, girls," she says. "Oh, my sweet girls. You're safe here. You're safe.

"You're home."

CHAPTER 8

Now

They usher us out after the feast, and we file into the sprawling courtyard behind the main hall. Cobblestone paths cut across the grass in ornate spirals, and lanterns sway from iron posts as they blaze red and purple against the dark. I don't know where I'm going, but the others seem to, so I walk with the crowd. There's a clarity in camouflage, a certainty that comes from surrendering your identity, if only for a minute, to blend in with a group.

At the end of the courtyard are five large dormitories, laid out in a wide half circle. Each one is unique, with architecture befitting its deity. The Order of Vanguard stands proud and ostentatious, with elegant marble columns and billowing golden flags. The Order of Zartan looks more like a fortress, down to its rounded parapets and an array of practice dummies set up on its lawn. The Order of Selura honors water with elegant fountains and spiraling blue balustrades, while the Order of Javellos sparkles with inlaid emeralds and shimmering filigrees. And the Order of Nethro stands at the very center, dark and cold and unadorned, its flags black, its lanterns burning an impossible obsidian flare.

The students divide themselves as they approach, sixty or so to each

Order. I see Marius and Dean and a bunch of others whoop as they pile into the Order of Vanguard, see the headmaster's niece Vyctoria stroll to the Order of Selura. Prince Talyn is out here, too, walking through the awning of the Order of Javellos. Our eyes meet, and he offers a playful shrug.

"The Xintari prince strolls through the doors of Javellos, while we're stuck in Nethro," Fyl grumbles next to me. "Unbelievable. He doesn't even look like he *wants* it."

"I think it probably suits him," I reply. "He was certainly quite cunning when we spoke."

Fyl blinks at me. "You talked to him. To the prince. When? How?"

"Outside, when I needed fresh air. He's very perceptive. Dangerous, too. And a flirt."

Fyl's jaw drops. "Who *are* you?"

We pace together toward our Order. A statue of Nethro, God of Death, stands outside, holding a scale in his bony hands, his empty eye sockets half hidden by a shroud that hangs over his face. It makes me uneasy, the way all religious sculptures make me uneasy, the way I find myself sweating and fidgeting whenever I've had to sit in a temple, trapped in the chasm between skepticism and belief. Religion and politics always go hand in hand; the high clerics serve the Senate, preach the gospel of the Republic, insist that it is divine will that Humbles serve and Wizards rule. For obvious reasons, I don't believe that. But I can't just renounce the Gods the way some of the other Revenants do, or accept that it's all a lie. I feel the Gods' power run through my veins every time I carve a Glyph, and I've spent enough time in the Null, seeing those terrifying shapes pass just beyond the veil, feeling that raw, ancient energy.

It was Pavel, of all people, who offered the best explanation, one night as we sat together gazing out at the ocean from the deck of a ship. *The way I see it, the Gods are like the tides, the moon, the stars*, he'd said, eyes glassy, cheeks red. *They exist, all right. Of course they exist. You can see them, right there, with your own two eyes. But if any man tells you he knows why they exist, what they want, what their purpose is... well, that man's either a liar or a fool.*

We pass the statue and walk up the stairs and into the dormitory itself. The first room we enter is a common area. Tall bookshelves line the walls, stacked dense with tomes. Leather couches covered with fluffy pillows fill the room. A bar rounds a corner, covered with tall multicolored bottles and crystal carafes. Portraits of accomplished Nethros line the walls: stern-faced Wizards in black robes; bearded, scarred men; and willowy gray-haired women.

It's a very nice room, but the air of the crowd around me is gloomy, despairing. No one speaks. A few students slump down on the couches, heads in hands. One, a chubby boy with a messy head of curly black hair, makes a beeline to the bar where he drinks wine straight from a carafe. I'd thought Fyl a bit overdramatic, but now I'm starting to worry. Is this Order really that bad?

As if to answer, a voice cuts through the silence. "Welcome, young krakens, to the Order of Nethro."

An older woman stands in the room's doorway. She wears a long black dress, one that clings tight to her lean frame, with elegant black gloves that rise up to her elbows. Her black hair is up in a bun, and her yellow eyes study us with a cold intelligence from behind a pair of gold-rimmed glasses. Her skin has a soft olive tint, and her lips are painted a crimson, almost bloody, red. The other students rise to attention as she enters, except for the boy with the carafe, who just keeps drinking.

"My name is Professor Iola Calfex," the woman says, crossing to the room's center. "Adjunct professor of Null studies. Scholar of Marovian history. And head of the Order of Nethro. For the next two years, you are all my wards." Her lips curl into a smile. "Try not to look so devastated."

Fyl snorts a little laugh, and Calfex's eyes flit our way. There's something about her that makes me uneasy, like she's seeing me, seeing through me, in a way that no one else has. I tense up, but then she's looking away again, toward the others, talking with the measured cadence of someone who's given the same talk a dozen times. "The other Order heads are currently giving their new students rousing speeches. They're talking about how lucky they are to be a part of their Order, singing the virtues of their most memorable alumni, promising them victory in the Great Game." She folds her hands together, lips pursed into a narrow line. "I'm not going to do that."

"Gods," the boy with the carafe groans. "Even our own Order head knows we're worthless."

"Not at all," Calfex replies, pacing toward him. "I wouldn't be here if I believed that. I choose to lead Nethro because I believe in this Order. I believe in our purpose. I believe in all of you, in your potential." She takes the carafe out of his hands, then turns to pour herself a glass. "The question is... do *you* know your potential? Your purpose?"

She phrases it like a question, but no one replies, so finally Fyl clears her throat. "Would you mind clarifying?"

"Fylmonela Potts. A delight to see you here." Calfex's smirk is a dagger. "And I'll clarify by way of a question back. I assume you all saw the statues outside. Vanguard is the God of Politicians; he wears a crown. Zartan, God of Soldiers, holds a sword. Selura the scholar holds a quill; Javellos the merchant, a goblet. All very clear. And yet Nethro, the God of Death, holds no shovel, no scarab, no bone. He holds instead a pair of scales. Why?"

The scales were an unusual touch; the Gods are typically depicted empty-handed. But even as the other students look at one another uncertainly, the answer seems obvious to me. "Because Death is the great balancer," I say, the words of scripture burned into my brain. "Death clears all ledgers. Death erases all debts. Death makes all equal."

Calfex's eyes narrow as they scrutinize me. "And you are?"

"Alayne Dewinter," I reply, and dread tightens in my stomach like a clenching fist. *I* know that quote because it's a standard at Humble funerals. But would Alayne?

Calfex just smiles. "An excellent answer, Lady Dewinter. You know your scripture well." She turns back to the others, taking a small sip from her glass. "I believe the Order of Nethro exists for a reason. I believe you have all been assigned here for a reason. And that reason is *balance*." She gestures up at the portraits hanging behind her. "Behind me, you do not see any famous Grandmasters or legendary warriors. You do not see any champions of the Great Game. And yet, you see truly influential people all the same." She makes her way down the line, tapping each portrait as she goes. "Visselyn Markos mediated the Compromise of 254, preventing a civil war. Ellaro Williamson deceived the Sithartic patriarchs in 432, allowing for the conquest of the continent. Caspar Wilshire discovered how to trap Glyphfire in glass, long after everyone had dismissed it as impossible. And Genevieve Auguste..." She reverently runs a hand along the center frame, a determined woman with a pox-scarred face. "She gave her life casting the largest flame Glyph in history, setting alight the fleet of Mad Grandmaster Sethis, and putting an end to his reign of terror. Do you all understand?"

A few heads nod. "We bring balance," the boy by the bar says.

"Exactly," Calfex replies. "And we do all the things they won't. The other Orders venerate one trait, and that traps them in single-mindedness. A Zartan will always stab a problem. A Selura will always study it. But us Nethros? We're unpredictable. We find new solutions. We brave new frontiers. And we keep the rest of them in line." She sets her empty wineglass down, turning back to us with arms open wide. "The others will say you are here because you're outcasts, because you're worthless, because you don't fit in to some clear role. I say, what's good about fitting in? I say, you're here because you're different." She smiles wide, her impeccably white teeth glinting in the light. "I say you're here because you're *interesting*."

The boy by the bar is the first to clap, and then others follow, a low cascade of applause that reverberates off the domed roof. It's not quite an enthusiastic roar, but the mood has changed. Even I feel a little swell of pride, before remembering that Calfex is still the enemy, as much as anyone else.

"It's a nice speech," Fyl whispers, even as she claps. "But being different doesn't earn your family honor. Being different doesn't get you power. Being different doesn't make you rich."

No, it doesn't. But I don't need honor or power or wealth. All I need is to make sure the Order of Nethro wins the challenges and I get into the Senate. And if these really are the students who can think differently, who can innovate around the strong and the wise? I can work with that.

The rest of the night passes uneventfully, which is a relief because I'm exhausted. I linger in the common room, have one last drink with Fyl, and try to steer clear of Calfex's scrutiny. I get to know a few of my other Nethros: Desmond, the boy with the carafe, quick with a joke; Jasper, a shy boy with enormous glasses who speaks like an encyclopedia; Tish, a nonbinary Kindrali who speaks softly but sees everything; Zigmund, a hulking Velkschen who laughs so loud it shakes the room. I can use them, I think. They're not perfect, but they'll do.

The night winds down, so we all collect our keys from Calfex and make our way upstairs, to our rooms. Mine is on the fourth floor, number 29. A single bed rests under a window. A writing desk sits against a wall, with a neat stack of papers, a quill, and a little crystal lantern that glows a soft white. At one end of the room is a wardrobe, at the other a full-length mirror. I imagine that for most of the students here, a room like this is a step back from the opulence they grew up in. But there's no question this is the nicest room I've ever had.

I step in and close the door, sighing the deepest, weariest sigh of relief. I'm finally, *finally* alone. I can drop the mask, drop Alayne Dewinter, drop the constant pretending and preening and lying. Tomorrow, I'll have to go back out there, but for now, for this precious *now*, I'm alone.

I collapse onto the bed, onto that cool, soft pillow. I close my eyes and let myself taste victory, however small. I made it. A Revenant in Blackwater. I'm in.

Sleep takes me like a gentle wave.

CHAPTER 9

Then

I am nine when I carve my first Glyph.

It's a hot summer night, the kind where you toss and turn and wake up slick with sweat, where the mosquitos hum and buzz, where the wide white face of the moon feels like a mockery. Not that I could sleep that night anyway. Not with the plans I've made.

I slip out of my tent and creep barefoot across the campsite, past the flickering embers of the firepit. We're sleeping in the forests of Galfori, our tents nestled under the tall redwood trees that reach into the skies. The Revenants I usually travel with have split up, forced to part ways after the Republic's Enforcers closed in on us in Laroc. Most of our fighters have gone north, to liberate the Velkschen labor camps and reinforce our numbers. Meanwhile, Sera, Whispers, and I travel south, along with a small company of guards, toward the lawless swamps of Morro. But it's a slow journey, a tedious ride across dusty backroads in rickety wagons, with nights spent sleeping in flimsy canvas tents under the stars.

I don't mind, not that much. Sera's there to tell me interesting facts from her books as we ride, to laugh by my side as we fish in creeks, and to snuggle up by the campfires. With Sera, I'm never alone. With Sera, I'm home.

It's her I seek out that sweltering night. I sneak into her tent, expecting to find her asleep, only to find her sitting upright, reading a heavy history tome by candlelight. She startles and I startle and she says "Alka?" bafflingly loud, and I shush her as intensely as I can before vanishing back outside.

A few seconds later, she crawls out of the tent, her red hair wild and messy around her face. "What are you doing?" she whispers. "We're supposed to be asleep!"

"*You* were awake."

"I was reading!" she insists. "What are *you* doing?"

"Getting ready." I grin. "I'm doing it. Tonight. I'm going into the Null. I'm going to do magic!"

"Wh—I—since—what?" her mouth opens and closes as she runs the gamut of emotion: confused, angry, intrigued, upset. "Gods, Alka. Why do you always come up with your worst ideas in the middle of the night?"

"Because that's when no one's up to stop me?" I beam back. "Come on! I want you to be there! I want you to see me carve my first Glyph!" I reach into my bag and pull out a folded cloth. Inside are my most prized, most secret possessions: Loci, two of them, a pair of crooked redwood wands.

"Did you *steal those*?" Her eyes go wide.

"From the armory!" I reply, giddy with excitement. "I took them one at a time, when everyone was distracted!"

"Why are you saying that like it's a good thing?" she replies, and if a whisper could somehow be a shout, she's doing it. "Are you out of your mind? Why would you do that?"

"I need to learn how to do magic, Sera!" I'm starting to get a little annoyed. I hadn't planned on this much conversation. If we keep it up too long, we'll wake someone up. "How am I going to do that without Loci?"

"From the books Whispers gave you," she insists. "They'll teach you what you need!"

I fight back the urge to roll my eyes. This is the great challenge Whispers faces. On the one hand, she has something no leader of the Revenants has ever had: a young Wizard with a Godsmark on her wrist, capable of unimaginable power and destruction. On the other, what she really has is a child, a child with no skill, no training, and, most important, no teacher. For me to be truly valuable to the Revenants, she needs me to learn to wield my power. But how can I learn with no one to instruct me?

So Whispers gives me what she can, what she manages to steal. Books about the history of Wizards. Dense tomes of magical theory that I can't begin to understand. A handful of notes stolen from raids here and there, with what might be Glyphs drawn on them.

But none of that addresses the yearning in my heart, the hunger. My body burns with the desire, the *need* to do magic. It wakes me at night. It tugs at me during the day. It's an itch that needs to be scratched, a thirst that needs to be quenched. I don't know how much of it is the Godsblood and how much of it is just me. But I can't keep sitting and reading and drawing. I need to *do*. And I don't want to do it alone.

"The books don't help," I tell Sera. "I'll never learn to be a Wizard like that. I need to try. To enter the Null. To carve Glyphs." I gesture to the Loci. "This is the only way I'll ever really learn, and you know it!"

"Alka..." she says softly. She's just eight, but she has the patience of an adult and the temperament to match. "I know you want to do this. But Whispers said it's not allowed. She said you can't risk it!"

I love her more than anyone in the world, but, Gods, can she frustrate me! I want this so badly, so badly, and I took a huge chance telling her. But of course, *of course*, she won't dare defy Whispers. She's Whispers's favorite, her prodigy. She gets to sit with her all day in their little lessons, learning about strategy and diplomacy and spycraft. She's being trained to be a leader. And I'm stuck staring at stupid old notes. "Fine." I scoop the Loci back up into the cloth. "We should just do whatever Whispers says. Even though she's not a Wizard. Even though she doesn't understand *shit*."

I practically spit the last word at her, and I see her wince, because I know she hates it when I swear. "You're not going to do anything reckless, are you?" she asks, grabbing my wrist. "You're not going to try on your own?"

"No." I jerk my hand out of hers and sulk off into the night. "I won't. I promise."

I wait a good hour to make sure she's asleep before I try. I don't want to do it alone. I'm scared to go into the Null by myself, but even more than that, this is something I want to experience with her. I want her to be there when I carve my first Glyph. I want to know she's there looking after me. I want this moment to be one we share, our secret, ours and ours alone.

But fine. She chooses Whispers over me? I'm not going to give up just because she's a coward.

I creep out of the camp toward a grove not far away, near a small bubbling creek. It's a wide flat circle of dewy, moonlit grass, sparkling like stars against the night. I take out the Loci and I grip them tightly, their polished wood cold against my palms. I square my feet in the dirt, the stance described in the books. I breathe in and out, in and out, five times.

And then I slip into the Null.

Going in is simple, instinctive, easy. It's not even really a conscious action; it's more like a release, like exhaling a breath I've been holding. I let go of that resistance, and the world vanishes. The bright moonlit sky, the grass below, the trees and the wind and the flickering embers of the fire, they're all gone in a rush, replaced instead by a dense gray fog that envelops me like a shroud. I gasp hard, but breathing feels different here, like I'm taking in something thicker than air, like water and smoke. Flakes of ash dance all around me, slivers of black with jagged edges that spiral like leaves. And the sound, like the roar of a river, like the howl of the wind, so loud it hurts.

The Glyph. Right. I raise up one of my Loci, but moving here feels so wrong and strange, like I'm trapped in amber, like every single action takes a hundred times more effort than it should. Just lifting my arm is an exertion, but beyond the physical strain, there's something else, a tugging on my mind, and I have to strain just to stay focused. I force my hand up and plunge the Loci forward.

It stabs into the world, *into the world.* I'd imagined it would feel like drawing in the air, but no, this is cutting, *carving.* There's resistance, something there, something soft and moist, like I'm plunging the Loci into flesh. My hand is trembling, trembling too much and it's getting harder and harder to breathe, and now the feeling in my head is like a gnawing, like something's eating my thoughts, eating away at me. I wasn't ready for this. I should have waited. But no, I'm in now and it's too late so all I can do is keep going.

I've already decided what Glyph I'm going to carve: the simplest one in the notes, a ball of light. Light is harmless, after all. It's just...light. Even if I go wrong, what's the worst that can happen? I don't know yet that light can turn quickly into heat. I don't know yet how viciously light can burn.

The Light Base is just a single vertical slash, and as I jerk my Loci down through this, this *whatever* I've stabbed, the line appears, hovering in the air, glowing the brightest, most luminescent white, so bright it hurts, so bright it'd make me cry if I could cry in this place. My mouth floods with the taste of blood and ash, and my head is hurting worse and worse, but I strain to stay on task and carve the second form, a pair of diagonal lines, one above, one below. The noise is getting louder, that rushing whir, like a swarm of insects closing in. I carve the bottom line, but, Gods, it's so hard to move, like I'm straining against a current, like my arm weighs a thousand tons. I carve the last line, the line above but—

My hand slips. My hand *slips.* The weight was too much, the noise too loud, and instead of carving a diagonal line at the top, I've carved a long slash down through the first Glyph, cutting clean through it. And instantly, something starts happening. Something wrong. The Glyph starts throbbing, pulsing, the air around it curdling and quivering. Tendrils of light snake through it with a desperate hunger, and everything trembles and buzzes and writhes.

I've messed up. Oh, Gods, I've messed up. And now I'm scared, really scared. I don't know exactly what happens when Glyphs are carved wrong, but I know it's *bad*, and it's happening now. I turn to run, and even though I'm not looking at the Glyph anymore, I can see its light, bright and hot and pulsing, and hear a crackling noise like shattering ice.

The Glyph behind me bursts in a blinding pop. Scorching beams of white light cut through the air like spears, slicing through trees and blazing streaks through the earth. I feel a rush of heat and air that lifts me off my feet, hurling me forward, deeper into the fog and the gray, where I hit the ground with a skid. My body burns with a shivering cold. I look down at my leg and see the flesh bubbling and blistering from where a beam hit me. But even worse is the feeling in my chest. I can't breathe, can't scream, can't gasp. It's like my lungs are filled with ash, every breath a wheeze. I try to pull myself back into the Real, but I can't. The buzzing of insects is a deafening din now, and the flakes of ash are swarming over me, crawling over me, and I swear there's something coming at me through the fog, stalking toward me, a shape in the gray, tall and lean and bony, chittering and snarling, with far too many limbs.

I've been in the Null too long. The Null is going to kill me. The Null is going to drown me. The Null is going to eat me whole.

Then a hand grabs my arm. I look up and she's there.

Sera.

In the Real.

Our eyes meet across the hum and thrash and buzz, and I can see the blood running through her veins like rivers of starlight, and I can see her hair, brighter than the brightest light, billowing out behind her like a river of flame. She opens her mouth to scream something, something I can't hear, but it doesn't matter because I wrench up to grab her, use every last bit of strength I have to pull myself into her arms.

And I'm wrenched back, hard, into the Real.

The gray fog is gone, and the buzzing, and the roar, and that thing, whatever it was, in the fog. I'm back in the forest, and I can feel the wind against my skin again and the grass below my feet. And I can feel Sera, feel her arms wrapped around me, feel her trembling body, her beating heart. "You idiot!" she sobs. "You absolute idiot!"

I know there are going to be consequences. I have a bad burn on my leg. The grove where I'd been standing is a blasted mess, the trees slashed apart by the beams of jagged light, the grass flattened and blackened.

But I'm just happy to be alive, to be here, with Sera. I'm so happy she came for me. I grab her and hold her tight and cry.

This is us, this is me and Sera. I'm the sister who swims too deep. And she's the sister who rescues me. This is who we will always be.

Until it isn't.

Chapter 10

Now

There is a precious moment when I wake up and I don't remember where I am. In that long, lingering second, I'm not a spy or a Wizard or Alayne or Alka. I'm just a body, savoring the soft sheets, gazing up at the smooth grain of the ceiling. That second is the best part of my day.

Then it's gone. I sit up and rub the sleep out of my eyes with the back of my hand. The little clock on my desk says that it's seven in the morning, which means class starts in an hour.

I wash quickly in the bath chamber by my room, where hot water comes surging out of polished bronze shower heads. The pipes must be lined with Fire Glyphs, warming the water as it rushes through. No one else seems impressed, so I have to pretend that I'm not, either, even though it's quite possibly the most amazing thing I've ever experienced.

Back in my room, I throw open my wardrobe to find a dozen school uniforms, all perfectly tailored to Alayne's measurements. Buttoned shirts, made of the shiniest silk I've ever seen, hang alongside elegant blazers with the Blackwater crest emblazoned on the backs. For bottoms, they've thoughtfully provided two options: pleated knee-length skirts or long, neatly pressed pants. All of the clothes are a dark Nethro black, and buttons in the shape of krakens adorn the blazers, presumably so we don't forget for a minute which Order we're in.

I opt for the pants today, and when I'm dressed, shoot a glance in the mirror. I instantly regret it. It's not that I look bad, because I look fine, maybe even good. But seeing myself dressed like this, head to toe in the uniform of the Wizards, is unsettling. It's like finding a note in your handwriting that you don't remember writing, like a stranger insisting you've met. It's me, but it's not me at the same time, and I recoil, instinctively, at the sight.

Breakfast is served in the dormitory's common room, at a pair of long wooden tables, where I find bowls of glistening fresh fruit, creamy yogurt drenched in honey, and sizzling plates of thick fatty bacon. I'm apparently a late riser, because most of the other Nethros are already down here, all in their matching uniforms, a sea of neat black blazers. Professor Calfex sits at the head of a table, sipping her coffee while reviewing some papers, seemingly uninterested in any of us. Fyl has been seated all the way at the other end, where she's chatting with Desmond, the curly-haired boy who'd made a beeline for the carafe. Humble servants linger around the room, refilling cups and restocking plates. I'm relieved to see Marlena among them, and when our eyes meet, she nods with silent gratitude. Then she bends over to grasp a water pitcher, and I see how she winces as she moves, the pain from her lashing.

Bastards.

I slide into one of the few free spots in the middle of the table, ladling up my plate as discreetly as I can. Which apparently isn't discreet enough, because someone to my left clears their throat.

It's Tish, the Kindrali I met last night. Their head is shaved bald, their eyes a dazzling brown. Elegant golden tattoos envelop their hands like ivy, dazzling against their light-black skin. But it's Tish's voice that stands out the most: husky, smoky, and low, like they're always whispering. "You must really like bacon."

I glance down at my plate, where I've scooped a tower of it. "We don't have bacon like this in New Kenshire," I lie, hoping that's plausible. "It's a luxury I can't resist."

"I can relate," Tish says with a smile, scooping themselves a heaping dollop of cream. "Is it true what Fylmonela says? Did you really tell Marius Madison to get lost?"

I shoot a glance down the table at Fyl, who throws me a wink back. Her big mouth could be a problem if I want to keep a low profile... but on the other hand, it could be an asset when it comes to winning the trust of my fellow Nethros. So I offer Tish a little shrug. "I was honest." They smile and laugh, so I lean forward, whispering low. "I take it you're not a fan of Marius."

"That is one way to put it." Tish speaks with a Kindrali accent, each syllable enunciated. "My House was once one of the wealthiest on the islands, my father a powerful merchant. Then Grandmaster Madison levied the transit tax. My father protested and tried to rally the other Lords of the Isles against the tax. So the Grandmaster sank my father's prize vessel at sea." Tish swallows deeply, a distant look in their eyes. "While my brother was on it."

"Tish..."

Their hand squeezes mine, lightly. "Any enemy of the Madisons is a friend of mine."

I squeeze back, even as my mind races with possibilities. The Revenants had always operated as though the Wizards were a unified front. Is there truly this much dissent in their ranks? Are there so many who would count the Senate's leader as an enemy? Or is it just that all the children of dissenters are put here, within the black walls of the Order of Nethro? Calfex said we were placed here because we are different...

but it feels more like a matter of keeping all the troublemakers in one place.

I don't have time to think more deeply on it, because a distant horn blows, announcing the start of the school day, and Calfex rises to her feet, her arms wide. "Be bold, my krakens. Serve Nethro well."

We make our way out into the courtyard, grabbing little paper schedules with our names on the way. I glance at mine, not knowing what to expect, and the words there provide little clarity: FUNDAMENTALS OF MAGIC. GLORIES OF THE REPUBLIC. INTRODUCTORY GLYPHCRAFT. The others seem to understand what they mean, murmuring among themselves, so once again, I'll just have to keep up.

It's a crisp fall morning outside the dormitory, the rising sun hidden by a thin veil of cloud, the fresh air tinged with the smell of smoke and pine. Tall trees sway on the outskirts of the campus, and dew glistens on the grass. I make my way over to Fyl and show her my schedule, which she reads with a nod. "Oh, good. We have two classes together."

"I'll follow you, then," I say with a smile. "I hear you've been telling everyone about me and Marius?"

"I mean—I—well—" she stammers. "It's a good story, you know?"

It is, even if it might end up painting a target on my back. "Are you feeling better about being in Nethro?" I ask. "I have to say, Professor Calfex knows how to give a speech."

"Words are air," Fyl replies, "pretty as they may be. When Professor Calfex convinces my parents I'm not a failure, then I'm interested." She pauses, a pretty flush dancing across her cheeks. "That Desmond boy's not bad, though."

We stroll together into the massive main building and, with just a little struggle, find our way to our first class, Fundamentals of Magic. We sit at long tables laid out in neat rows in a cozy half circle of a room. Sunlight streams in through tall windows, long golden beams sparkling with dancing motes of dust.

Professor Hapsted is a hunched old man with eyebrows like bushy white caterpillars. He paces back and forth along the front of the room, his cane clanking loudly on the floor. "Let's start from the beginning," he says, a sly twinkle in his eyes, and I can tell he's setting someone up for a trick question. "Who can tell me what the Null is?"

A hand shoots up in the front. It's Vyctoria Aberdeen, the bored girl from Marius's side on the ferry, and she's wearing the Selura uniform, a dark-blue robe with a trim of long black raven feathers. "The Null is a transitory plane of reality, existing on a liminal level between our material world and the immaterial abyss. It holds properties of both and yet is neither, at once tangible and ethereal."

Next to me, Fyl rolls her eyes. But my mind is elsewhere. Vyctoria is the niece of Headmaster Aberdeen, and I can see the resemblance now, in the high cheekbones, the pointed chin, the gray eyes. Does she have any idea the kind of man her uncle really is? Would she even care?

Professor Hapsted, for what it's worth, doesn't seem all that impressed. "A pleasantly technical answer, Lady Aberdeen, and one, I imagine, of no meaning to most of the others gathered here." He's got her there. "If I may, with a bit more poetry: Think of our reality as a house. It has walls. A roof. Windows. A floor." He raps his cane on each, demonstrating. "To the Humbles out there, this house is all they will ever see, all they will ever know. As far as they can tell, the house is all there is. But we Wizards... we know there's more." He grabs a wooden panel of the wall and jerks it aside, revealing a dusty, narrow cavity behind it. "We can slide into the hidden places between the walls. We can lift the floorboards and move through the crawl spaces. We can see the beams that built the house, admire its bones, the dirt beneath the floor. The Null is the realm of the Gods, where they once lived, and while there, we can see how they built our reality, how they erected those beams, those walls. The Glyphs are the language of the Gods, and they used that language to build our entire world. We can't quite do that, and yet... we can still leave a few

Glyphs of our own. And in doing so, we can channel their ancient language to change the world itself, to create fire and light and ice, to bring life and rain down death." Hapsted slides the panel back into place, and it would've been a slick move if he didn't fumble a little.

I raise my hand. "If the real world is the house, and the Null is the hidden spaces within the house... then what's the outside? What's beyond the Null?"

Hapsted shrugs dismissively. "No one knows," he says, and he's half turned around when someone else in the room speaks.

"I do."

The voice comes from a table in the back of the room, and when I crane my head to look there, I find a familiar face. Prince Talyn. He leans back in his seat, hands folded behind his head, lost in the long braids of his hair. The Javellos uniform comes with a dark-green blazer but Talyn hasn't bothered to wear it, heading out instead in a loosely draped silk shirt, its low collar showing off the curve of his collarbone, the soft hairs of his chest. His eyes flash to mine, and my cheeks burn.

I imagine what Sera would do if she could see me, blushing at a glance from some handsome prince in the middle of the most important mission of my life. She'd drown me in a creek.

Professor Hapsted doesn't notice any of that. He just turns to Talyn, head cocked with curiosity. "Our esteemed foreign visitor speaks! Please enlighten us, Good Prince. What lies beyond the Null?"

"We don't call it the Null," he explains. "The place you go when you use your magic is the Realm Between."

"Between what?"

"Between our world, the world of the living," he says, gesturing around our room. "And the land of the dead."

I remember that shape I saw through the fog all those years ago, tall and lean and blurry, with way too many limbs. I shudder.

The rest of the class goes on pretty much the same, with Hapsted droning on about the nature of magic, the perils of the Null, and for some reason an odd digression on the history of luggage. I'm bored out of my mind. If I wanted to study abstract theory, I could bury my nose in a book. I came to this school to learn new Glyphs, to become a skilled Wizard. I came to this school to *do*.

My next class is even worse. Besides teaching us magic, they want us to learn things like history and politics, which is absolute torture. Professor Pentacoste, a plump middle-aged woman with her red hair up in a bun, strolls back and forth, expounding on the glorious First Fathers, the brave men blessed by the Gods to master magic, who tamed a wild and lawless continent to create the Republic of Marovia. Never mind that the First Fathers were brutal tyrants who slaughtered thousands of Humbles and enslaved thousands more. Never mind that every word she speaks is pure unabashed propaganda. I have to bite my cheek just to stay silent.

Talyn is in this class, too, and he's struggling as much as I am, maybe more. At one point, he lets out a groan, and at another, a weary sigh. I catch up with him after the class ends, and we walk side by side through the quad, our feet crunching neatly over the fallen leaves. "Tell me you found that class as excruciating as I did," he says. "Tell me I'm not alone."

I know he's reaching out, but the footing here is treacherous. I want to agree with him, but in a way that won't attract suspicion. So I deflect. "I take it you're not a fan of how we teach Marovian history?"

"Am I a fan of being fed horseshit and told it's cake? No. No, I am not." He cranes his head up to the sky. "It's going to be a long two years."

"And do all scholars in your kingdom tell the truth?"

"No, our scholars lie as well," he admits with a shrug. "But they're much less self-righteous about it. Funnier, too." He turns to me, a single eyebrow cocked as his intelligent brown eyes take me in. "I have to admit, though, you surprise me. A girl who charges Marius Madison with a knife *and* admits the Marovian history lecture is a lie? Are you sure you really belong here?"

I keep up the smile, even as I'm cringing inside. I've shown too much, and he's too close to the truth. "In New Kenshire, we value skepticism and independence," I say, because if he's going to mark me as an outsider, I might as well lean into it. "We're part of the Republic but we do things our own way."

Talyn lets out an appreciative laugh. "It's funny. When I arrived, I assumed you Marovian Wizards were all the same. But now I see how divided and different you really are." Hierarchies within hierarchies, castes within castes. He's seeing the same things I am, even if I can't acknowledge it. "May I ask a favor of you, Lady Dewinter?"

"You may."

His mouth twists to a crooked smile. "Will you walk with me after class again? I suspect I'll need another outsider to talk to so I don't entirely lose my mind."

I smile back, genuinely this time. "I think I can agree to that."

Finally, at my last class of the day, I get what I was looking for: Introductory Glyphcraft. Fifty of us meet in a wide outdoor amphitheater on the western side of the campus, sitting on tiered benches around an elevated stage. Fyl's in this class, too, along with Desmond, so I slide up next to them. They've got their Loci out. Fyl's holding a nice old-fashioned set of sandalwood wands, engraved at the handle with the Potts House crest, while Desmond has a pair of jagged obsidian knives that sparkle darkly in the light. I eagerly roll my bone knives out. "Do we finally get to use these?" I ask.

"Really? You're that eager to start carving Glyphs?" Desmond asks. "I've been dreading this humiliation all day."

"It's better than falling asleep in Basics of Rhetoric," Fyl groans, burying her face in her hands. "That's not an exaggeration. I literally fell asleep. On the *first day*. Professor Reens decided to demonstrate her art of rhetoric by yelling in my ear."

"In her defense, it was really funny," Desmond says, and Fyl punches him in the arm. Grinning, he turns toward me. "Neat Loci. Are those military issue?"

"My father was given them as a ceremonial honor for his service," I lie, because the real truth is, we pulled them from the cold, dead hands of a decorated Wizard after we attacked his caravan. "Can you back up a moment and explain why this is going to be humiliating?"

"Because none of us know how to carve Glyphs?" Fyl says. "I mean, my mother tried to teach me, but she's not exactly some great master Wizard herself...."

"My father can make a pot of water boil," Desmond says. "I don't know how he graduated from here. I really don't."

"And it's not like we can afford fancy private tutors," Fyl follows up. "Not like some people."

I follow her eyes and there he sits on the opposite side of the amphitheater. Marius Madison. He's wearing the Vanguard uniform, a crisp gold suit with stag heads for the buttons. His friend Dean, the hulking boy from the ferry, slumps next to him, scratching at his curly beard. I make the mistake of meeting Dean's gaze, and his mouth crinkles into a cruel grin. "Hey, New Mark!" he shouts. "You sure you're sober enough for this? I'd hate to see you accidentally blast a servant girl into twenty pieces!"

"No, she's merciful, remember?" Marius replies. He's not pretending to be better than Dean, not anymore. Why bother when the lines have been drawn? "She'll make sure the girl is just blown into *ten* pieces."

A raucous laugh rolls across the room, even as Fyl rolls her eyes and Desmond glowers. "Welcome to the Order of Nethro. Where things can only get worse."

A rap of knuckles cuts off the laughter, and we all turn to the front, where the class's professor has entered the amphitheater. "Now, settle down, pupils," Headmaster Aberdeen says with a chuckle as he strides onto the stage. "You'll have more than enough time for merriment later."

Of course it's him. Of course. Even with my newfound resolve and purpose, seeing him makes my blood run cold. I breathe hard through my nostrils and dig my nails into my palms and force myself to swallow down that anger. Right now, he's not the monster who slaughtered my parents. He's just the professor who's going to teach me to carve Glyphs. Glyphs I'm going to eventually use to kill him, sure, but he's just the teacher for now.

"I imagine you're all very eager to get started," he says, moving to a wooden table at the center of the stage. "This is, after all, why you're really here. To learn the ancient art of Glyphcraft. To become Wizards! I remember when I was a young man, arriving at Blackwater. It was long ago, far longer than I'd like to admit. I've forgotten much of that time..." he says to mild chuckles. "But I'll never forget how excited I was the first time I laid eyes on the *Codex Transcendent*."

Then he reaches down to pick up a massive book, which he slams down on the table before him with a resounding thud. We all go silent, our eyes transfixed. This book is enormous, so thick he has to grip it with both hands, overflowing with pages. It's bound with thick worn leather, and a half dozen chains are wrapped tightly around it, connected to a shifting crystal lock. "The *Codex Transcendent*," Aberdeen repeats. "The single most valuable book in the world. The sum of all the knowledge of every Wizard who has passed through these halls. Every Glyph known to us lies in these pages. Basic Glyphs. Advanced Glyphs. Forbidden Glyphs." He runs a hand across the top, almost lovingly. "All of them are here." His eye twinkles as he gives us all a warm smile. "And no, I won't let you borrow it."

He pivots, turning the book sideways, so we can get a look at how thick it is. Gods. There's got to be hundreds and hundreds of pages. Are there really so many Glyphs out there? Is there really so much to know? "When I first saw this book, I thought, well, that's not so much. I could memorize all that. I could become a Master Wizard. After all, I've got that keen Selura intellect." An amused murmur ripples through the room, and a few Seluras cheer. "But you may be surprised to know that even now, as the headmaster of this school, I can only carve maybe half of them. And only a hundred or so well. Why? Because it turns out, to my great chagrin, the secret of Glyphcraft is not memorizing Glyphs. It's learning how to carve them well. The precision of your stroke... the deftness of your cut... the subtle arcs, the delicate curves... all of these are what truly matters."

Of course. Sera had always emphasized that precision mattered, and she sat with me night after night trying to help me perfect my strokes.

"And yet I imagine you've had enough theory and abstraction! Perhaps a demonstration is in order." Aberdeen presses his hand on the book's front, and the chains unlock, sliding back into the crystal lock like serpents retreating into their burrows. He opens the book to the first yellowed page, which shows a Glyph I recognize: on the left, the triangle of Ice Base, on the right, two diagonal cuts for Sphere Form. Sphere of Ice. Even I can do that.

Clearly, I'm not the only one who thinks that, because a groan runs through the room. Aberdeen notices it, nodding. "Ah, yes. I know what you're thinking. You know how to do this. Everyone knows how to do this. Even the lowest, commonest, most disreputable Wizards in this Republic can make a Sphere of Ice." He claps his hands together. "So let's see it, then. Marius Madison, if you'll do the honors?"

"Of course, Headmaster," Marius beams, hopping up to his feet.

"And another." His eye roams the room, like a hawk searching for its prey, before alighting on us. "Fylmonela Potts! Would you care to join him?"

Fyl looks like he just threw a spear through her chest. Her mouth opens and closes wordlessly as the blood drains from her face, before she finally swallows deeply. "Yes, Headmaster," she chokes out. "I—I would be honored."

Desmond and I share a worried glance, but it's too late. The ship is in motion, and there's no turning back. Fyl makes her way to the front of the amphitheater as everyone stares at her. She and Marius take the stage, and the contrast between the two couldn't be clearer. Marius is preening, confident, taking out his fancy Loci with a little spin, even as Fyl raises hers with a trembling hand, her face paler than I've ever seen it. I feel that deep, aching secondhand embarrassment, the kind that is somehow so much worse than when it's your own. "Hail Vanguard!" Dean shouts from the stands. "Show that Nethro how it's done!" A few other students, some of whom aren't even Vanguards, cheer.

"All right," Aberdeen says, turning the book toward them. "Let's see it!"

I feel them enter the Null before I see it, that aching pull within my chest drawing toward them. Their heads jerk back as their eyes turn to a glassy glimmering starscape, black speckled with twinkling white and spiraling blue. If I joined them in the Null, I'd see them actually carve the Glyphs, but I stay in the Real, so all I see is a single flicker of motion in front of them, feel the world throb with the electric pulse of magic. In the Real, it's a second, less than a second, and then they're both back, and hovering in front of each is a glistening sphere of ice. I shoot Fyl an encouraging smile. She did it, right? She made the sphere?

Then I see Aberdeen's face as he observes the orbs, see the smug twitch of his smile. "And here we have it. A perfect demonstration." He paces in front of them and takes Marius's sphere, raising it for all of us to see. "Examine this. A wonderful specimen, if I may so myself. Perfectly spherical. Its surface smooth as silk. Its size ideal for a hand. And its density..." He smashes it down against the table, hard, so hard a few students jump back, startled. The table shakes, but the ball remains intact. "Solid as a rock."

He sets it down, then reaches out, taking Fyl's, as her face drops with embarrassment. He holds it up for us to see, and even I have to admit, it's a bit of a mess. "And here we have a counterexample. The shape is uneven, lopsided, more like an oval. The surface is brittle and jagged. It's far too small, hardly more than a pebble. And as for the density..." He squeezes, barely, and it crumbles to slush in his hand. "The less said, the better."

Everyone in the room laughs, except for me and Desmond. Fyl stares down, her cheeks bright red, her Loci limp in her hands at her sides. And Aberdeen is there all the while, that kindly old smile on his face. This is theater, all of it, theater to establish those with power and those without, theater to make the Mariuses of the world feel strong and the Fyls of the world feel weak. Theater to put us in our place. I feel that anger again, burning behind my eyes, balling my hands into fists. It's all built into the system here. The cruelty, the competition, the constant humiliation and hierarchy. This is the Republic at its purest.

"Don't worry, Lady Potts." Aberdeen gently squeezes her shoulder. "We all need to start somewhere." And she nods politely, because what else can she do? Marius takes a grandstanding bow, and she makes her way off the stage back up to us. When she sits down, her breath is caught tight in her throat and her eyes shine with tears.

"Fyl," I say, "That was—"

"It was nothing," she cuts in, swallowing hard to get the words out. "It was my fault. I know those Glyphs. I could've done better. I could've practiced more." I reach out to try to pat her shoulder, but she swats my hand away. "It's *my* fault. Don't try to make this better."

"Would any others care to try?" Aberdeen asks, as if he were being sincere.

And before I can think better of it, my hand shoots up.

Fyl glances at me, stunned, and Desmond just shakes his head. "Lady Dewinter," Aberdeen says, somewhere between surprised and amused. "Come on down."

Gathering my Loci, I stride down through the seats and climb onto the stage. Aberdeen calls on another student, a broad-shouldered Zartan girl named Terra, and she lumbers down to stand by my side. I barely even notice her, though, because it's taking every ounce of restraint I have to maintain my composure around Aberdeen. He's standing right there, just a few feet from me, no idea who I am. He smells like old books and sawdust, and I can make out every sparkling little moon on his robe. I could kill him right now if I wanted. I could kill him right now.

No. The mission. I take a good look at the *Codex Transcendent*, overflowing with knowledge, possessing every secret I so badly want, and pretend I'm just studying the open pages closely. The Zartan girl lines up next to me, holding two long curved daggers as Loci. "All right," Aberdeen says, "Begin!"

I take a deep breath and slip into the Null.

The world fades away around me. I've never been in the Null near this many people, and I can see all of the students in the audience through the haze, see the dozens of flickering red lights that are their slowly beating hearts, like a sea of lanterns on the other side of a storm. The fog seems thicker here, like the Null is denser, and it takes more effort than usual to push through it, to raise my hands and carve. I glance to the side and see the Zartan girl stab her dagger into the skin of the world, see her thick biceps tense as she drives the Loci deep. Sweat streaks down her brow, and in the molasses fog of the Null I can actually see her exertion, see her intensity radiate off her like plumes of purple smoke.

I turn away. Eyes on my own. My Glyphs have always lacked precision, but I suspect I'm better than Fyl and probably better than this Zartan. With a solid inhale I raise my right hand and press my Loci in, gently, cutting in just enough. I carve the triangle Glyph of an Ice Base, and it glows a vivid blue before me, and I feel its cold soak through my skin, feel frost dance at the edges of my hair. Then I raise my left hand

and carve the second form, the two diagonal cuts. The Glyph solidifies in front of me and starts to take shape, folding in on itself to form a hovering frozen sphere. It's not as good as Marius's, but it's not bad, not bad at all.

I glance back at Aberdeen, and he's in the Null with us, flesh and blood, observing everything we do. His eyes flit to my sphere, and I see a glimmer of approval.

So I jerk my left hand down hard, cutting my Glyph in half.

In the real world, it's barely been a second. But here in the Null, a whole crisis plays out. My sphere of ice throbs, pulses, trembles with untamed energy. Its smooth surface cracks and shatters, tendrils of ice bursting out like grasping hands. There's a noise coming out of it, a terrible rending noise, like a knife scraping against the inside of my skull. The Zartan girl screams.

Aberdeen's on it. Moving faster than I would've thought for a man his age, he shoves past me, and in each of his hands is a Loci, gnarled ivory shafts twisted in spiral strands. Unicorn horn, the rarest of all materials. Aberdeen weaves them through the air with incredible precision, like an artist dazzling a landscape onto canvas with a pair of brushes. His Glyphs are like nothing I've ever seen, the base a whirling sequence of increasing horizontal bands, the form an interconnected cage of at least two dozen diagonal cuts, forming a glowing golden mesh. And even more amazing, he carves both Glyphs *at the same time*, one with each hand, moving independently of each other. I've never seen anything like it. I didn't even know it was possible.

So this is what a Master Wizard is like. This is what I'm up against. Even here in the Null, my heart plunges. How the hell am I ever going to take on *that*?

I jerk back into the Real, just as Aberdeen carves the last line of his Glyphs. My sphere explodes with a deafening crackle, like an ice shelf breaking off a glacier, shooting shards of jagged blue in all directions.

The Zartan next to me throws up her hands, and I dive back, knocking over the table, sending the *Codex Transcendent* tumbling. In the stands, students scatter and duck.

But there's something else in the air, just in front of Aberdeen, something that *isn't* there, until it suddenly is. With a rush of air like a cosmic sigh, an obelisk appears where my sphere exploded, a tall translucent crystal made of glowing golden light that spins like the world's slowest top. It traps the exploding shards within it, and they shatter against its sides, dissolving into nothingness in a cascade of dazzling sparks. Just like that, the crisis is averted. Without breaking a sweat, Aberdeen contained my disaster. Everyone lets out a gasp of awe, and even I find my jaw hanging open.

Aberdeen spins back around to face me and I realize that actually the crisis might be far from over. "Dewinter!" he growls. "What the *hell* was that?" And there, there at last, I see it. The vicious snarl, the glaring beady eye, the radiating contempt. He hides it well behind the facade of the kindly headmaster. But here he is, unmasked, the real Magnus Aberdeen, the man who killed my parents.

Even as he drops his facade, I have to commit to mine. "I—I—I'm sorry!" I stammer, scrambling back on my hands and knees. "I've never carved that Glyph before! I just slipped! I'm so sorry!"

He inhales sharply, nostrils flaring, long gray beard billowing. Then he forces a patient nod, offering a warm patrician smile. "Of course. I understand. Everyone makes mistakes when they're just starting. Believe me, it's not the worst thing I've seen happen in this class. At least no one lost an arm!" Another laugh goes through the room, though this one is a bit more nervous. Aberdeen kneels right in front of me and oh, Gods, he's *so close*, my heart thunders and my hands dig into the grain of the floor. "Your dormitory has practice rooms where you can refine your Glyphs. The next time you take this stage, I expect a better outcome."

"Of course, Headmaster," I say, and I look away, and I hope he takes that as my embarrassment. "I'll do better. I promise."

He nods, satisfied, and I rise to my feet, my head down as I hand him the *Codex*. He takes it out of my hands and lays it back across the table. "All right, then." He turns back to the class. "Who'd like to try next? Perhaps with a bit less excitement?"

I make my way back to my seat as everyone laughs, and I slide in next to the other Nethros. "Look on the bright side," Desmond says. "We're setting expectations low enough that we can only really go up from here."

I kind of hope that'll be the end of it, but Fyl's looking at me, head cocked to the side. She's suspicious. Maybe I overplayed my hand. "Alayne," she asks, and I can tell she's not sure if she even wants to finish the sentence. "Did you do that on purpose? To make me feel better?"

"No, Fyl," I say, patting her hand, "I'm really just that bad."

Desmond laughs, shaking his head, and Fyl smiles a little, too. "All right. Good. Then we can both be awful together."

She turns back to the front of the room, where two new students have taken the stage. It's odd. I actually feel a pang of guilt lying to her. Which makes no sense because my very presence here is a lie to her, because she's one of *them*, because she's my enemy, because if she stands between me and my mission I'll have to cut her down. But despite knowing all that, I still feel that pang.

The worst part is, she doesn't even know why I'm lying. Yes, I destroyed my Glyph on purpose. But it wasn't to make her feel better.

I shift back into my seat and feel them crinkle under my shirt. Four pages from the *Codex Transcendent*, pages I tore out when everyone was watching Aberdeen's crystal. Four pages from the very back, where I'm sure the most powerful and forbidden Glyphs are. Four pages that are now mine.

My social status at Blackwater couldn't be lower. For days, everyone will gossip about what a disaster I am, how my Glyph blew up in my face, how I don't deserve my Mark. Even the other Nethros will probably keep clear of me. But I don't care. Because I've been here for just one day and I already stole four Glyphs from right under Magnus Aberdeen's nose.

These Wizards have no idea who they're dealing with.

Chapter 11

Then

I am twelve when I make my first kill.

He's a Humble, a City Watch recruit, maybe twenty years old. Our paths cross through pure bad luck. I'm rushing through the alleys of Hellsum with a crew of Revenants, fresh off a raid on a Wizard merchant's warehouse. He's on patrol, a lonely night shift, whistling to himself as he walks. We round a corner and see him, just as he sees us. There's a moment as we all freeze up, a moment of stunned recognition that lasts an eternity.

Whispers sent me on this raid because I'm small and nimble and I can use my magic to melt metal, all of which makes us perfect for a smash and grab. It was supposed to be quick, easy, risk-free. No one was supposed to know. No one was supposed to get hurt.

The recruit reaches for his whistle.

My hands move, whipping out my Loci, and I'm in the Null before I can even consider what I'm doing, before I can even think. Had I slowed down and considered, I might have hesitated, maybe let one of the other rebels try to knock him out. But I can't think now, because everything's happening too fast, because his whistle is halfway to his lips, because I'm doing what I've been trained to do.

I carve fire and push.

A lash of flame shrieks through the air like a whip, scorching the brick wall of the alley. One moment the recruit is there. And then he's gone, this fresh-faced boy, with a nose covered in freckles and a wispy barely-there beard. The flame swallows him whole, and all that's left is a charred husk.

I don't speak to anyone as we rush back to our safe house on the city's outskirts, as we divvy up the loot, as we lock down and set up watch. Sera's there waiting, and she tries to talk to me, and I shove her aside, unable to even look her in the eye. But that night, I wake up screaming, and Whispers is there to hold me.

"I killed him," I tell her, tears running down my cheeks, every word a jagged stone in my throat. "That city watchman. I *killed* him."

"You did," Whispers says. We're up in the loft of the farmhouse at the property's edge, on a pile of soft hay, the pale moonlight streaking in through the cracks in the roof. "If he'd blown his whistle, he would've brought the rest of the guard down on all of you. You would've been caught. Tortured. Killed. You saved us, Alka. You saved us all."

"He wasn't a Wizard," I choke out, but there are so many feelings bursting through me it's impossible to put them into words. "He was a Humble. Like you, like my mother, like Sera." I'm sobbing now, and Whispers holds me tighter and tighter, enveloping me in her strong arms. "I killed a Humble! I'm no... no better than any other Wizard!"

"No, my darling," Whispers says, and she kisses me, actually kisses me on the forehead, which is more affection than she's ever shown. It startles me enough that I stop crying, if only for a second. "What you did was preserve your mission. What you did was fight for our cause. What you did was *the right thing*."

"Our cause is fighting Wizards," I whisper back. "Helping Humbles. Not killing them."

Whispers sighs deeply, pressing her forehead to mine. Her skin is cold but surprisingly soft, and for a fleeting second I can almost remember what my mother felt like. "Oh, sweet child," she says. "I wish life were that simple."

"It isn't?"

"For as long as there have been oppressors, there have been collaborators. For as long as Wizards have terrorized, there have been Humbles who aided them. There will always be those who place their own comfort over the good of their people." Whispers still holds me, but there's a coldness in her voice, a blade unsheathed below. "That man today chose his fate. He could have sought us out. He could have stood with those fighting for liberation. Instead, he chose to aid the oppressors. He made his choice, Alka. And you did what you had to."

"Have you killed Humbles?" I weakly ask.

"Yes," she replies. "More than I can count."

"Will I have to kill a Humble again?"

"Yes," she says, without hesitating. "Almost certainly. We're at war. Wars have casualties. That's the price we pay, the burden we take on. We stain our hands with blood so that others can live in peace." With that she takes my hands in hers. "Do you understand, Alka? If *anyone* stands between you and our cause, cut them down."

"But what if—"

"Alka." She gazes at me, her hair silver in the moonlight, her lean features as cold and distant as a statue's. "Do you understand what your cause demands of you?"

"I do," I say. I'm not entirely sure it's the truth.

Chapter 12

Now

I desperately want to dive into the stolen *Codex* pages, but I also want to not get exposed on my first day, so I have to bide my time. I stash the papers in my room and try to put them out of my mind through dinner, through the socializing hours after, through the long stretch of evening when I can still hear people doing their homework and puttering about. Only at three past midnight, when I'm sure it's safe, do I dare take them out again, and then it's just to tuck them back into my pocket and skulk into the hall.

Even I'm not reckless enough to try forbidden magic in my room. The odds of this going wrong are incredibly high, and I can't risk that there, where the walls are so thin I can hear my neighbor snoring. So I sneak down the hall instead, pacing lightly on the balls of my feet like Whispers taught me, silent as a ghost. I creep down the stairs and through the common area (where that giant Velkschen boy, Zigmund, is passed out on the couch) to a heavy door that leads down to the dormitory's basement. There, down a narrow flight of stairs, are the practice rooms. Calfex walked us through them last night: six private, windowless rooms, their walls made of dense cold steel, imbued with powerful warding Glyphs of magic entrapment. No matter how badly a Glyph goes, the rooms will make sure to contain it. In theory, anyway.

As novices, these are the only rooms where we're allowed to practice magic, and even then, under strict parameters: rooms must be reserved with the Order head and can only be accessed exclusively during evening hours from six to ten, and all students must practice with one of the Order mentors, a trio of young Wizards who live on the upper floor of the dormitory and are here just to ensure we're safe. To make sure the rules are followed, the heavy metal doors to the practice rooms are locked at all times.

Which is why I swiped a key off a mentor the first chance I got.

I unlock the first practice room and duck into it. It's decently large, maybe three times the size of my bedroom, but being inside still feels like being trapped in a dungeon. Every surface is cold metal, lit up by a single lantern built into the ceiling that bathes the room in a pale yellow glow. I fight back a shudder as I close the door behind me, sealing myself in, and lay the pages on the floor.

Right away, I realize I may be in over my head. For one thing, while the Glyphs are accompanied by instructions, they're all written in Old Marovian, a language I've only heard in temple sermons and one that I very much cannot read. For another, out of the four Glyphs, two look impossibly complex, geometric puzzles made of dozens of interwoven lines requiring precision worlds beyond what I can do. Of the remaining two, one uses the hatched line of fire at its core, and there are a dozen skulls drawn on the page, which cannot be good. That means there's just one of these I'll even consider trying. My great win is already looking a lot more meager.

I lay out the page and study it closely. The Glyph itself doesn't look overly complex: a series of four circles, nesting within one another like an archery target. I'm pretty sure I can carve it, but it's a little worrying that I have no idea what it'll do. It's a second form, which means that it's used to guide the power of a base, like push or sphere or shield. I squint as hard as I can at the Old Marovian, hoping it'll make sense, but it's just a mess of squiggly lines and the few things that look like letters don't spell anything.

A part of me feels like I ought to just call it off and head back up to my room. But I'm not going to be able to best the likes of Marius Madison if I'm afraid to take some risks. And isn't the whole point of this room to make practicing magic safe? What's the worst that could happen?

I tuck the pages back into my pocket. Then I draw my Loci, take a deep breath, ground my feet, and slip into the Null.

Right away, I realize how powerful the room itself is. In the Real, it looks like a cold metal cell, but here in the Null, I can see Glyphs everywhere, dozens and dozens of them. Spells of containment, like the one Aberdeen used during the lecture. They glow all around me beyond the ash, complex shapes shining a dazzling gold, carved into every panel of the walls and ceiling and floor. This is the brightest I've ever seen the Null, the light of the Glyphs dancing off the usual flakes of gray, turning them into falling golden petals. It's like being trapped in a field of stars. I'd never known the Null could be so beautiful.

Feeling a little safer, I raise my Loci and carve. Aberdeen said Ice was the safest Glyph, so I take him at his word and cut that as my base. Then I raise my other arm and carve the second form, the Glyph from the page, circles within circles within circles. It glows a cold steely white in front of me, and I can't help but smile. First try.

I slip back into the Real.

Right away, I realize I've done something wrong.

The air in front of me, where the Glyph ought to be, is flickering, like light from a candle blowing in the wind, like sparks of lightning in a storm. I hear crackling ice, but I smell burning instead and something else, like blood on metal. The little hairs on my arms stand on end and a horrible curdling feeling twists my stomach.

I jerk back, and it appears floating before me, a single crystal of ice, no bigger than my first. Then a little branch shoots off it, then another, then another, all cold blue and jagged, tiny icicles stabbing through the air. It's like frost growing on a windowpane, like glass cracking, but the glass is the world itself. This mass of ice expands, each offshoot crackling into its own offshoots, a spiderweb growing across the room, and growing fast.

I don't know what I've done here, but I don't have to know that something very bad will happen if one of those jagged spokes touches me. I jerk away, and just in time, because the web has doubled in size, as big as me, and it's growing and growing, a crystalline structure of jagged blue, an impossible fractal of interconnected lattices, and the room is so cold all of a sudden, the air so thin I can't breathe, and I know with absolute certainty that if I stay in this room I'm going to die.

I stumble back, grab the doorknob behind me, throw open the heavy steel slab, and tumble out into the hallway. Not a moment too soon, because the crystalline mass has filled up the entire room now, massive, frozen, pulsing with magical energy. I wince, because there's no way I'm going to be able to cover this up, and then the sharpest furthermost spoke stabs into the practice room's wall.

The structure trembles, shudders, flaring with tendrils of golden light that lash through it like blood through veins.

Then it crumbles instantly, shattering into nothingness. The spokes, the lattices, they all break like glass. The feeling of wrongness, the pulsing of energy, the curdle in my stomach, they're all gone. The Glyphs I carved are gone. All that's left is a hundred thousand chunks of slowly melting ice, scattered over the practice room's floor.

It's a long time before I move. I just lie there on my hands, staring, panting. On the bright side, those containment Glyphs really do work. On the downside, I feel like my heart exploded in my chest. I'm in so far over my head. I have no idea what I'm doing. I—

The thought sputters and dies. Because as I pull myself up to my feet I see someone, a figure standing at the end of the hall, a girl, staring at me.

Marlena.

Her eyes are wide, her jaw hanging open, and before I can do anything, before I can even think about doing anything, she runs my way. "Are you all right, my lady?" she asks as she slides up to my side.

"I'm fine," I stammer, trying to come up with some way to possibly explain this. "I was just—see, I—a Glyph—and I mean—"

Marlena turns to look into the practice room, where the last vestiges of ice are melting away, and I see the moment recognition dawns. "You're not supposed to be here," she says. "These rooms are locked at night. You broke in." Then her eyes drift down to the floor between us and I follow her gaze and die inside. There it is. The page from the *Codex*, the Glyph I'd tried to carve. It must have fallen out of my pocket when I tumbled out of the room, and it's just lying there, crumpled, unmistakable.

"Is that from the headmaster's book?" Marlena whispers. "How did you get..." and she doesn't have to finish the sentence, because she's already guessed how, and she's maybe just realized how serious this situation is. Breaking into the practice room is bad, but it's a transgression that could be forgiven. Ripping a page out of the *Codex* is unforgivable.

The weight of the moment hits both of us like a wave, freezing us in our tracks. I can't believe it. For all my efforts, I've been caught already. If

Marlena tells Professor Calfex about this, it's all over. I'll be arrested. I'll be tried. I'll be dead by the end of the week.

I wanted to help Marlena. I had vowed to protect her. To save her. But right now, she's the biggest threat to me on this entire island.

I know what I have to do. I know what Whispers would want me to do. I know what the mission demands. My hand flits down to my Loci, sliding into my palm behind my back. I could do it so easily. We're the only ones down here. I could grab her and pull her back into the room, slit her throat, and hold her still as she bleeds out. I'd burn her body with a Fire Glyph, and dump the ash into the ocean. She'd just be a Humble who disappeared. No one would ever know.

The Loci trembles in my grip, but my hand doesn't budge. I think Marlena can sense it, feel the danger radiating off me, because she pulls back a little, like she might run. My other hand shoots out, grabbing her wrist tight, so tight she flinches. I have to do it. I *have* to. She could expose me. She's a liability. Wars have casualties. Her life can't be worth the hundreds of thousands I could save if I bring the Senate down. This is the right thing to do. It's the only thing to do.

I have to kill her.

Then I look into her eyes. I expect them to be frightened. But Marlena just stares right back at me, those deep-amber eyes blazing with curiosity and a hint of uncertainty. She's not afraid of me, I realize, even though she senses the danger. She's *intrigued.*

I swallow hard, even as I keep my grip tight on her wrist, even as my Loci's point angles her way, even as I can't pull my eyes away from hers. I can feel the pulse in her wrist beating against my palm, her skin warm and soft. The air feels charged, electric. She should be afraid. Why isn't she afraid?

Then her eyebrows raise, just a little. A challenge. A dare. *If you're going to do it*, her eyes whisper, *then do it.*

I can't do it. I let go of her wrist and she jerks her hand back, her chest rising and falling fast. She could run now. She could bolt for the door. I wouldn't stop her.

But she stays, watching me, rubbing her wrist where I grabbed her. "I won't tell anyone," she says. "I promise."

"Why would you do that for me?"

"You defended me to the headmaster," Marlena replies. "Even though I embarrassed you in front of all the others. You still asked for mercy." She reaches to her back, wincing just a little. "Most of the students here would've demanded I be lashed more. I owe you a debt."

I know if Whispers could see this, she'd be livid at my weakness. And maybe I am weak. Maybe I'm naïve and gullible. But I decide I'm going to trust Marlena and take her at her word. "Thank you," I say, and slide my Loci back into their sheaths. She relaxes a little at that, and I relax at her relaxing.

"I don't mean to pry, my lady, but may I ask why?" She kneels, picking up the *Codex* page. "Why would you do this?"

"Because I need to win the Great Game," I say, and at least that's not a lie. "But I'm not going to do it unless I learn some advanced Glyphs, and fast."

"And this was the Glyph you wanted to learn?" She glances down at the page, her eyes darting across the text. *"Third-Degree Delayed Elemental Infusion?"*

There is a long moment of silence.

"You can read Old Marovian?" I say at last.

"Of course," she replies, "I assist many of the professors with transcription and note-keeping and..." She stops. "Wait. Can you *not* read Old Marovian?"

"It isn't commonly taught in New Kenshire," I try. Can everyone else here read it? Am I hopelessly behind?

"Oh," Marlena says, studying me carefully, and I can see the glint of suspicion dance across her face. Out of everyone here, the first person to doubt me is a Humble servant. "You're not like the other students, are you?"

No, I'm very much not, and since I can't deny it, I might as well lean into it. "The rest of the students grew up in Arbormont, in old noble Houses. I'm a new Mark. My father was a Humble commoner until he proved himself in the war. I didn't have a fancy tutor to teach me Old Marovian. I have to learn here, now, as I go." I swallow deeply, hoping she's buying it. "That's why I had to steal the page. That's why I have to do this."

She looks at me thoughtfully, and it feels like the mood between us has changed instantly. The tension is gone, replaced by something else, a shared conspiratorial air. "My lady..." She hands me back the page with one hand, and with the other she brushes her black hair out of her eyes. "I would like to make you a proposition."

"A proposition?"

"I can teach you Old Marovian," she says. "I can read these pages. And I can get you more. I work in the library, helping with transcription and organization. There are other pages like this. I can get them for you."

That is a hell of an offer. Too good. "And in exchange?" I ask.

She hesitates for just one moment, like she's gathering her courage, like a diver on the edge of a lake bracing herself to jump in. Then she looks up, her eyes again meeting mine. "I want you to take me with you," she says. Her voice is even, but her gaze burns with an emotion I can't quite place. "When you graduate and leave this island. Take me with you wherever you go."

"Is that permitted?" I ask. "I thought you had to stay on this island."

"In special cases, exceptions may be granted," Marlena explains. "Last year, when Vicus Sinclair graduated, he asked for his favorite servant from the Order of Vanguard to be released from his role here and to join his staff instead. Headmaster Aberdeen granted it. You could ask the same for me."

"I don't know that I'll have the sway to move the headmaster...."

"You will if you take the Order of Nethro to victory," she says, and then for the first time she smiles, her cheeks dimpling, her eyes dancing with cunning and mischief. For the first time I think I see her, the real Marlena, not the servant humbling herself to please a Wizard, but the cunning, calculating girl behind that facade. She's smart, I realize, exceptionally smart, wearing a mask just as much as I am.

Am I manipulating her? Or is she manipulating me?

Does it matter?

"All right," I say. I have no idea if I'm stumbling into a trap, but we're so far off the rails of strategy that I might as well go with what feels right. Marlena might be using me. She's *probably* using me. But the fact is, there's no way I'm going to read these pages without her, so maybe we can just use each other and hope it works out.

"You promise?" Marlena asks. "You swear?"

I nod. "I swear by the Gods, by my mother and father, may my name be cursed and my line ended. When I leave this island, I'll do everything I can to take you with me."

That's not a lie.

She smiles again, widely and delightedly, maybe even a little giddily, and I notice for the first time how radiant she looks. My heart beats against my ribs, and I feel something I've only felt a few times in my life, the pull of destiny, the sense of significance. This moment matters. This choice matters. "Would you like me to read it now?" she asks. "I don't have to if you don't want to, if you're tired, I just mean, in case..."

"Please," I reply. "Let's do it. I could use a victory tonight."

Marlena nods, then turns to the page. *"Third-Degree Delayed Elemental Infusion. This Glyph allows the caster to temporarily imbue a given receptacle with the lowest level of power from a base elemental Glyph. The base Glyph and this secondary form must be carved directly into the receptacle, which must weigh less than one stone. The effect will persist for up to seventy-two hours but may go dormant until the receptacle is touched. When carving the second form, carve it in reverse order, starting with the smallest circle and working up."* She turns to look at me. "Did you do that?"

I blink. "Not necessarily. I mean, not all of it. I didn't really use a receptacle. I just carved it."

Marlena stares at me. "Into the air? You know that treats the air as the receptacle, don't you?" She looks back into the room, where the last vestiges of my mess are melting away, then back at me with increasing alarm. "You infused the *air* with ice?"

My cheeks burn with embarrassment. "You know an awful lot about magic for a Humble," I manage to get out.

"And you know shockingly little for a Wizard," she replies, which is fair but still hurts. "I've spent my life here, helping professors and students. I've picked up quite a bit." She walks over to a set of wooden shelves against the hall's wall and picks up a wide stone plate, the size of a floor tile. "Here. These are meant for infusion practice. Try carving the Glyph into this."

The plate is surprisingly light, its surface smooth and polished. "Into the slate? Like, right into it?" Marlena nods. "All right. I'll just go into the room then and try it out."

"I'll go with you."

"Are you sure? If I make a mistake, it can be dangerous."

She glances over her shoulder with a coy smile. "Then don't make a mistake," she says.

I'm lost as to how quickly the dynamic between us has changed. I don't understand her, this Humble servant who stared me down without hesitation, who grins as she teases me like an old friend. A part of me wants to jerk away, to run, to take a deep breath and think this all through before committing any deeper. But no. She's here right now, and if she's this willing to help me gain an edge, I'm not going to pass that up. I make my way back into the practice room, shivering a little as my bare feet pad over the icy floor. Marlena follows, carrying a small wooden pedestal, which she sets in the center of the room. "For the slate," she explains.

"I gathered," I reply, though honestly I hadn't thought that far ahead. I lay the slate down on the pedestal, take one last glance at Marlena, then draw my Loci and slip into the Null.

The room is just the way it had been before, except the Glyphs on the walls are glowing a little brighter in the fog, and I can see fragments of my ice Glyph flickering blue all over the floor. I can vaguely make out Marlena, her shape a dark silhouette, her heart a steady beating beacon in the gray. I take a deep breath, then raise my Loci, pressing its tip right against the cold stone of the slate.

I've never carved a Glyph into anything. I know it's possible, certainly, but none of the Glyphs Pavel taught me worked that way, and I never dared try on my own. With a wince, I push down, and my knife slides forward, *into* the slate, like the hard stone is as soft and malleable as butter. It's amazing but also wrong, profoundly wrong, a violation of everything I know about how physics should work, the uneasy, sickening friction of a nightmare.

I carve my first elemental base (picking wind this time, after the disaster that was ice), and it glows a gentle white on the surface of the stone, like a tattoo on skin. Then I carve the second, the one from the page, the four concentric circles, taking just a moment to remember the order I'm supposed to carve them in. As I cut the final stroke, the second form merges into the base, melting into it, the soft white of the shapes intertwining.

And then the Glyphs expand, blossoming out in a network of luminescent vines that wrap around the slate, crisscrossing over one another again and again like it's being wrapped up in ribbon. I step back, gaping, and within moments, it's so enveloped that I don't see the Glyphs at all, just the slate itself, glowing a beautiful, radiant white.

I jerk back into the Real. I'm not sure what I expect to see, but the slate is just sitting there on the pedestal, doing absolutely nothing. "It didn't work?" I ask. "I swear I carved it right...."

"Try touching it," Marlena offers. "I often see students do that after an elemental infusion."

I step forward and poke the slate carefully with one finger, like it might explode. It doesn't. Instead, there's a soft, low rustling sound, like the wind blowing through the trees, and the slate buzzes with that gentle white light of the Glyph. I jerk back, jaw open, and then before my eyes the slate lifts up, leaving the pedestal, spinning like a leaf as it rises up, up, up over my head toward the ceiling.

I clasp a hand over my mouth to suppress the laugh. I did it. I actually carved an advanced Glyph, infusing the slate with the element of wind. It's not the most graceful magic, not by any means. The slate wobbles back and forth uneasily, then after a minute comes crashing down. But I don't care. I did it.

I glance back at Marlena, and she's grinning. "Nicely done," she beams.

"I couldn't have done it without you. Very literally. I probably would have ended up killing myself."

"Do you want to try again?"

I do, in theory, but I'm starting to feel a growing ache in my arms, like someone's crushing them in a vise. My eyes are starting to burn, too, and my temples throb with an incipient headache. Magic fatigue. Every action you take in the Null causes ten times the exertion the same action would take in the Real. "I think I should rest for now."

"All right." Marlena picks up the slate. "You go to bed. I can clean up here and put everything back the way it was."

"You'd do that for me?"

"I'm a servant of the Order of Nethro. It's why I'm here."

I arch an eyebrow. "You know what I mean. You're not my servant anymore, Marlena. Not after this."

"Then what am I?"

It's a good question, honestly. I take a step back and look at her, really look at her. The way her black hair makes her pale skin look almost ghostly. The way she stands, confident and tall, her white shirt clinging tightly around her lean frame. And above all, her eyes sparkling bright with intelligence, earnest and unknowable and intoxicating all at once. I don't understand this girl, *can't* understand this girl. She's like a riddle whose solution's dancing at the edge of my mind, like a word whose definition you can almost recall. I know I should keep my distance, that I should keep up my guard, that I should fear what she knows. But all I want is to get closer. All I want is to understand.

"You're my partner," I say at last.

She smiles again, almost glowing, then she gently places the slate, which still feels warm, in my hands. "All right, then," she says. "Partners."

She turns back, bending down to sweep away the last fragments of ice, and I make my way back through the basement, to the flight of stairs up into the common room. Even as my body aches, my mind reels, trying to make sense of it all.

If Whispers had been here, she would've told me to kill Marlena the minute I was exposed. But if I had done that, I wouldn't have gained her as an ally. If I had done it Whispers's way, I'd be stuck uselessly staring at the Old Marovian. I'd be alone.

Maybe Whispers's way is wrong. Maybe I can do this my own way. Maybe I can carve my own path.

I collapse hard onto my bed and feel sleep taking me like an enveloping shroud. This could all still backfire, of course. Marlena could still report me. But I don't think she will. Not after what she did. The moment she broke the rules and read me that page, she sealed her fate alongside mine. Like those vines weaving across the slate, our fates are intertwined, two strands bound together.

One way or another, we're in this together.

Chapter 13

Now

I spend the next three days in an excited blur, a giddy haze of my newfound strategy and power. During the days, I slog through class, I joke with Fyl, I walk with Talyn, and then I sit alone in my room at night, counting down the hours, minutes, seconds, until I can creep down into the practice rooms with Marlena, until I can learn more forbidden Glyphs, until I can huddle together with her over stolen pages and listen rapt as she translates their secrets. At the end of every session, I feel overwhelmed, exhausted, light-headed. My body aches, but it's the good kind of ache, the kind of ache where you can feel yourself getting stronger, harder, more skilled.

Then, on the fourth night, Marlena says, "No."

"What?" I ask. We're both in my room, sitting side by side on my bed with the door shut, the sunset outside lighting up the room with a bright-orange glow. In theory, Marlena is making the rounds through the Order to change sheets and collect silverware, but really, she's here to talk to me. "What do you mean, no? I need to practice!"

"We can't spend every night together," Marlena explains. "It'll draw suspicion on me and then on you. Besides, if you want to win the Great Game, there are other skills you'll need to cultivate."

"Like what?"

"The challenges are all team based," Marlena says, with just the subtlest hint of *do I really have to explain this?* "You can be the greatest Wizard in the school, but if you haven't built a team that has your back, you'll still get crushed. Right now, all your fellow Nethros are downstairs in the common room, socializing, mingling, making friends. It's the perfect opportunity for you to find your allies."

I arch an eyebrow. "Are you giving me strategic advice now?"

Marlena shrugs, but I see that slight twitch in the corner of her lips, the mischievous glint in her eye. "You're the Wizard, Lady Dewinter. You can make all the strategic decisions you want. I'm just the Humble servant who knows how the game is actually won."

Now I'm the one fighting backing a smile. I know I ought to be more wary, more cautious. I know Whispers would be screaming if she could see this. But I can't help myself. Our sessions together, the two of us huddled together as we pore over stolen pages, as the air around us pulses with magic, are the best part of my day. "All right," I tell her. "If you insist. But tomorrow night . . . ?"

"Tomorrow night." She nods.

So I get out of bed and throw on my blazer and head downstairs to the common area. Like Marlena said, it's packed with other Nethros. The dining tables have been stripped of their tablecloths and are now lined with students working, poring together over loose papers and thick tomes. Others lounge on their own in comfortable chairs by the roaring fireplace. Tish is there, their nose buried in a massive leatherbound book titled *The Rise and Fall of the Izachi*, and they don't even glance up as I stroll down. On the other side of the common room, there's a less studious atmosphere. Several Nethros sit around a circular board, brows furrowed in consternation as they slide colored stones around in some elaborate game. Two boys cuddle up, resting their heads together as they read a romance novel. And a few others, like that hulking Velkschen Zigmund, just sit on the couches and chat, laughing noisily with goblets of wine in hand.

I don't know where to begin, but I don't have to. "Alayne!" a voice calls. "Over here!"

It's Desmond. He sits alone at a small table, a glass of wine at his side and a loose stack of papers in front of him. I don't see a better option, so I pull up a chair opposite him. "Hey," I say. "Is Fyl around?"

"She was too worn out after Glyphcrafting, so she went to take a nap. You're stuck with me for now."

"How tragic," I say, and he snorts. "What are you reading?"

"Oh, these?" Desmond holds up papers, which are covered in dense text. "Transcripts from the latest Senate session. I made my father promise he'd send them to me."

I try to read the first page, but the text is so dense and ponderous, I give up almost immediately. "Is this for a class?"

"No. Believe it or not, I actually enjoy following politics." He takes a sip of wine, and when he sets his glass down, his lips are purple. "When I got here, I hoped I'd be sorted into Vanguard. But no. Apparently, no matter how much you know or how passionate you are, that Order is only for the most upper of the upper crust, even if your father's a senator himself."

I pause. What I know about the Senate could probably fill a single page, but this feels important. "Your father's a senator?"

"Yeah." Desmond shrugs. "But not one of the important ones. I doubt you've heard of him. He's just a minor Traditionalist from Westphalen."

"Traditionalist?"

Desmond blinks at me. "Good gods, what are they teaching out in New Kenshire? I mean, I knew you were a bumpkin, but sheesh!"

I feel like Alayne would be offended at that, but I'm more interested in learning what I can. "I don't suppose you could offer a primer?"

"Right. Okay. Yeah." Desmond takes another sip of his wine. "So, there are ninety-nine senators total, from all over the Republic, that make up the Senate. In theory, they're all supposed to operate independently and represent their regions. But realistically, they've split off into factions and formed a bunch of different parties. The Traditionalists are the largest party, with forty-three senators. Their leader, Marius's father, is the Grandmaster of the Senate, the most powerful member, who sets the agenda and controls the military."

"And I'm guessing from the name, the Traditionalists are..."

"Traditional? Yeah," Desmond says with a laugh. "When you think of the Senate, you're probably thinking of them." He raises a fist dramatically as he speaks in an exaggerated voice. *"Conquest and capital! For the glory of the Republic! Honor thy fathers and serve thy Gods!"*

"I take it that's not how you feel?"

"My father and I don't see eye to eye politically, no," Desmond sighs. "The worst part is, when we talk in private, he's as critical of the Traditionalists as I am. But Madison's too powerful, and my father's too timid. So when it comes down to it, he always votes what the Grandmaster says."

Hierarchies within hierarchies, ladders within ladders. "You said there were only forty-three Traditionalists. That's less than half," I say. "So why don't the other senators team up to take power?"

"Because the rest of the Senate is a damn mess?" Desmond replies. "The closest you've got to a real opposition party is the Reformers. They want better treatment of Humbles, an end to wars of conquests, that kind of thing. There's maybe twenty of them. Then you've got the Gods' Glory party, who want the high clerics to run everything. You've got the senators from Sithar and the Velkschen north and the Kindrali Isles, who are just looking out for their regions. Add them all up and you've got a group of people who can't decide what to order for lunch, much less how to be an opposition."

He flips his paper over, and I suck in my breath. Because I can't make out all the words printed there, but I can make out one, clear as can be, big and bold. A name. "How does Headmaster Aberdeen fit into this?"

"Aberdeen?" Desmond repeats. "He's 'The Great Unifier,' one of the most respected men in the Republic. All the senators look up to him, no matter what party they're in. He'll sometimes get called into the Senate when there's some big debate or complex issue, to offer his wisdom and guidance. He's famous for his neutrality, for his compassion, for his dedication to the Republic above all." Desmond has sounded cynical this whole time, but when talking about Aberdeen, even he seems to believe it. "My dad always said that Aberdeen could've been Grandmaster if he wanted. But he passed on all of that, gave up all that power, to stay here and teach the next generations. You have to respect that."

You very much do not, but I'm not going to get into that now. I'm just trying to square what he's telling me with the monster I remember, the murderer who sneered into my father's dying face. Where was his neutrality then? Where was his wisdom, his compassion?

"Anyway," Desmond says, folding the papers back. "I could go on all day about the intricacies of Senate floor decorum, but the truth is, none of it really matters. Maybe fifty years ago, there was real democracy, real debate. But it's all a farce now. Madison and the Traditionalists run everything. And they're always going to."

There's something new here, a flash of real anger, a hint of turbulent depths. I have to pry more. "And if you were a senator, if you could change things, what would you do?"

He hesitates a minute, choosing his words carefully, and when he talks again, his voice is low, hushed, conspiratorial. Maybe it's the wine hitting, or maybe he can sense what I'm getting at, can sense where my sentiments lie. "Look," he says. "My mother died when I was born, and my father was gone all the time to be in the Senate. You know who that left to take care of me? Brenna, our Humble servant. She was the only person there for me in my childhood. She raised me. She taught me. She took care of me. As far as I'm concerned, she was my real parent."

"'Was'?"

"Yeah. One day while we were at the park when I was nine, another boy attacked me, hitting me across the head with a rock. He was going to do it again, so Brenna grabbed him and stopped him, knocking him down into the grass. Turns out that was a mistake, because he was the mayor's son. For the crime of striking a Wizard, Brenna was sentenced to a month's labor in the mines. She was sixty-five at the time. She didn't survive." Desmond's brow furrows, and rage, hot livid rage, flashes in his eyes. "That's not who we are. That's not who we should be. So yeah, if I were in the Senate, I'd change things. Which is why I'm guaranteed to never end up there."

"Desmond..."

He stands up, clears his throat, turns away. He's realized he's gone too far, bared too much. "I'm sorry. I shouldn't have gotten into that. That... it's not what I... I should go." I reach out to stop him, but it's too late. Head down, he vanishes up the flight of stairs, leaving me alone at the table with his stack of papers and a mind whirring with thoughts.

For a moment there, Desmond hadn't sounded like a Wizard. He'd sounded like one of *us*, a Revenant, full of fire and ready to burn. In the right situation, with the right guidance, would he join the cause? Would he turn on his world, his country, his father? Instinctively, I want to say no. But when I think about the way he looked, the fury in his eyes...

Marlena sent me down here to make allies. I think I just found one.

Chapter 14

Then

I am thirteen when I have my first drink.

I wait alone, pacing nervously in the sprawling wheat field by our hideout. It's a warm summer night, the moon a pale crescent overhead. I told Sera to meet at midnight, and it's already an hour past, and just when I'm starting to think she's not coming at all, the wheat stalks in front of me part like a curtain.

"Well?" she asks. She's wearing a long pink nightgown, her bare feet padding softly over the earth, and her curly red hair hangs down her back in a long woven braid. "What's this big secret you had me sneak out for?"

I grin and pull the triangular bottle out from behind my back, its green glass sparkling in the light. "Look at this. Raspberry sherry. I stole it when we raided the merchant's manor."

Sera blinks. "And what are we going to do with that?"

"We're going to pour it on some tulips and make a magical garden," I say with a laugh. "What do you think we're gonna do, Sera? We're going to drink it!"

"Are you serious right now?" she says, looking around like someone's going to walk in on us. "No. Absolutely not. Whispers forbade us to drink until we're sixteen."

"Whispers is on a pirate ship five days' ride away," I reply. "Come on. This will be fun. I promise we won't get in trouble."

"Oh, really? That's what you said about dagger-throwing practice and stealing the pies from the market and that time with the masks!" She folds her arms across her chest, but I can see it in her expression, the way her eyes focus on the bottle with curiosity. I know Sera, so I just patiently wait, five seconds, ten seconds, and at fifteen, she clears her throat. "Have you already tried some?"

"No, silly, I've been waiting for you." I pat the ground next to me. "Look. Think of it as practice. This way, when you turn sixteen and have your first drink of wine with Carlita, you'll seem smart and sophisticated and not make a mess of yourself."

Sera rolls her eyes. "For the last time, I do *not* have a crush on Carlita," she says, but she sits down next to me all the same. "One drink. That's it. Just to try it."

"That's the spirit!" I pry out the wooden cork and raise the bottle to my nose, sniffing it like I sometimes see the older Revenants do. It smells nice, nice-ish anyway, raspberry mixed with the distinct tang of alcohol. I feel a little nervous, but I know that if I show that, Sera will use it as an excuse to back out, so I raise the bottle to my lips and swig.

It tastes nice, sweet and tart, and then the actual alcohol hits me and I lurch forward, hacking and coughing. "Are you all right?" Sera gasps.

"I'm fine," I wheeze out, eyes burning. "It's just the taste. Kind of like burning. Like I'm drinking the feeling of burning. Like there's a fire inside my throat."

"How is that *possibly* supposed to convince me to drink?"

"It's good, it's good," I sputter, pulling myself back up. "It's like a good burning." And that's not actually a lie. The worst of that first swig has passed, and I'm feeling something else run through me, a pleasant warmth in my stomach, a gentle tingle in my hands. "Oh. Yeah. That is nice."

Sera raises an eyebrow skeptically, then takes the bottle from my hands. I nod encouragingly, and she raises it to her lips, taking a long, slow sip. I expect her to sputter the way I did, but she keeps it together, just coughing a few times gently into the back of her hand. "Oh, Gods. That's rough. That's really rough. Are you sure it's supposed to taste like that?"

"Why wouldn't it?"

"I don't know!" Sera stands up. "It feels weird. All tingly in my stomach. Are you sure this is sherry? What if it's actually a poison the Wizard kept and he just labeled it sherry?"

"Why would he keep poison in a bottle labeled sherry?" I demand, even though, honestly, that does seem like something a Wizard would do. "I'm sure it's fine. It's supposed to taste this way."

"Blech." Sera sticks her tongue out. "Why do adults like this stuff so much?"

"I don't know." I shoot her a mischievous grin. "I guess we'll just have to drink more to find out."

So we drink more, passing the bottle back and forth a few times, later in the night, dropping it halfway. And we have fun. We share funny stories about our studies, Sera admits she absolutely *does* have a crush on Carlita, and at one point we both have a good cry over everyone we've lost. Maybe two hours after we started, the bottle is empty. I sit cross-legged, my cheeks burning, while Sera lies with her head in my lap.

"We're drunk now, right?" she asks. "This is what drunk is?"

"A minute ago, you asked me if birds have butts," I reply. "Yes, Sera. This is what drunk is."

"It's not bad. It's okay. I like it." She blinks, her eyes glassy. "Don't like how everything's all spinny, though. I could do without that."

I grin, craning my head up to the sky. A soft breeze washes over me, cool and nice against the summer night's heat. The air hums with the song of cicadas, and the wheat stalks ripple like the surface of a pond. "I like it here. It's peaceful. I think it's my favorite place we've stayed."

"It's wonderful," Sera says. "Thank you for this. For this night. For sharing with me. Things are so hectic all the time, so stressful and dangerous . . . I sometimes forget how much fun we have together."

"Well, I never forget," I say, squeezing her shoulder. It's funny. Because Sera's smarter and more studious and more mature, it's easy to think of her as the older sister. But in moments like this, she just looks so unfathomably young, so vulnerable. "And I'm glad you came."

A long silence hangs over us, and in that silence, something changes. When Sera speaks again, her eyes are shut, and her voice is low, heavy. "Do you think we're going to die soon?"

"What? No. Why would we die?"

"Because that's what Revenants do," she says. "Like Tasha. Or Baelyn. Or Valay. Sooner or later, it's everyone's turn."

"Ours won't come for a long time," I tell her. "Whispers won't let us. You know that."

The silence lingers between us like we're underwater. When she speaks again, her voice is barely a whisper. "We could run away."

"What?"

"You and me. We could run away." Her head's turned to the side, like she can't even meet my gaze. "Right now. Grab the money from Whispers's stash. Steal a pair of horses from the stables. Ride into town, buy passage on a ship, be gone by sunrise. They'd never track us down."

I suck in my breath. I can't tell if she's joking or if she's serious or if this is just the alcohol talking. "What would we do?"

She rolls over, and now she looks at me, right at me. "I don't know. Sail somewhere nice. Maybe the Kindrali Isles. Maybe farther. Find some little town and hide out there. If they have a library, I could be a scholar, and you could work in the town watch. We could get houses side by side. We could meet people and get married and have kids and our kids would play together. We could be happy."

"Sera, are you being serious?"

"Yes. No. I don't know." She breathes deeply. "Yes. I am. I mean, we could do it. We could live. Just... *live*."

I close my eyes. Because I want it. Of course I want it. Of course I've fantasized about it thousands of times. When I dare to think of myself happy, dare to even consider the idea, a quiet, peaceful life with Sera is all I can picture. There's nothing I'd want more.

But then I think of our parents. I think of our father screaming as the flames swallow him. I think of our mother's body, still, shattered, her chest a sunken ruin. I think of all the other Humbles out there, all the people struggling and bleeding and dying under the Wizards' reign. And I feel that hate inside me, that anger, that bloody, screaming rage. I'd never be happy with a peaceful life. It's like I have this toxin in me, this black ink of hate running through my veins, and I have to do what it wants, no matter how much pain it brings me.

"We can't," I tell her. "You know we can't."

"I know," she replies, rolling to the side. "It was just a nice dream."

I hold her until she falls asleep.

Chapter 15

Now

Just when I'm settling into a routine and starting to get a handle on life at Blackwater, the weekend hits, and Fyl is at my door, pounding away. "It's the weekend, Alayne! Come on! It's time to go out!"

All I want to do is lie in my bed and read a book in peaceful solitude. But Fyl keeps banging away, so I grumble to the door and throw it open. "Go out where?"

"When the school week ends, everyone heads down to the Barefoot Archer. It's a pub in the Humble village. They've got drinks and music and dancing and everything."

Going to a pub for drinks and dancing with a bunch of Wizards sounds worse than death. "I'm really tired, Fyl," I try. "I think I'll skip this one."

"Noooooo," she pleads. "Please? It'll be so much more fun if you're there. And everyone's going."

I wince, because those are the absolute only words that could convince me to go. I've already made myself suspicious enough. The last thing I want is a bunch of my peers sitting around, speculating about my absence. Besides, Fyl's giving me the big pleading eyes, and I still need to work on making those allies. "All right. Fine. I'll go. But I'm not going to stay long."

"You absolutely will," Fyl says, grabbing my hand and dragging me out.

Desmond and Tish join us as we leave the house, and the four of us walk together on a long, winding trail to the north. I'm wearing my uniform, but everyone else is all dressed up: Fyl's in a sharp blue gown, Desmond's wearing a brown suit, and Tish is wearing a sleeveless Kindrali robe, its fabric a lush deep purple, and a delicate golden circlet across their forehead. Fyl wasn't kidding about everyone going there. There are groups behind us and in front of us as far as I can see, all making the same trek. The Humble village is nearly forty-five minutes away, our trail winding through dense forest. It's a dark night, the moon mostly hidden by clouds, but I can occasionally make out shapes amid the trees, wooden towers with swaying ropes, odd little huts, even what looks like a set of cages. "What is all that?" I ask.

"Some of it is for classes, I think," Desmond offers. "In our second year, we get much more hands-on with magic. They've got courses for us to practice on, that kind of thing. I think there's even a Balitesta arena."

"And some of it is for the professors' research," Tish adds. "I heard a rumor that Professor Calfex is trying to make a Glyph that can let her meld together different creatures. I heard she's trying to make a killer wolf-bear."

"Come on. There's no way that's true," Desmond says, and just as he does, something rustles in the trees to our left, and he lets out a surprised little yelp. "On the other hand, maybe we ought to walk a little faster? Just in case?"

I hear the village before I see it. The Blackwater campus is packed with students, but it has a quiet tone: the hum of a library, of people chattering softly. The Humble village, on the other hand, is alive with sound. Even when it's just a distant set of lights beyond the trees, I can hear the loud commotion of a market square, voices shouting and arguing and laughing, music playing, dogs barking, children running. It reminds me of the docks in Laroc, of the main square in Hellsum, of every city I grew up in.

The village is bigger than I'd imagined, maybe four dozen little homes, with sturdy wood frames and red-shingled roofs, clustered around a cobblestoned square. I'm not sure what I expected, probably something more ornate or magical, but it's almost striking how familiar it is: a brick well surrounded by buckets, horses tethered to posts, scruffy cats prowling the rooftops, and the whole thing lit up by the flickering light of dozens of mounted torches. This could be any Humble village anywhere in the Republic.

Except for the tavern, that is. It stands at the end of the town square, a two-story building as big as half the homes put together. Where everything else in the village is made of stacked wood, the tavern is made of smooth polished brick, with ornate marble windowsills and flowering yellow ivy creeping elegantly down the walls. Music wafts out of its wide swinging doors. A giant swinging sign identifies it as THE BAREFOOT ARCHER, with a woodcut of a sprightly figure holding an oversize bow.

Humbles are everywhere, and they bustle toward us as we approach. "Greetings, my lords and ladies!" a portly man with a bushy white beard bellows, arms stretched wide. "Welcome to our village! Enjoy the sights and sounds! Grab a scone at the bakery, some new clothes from the tailor, or a drink at the Barefoot Archer. Anything you want, anything you need, just ask!"

The others laugh, but I fight back the urge to cringe. I can see it even if the others can't: the way he has to force the smile, the fear dancing behind his eyes. All the Humbles are looking at us like that, from the baker holding out tarts by his wagon to the two children loitering in the shadows. The charade makes me sick. It's not enough that the Wizards have total power over these people, that they live to serve, terrified of punishment for the slightest failure. No, the Wizards also need this pantomime, these pained smiles, this forced friendship. The powerful don't just want to be feared. They need to feel loved.

I'd been so swept up in studying, I'd momentarily forgotten my mission. One minute in this village brings it all back.

We head straight for the tavern. It's even fancier inside than out. A sparkling chandelier with at least a hundred prisms spins overhead, casting the whole room in a dancing light. Two wide staircases lead up to a second-floor balcony. A long, slick bar runs along the back, with a half dozen bartenders running it and a massive wall of bottles and barrels behind them. Small, round tables dot the floor, and wide, comfortable booths line the walls. On a wide central platform, a band is playing a jaunty jig: two dancing fiddlers, circling each other as they strum away, while a pair of women back them up on flutes.

There are at least a hundred people in here, probably more. Blackwater students crowd the tables and jostle for spots at the bar, as servants bustle about with trays covered with cups and goblets. I can make out a few familiar faces: Zigmund is arm-wrestling with that Zartan girl from my Glyphcraft class, while Dean Veyle downs a stein by the bar. Marius is here, too, sitting in a booth with his arm around Vyctoria Aberdeen, her head resting on his shoulder. They're a couple, I guess. The Grandmaster's son and the headmaster's niece. That seems like it could be a problem.

The one person I don't see is Marlena, even though it's packed with Humble servants. Maybe that's for the best. This way I won't have to pretend that we haven't been secretly studying the stolen Glyphs every night.

"Come on!" Fyl shouts, and she has to shout because the room is unbearably loud. "There's a booth over there!"

We pile into the booth, squeezing tightly, and place our orders with a cheerful Humble waiter. Desmond gets some beer; Tish, a glass of water. I barely have time to think about what I want, so I just get the same raspberry sherry Fyl orders. Within moments, the waiter slides back up, laying our drinks out before us. The tavern clearly spares no expense. Desmond's beer is in a carved metal stein, Fyl and I have pretty copper goblets, and Tish even has an ornate crystalline cup for their water.

Desmond cocks an eyebrow their way. "Just water? You don't drink? Is that a Kindrali thing?"

"No. It's a *me* thing." Tish shrugs. "I don't like the taste."

"Well, I do!" Fyl raises her cup high. "To our first week at Blackwater! We made it!"

"One down, just ninety-nine to go," Desmond replies, and we all clink together. "I feel like we've got good odds of making it to graduation. Well, decent odds. Well, not terrible. That's something, right?"

"Speak for yourself," Fyl says. "You're the only one here who didn't make an ass of himself carving an ice sphere."

"Tish didn't!"

"I got lost on my way to Political Theory, and I was so embarrassed to be late that I just never showed up," Tish quietly admits. "I've missed three classes now. I'm hoping no one notices."

"All right. Fine. You win. I'm the only one here who's going to make it, and I'm going to have to graduate alone." Desmond raises his stein to his lips and takes a long sip. "Mmm. That's good. That's really good."

"You've got a foam mustache." I grin and take a sip of my own.

It hits me like a hurricane. I'd ordered the drink without thinking about it, just copying Fyl. But that flavor. Raspberry sherry. Sweet and tart but still strong, a burn that tastes like summer. It takes me back instantly. That wheat field. That humid night. Sera's head resting in my lap. The way she smiled. The way she laughed.

The way her body looked in Von Clair's manor, trapped under that flaming beam, the way she gasped and sobbed as the flames closed in.

Shit. *Shit.* I jerk back, like I'm stung, and the whole table rattles. "Alayne?" Fyl says. "Are you all right?"

"I'm fine," I choke out, though no, I'm not really fine, not at all. My eyes are burning, and my heart feels like it's collapsing in on itself, and I can't breathe. There are memories I just can't revisit, memories I have to bury, memories I have to encase in stone and send plunging down to the darkest depths of my subconscious. This is one of them, the worst one, and now I'm thinking about her, and I'm thinking about that night, that terrible night, the night it all went wrong.

"I just drank too fast," I say, fumbling out of my chair. "Burned. Wrong pipe. Need to use the bathroom." The others are staring at me bewildered, but it's better they think I'm some novice who can't hold her sherry than they know the truth.

I stagger toward the restroom, but the bar is too noisy, too chaotic, the band reaching a feverish climax, the crowd surging around me. I push forward and end up slamming right into a burly boy's back. He lurches forward with a yelp, spinning around, and I can make out beady brown eyes glaring at me from above a mossy beard. Of course.

"Dewinter!" Dean Veyle hollers, and I can see that he's spilled beer all down the front of his shirt. "You are a godsdamned blight, you know that?"

"Sorry," I stammer out, but I'm still all thrown off, my pulse still racing, my body still afire from excitement. A confrontation is absolutely the last thing I need right now.

Dean wobbles back, his now-half-empty stein in his hand, wide nostrils flaring. His cheeks are red, his eyes glassy. He's already drunk, mean drunk, which is impressive given that night just fell an hour ago. "You ruined my shirt!" he yells, and now heads are turning our way, more people looking at me, which I do not need, which I cannot handle. I need to be alone. I need to get it together. I try to push away, but Dean grabs my shoulder and shoves me back across the floor, and now this is getting really bad because my instincts are kicking in, instincts forged on Revenant sparring mats. My body is screaming to fight, my hands balling into fists, my vision flaring red. And I'm fighting it, because *Alayne* wouldn't do that, wouldn't grab him by the back of the head and smash his face against a beam, but I'm losing that fight and sooner or later Alka is going to take control.

"Now, let's all just calm down," a meek voice says. It's Jasper, the shy Nethro with the enormous glasses that I met on the first night. "We're all Wizards here, are we not? We—"

But before he can finish, Dean shoves him, and Jasper plummets back, falling hard onto the floor. A crowd is forming all around us, gawkers and agitators, shouting and pointing and laughing. That just makes Dean bolder. He turns in a circle, soaking up the attention with an intolerably smug grin. "You like spilling beer on people, huh?" he taunts. "Well, two can play that game!" He winds up his goblet, beer sloshing out and I grimace because I know as soon as it hits my face I'm going to snap and then it's all over.

But it never hits me because there's a hand on his wrist, holding him back. He spins around and there's Prince Talyn, towering over him, his body relaxed but his eyes blazing with intensity. "No," Talyn tells him, his voice iron. "We don't do that."

Dean jerks free, his stein flying out of his grip. "Get your hands off me!" he growls, and this was apparently the last straw because he winds up and takes a swing at Talyn's face.

Which Talyn casually dodges, listing to the side with incredible speed, his expression calm, even bemused. Dean hurtles past him then spins around and swings again, and again, and again. The crowd hollers and cheers as Talyn weaves around his punches, practically dancing as he slides on his feet. He makes it look effortless, but I see the skill, the precision in each move. He's wearing a sleeveless purple shirt, its silk loose and billowy, and I can see the muscles in his shoulders tense and relax, see the way his eyes follow and anticipate every one of Dean's strikes. Talyn isn't just some pampered, smooth-talking prince. He's a trained fighter.

The ninth time's the charm, as Dean's fist very lightly grazes Talyn's cheek. The crowd bellows, and Dean lets out a triumphant whoop. Talyn smiles, too, and then there's a dark blur as his fist shoots forward in a brutal jab, so fast even I can barely see it, like a striking hawk. There's a wet crunch and Dean falls back, clutching his face as blood streams out through his fingers. "You broke my nose!" he warbles, and Talyn just shrugs.

I'll grant Dean this much. He's not a quitter. With a primal howl, he grabs a chair and rushes right at Talyn with it raised overhead, even as Talyn leans back, preparing to dodge.

"Stop!" a voice calls out, and amazingly Dean does, freezing in place, like he's been hit with a blast of ice.

The crowd goes instantly silent. Every head turns to the back of the room, to the booth where Marius is sitting, his arm still around Vyctoria, watching the whole thing play out. "Seriously, Dean," he says. "Enough."

Dean listens, dropping his chair. "He broke my nose, Marius!" He jabs a bloody finger at Talyn. "He broke my godsdamned nose!"

With a sigh, Marius rises to his feet, stepping away from the booth. Vyctoria shoots him an annoyed glance, then takes out a book and starts reading. Marius paces toward us, and I scuttle away, trying to push into the crowd and avoid getting any more involved. "Now, now, Dean," he says, his voice soothing on the surface, with an undercurrent of menace growling beneath. "You *were* trying to hit him."

"But—he—" Dean sputters, blood still streaming down his face. "Marius, are you serious right now?"

Marius clasps a hand on Dean's shoulder. "What's *serious* are my father's instructions that the prince here be treated with the utmost hospitality, to ensure a sound diplomatic relationship between our great nations. And I don't know about you, Dean, but I don't think smashing a chair across his head really qualifies."

"That chair was never going to hit me," Talyn says. "Just to be clear."

Marius ignores him, squeezing Dean's shoulder harder. "Well, Dean? I think you owe our guest an apology."

"I'm sorry," Dean says through gritted teeth. Even piss drunk and full of adrenaline, he knows who his boss is. "Won't happen again."

"If it happens again, you won't walk away." Talyn takes a cloth towel off the bar and wipes his knuckles with it. "Now then. I think I've had enough of your Marovian hospitality. If no one minds, I'll head back to campus." He pauses, and across the crowd, his eyes find mine. "Lady Dewinter. Would you care to accompany me?"

I swallow deeply. One thing's for sure, I need to get away from this tavern, and Talyn just offered me an out. I turn back to my friends' table to make sure it's okay. Desmond's jaw is hanging wide, Tish's eyes are as big as saucers, and Fyl is nodding so hard her head looks ready to pop off. *Do it*, she mouths.

"Yes. Yes, I would," I reply. Talyn offers me a hand, and I take it, and we walk out together. I shoot one last glance over my shoulder at Dean hunched over, panting with fury, at Marius studying me with a furrowed brow, at the crowd gaping and gawking. Lying low might not be an option anymore. Perhaps it's time for Alayne Dewinter to commit to being bold.

The night air is brisk, a pleasant change from the sweltering heat of the tavern. We walk through the village square side by side and don't say a word until we're out of earshot, alone on the trail. With every step, I can feel my heart slowing down, feel the panic and the anger fading. Finally, when we're deep in the woods, I turn to him. "Thanks for the help back there. My night was bad enough without getting soaked in beer."

Talyn glances down at me with a low little laugh. "I wasn't worried about the beer. I was worried about you. I saw the look in your eyes. You looked ready to kill him." I find myself staring at the curve of his long, lean neck in the moonlight, the tiniest traces of stubble on the underside of his chin. "Honestly, I was probably going to end up punching that boy no matter what." He glances down at his knuckles, still flecked with blood. "My father told me to play nice and make friends. But I doubt that goes for loudmouthed bullies."

What can I say? I like him. "Well, Dean's from a rival Order, anyway. I think you're supposed to be enemies. Are you making friends in the Order of Javellos?"

"The Order of Javellos," Talyn repeats. "The problem with an Order full of students chosen for their cunning is that every single one thinks they're the smartest person in the room."

"And you?"

Talyn grins. "Well, I'm *actually* the smartest person in the room."

I can't help but laugh. I don't know what it is about Talyn, but something about him relaxes me. With all the others, whether it's Fyl or Desmond or even Marlena, I still have to pretend, to keep up the front of Alayne. But it's like Talyn sees right through it anyway, like he sees the real me. So I can just be myself. "You don't seem to like it much here."

"Is it that obvious?"

"Very," I reply. "Is this school not up to your princely standards?"

"Well, no, it's not, but that's not the problem." We cross into a wide glade, and the moonlight hits him just right. The runic symbols are still painted onto his arms, but they're faded, duller, like a mural after a rain, an afterimage ghosting across his black skin. "The truth is, I miss my home," he says with a sigh. "I miss the desert heat on my face. I miss floating in the salt lakes. I miss the singing of the dawnswallows and the taste of elderfruit. I miss the *smell.*" He shakes his head, and the little silver beads at the ends of his braids tinkle like a wind chime. "Look at me, getting all sentimental." He glances back my way. "Do you miss your home?"

I know he means New Kenshire, but I think of that little apartment in Laroc, the one by the beach, the last place I saw my parents. *Find the truth behind the lie*. "More than anything."

Talyn nods. "I don't fit in here. I don't like the chill winds, the cold stone, don't like the way the trees seem to follow me. And the people, the other students..."

"You don't like Marovians?"

"I don't like *these* Marovians," Talyn says. "The constant squabbling over status, the obsession with rank and perception, everyone smiling those shark smiles while thinking about how they can knife one another in the back. Every single thing we do is a competition, and for what? A pat on the back from the headmaster? Pah." Something flits across his face, a real hint of anger. "And the servants back there, the way they're treated? Forced to grovel before us with fear in their eyes, terrified at every turn that they'll be lashed or killed. It makes me sick."

Talyn has been full of surprises, but this is probably the biggest of all. "You don't have Humbles in the Xintari Kingdom?"

For once, he doesn't have a quick reply, choosing every word carefully. "Things are different in my home. Those without magic, the Humbles as you call them, are protected by the law as much as we are. Wizards may not hurt them or mistreat them, and there are grave punishments for doing so. In the kingdom, the Humbles are not servants but fellow countrymen, who may live their lives as they please."

"But... you still rule," I say. "The Wizards, I mean. You're still in charge."

Talyn blinks, for once surprised. "Well, yes," he says. "It's the will of the Gods, after all."

I say nothing, turn away, let the moment linger in silence. Because of course. As different as Talyn is from the others, as much as he seems to understand me, he's still a Wizard, a noble, a *prince*. As alike as we might be, there is still this yawning chasm between us that I can't imagine how we'd begin bridging. He might be charming and handsome, he might have those impossibly deep eyes, but in the end, it's not me he's flirting with. It's Alayne. And I can't forget that.

We're almost back at campus now, the tall spires of the main building looming high over the trees, the glow of lanterns swallowing the moonlight. As we step onto the courtyard, Talyn turns to me, his brown eyes meeting mine, the flecks sparkling like gold in a river. "What about you, Alayne? How are you liking it here?"

"I'm not," I reply, before I can really think it through, and then the words are just tumbling out like a waterfall. "I'm an outsider, like you. I mean, not exactly like you, but... I don't come from some big powerful family. Everyone looks at me like I don't belong, like my presence here is an insult to their hallowed institution. Everyone stares at me like they expect me to fail, and every system I encounter seems designed to make me fail. I thought once I made it in here, I'd be in, that I'd be one of the elite. But all I've really found is just more levels of exclusion, more rungs on the ladder of hierarchy. And it's a struggle, a constant struggle to put on a face, to not show them who I really am, to hide anything I'm really thinking in case it's used against me. It's exhausting and it's maddening and I hate every second of it." I take a deep breath. "Sorry. That was a lot."

"No, it was good," Talyn says. "I feel exactly the same way." We've reached the campus's central quad now that splits off into our dorms, and we linger there a minute in silence.

"Thanks for walking me back," I say at last.

"It was my pleasure." Talyn reaches out and gently rests his fingers under my chin, lifting my head up to look into my eyes. His hand is calloused, rougher than I would've thought for a prince, and warm, blazingly warm. I feel something inside me, a part of me I've long cut off, stir. I know that I ought to step back, to cut this off now, to keep my focus on the mission. But I don't, because that other part of me really likes how his hand feels.

I look up into his brown eyes, and he smiles. And not the cunning smile or the playful smile or that smile of slight amusement. This smile's genuine. "This is why I like you, Alayne. In a campus full of liars… you're the one honest person I've met."

Me. The one honest person. The irony is so thick I want to laugh.

It's not until later that night, when I'm lying in my bed, that I realize he was actually right. I spoke many words to him tonight. And every single one of them was true.

Chapter 16

Now

I want nothing more than to sleep in, but Fyl wakes me early the next morning, pounding on my door. Well, technically, it's just before noon, but it feels early to me. "What is it?" I demand, rubbing the sleep out of my eyes. "What do you want?"

"Sorry, but you've got to come to see this," Fyl shouts through my door. "They're having a *krova-yan*."

Now that gets my attention. I might have been raised by Humbles, but even I know about krova-yans. Duels of honor between Wizards, fought to the death, no Glyphs forbidden, no mercy shown. It seems like every epic poem ends in some doomed lover or another meeting his fate in one. "Like a real one?" I ask, pulling myself out of bed, grateful for once I fell asleep in my clothes. "To the death?"

"Yeah, that's what a krova-yan is." Fyl slams an impatient palm against my door. "Come on. We're going to miss it!"

I follow Fyl down the hall, down the stairs, through the common area. I'm still forcing myself awake, still tingling at the memory of Talyn's hand on my chin, but I know damn well a real Wizard duel is something I can't miss. "Are krova-yans allowed?"

"It's a touchy subject," Fyl replies. "Many of the more progressive Wizards have tried to have them banned, and Aberdeen's done his best. But the Traditionalists like Madison have too much sway. So the compromise is, they're still allowed but discouraged."

They don't feel particularly discouraged to me, given that we're going to one, but I'm not about to bring that up. "Who's fighting?"

"Dean Veyle and Jasper. Have you met Jasper?" Fyl asks, and I nod. The shy boy with the giant glasses, the one who stood up for me last night. "After you left, things got ugly. Dean Veyle was mad and drunk and looking to take it out on someone. He kept picking on Jasper, calling him a little runt, mocking his mother, spilling beer on his head. Jasper snapped and challenged him to a krova-yan." Fyl shakes her head as she pushes open the front door. "Poor kid. I think he's in way over his head."

There's already a large crowd gathered out on the quad, their murmur washing over us like a crashing wave. I'm still barely awake, vaguely aware of how scruffy I look, but Fyl's urgency is contagious. "How often does this happen?" I ask, trying to sound as normal as I can. "On the continent, I mean. We don't duel much in New Kenshire."

Fyl shrugs. "Often enough? I've been to a few. They're never pretty." She elbows her way through the crowd, pushing students aside, and I follow in her wake. "You're not squeamish, are you? Because these can be pretty bad."

I think of the real Alayne's frozen scream, of the blood trickling out of Drell's shattered skull. "I can handle it."

Fyl shoves her way to the front of the crowd, and I join her. We all stop in a line, and I can see the dueling grounds now, a smooth rectangle of freshly cut grass, maybe fifty paces in length and twenty paces in width. The crowd stops neatly on the rectangle's end, all of us pushing and gawking.

It's early autumn, the sky blue, the sun bright above, but the morning air still bites with an unusual chill. The two combatants are on the field, standing on opposite ends. Dean Veyle is on one, cracking his knuckles with a lazy stretch. Jasper paces restlessly on the other. He's pale as fresh-fallen snow, sweat streaking down his brow.

"Duelists!" a phlegmatic voice cries out, and Groundskeeper Tyms steps out onto the field, his bald head glistening in the bright morning light. "You have met here to fight for your honor, to defend your names, to bleed, to die! You have come here before the very Gods to honor the sacred rite of krova-yan!"

I lean over to Fyl and whisper, "The professors are all right with this?"

"It's a sacred duel," she says, and her cocked eyebrow is a clear sign I need to stop asking questions. "They honor the laws, same as anyone."

"Dean Beauregard Veyle! Do you relent, drawing the shame of the Gods unto your line?" Tyms bellows.

"Hell no," Dean replies, and flicks his wrists, drawing his Loci out with an unnecessary flourish. Way too many people cheer.

Tyms turns to the other side of the field. "Jasper Nesbitt Vancross II! Do you relent, drawing the shame of the Gods unto your line?"

"I—I—" Jasper stammers, and it's clear even from here how badly he wants to. He struggles for a moment, breathing hard, and then finally caves in, head falling low. He draws his Loci, plain wooden wands, and holds them at his sides. "I do not, sir."

"Then let the krova-yan commence!" Tyms brings his hands together with a booming clap. "Begin!"

It's over in a heartbeat.

I don't even have time to slip into the Null. Jasper whips his Loci up, trying to carve a basic Shield of Earth, but Dean is so much faster, so much more precise. Before Jasper can even finish, before his shield can even materialize, a perfect orb of flame scorches across the dueling grounds, catching him in his right shoulder and scorching clean through him. Jasper shrieks and falls onto his knees, his shield crumbling uselessly in front of him. The crowd *oohs*, and Dean stands there, a triumphant grin on his face.

"Well," Fyl whispers, and whatever excitement she had has quickly curdled. "At least it was quick."

Jasper gasps, blood trickling out between his lips. The flame hit him hard, nearly taking off his right arm at the shoulder, cauterizing the wound so it dangles weakly by a thread of bone. Jasper reaches for it with his other arm, moaning, and if he had even a shot at fighting back, it's passed.

"Well?" Dean shouts. "Should I finish him?" And he doesn't even wait for a reply before raising his Loci again.

Maybe I want to deny Dean the satisfaction. Maybe I can't stand seeing someone suffer. Or maybe I just want to protect my fellow Nethro, as much as a Wizard can ever be my fellow. But whatever the reason, I step toward the dueling grounds.

Fyl grabs my shoulder hard. "Alayne! Are you crazy?"

"Dean's going to kill him...."

"Yeah," she says, utterly incredulous. "That's what a krova-yan is! Do you not know the rules?" I try to push her off, and she just digs her fingers in harder. "If you cross that line, you enter the duel! Your life becomes forfeit as well!"

"But I—" I say, but it doesn't matter, because it's too late. Dean's Loci cuts through the air with the rush of magic, the scorching of heat, and a second ball of flame shoots across the field. This one strikes Jasper right in the face, boring a sizzling hole clean through his head, and that's it for poor Jasper Vancross.

A deflated murmur runs through the crowd. Dean throws up his hands, preening, and his fellow Vanguards gather around him, clasping his shoulders. No one moves toward Jasper, whose body lies smoldering and still, save Groundskeeper Tyms, who nudges him with a foot. "Pitiful showing," he grumbles under his breath.

"Right," Fyl says next to me, swallowing deeply. "That's that, I guess."

My gaze is fixed on Jasper, on the smoldering crater where his face used to be, at the way his outstretched hand twitches, like it's trying to grasp something that's not there. I feel something prickle within me, something old and angry and loathing. This is what Wizards are. Not the philosophical discussions in classes or the friendly students or the tables piled high with sweets or the taverns with the free ale. This scared, fragile boy, killed for no reason at all, his life snuffed out for sport. This gawking crowd watching him die, already bored and turning away.

Three hundred students arrived on that ferry. Two hundred and ninety nine are left. Jasper is the first of us to die.

He won't be the last.

Chapter 17

Now

Fall is my favorite season, and it sets in gradually on the island. The trees turn a vivid scarlet and gold, shimmering like the sea at sunset, and the air is crisp with the honey-sweet smell of earth and rain. Every morning a soft mist lies over the campus like a veil, and I stroll through it alone, leaves crackling underfoot. There's a peace in that fog, a solitude, and I'm enjoying it the morning that Tish comes wandering up to me with a concerned look on their face. "Professor Calfex wants to see you," they say, "in her office."

I've been at Blackwater for almost two months, and I've managed thus far to avoid being called into Calfex's office. It's not that I don't like her. Of all the professors, she seems the most interesting. But there's something intimidating about her manner, something inscrutable. I can't read her, and that makes me profoundly uneasy.

Calfex's office is a wide room on the third floor of the Order of Nethro, and it's an absolute mess. Books are everywhere, spilling off the shelves lining the room, sitting in stacks on the floor, one heavy leather-bound tome serving as a doorstop. The wide blackwood desk at the back is covered with papers: maps, notes, even what appears to be a detailed drawing of a flayed man. Dark curtains block out most of the tall, angular windows, bathing the room in a wan, eerie light. A dozen teacups rest on surfaces all over the room, their empty porcelain frames stained green and brown. The smell of dust and paper hangs heavy in the air. Something rustles around in the far corner, a mess of orange fur that I'm hoping is a cat.

"Have a seat," Professor Calfex says, from behind her desk. She's wearing a dark suit, long gloves, and a tiny pair of golden glasses on her nose. Her hair is down now, hanging long and curly around her shoulders, its impeccable black speckled with strands of gray. She gestures to a chair opposite her, and I slide in. "Lady Alayne Dewinter. What a pleasure it is to finally talk. If I didn't know better, I'd think you were trying to avoid me."

There's that intimidating air. "Not at all," I say, "I've just been busy."

"That you have." She taps a series of papers laid out before her. Reports from the other professors. Ones with my name on them. "Excellent attendance. Consistent participation. And outside of a rough start in Glyphcraft, solid performance in all your classes. As far as I can tell, you're a perfectly capable student."

"Thank you, Professor." I'm a good student all right, thanks mostly to Marlena. Our private sessions in the practice rooms below the dorm have given me a huge advantage in improving my Glyphs, as has the steady supply of stolen pages from library books she's brought me.

Also, she wrote all my papers for History class.

Calfex stacks the pages in a neat pile and slides them aside. "As we approach the end of fall, the Great Game will begin. The First Challenge is in two weeks. One of my responsibilities as the Order head is to choose which of my students get to be team captains." Her penetrating gaze bores into me. "I'd like to nominate you."

It takes a lot not to leap out of my chair in triumph. "I'm honored!" I beam. My plan is actually coming together. I've been chosen for the game.

"Don't get too excited. The odds aren't exactly in our favor," Calfex says with a weary exhale. "For the First Challenge, our esteemed headmaster has chosen a Balitesta match."

"Balitesta," I repeat. I've heard of it vaguely. The great sport of Wizards, some epic contest of magic and skill. There were giant arenas for it in Hellsum and Laroc, and even some Revenants would chatter about it, gossiping about their favorite teams as they bet on the games.

Calfex picks up on my confusion. "Are you not familiar?"

"It's not common in New Kenshire," I try.

She arches an eyebrow. "Really? I thought your team made it to the Republic semifinals last year."

This is precisely why I've avoided talking to her. "They did," I stammer. "I just meant it's not common in my family. My father thinks it's not a good game for... women?"

That works. Calfex shakes her head in annoyance. "Your father's a fool, but that's to be expected from a general. The game is played in three rounds, each with a different team led by a different captain. I'd like you to be captain in the third round."

I wait for more, and nothing comes. "Is that all you can tell me? About the game or the challenge or any other insights?"

Calfex actually rolls her eyes. "The library has a wealth of books about Balitesta, Lady Dewinter. If you need help, I recommend starting there."

"Right. Of course. The library." I rise from the chair, eager to get out of this room before I slip up worse. "Thank you for nominating me, Professor Calfex. I won't let you down."

"Wait a moment. I'd like to ask you a personal question, if you don't mind." Calfex's voice drops low, and her yellow eyes study me closely. "Do you perchance have any Izachi heritage?"

I freeze. Everything about this question feels like a trap. The truth is yes. My mother was Izachi. The obvious answer, however, is no. The real Alayne Dewinter was pure-blood Marovian, so that's what she would have said. But just the fact that Calfex is asking me this question means she senses something, and lying here might make her dig more. I need to hedge my bets. "Not officially," I reply. "But there have always been rumors about my grandfather."

"I suspected as much." Calfex rises to her feet. "You may not know this, but I'm actually half Izachi myself."

"Really?" I ask, but I can see it. She has the olive skin, the curly black hair, the short stature. If I squint an eye, she looks a bit like my mother.

"Oh, yes." Calfex turns away, staring out the window. "Or did you think that after four decades of teaching here, I'm still an adjunct because I'm not good enough?"

"I—I didn't—"

"Of course you didn't. How could you have?" Her voice is bemused, but there's an undercurrent of acid. "There's no bigotry at Blackwater, after all. All Wizards are equal. And if some never seem to advance, no matter how hard they work, why, there must of course be some perfectly logical explanation."

"Professor…"

"Did you know," she asks, turning back to face me, "that the first Wizards were Izachi? It's true. Long before the First Fathers picked up their Loci, the Izachi Wizards ruled this continent. Our ancestors were the first to get the Godsmark, the first to be chosen by the Gods. Most records of their era are lost, but by all accounts we have, it was a time of peace and prosperity."

"What happened?"

"The Marovians got their own Godsmarks," she says coldly. "But where the Izachi had carved Glyphs of life and growth, the Marovians learned the Glyphs of war and bloodshed. They overthrew our priests. They conquered the continent. And they slaughtered our people without mercy, men, women, and children, with the goal of wiping the Izachi line off the earth."

I'd heard that part before, from my mother, but never in context. "Gods…"

"We survive, though. Just enough of us. Scattered across the continent and beyond in a diaspora. Hiding our heritage, practicing in secret. And despite their best efforts to wipe us out, we persevere, again and again and again." Calfex's voice is low, but it's also tinged with growing pride. "The fact that you and I are standing here, talking? That's a miracle. That's a testament."

"Oh," I say, because what else can I say? "Is that why you chose me?"

"You're not my smartest student, Dewinter. Nor my strongest. And certainly not my most skilled Wizard. But you have something the others don't." She walks out from behind her desk, pacing toward me. "The other Nethros, they've accepted their place in the world. They've internalized that they'll never be at the top. They're fighting for fourth place, maybe third. But you? You've got the fire. I can see it burning in you. You'll settle for nothing but victory. And you'll do whatever it takes to claim it." She leans in close, her voice almost a whisper. "You want an insight? Marius Madison is the top player in the entire Republic Youth Balitesta League. He'll be the best player on the field. Whatever strategy the Order of Vanguard has, they'll be leaning on him. Find his weakness. And exploit it."

Then she pulls back, curt and formal, a professor again. Whatever that was, that quiet little conspiracy, is gone. I take the hint. "I'll do you proud, Professor," I say.

"Good," she replies. "Because I'd hate for you to prove me wrong."

Chapter 18

Now

Until now, I've barely spent any time in the Blackwater Library. Why would I need to, with Marlena helping me out? But I spend the next two weeks there, night after night, hunched by candlelight over books about Balitesta. It's a beautiful building, certainly, maybe the prettiest on campus, with tall marble columns and stained-glass windows and enormous black-iron candelabras swaying overhead. But I have no appreciation for that, because I'm busy tearing my hair out trying to find a strategy for this stupid game.

Balitesta translates in Old Marovian to the Game of Gods. It's the oldest sport in Marovia, as old as the Republic itself, played by the First Fathers after their conquest. It is at once incredibly simple and staggeringly complex. The game is played in a circular arena six hundred feet in diameter, on a field of freshly cut grass. Five teams compete at once, made up of five members each. Each team has a fort positioned on the outside diameter of the circle, where it can retreat and strategize. At the center of the circle, behind an array of barriers and obstacles, sit ten daises, each with a gemstone. At the blow of a horn, a round begins, lasting ten minutes. The aim of the round is to collect as many of the gems as you can and bring them back to your fort where you can store them in a chest. A game takes three rounds, and in each round a new group of five players takes over on each team. At the end of the third round, each team's chest is opened and the gems inside are counted. Whoever has the most gems wins.

The actual game plays out entirely on the field, in the scramble to get the gems and bring them back to the fort. To do that, players can use magic from an approved list of fifty Glyphs. Some are obvious, like Blasts of Wind or Shields of Ice. Others feel more obscure, like Orbs of Shadow and something called Shawl of Radiance. The list is meant to exclude the more explicitly violent Glyphs, but there's only so much they can do. The books are heavy with stories of players getting injured, maimed, even killed.

Remarkably, that's pretty much it. Sure, there are a few small details here and there, like "No leaving the field of play" and "Magic cannot be used on the referees." But that's basically the whole game. Anything not explicitly forbidden is permitted. You start in your fort and you fight to get the gems and then you fight to get them back, and you can use any strategy you want to win.

That open-endedness means the game has infinite permutations. Many matches play out like mock battles, with players scurrying from barrier to barrier as they fight to the center. Some teams have won through brute force, battering their way to victory with volumes of powerful, well-cast Glyphs. Others have won through speed and trickery, by creating magical barriers of their own that block the other teams or by hurling the gems along on gusts of wind or torrents of water. Some teams fight as one, combining their magic into unstoppable salvos, while others divide, attacking all over to create chaos. The battle doesn't even have to stay in the center of the arena! Players ambush one another on the routes back to their forts, and a few games have even been fought within their walls, victory wrenched away at the last second as the players are unable to deposit the gems into their chest. The possibilities are endless, a never-ending series of strategies and counterstrategies and countercounterstrategies, built up over centuries.

I can see why Wizards like it. Hell, reading through the books, I find myself starting to enjoy it, especially some of the more cunning plays. But after two weeks of study, all I've got is a list of things I can't do. "There's a million strategies, and we won't be able to pull any of them off," I tell Marlena late one night, as we sit huddled together over a table in the library. "We're not going to be able to overpower the other teams, that's for sure. But we're not going to beat them on Glyphcrafting, either. And I don't think we have the speed or coordination to pull off some of these elaborate gambits."

Marlena sighs. For every hour I've spent reading the books, she's spent three, and heavy bags hang under her eyes. I've begged her to take a break and let me handle it, but she's insisted that she's better at research (factually true). This matters to her, matters enough that she's willing to push herself to her limits, to dedicate every free hour she has. Is this all still about getting off this island? Or does she genuinely care about me winning? Does she genuinely care *about me*?

Now isn't the time for those questions. "So what other options do you have?" Marlena asks.

"Only one I can think of," I say. "One path to victory." And then I smile. "Luckily, it's what I do best."

Chapter 19

Then

I am nine when I learn, really learn, what magic is.

We're back in Laroc, in that ramshackle city by the sea, in a cluster of warehouses not so different from the ones where I first met the Revenants. It's midday when Whispers comes to get me, leading me by the hand to a room at the back, while Sera trails curiously after us. I don't know what's going on, just that it's important. A group of Revenants came back from a big mission the other day, and since then everyone's been whispering and looking at me.

The room is sparse, just a dusty floor and a few rotting pillars. There's a table at the back and a man sitting at it. He's a Marovian, a burly man with a round face and a big belly. His long brown hair hangs in greasy strands around his face, and patches of uneven beard dot his chin. His breath comes in heavy wheezes. When he looks up at me, his eyes are bloodshot, framed by deep-purple bruises. "This is her?" he grumbles.

"It is," Whispers says, then turns to me. "Alka, meet your new teacher, Pavel."

In the years to come, I'll learn Pavel's whole story. I'll learn that he's an apostate, a Wizard stripped of all rank and title, disowned by his family. I'll learn that he was a year into his magical schooling when he killed a boy in a fight, a boy related to a powerful senator. I'll learn that he spent the next fifteen years in a brutal prison labor camp, his magic used at sword point deep in the Galfori Mines. I'll learn of the tortures he suffered, the cruelties. I'll come to look at him with, if not kindness, then at least sympathy.

But that's all later. Right now, all I see is a slumped, surly man gazing at me with a scowl. "This is the girl? Gods, she's young." Pavel sits back up in his seat, brushing some hair out of his eyes. "Going to be hard to teach her without a Loci."

"You'll manage," Whispers replies.

Pavel sighs deeply. "All right, girl. These people say you're a Wizard?" I hold up my wrist, showing him my Godsmark, and he lets out a low, wheezing laugh. "Well, I'll be damned. A Wizard brought up by the Revenants. Those bastards in the Senate would shit themselves if they knew." Whispers clears her throat, and he gets back on task. "So you've got the Mark. That's a start. Can you carve any Glyphs?"

I shake my head. Ever since the incident in the forest six months ago, when I'd nearly killed myself by accident, Whispers has forbidden me to even think about magic. Just to be safe, she's had someone watch me day and night.

Pavel isn't pleased. "Nothing? Not a one? I'm supposed to teach you from scratch? I think I was better off in the mines."

Whispers shoots him a withering glare. "We'd be happy to return you."

Pavel throws up his big dirty hands in defeat. "All right, all right. We'll start from the beginning. What *is* magic?"

I look back to Whispers for guidance (she's a stone slate), then to Sera (she shrugs). "Magic is power," I try. "The power to do whatever you want. The power to kill whoever you want. The power to be strong."

Pavel cracks a smile, the corner of his mouth bloody. "Good guess. Wrong, but good. I'll show you the truth. Can I get three cups?" He looks to Whispers, who narrows her eyes. "Come on, lady, I've got my arms bound, no Loci, and there are dozens of your goons. I'm just trying to demonstrate to the kid."

"Fine." Whispers jerks her head at Sera. "Bring the man three cups."

Sera leaves and returns with three tall tin cups, which she lays out before him. "Perfect," Pavel says, and reaches into a little pocket on his vest to take out a round bronze coin. "We're going to play a game, girl. You like games?" I nod. "This one's called Find the Coin." He places the coin flat on the table, under the middle cup. "Watch it go." Then he moves the cups, sliding them around in lazy circles. I've seen street hustlers play this game, but Pavel isn't anywhere near as good as they are. He moves the cups slowly, clumsily, his shaking hands threatening to knock them over. I have no trouble following the coin, and when he's done, I point at it with a grin. "That one!"

Pavel flips the cup, and it's empty. I blink in surprise, and Sera lets out a snort of laughter. "Again," I demand.

We go again. And again. And again. Every time, I follow it perfectly, and every time, the cup is empty. After a half dozen tries, he offers to make it simpler for me by going down to just two cups, so we do that and I still get it wrong. I'm getting angrier and angrier, and Sera just finds this to be so funny, which isn't helping. Finally, with a reluctant sigh, he goes down to just *one* cup, which has to be mocking me, but when I tap on it and he flips it, there's no coin.

"This game is stupid!" I shout.

"Now you're getting it," Pavel says. "You want to see how it's done? Join me in the Null. You *can* go into the Null, right?"

I can, but I'm strictly forbidden to. I look back to Whispers for approval, and she nods. So I turn back to Pavel, and even though I'm still a little afraid, I take a deep breath and slip in.

The world recedes into that ashy fog, so thick around us that the room is gone, Whispers is gone, Sera is gone. But Pavel is there, sitting across from me, as vivid and colorful as if we were in the real world. It's comforting to have someone else in the Null with me, even if it's this strange, surly man. He smiles at me, across the gray, and then he raises the coin up high. In the Real, it was a dull, faded bronze, but here it shines impossibly bright, glistening like a jewel. He turns it around, and I can see the Glyphs carved into it, bright and dazzling, a grid of cross-hatched arcana. He spins the coin across his fingers, and as he does, it vanishes, then reappears, then vanishes again.

I jerk back into the Real with a gasp, the color flooding in quickly, and Pavel is back, too, sitting across from me with a satisfied look. "The coin is magic!" I shout. "You were cheating the whole time!"

"Now you've got it," Pavel says. Whispers crosses over, plucking the coin from his hands, and he barely even notices. "That's what magic is, girl. It's *cheating.* All those poor Humble bastards out there, all the people in this room, all of them have to go through life playing by the rules. The rules of the world. But people like you and me? We're different. We're special. We can break all those rules. We can make up down and black white. We can rig any game and get any outcome. Because that's what we are. That's what *Wizards* are."

Whispers has an uneasy look on her face, and Sera looks upset, but I'm on board. "Is that what you're going to teach me?" I ask.

"Damn right. And you've already had your first lesson. When a game's rigged, there's only one way to win," Pavel says, lacing his fingers together to crack his knuckles. "Break the game."

Chapter 20

Now

The First Challenge of the Great Game plays out in the crisp fall air on a weekend afternoon, the sun bright even through a thin canopy of clouds. There's a full-blown arena on the island's western coast, a tall open-air colosseum built around a grassy Balitesta playing field. Everyone's there, all the students, the professors, even the Humbles, piled up on rows of tiered benches to watch the big game. I spot Marlena, bustling about with a tray of drinks, and we share a conspiratorial glance. She knows what's coming next, even if no one else does.

We sit grouped by Orders, with the students below and the professors at the top. My team isn't up until the third round, which means we're spectators just like anyone else for the first two. The others around me are nervous, Desmond's face slick with sweat and Fyl's knee bouncing wildly. But I feel oddly calm, the calm I always get before a dangerous mission, the calm that feels like I'm not even really in my body anymore. My life's not on the line, but in a way, I suppose it is. One way or another, today determines my course, and so much of it is out of my control. So for now, all I can do is sit back and watch.

Groundskeeper Tyms descends to the center of the field to kick off the game. Everyone cheers for him, which is baffling because he's awful, and he casts a Glyph up into the air, a dazzling firework that bursts into a multicolored bird. The players for the first round rise from their seats and descend into the arena, vanishing into their Orders' respective forts.

A massive horn blasts, a low warble like a whale's cry, and the game is off. It's absolute chaos to watch, twenty-five players coming from all sides to clash in a dazzling, deafening explosion of magic. Tornadoes howl across the field, lances of light streak and shatter, clouds of dirt billow with thunderous blasts. Players run and duck, slide and scream, cowering behind barriers and battling to the center. Referees rush about the outskirts in full-body plate armor, their faces hidden behind shining helms as they check on the fallen and monitor for forbidden Glyphs. The crowd whoops and hollers, leaping to their feet with wild excitement.

The first round plays out brutally. The Vanguard players dominate, smashing to the center with wave after wave of offensive magic. The Zartans try to rush in and get bowled clean over, while the Javelloses settle for sneaking a single gem back. Only the Selura team, captained by Vyctoria herself, puts up a decent showing, shielding itself in perfectly carved ice and withstanding long enough to grab three gems. The less said of the Nethro team, the better. Captained by a pompous Kindrali I've never liked, they rush into the fray and are tossed aside by the Vanguard like rag dolls, with two of the students carried away on stretchers.

After a lengthy intermission, the second round kicks off, and it goes better, but barely. Talyn captains the Javellos players and they rush onto the field with a clever play, combining their magic to disrupt the terrain with barriers of dirt that funnel the Selura and the Vanguard into one another and leave the center open for the others. It works briefly, long enough to stall the Vanguard from their usual rush, and Talyn makes it back to his fort with three gems before the barriers fall. A single Nethro player manages to get his hand on a gem and get it back to our fort, while the other players are all swallowed by the chaos of the center. In the end, the Seluras walk away with nothing, the Zartans claim two, and Vanguard still manages to take the rest.

The second intermission commences, which means it's time for my team to take the field. I stand up, crack my knuckles, stretch my neck. A banner hangs from the professor's platform, with the current standing clear:

Vanguard—10

Javellos—4

Selura—3

Zartan—2

Nethro—1

Just what I need.

My teammates get up around me, and we begin the long march down to our fort. I chose for loyalty, not skill, so I've got a ragged crew behind me: Fyl, Desmond, and Tish, my closest friends and the only Nethros I halfway trust. Rounding out the group as a fifth is Zigmund, the hulking blue-eyed Velkschen with biceps the size of my head. I don't know him well, which is a problem, but I like him. When I asked them all to join the team, he got so excited he slammed his fist through a table. That's the kind of spirit I need.

We don't talk as we pace down the stairs and onto the field, but I can tell everyone's nerves are running high. A referee, his plate armor clanking, straps us into heavy padded chest plates and thick leather helmets, painted black for the Order of Nethro. Our Loci rest in hip sheaths, and we've also each got a small leather bag hanging off our belts, for storing gems should we get them. I can feel the eyes of the crowd on me, all watching, and a few even boo us, chanting "Just one point!" Fyl's expression sours, but I don't mind. Let them underestimate us.

Our fort awaits us at the edge of the arena. It's a one-room structure made of stone brick, like a miniature castle from a picture book, down to the toothy parapets on the roof. It's almost comically old-fashioned, but when it comes to Balitesta, tradition beats all. The inside is sparse, save a ladder up to the roof and the single most impressive chest I've ever seen. It's made of cold, hard steel, with enormous bolts holding it shut and a wide, flat plate, like the kind I carved on in the practice room, at the top. Desmond wanders over and presses his hand to the plate. There's the soft pulse of magic, and it slides open with a *whoosh*. I read all about these chests in my research, how they use a dozen intricate, interwoven Glyphs to ensure that only members of the team can open them.

Desmond reaches into the chest and plucks out the one gem inside. It's beautiful, a teardrop of vivid blue, smooth as glass. He turns it over in his hand, letting out a low whistle. "One point. Not bad. If we do this right, we might actually manage to take fourth place."

"I don't even care," Fyl says. We all look ridiculous in our gear, but she looks *especially* ridiculous, her helmet twice as big as her head. "My parents are going to be proud I just played in the game at all."

"We're not going for fourth," I say, and they all turn to me. A horn outside blasts. Ten minutes until the match begins. I'll have to talk fast. "We're playing to win."

"I don't think that's mathematically possible," Fyl responds.

"I mean, it's not *mathematically* impossible, just practically," Desmond unhelpfully clarifies.

"What are you talking about, Alayne?" Tish asks.

I fold my arms across my chest and try to put on my most confident smile. "I'm the team captain, aren't I? Well, I have a plan."

I tell them my plan, and I watch the looks of shock and disbelief pass across their faces. I'd debated telling them earlier but decided against it. Part of that was to remove any risk of it leaking to the other teams. But more important, I need to put them on the spot, to let the pressure of the ticking clock push them to doing something rash. If I give them any time to think this through, at least one of them will back out. And I need them all in.

When I'm done talking, Desmond is staring at me, mouth agape in horror. "No. Absolutely not. That *has* to be against the rules."

"It's not. I made sure of it. There's nothing about this. And you know the main principle of Balitesta. Everything's that's not forbidden is permitted."

"But what if you're wrong?" Fyl asks. "We could get in huge trouble."

"If I'm wrong, I'll take all the blame. You can say I forced you to do it." She's not buying it, and neither is Desmond. "Come on, Fyl. If I'm right, we can actually win this. We can prove everyone wrong. We can show them how great we are." The horn outside blows, three minutes until the start. "Think of how proud your parents will be."

"That's a low blow, Alayne," Fyl says, but I can see it wearing her down. She bites her lip so hard I think she's going to hurt herself, and then finally shakes her head in resignation. "Okay. Fine. Let's do this."

"Hells yeah!" Zigmund shouts, though his accent make it *Hulls ja*. "This is how I like to play!"

"I'm in, too," Tish says. "It's a good plan. We should see it through."

We all turn to look at Desmond, who's the palest I've ever seen anyone. "What you're talking about... if we pull it off... we'd be making enemies of the Order of Vanguard. Of Marius Madison. You see why that's a problem for me, right? Or have you forgotten that my father is a senator in Grandmaster Madison's party? Your parents might be proud...but mine will be livid."

I'd worried Desmond would be the hardest to win over, so I play the last card in my hand. "Do you remember what you told me when we talked, Desmond? About how your father didn't agree with Madison, but he was too timid to stand up for himself?" I see the words hit him like a slap, see his jaw work as he takes it in. "Do you want to be your father's son? Or do you want to be the man Brenna raised?"

Desmond gazes down, and when he looks back up, his eyes are narrowed with determination. "Fine. All right. But when we're all expelled, I'm blaming you."

"That's my boy," I say, grinning, and just in time as the last horn blows. "All right. In positions."

There's a cheer from outside as the game kicks off. The other teams must have started rushing the center, because I can hear thunderous bursts and crackling ice, can feel the ground shake underfoot. But our first step involves hunkering down. I nod to Tish, our best Wizard, to kick off the plan, and they take a deep breath before turning to the doors and raising their Loci. "Cover your eyes," I tell the others.

I stay in the Real, so I don't actually see them carve the Glyph. I just see them raise their hands one second, and the next there's a deafening blast of hot white light that shudders the fort and blows the door clean off its hinges. My ears are ringing hard, but I can still hear the crowd laugh, because what's funnier than the Nethros blowing themselves up before they even leave the fort? Behind me, the others scramble to get alongside the walls, Desmond clutching the side of his head in pain. I pat Tish's shoulder, and they give me a little shrug. "Sorry if that was too much."

"It was perfect," I say. Outside, a horn blows, signifying we're one minute into the match. And not a moment too soon, because I can hear footsteps thundering toward us from outside, the heavy clank of plate armor. The referee. This is it. The point of no going back. I look at the others, one at a time, and they all nod, even Desmond. We're in.

The referee lumbers into the room, a bulky woman, her face hidden under the polished helm. "What happened in here?" she bellows. "Is everyone all right?" She stops in the center of the room, looking at all of us standing, unhurt. "What is this?"

I kick her as hard as I can in the back of the legs. With a startled yelp she drops to her knees, and then Zigmund slides in, wrapping a thick bicep around her neck, just under her helmet, and choking, hard. She lets out a muted gurgle, flailing, her feet kicking and thrashing. Fyl and Tish stare in horror, and Desmond can't even watch, his hands over his eyes. She swings up, batting a gauntlet at Zigmund's head, and I have to jerk her arm down to keep her from hitting him. "Just go to sleep," I hiss at her. "Knock out. Make this easy."

"Oh, Gods, we're so dead," Fyl says, as the referee gives one last judder and slips into unconsciousness, her head limp on her shoulder. Zigmund lowers her, panting, and I rush forward. The horn outside blows. Seven minutes left.

The rules on this are very clear. No magic of any kind can be cast at a referee. But they don't say anything about a good old-fashioned choke hold.

I slide forward, pulling off the referee's helm. It's heavier than I'd thought, bulky and cold. Tish and Fyl get to work pulling off her chest-plate, but the damn thing's complicated, a mess of latches and buckles that takes forever to undo. By the time they've gotten it off her and onto me, we're down to five minutes, and I'd counted on at least six. We don't have time for the boots or the leg plate, so I'm just going to have to hope no one looks closely in the chaos.

"All right," I tell the others. "Time to get out there. Remember, go as flashy as possible. Make a lot of noise, cause a lot of confusion, draw all the attention your way." They look absolutely terrified, except for Zigmund, who looks thrilled. "Time to prove everyone wrong."

With that we rush out, through the doorway, onto the field. The others bolt a hard left for the center of the arena, but I break off them, sprinting along the diameter. My heart starts to thunder, my palms clammy, my eyes blinking away the sweat streaking down my forehead in this tight, stupid helmet. It's loud out here, a cacophony of shrieking crowd and explosive combat. Out of the corner of my eye, I see the center of the arena, where crags of earth shoot up like giant nails, lattices of light race like whips; a student flies fifteen feet into the air and comes crashing down. I hope my Nethros are okay, but right now, I can't think about them. My concern is up ahead.

It's a fort, the same build as ours, but with the flag of the Order of Vanguard flying overhead, a rippling gold banner with a white stag. There's a husky figure standing by the door, one of the teammates left behind to guard the place. It's a common tactic for teams in the lead, to prevent others from ambushing them on their return from the center. I'd counted on it.

The figure looks my way as I approach, and I wince as I see the face under the leather helmet, recognize that mossy beard and those reddish sunken eyes. Dean Veyle. Of course. My face is fully covered, but just to be sure, I put on the deepest, gruffest voice I can. "Out of the way. We need to inspect your fort!"

Dean gawks at me, genuinely startled, but there's no flicker of recognition. His face is flushed, sweat-streaked. I'm counting on him being too flustered to question it, and it looks like I'm right. "Uh, sure, all right." He steps aside. "Go ahead."

I shove past him, and I'm in, actually *in* the Vanguard fort. I stomp forward, right up to their chest, and this right here is the most dangerous part of all, the moment in which the plan either works or blows up in my face. I turn back to Dean and growl, "I'm going to need you to open this."

"What? Why?"

"Some of the Nethros reported that your team is cheating. That you've smuggled in contraband items and are storing them in your chest to avoid detection. I need to make sure."

"Those little shits said *what*?" Dean yells. "This is ridiculous! This is an outrage!"

It absolutely is, but I need to keep stringing him along, so I lay on the pressure. "Do I need to report you for denying a referee's order? Just open the damn chest so we can get this over with!"

"Gods, what a mess. This school has completely gone to shit," Dean grumbles, but I can see the panic dancing in his eyes, the urgency with which he wants to get back to the game. "Fine. Here. Let's get this over with."

He presses a hand on the plate at the chest's lid. It crackles, pulses, and then with a *whoosh* of air, springs open. There they are inside, bright and beautiful, a rainbow of perfect tears. Ten godsdamned gems. "Satisfied?" he says.

"I'll need to check the chest out, look for anything hidden," I reply. "You can get back to the game."

"Fine, whatever," he grumbles, and turns to go back to the door. His back is turned to me, and I grab the gems, as many as I can, and shove them into the bag at my hip. Dean takes one step, two steps, three steps, four, and he's almost at the door when he freezes mid-stride, and I can see the second when he realizes he's being played.

We both draw our Loci, but I'm fumbling with the bag so he's faster. By the time I hit the Null, he's already started carving his Glyph, forcing me onto the defensive. The gray howls around us, louder and wilder than usual, turbulent from the chaos of the battle outside. Across the fort, Dean glares at me with a vicious scowl, his curved steel blade stabbing hard into the skin of the world. He's carved a backward *L*, which means he's going to be making a square. Earth Base. And since he's not making a shield or building a wall, the only option left is an orb. A hard ball of packed dirt, formed out of nothing, hurtling my way.

If I had more time to think, I'd come up with a clever counter-Glyph. But he's already almost done with his base before I even raise my first knife so I just need to go with my gut and do something fast and simple. I slash four notches for a Wind Base and by the time I'm done, Dean is already onto his second form, a hard clod of earth the size of my head twisting into existence in front of him. I can't block it with wind, but maybe I can push it out of the way, so I slash a circle for push around my Glyph and not a moment too soon because Dean has finished and his earth ball is on the move, hurtling my way like a cannonball.

I jerk back into the Real to see my gust of wind rush out. I'd hoped to knock the ball back at him, but I carved sloppy and slow, so instead it hits the sphere from below, a jet of air rushing up from the floor like a geyser. The earthen ball hurtles upward and shatters explosively against the ceiling, showering a rain of clods onto us. Dean throws up a hand, blocking himself. I turn around and sprint, grabbing the ladder to the roof and leaping up it in three bounds. Behind me, Dean howls in impotent fury but it doesn't matter because I'm already out of his range. Dean's a better Wizard than I am, but I'm a whole lot faster.

I leap onto the roof of the Vanguard fort, back outside in the hot sun. A horn blows loudly. Two minutes left. As Dean scrambles below me, I sprint forward, bounding across the roof's hexagonal stone tiles to the parapet at the edge. I can see my fort from here, just a sprint away, and I know what I have to do. The fort's only a story tall. I can leap down, take the fall, and make it to our chest before the round ends. It's tight but doable. Tight but d—

I hear the crackle of magic from below me and then something wraps around my ankle, something sharp and tight. A vine, covered in thorns, growing up from the roof like a grasping hand. I lurch forward and slam face-first onto the hard stone. My chin splits, my vision flashes red, and my Loci spin out of my hands, skittering out of reach.

"You little bitch," Dean growls, hoisting himself up through the opening in the roof, Loci in hand. I jerk forward, trying to scramble up, but the vine is holding me in place, a thick green rope bursting out of the hard stone, tethering me like an anchor. That's an advanced Glyph, and he cast it up through the floor; if it weren't for the situation, I'd actually be impressed. Dean stands up tall, pacing toward me, a shadow blocking out the sun. "You really thought you could pull a fast one on me? You thought you could make a fool out of me?"

"I already have," I spit back, jerking as hard as I can with my leg. The vine strains, just a little, its roots in the tile starting to tear. "Everyone's going to know how you let me pluck the gems right out of your chest."

"Like hell!" he screams, spraying spittle, his cheeks burning. His eyes are wide and crazed, and then they flash a hard black, dotted with a starscape of light. I slip into the Null instinctively with him, even though I can't cast without my Loci. As the world howls gray around us, he flashes me a sadistic grin and raises his Loci to carve. A long slash at forty-five degrees, bisected in the middle, glowing a hot raging orange.

My heart leaps into my throat. Fire Base. It's forbidden in the rules of the game, but Dean's clearly decided he doesn't care.

He's not trying to win.

He's trying to *kill me.*

Then, as he starts to carve the second form, a lance or an orb or a cutting whip, he steps forward. His foot presses down on the wide round tile at the roof's center, and as he does, something happens. It starts to vibrate, to pulse, to glow a gentle white. It starts to rise.

Third-Degree Delayed Elemental Infusion.

Now it's my turn to grin.

Chapter 21

Then

I am seventeen when I rig the First Challenge.

Finding the arena is easy enough. There's a massive map of the island in the library, and it's clearly labeled. So two weeks before the challenge is played, I sneak down there in the middle of the night, when everyone on the campus is asleep, creeping through the island's underbrush. There's a tall wooden fence blocking it, nothing I can't scale, and no one, *no one* guarding it. It's like it didn't even occur to them that someone would try this, which makes me either a lunatic or a visionary.

Being on the field makes it easy to test my plan. I sprint back and forth between the forts, timing myself, verifying that it's doable. I practice scrambling up the ladders, leaping off the roof to hit the ground with a roll. I run through every scenario I can think of, modeling them out, rushing around and practicing my dashes and jumps and recoveries. I come here every night for two weeks, training until I know the route by heart.

And then, just to be safe, the night before the challenge I hunker down on the roof of the Vanguard fort and carve that Elemental Infusion Glyph into a few of the round tiles. It won't do much, just make the tile rise a little, but it might throw off anyone pursuing me long enough for me to escape. I carve so shallowly that the magic should last, at most, twelve hours, before fading away.

It's cheating, of course. Actively against the rules. But like Pavel always said... that's what magic is.

Chapter 22

Now

The tile under Dean's foot buckles, jerking back hard. In the foggy slow motion of the Null, I see him stumble, see his mouth open in surprise, see him fall back. That's all I'd wanted, all I'd hoped for. But Dean is in the middle of carving a Fire Glyph, and as he falls back his Loci jerks down, cleaving the Glyph clean in half. It pulses and throbs, flames licking out, the world around it quivering and writhing. The Null roars with the churn of gathering thunder.

A miscast. A *fire* miscast.

Oh, shit.

I snap back into the Real and throw my hands up over my face. I don't see the explosion, but I hear it, a scorching blast that makes the fort shake, that sets both my ears ringing, that washes over me in a wave of singeing heat. When I open my eyes, the spot where Dean was standing is a sunken crater, the stone scorched black. Dozens of little fires burn on the edges of the parapets. As for Dean, he's gone, hurled over the roof. He lies on the grass below, his body a bubbling, burned ruin, twitching and rasping, flesh charred black.

This is going to have consequences.

The one-minute horn blows, and I snap out of my trance as the rest of the world comes back in a rush. The crowd is shrieking. Referees are scrambling. People are shouting from the center of the arena, probably the other Vanguard as they realize what's going on. I don't have time to think about Dean. I have to move.

I rip as hard as I can on the vine, tearing it off, and scramble to my feet. The bag with the gems is still at my hip, full and jangling. In one fluid motion I scoop up my Loci and hurl myself over the parapet. My roll isn't as good as I practiced, but it's not bad, and soon I'm up on my feet, streaking back to our fort. The howls of the other Vanguard grow louder and louder, the crowd utterly thunderous. The ground vanishes beneath my feet. My thoughts melt away. The world is a blur. In this moment, I'm barely a person. I'm a creature of pure adrenaline, a thundering heart, a will to win made flesh. All I know is the bag of gems at my hips and the Nethro fort, standing tall and proud, drawing ever closer.

A lance of wind streaks past me, slamming into the arena's barrier with a resounding boom. A pillar of earth erupts right behind me, hurling fragments of dirt like shrapnel. Footsteps pound after me, loud and furious and gaining. I'm not thinking about them, though. I'm thinking about that horn that's going to sound any second now, the horn that ends the match. If I don't make it back in time, then all of this was for nothing. I can't lose. Not when I'm so close.

The door to our fort flies open, and there's Fyl, her face smudged with dirt and maybe blood, her black hair frizzled and wild. "Alayne!" she screams, and I grab the bag of gems off my belt and throw it and it hurtles through the air and she leans out far and just barely catches it and she's running into the fort to get it into the chest and this is all just in time because someone grabs me from behind, a pair of muscular arms wrapping around my waist, and tackles me hard onto the grass.

My vision flares red and I taste blood and I realize in one rush just how much pain I'm in. Every muscle in my body aches. My face feels singed from the blast. The back of my head throbs from the impact against the parapet, and there's the matter, of course, of the guy on top of me, the student who slammed me into the ground so hard I'm afraid I broke a rib. Gasping for air, I roll around and see him. Marius Madison.

"What the *hell* do you think you're doing, Dewinter?" he growls.

I shoot him a bloody-toothed grin, my eyes wild with triumph. "Winning."

The final horn blows. The match is done.

Referees descend on us, hurling Marius off me, jerking me up to my feet and dragging me away. Everyone is screaming, everywhere, in the stands, on the field around us. The professors are trying to maintain order, shouting something about "this all being sorted out," but they're drowned out by the din. Marius glares at me with eyes full of utter hate. Behind him, just past the Vanguard fort, I can see a pair of referees loading Dean onto a stretcher. His hand hangs limply at his side, the skin charred like a roasted hen. I'm no doctor, but I don't think he looks good.

Groundskeeper Tyms grabs me by the shoulders and ushers me back into the Nethro fort. The referee I stripped is gone; maybe she woke up, or maybe she was carried away. The other Nethros are all in there, looking like survivors of a great battle. A long, bloody slash runs along Tish's cheek, Desmond is caked in dirt, and Zigmund cradles his left arm, which is obviously broken. At the sight of me, he breaks out into booming laughter, and Tish shoots me a small grin. "We did it," Fyl says, slumped over by the chest. "We got the gems in. Your plan worked. We actually *won*."

"You didn't win a thing," Tyms growls. "Not until the judges decide your play was valid. And good luck with that." I'd argue he's being a bit biased, but on the other hand, I guess I did choke out one of his referees. So I say nothing as he slams the door shut, sealing us in.

"What happened out there? At the Vanguard fort?" Tish asks. "I saw an explosion."

I slump down against a wall, wincing as my whole body aches and throbs. "That was Dean Veyle. What's left of him."

Desmond practically faints.

It takes more than an hour for the judges to come to a decision, an hour of us cooped up in that fort, an hour that feels like a week and a half. A nurse comes by to put Zigmund's arm in a sling. Tish passes out from exhaustion. Desmond paces so much he practically wears a hole into the floor until Fyl comforts him with an arm around his shoulders. I mostly just slump on the ground. I'm at that point beyond anxiousness, when you just close your eyes and wait for the inevitable. One way or another, it's all out of my hands.

The door flies open, and Tyms leans back in. "Come on," he barks. "Follow me." We stagger out after him into the light, and the first thing I notice is how quiet it is. The stands are still packed, but everyone is dead silent, the tension so thick it's suffocating. All of the other contestants in the game are already out on the field, all the ones who can still stand, anyway, gathered around their respective forts. Tyms rushes us out to join the other ten Nethros, the ones who played the previous two rounds, in a neat line. Professor Calfex stands at the front of our group, and when our eyes meet, I can't read her expression. Admiration? Concern? Distrust?

Then all eyes turn to the front as Headmaster Aberdeen emerges, pacing down to a platform at the edge of the field. His expression isn't hard to read. He looks absolutely livid. A tight knot clenches in my stomach. I hadn't realized Aberdeen would be involved in the ruling. Anxieties race through my mind like invasive species. What if I got something in the rules wrong? What if the judges are biased and don't care? What if they noticed the tile moving and link it to me? If the judges rule against us, I'm not just going to lose the game. I'm going to be expelled.

Headmaster Aberdeen clears his throat. When he speaks, his voice projects out of every horn in the arena. "After great consideration and exhaustive review, the judges have reached their verdict," he says. "The play was valid. With eleven points total, the Order of Nethro is the winner of this challenge."

The roar of the crowd is the loudest thing I've ever heard.

CHAPTER 23

Now

The next few hours are a haze.

I remember a few scattered images: the Nethros lifting me up on their shoulders, the crowd swarming the arena, the professors shouting and arguing, the heat, the din, the light. I remember my heart thundering against my ribs, the world throbbing red and black, the pain and exhaustion and exultation and relief. I remember the world growing dark before collapsing hard onto the grass.

I awake in the infirmary, a long stark-white building at the far end of campus, in a firm bed hidden behind a billowing white canopy. I can't see the other students there, but I can hear them, other victims of the Balitesta game. The room hums with moans and groans, a few scattered sobs and other more awful sounds, hacking gasps and crunching bone. There's a bandage wrapped around my head, holding a gauze to the cut in the back, and my skin is glowing a soft, sparkling green. Healing Glyphs. Good ones too, because all those aches and pains are gone, replaced by a floaty numbness.

"Welcome back," a voice says.

I roll over. It's Talyn, sitting in a chair by my bedside. He's still wearing his gear from the Balitesta game, dirt-stained leather, and he looks rougher than I've ever seen him, with messy hair and a long gash running along his forehead. "What are you doing here?" I ask.

"I wanted to make sure you were all right. You fell pretty hard back there." His lips twist into a playful smirk. "If you died, I wanted to make sure I was here to hold your hand and hear your dramatic last words."

"You're out of luck then, because I'm definitely not dying." I sit up. A dull pain flares in the side of my temples, but otherwise, I feel fine. "Are you even supposed to be in here?"

"No." He shrugs. "That's what windows are for."

I have to fight back my smile. "You didn't have to come here."

"I know. But I wanted to." He slides forward, extending me his hand. "Now, are you going to lie there for another hour until a nurse comes to check on you, or do you want me to show you just how I did it?"

Now the grin's too strong to fight. I take his hand, savoring its warmth, and I let him help me up out of the bed. My body aches but I can still move well enough, and we sneak out of my canopy, ducking behind a pillar and then sliding out through an open window. We're on the first floor, but the window is still up pretty high, so Talyn goes first and then helps me out, one hand firm on my hip and the other holding mine. He's strong, deceptively strong for that lean frame.

Once we're both on the ground, he steps back and offers me his arm. "Now then. May I have the honor of escorting the glorious victor back to her dorm?"

"Only if you promise never to call me that again," I say, and slide my arm through his, and, Gods help me, I love how he feels. We stroll side by side over the cobblestone paths of the quad, passing between the other Orders. It's a bright night, the moon a wide, round disk overhead, but most of the other students are indoors, recovering from the day's events. The few who are out stare at us, pointing and whispering. I try not to make eye contact, try to just keep going, but it doesn't matter. The days of lying low are done. This is my path, whether I want it or not.

Two students walk past us, wearing cloaks in Vanguard gold, and they glower at me with so much hate I almost expect a fight to break out. "I take it the Order of Vanguard is not pleased," I say when they're out of earshot.

Talyn lets out a low chuckle. "Oh, they are very much not. Marius is absolutely livid. After you fainted, he stormed off the field, red-faced, shaking. It was glorious." Talyn's blinding white smile shines through the dark. "I'd recommend watching your back, though. They're not going to let this go."

"That's the price of winning."

"You didn't just win. You served them the humiliation of the century. You made history." It sounds like he's making a joke, but when I look at him, he's absolutely sincere.

"Please. It was nothing." I'm actually embarrassed. Why am I embarrassed? "I found a loophole in the rules and I took advantage of it, that's all."

"You found a loophole in a seven-hundred-year-old game. That is very much something." He stops, turning to me with his head thoughtfully cocked to the side. "Look. I'm no model of modesty. I'd like to say I hold my own cleverness in pretty high esteem. But I spent a month poring over Balitesta strategy and didn't come up with anything half as clever as you. The boldness of your vision, the confidence, the way you moved out there..." He shakes his head, and there's something in the way he's looking at me, in the admiration, in the respect, that makes my breath stop in my throat. No one's *ever* looked at me like that. "You were like a Goddess."

I turn away, because I have to. "You're flattering me."

"I'm not," he says. "But it looks like this is where I must leave you."

We're at the steps of the Order of Nethro, where the heavy blackwood doors are shut. The two of us stand there, and I think neither of us wants this moment to end. "Right," I say at last and reluctantly let go of his arm. "Thank you for coming to see me."

"Anytime," he says, and with one last nod of his head, walks off back into the night.

I let out the deepest possible exhale. There is so much I'm feeling, so much to process, and all I want to do, more than anything, is collapse onto my bed.

So of course when I throw open the doors, every single student in the Order of Nethro is gathered in the common room. "Congratulations!" they all shout at once, a wave of cheers and hollers so loud it nearly knocks me back.

I was only in the infirmary for an afternoon, so they must have been busy. The hall has been set up for a grand party. A giant hand-painted banner reading HOUSE NETHRO WINS hangs across the ceiling. The dining tables are covered with carafes of wine and trays of bread and cheese and delicate strawberry sugar cakes. The regular lanterns have been replaced with multicolored ones that spin on little clockwork axes and bathe the whole room in dancing light. Given how red everyone's cheeks look, I'm guessing they've been celebrating for a while.

"Alayne! ALAYNE!" Fyl pushes her way through the crowd to me. "Oh, thank the Gods you're here!" I stagger back, because it's a lot, but Fyl grabs me and jerks me into the room. All the Nethros crowd around me, patting my back, clasping my shoulders, and in the case of one especially drunk girl, planting a big kiss on my cheek. Tish winks at me from across the room. Zigmund grabs me in a bear hug and lifts me off my feet. And Desmond scrambles up onto a table, raising his goblet high as he wobbles on his feet. "To Lady Alayne Dewinter! The new captain of the Order of Nethro!"

I turn to Fyl. "Captain?"

"We're supposed to spend the next week figuring out who our Order

Captain is and having a vote and all that. But in this case, we all agreed it was pretty obvious." Fyl shrugs, a shrug so big I have to wonder how many drinks she's already had. "We did it, Alayne. We won! And we never would've pulled it off without you. You're *amazing*."

"Oh, Gods, oh, Gods," Desmond says as he staggers up, and he is *very* drunk. "My father is going to *kill* me! And you know what? I don't care!" He turns back to the rest of the hall, throwing his arms out wide. "I! Don't! Care!"

"He's going to care tomorrow," Fyl says, and puts an arm around my shoulders, hugging me close. "When my father finds out I was part of the winning team, he's going to absolutely lose his mind. I almost don't want to write a letter just so I can tell him in person."

"Good for you," I say, and I try to smile, but I'm feeling something new, a stab of guilt that I have no business feeling. This is the happiest I've seen Fyl, the most confident and outgoing. And it's because of me, because she believes in me, because she believes in us. She has no idea who I really am.

I down the goblet in a massive swig.

The night's a blur. I dance with Fyl as a lanky boy plays the lute, twirling her around the floor until we both collapse. I arm-wrestle Zigmund and lose disastrously. At one point I slump on a couch with Tish as they explain the nuances of Kindrali Isles politics. I drink another goblet, and another, and a shot of a green liquor from Zigmund that tastes like horseradish and makes every inch of my body burn. The world slips away in a warm, hazy blur, and I flit from corner to corner, from person to person, laughing and chatting and vanishing into myself.

Is this what it's like to be one of them? To grow up surrounded by this kind of camaraderie, this luxury, this uninhibited, unabashed joy? To not worry about when the next meal is coming, to not dread being discovered, to not have that simmering undercurrent, always present, of hate and rage? To just go through life without seeing the injustice and the suffering? To go through life without pain?

To be loved?

Then I see her. Marlena. She kneels at the far end of the room, framed by a throng of guffawing students, wiping up some spilled wine with a dark rag. Our eyes meet through the fray, and it's like the sight of her is a splash of cold water, sobering me instantly, jerking me out of that glow. These aren't my real friends. This isn't real love. And I'm not Alayne Dewinter.

I need to get out of here.

I jerk my head at her, and she gets the message, responding with a curt nod. "I need some fresh air," I say to no one in particular, and push my way through the partying crowd, out the doors, and into the night.

The air is cold, bracing, and I welcome its bite. The rest of the campus has gone dark, the courtyard lanterns out, and there's no noise save the rumblings of the party. I pace toward a bench and sit down, closing my eyes, in part to let the cold wash over me but also because the world was starting to spin a bit and I need it to stop.

There's a rustle of motion and I look up to see Marlena sliding onto the bench next to me. "Oh, good," I say. "I wanted to talk to you, but I didn't know if you could get out of there."

"It's fine. Everyone in there is too drunk to notice a missing Humble." She turns to me, one narrow eyebrow perfectly cocked. "I'm just impressed you were able to make it to a bench."

"I'm not that drunk," I protest, gently resting a hand on her shoulder. "I'm just a little pipsy."

She looks at me, at my hand on her shoulder, then back at me. "You *just* said 'pipsy.'"

"Okay, I'm drunk." I pull away, leaning my head back against the cold metal of the bench's railing. My stomach feels warm, and every word takes just a little too much effort to get out right. "Too drunk. Should've been more careful."

I'm starting to realize that having this conversation drunk is a bad idea in and of itself, but she doesn't react. "Please. You deserve to enjoy yourself and relax. After what you did today?" Her features are hard, her face lean and angular, but when she smiles, it's like she's someone else altogether. "Honestly, I didn't think your plan would work, but you pulled it off. You won against all odds. You were amazing, Lady Dewinter."

"Call me Alk…call me Alayne," I get out. I don't know why, but it somehow feels like less of a lie. "And I couldn't have done it without you. Your lessons, your help with the rules, all of it. This is as much you as it is me."

"No. I helped you learn but you're the one who took the field. You're the one who actually did it," she says, head tilted to the side. "Maybe it's foolish but I really believe you can do this. I believe you're going to win the Great Game. I believe you're going to take me out of here."

The sting of guilt I felt earlier is now a lance, driven clean through me. The admiration of Fyl and the other Nethros was bad, but even if I let them down, they'd still go on to lead privileged, happy lives. But there's a desperation in Marlena, an intensity that rattles me to my core. She's bet it all on me. If I fail and let her down, if I somehow get caught and this gets traced back to her, she'll die a brutal death. This stranger who's barely known me has staked her life to mine. "Why?" I ask.

"Why what?"

"Why are you doing this? Why are you risking everything?" I feel bad asking, but I'll feel worse not knowing. "What is it that you're so desperate to run away from?"

There is a long pause, incredibly long. I can see her brow furrow as she thinks, see her eyes dart around as she considers the possibilities of what to say. She breathes deeply, her chest rising and falling, and at last she speaks. "I'm not running from anything. It's what I'm running *to*," she says at last, gazing off into the dark of the distance. "I'm running to freedom. I'm running to be me."

"I don't understand."

When Marlena speaks, her voice is tight, choked, like it's hard to even get a word out. "I was born on this island, like my mother before me, and her mother before her," she says. "Born under a contract that obligates me to serve here. Born into this life. From the minute I could walk, all I knew was service. Washing dishes. Dusting shelves. Carrying water and serving food and changing sheets. Girl, bring me a drink. Girl, sort my books. Girl, girl, girl." She spits the word like it's poison. "And if I did everything right, if I tried my hardest and was the brightest and the best, then I could earn a spot at some professor's side, transcribing his lectures and sorting his books. That was the most I could ever hope for, the most I could even *dream* of being, the most I could ever aspire to. Being a *slightly* better servant."

I breathe deeply, and the moment has changed, become heavy, somber, raw. "Marlena..."

"My mother was the most brilliant woman I've ever known," she says. "Smarter than all of the Wizards, with a mind that could solve any challenge, with more wit and wisdom than that entire school combined. She could have changed the world, and all she ever got to do, after a lifetime of service, was take notes at the faculty meetings."

I linger on the past tense in her words. "Did...did the Wizards kill her?"

"The red fever took her life," she replies. "But this place killed her spirit. I saw it die slowly, day after day, saw the light fade in her eyes, saw the crushing weight of the drudgery, of the cruelty, of the indifference wear her down until she broke." She stares out at the night, her eyes wet, her breath tight in her chest. "I don't want to be like that. I don't want that to be me. I'm more than this place," she says, and she's whispering so loudly it's almost a shout. "I could be so much godsdamned more!"

Gods. I know there's nothing I can say. Despite everything I've lost, at least I've been free. At least I had a purpose. We sit in silence for a few minutes as her breathing slows. "You've really never been off this island?" I finally ask.

She smiles, the kind of smile that's achingly sad. "Just once. When I was thirteen, Professor Barclay took me on a trip to the mainland with him, to help transcribe some papers. I saw the tall spires of the city, saw so many new and different people, got to do so much." She shakes her head. "It was just for a week, though, and then I came right back here. But it was the best week of my life." She looks up at me, right at me, her gaze burning. "I think about it every day."

There is so much yearning in her voice, so much raw longing, that my heart hurts. I see her now, really see her, this girl who's spent her whole life in a cage, this spirit so desperate to be free. I've spent so long focused on the violence and brutality of Wizards that I've forgotten about their everyday cruelty, how stifling and crushing this system is even when no one's bleeding. Marlena deserves so much better. They *all* deserve so much better. "What would you do?" I ask her. "If you got off this island?"

"I'd do *everything*," she laughs, even as she brushes aside a tear. "I would travel the world, see the blue mountains and the golden deserts and feel the ocean breeze. I'd visit every city I could get to, I'd drink new drinks and try new foods, I'd dance on rooftops and run through fields. And I would read, Gods, I would read so much." She exhales sharply, her voice trembling. "I'd fight for what I believed in. I'd speak my mind. I'd do what I want to do." Her eyes drop, not quite able to meet mine. "I'd love who I want to love."

My breath is tight in my chest, my stomach fluttering, my knees trembling. I'm scared and excited and overwhelmed all at once, like I'm about to plunge into something great and unknown. "Marlena…" I whisper.

"That's why I was drawn to you," she says. "You do whatever you want, rules be damned. You fight for yourself. You stand up to your enemies. You don't let anything break you or hold you back." She reaches out and touches my cheek with the back of her hand, and her skin is so soft and warm, and it's like her touch is electric, like she just sent lightning shooting through my veins, like I can barely breathe. "I want to be like you."

I want to say something, anything, but I can't find the words. Because I finally understand her, finally see the truth behind this girl who's been such an enigma this whole time. From the moment I set foot on this island, we were drawn to each other, and now I see why. I see who she is, and she's so much more than I could have imagined.

I take her hand, the one touching my cheek, and gently cradle it in my mine. It feels like magic, like the moment when I conjure flame and the heat flares through the Loci in my palm. And in that moment I know, with absolute certainty, that I'm not going to let her down. This isn't just about being partners anymore, about helping her so she can help me. She deserves to be free, deserves it as much as anyone can deserve anything. She's not a means to achieve my mission. She *is* my mission. "I'll get you off this island," I say.

She looks at me, and for the first time there's a sense of uncertainty in her eyes, a nervousness, like when you can't quite let yourself believe something's real. "You promise?"

"I swear on my life."

Something flutters down, something soft and white, landing on my shoulder. She gasps. "Alayne. Look. It's snowing."

I glance at my bare shoulder, at the perfect little drop of white slowly dissolving against my skin. Another flutters down onto my nose, and another into Marlena's hair, and then they're all around us, hundreds of dazzling little snowflakes, enveloping us like a field of stars. She cranes her head up, beaming, as they settle onto her cheeks, melting on her skin. "Wow," I whisper, because I've never actually seen snow. It might just be the most beautiful thing I've ever seen.

She looks at me with her eyes wide and awestruck. "My mother always said that sharing the first snowfall of the year with someone bound your souls together. But I suppose we've already crossed that bridge." She squeezes my hand tightly, and in that moment, snow on her cheeks, the stars in her eyes, *she* might be the most beautiful person I've ever seen. This feels impossible, magical, like we're in the Null, like time has slowed down for us and this could last forever. We both exhale at the same time, our breath swirling together in the air between us like a gentle mist, and my heart thunders against my ribs, and my whole body tingles like a storm, and I want this, I want this so badly, to cross the distance between us, to feel her skin, her lips, to breathe her in and lose myself in her.

Then clarity strikes, like a dagger in the back, like a lance through the chest. Because I can't. I *can't.* For everything we have in common, for everything we share, we're just too different. I'm a student and she's a servant. I'm a Wizard and she's a Humble. And for all her honesty, for all her yearning, she still has no idea who I really am. She doesn't know the blood on my hands, the pain in my past, the dark and ugly road I'm going to walk. She sees what she wants to see, what she aspires to see, but she doesn't see *me.*

She doesn't see the danger.

I have to be guarded. I have to have walls. For my safety, and for hers. We can be allies and partners and friends, but it has to end there. I can't get close. I can't risk hurting her. So I pull away, even though it physically hurts. "Right," I say as I rise to my feet and clear my throat. "We should head in."

Disappointment flickers across her face for just one second, and then she nods, herself again. "Of course. You ought to get back before anyone notices." Then she leaves, pacing inside, and I follow her back in, taking one last glance at the quad around me, at that first layer of perfect snow coating everything like a veil.

Inside the Order of Nethro, the party has wound down, by which I mean most of the students have wandered up to their beds or passed out in the common room. The lanterns are out, the room dark and still. Zigmund snores, splayed out shirtless on the floor. Desmond and Fyl are against the far wall, slumped together, her head on his shoulder, his arm draped around her. Opened bottles and half-drunk goblets rest on all the tables, and I debate having another drink, decide not to, reconsider that, then definitely decide no, not worth it. I need to sleep this off, and fast.

I'm up the stairs and halfway to my room when someone clears their throat to catch my attention. Professor Calfex rests in an alcove under a window, a glass of wine in her hand. I swallow deeply, trying to force myself sober, and she clearly notices because she snorts a barely suppressed laugh. "Relax. It's a night of celebration. You don't have to pretend." She raises the glass to her lips, finishing it, and sets it aside. "I probably should have stopped the party hours ago, but, well, it's my first time celebrating a victory in nearly two decades as Head of the Order of Nethro. Who knows when I'll get to again?"

I relax a little, though there's still something in her manner that makes me uneasy. "I'll just have to win the next two challenges and give you more opportunities."

"Gods, you're a cocky little thing, aren't you?" Calfex rises to her feet, chuckling under her breath. "Do you even understand the significance of what you did out there?"

"I just did what you told me. I found Marius's weakness and I exploited it."

"Oh, you did more than that. You found a weakness in the game itself. You made a mockery of the Republic's most celebrated pastime. You made many enemies today, Alayne Dewinter. You painted a target on yourself, on your friends, on this entire Order." The edge of her lip twitches, betraying her look of severity. "And you made me proud."

There is absolutely no good reason I should care what a *Wizard professor at Blackwater* thinks of me, but my heart still swells. "Is it really that bad out there?" I ask. "Are people really that angry?

"Some are. Wizards maintain their Order loyalties long after they graduate. There are many Vanguards out there who will be screaming that your play was illegal until their dying days. One of them happens to be the Grandmaster of the Senate."

"If my strategy is so controversial and humiliating, why didn't the judges just rule it an illegal play?"

"Because it was objectively legal," Calfex says. "Headmaster Aberdeen is the Great Unifier, the voice of reason and neutrality. If he and the judges were to rule against you today, he would be signaling his loyalty to Madison, to Vanguard. He'd be shattering his meticulously constructed role as the Republic's impartial arbiter. So no matter how much he personally disliked your play, no matter how much trouble it's causing him, he had to allow it. You forced him into a position where he had no choice." Calfex shakes her head. "Which brings me to the reason I'm up here. The headmaster has relayed a message. He would like to meet with you in his office, first thing tomorrow morning."

My blood runs cold, all the pleasant warmth of the drinking vanishing instantly. "What? Why?"

"Aberdeen is a man obsessed with control, a man who must know everything and who absolutely despises surprises," Calfex says, and maybe she's had a little too much, too, because she can barely hide her contempt. "I imagine he'll want to know exactly who you are."

Her words cut like a dagger, and I can feel the small grasp of panic tickling red at the corner of my vision, a hitch growing in my breath. What was I thinking, getting drunk and relaxing? "Tomorrow morning" is just hours away. "Am I in trouble?"

"That depends on what you say to him," Calfex says. "My advice? Don't lie."

I swallow hard. "Right. I'll do my best."

Calfex brushes past me, walking to the stairs, but right as she reaches them, she stops. "One more thing you ought to know," she says, her back turned to me so I can't see her face. When she speaks, her voice is flat, distant, cold as an Ice Glyph.

"Dean Veyle died an hour ago."

Chapter 24

Then

I am thirteen when I learn to lie.

We sit together on the upper loft of the barn, cross-legged opposite each other on hay-strewn beams. It's a beautiful day, a clear blue sky, and Sera's long curls are dazzling in the sun's warm light. She's wearing a red sundress, freshly acquired from the pirates of Midgar Bay, and even I've got a pair of new breeches on. Revenants practice all around us in the early morning light, sharpening new blades and sparring in the dirt. Spirits are high in the camp.

You wouldn't know it from Sera's stern expression. "All right, from the beginning," she says. "Lie to me."

I roll my eyes. "Come on, Sera. This is dumb. I know how to lie."

"Not according to Whispers you don't." She folds her arms across her chest. "This is serious. This mission is really important, and Whispers tasked me with making sure you can handle it."

I let out a weary moan. She's not wrong; the mission is important, maybe the most important one I've ever been on. After almost a year in Hellsum, we're finally going after our target, Reginald Von Clair, a powerful senator. We're going to break into his manor, take out his staff, and steal his prized red ledger, which contains all kinds of Republic secrets. I think we're also going to kill him, but Whispers hasn't been entirely clear. Either way, the plan relies on Whispers and me getting into the mansion by pretending to be a visiting merchant and her daughter, which is where the lying comes in. *If he sees through us, we're both dead*, Whispers insisted, *so you better make damn sure you can be convincing.*

I understand the importance. But I still resent being cooped up here on such a beautiful day. "What am I supposed to lie about?"

"If I tell you, dummy, you can't lie about it," Sera laughs. "How about this? We'll play that drinking game the soldiers play. Tell me two truths and one lie."

"Not a fun drinking game if we're not drinking," I grumble, though honestly, my head *still* hurts from our misadventure with the sherry. "Fine. How's this? I'm scared of spiders. I like jasmine tea. I—"

"Lie."

"What?"

"That last one. About the jasmine tea. That was a lie."

"You're cheating. You just already knew that! This game's no fun since we already know everything about each other!"

"Oh, do we now?" Sera says, and I realize I've run right into her trap. "I dream of falling all the time. I don't like Carlita anymore. That night we drank the sherry was the best night of my life." I blink at her, and she just stares back with a smug little grin, cheeks dimpled, eyes sparkling with satisfaction. "Well?"

"The first one? No, the third one. No, none of them, they're all true, that's the trick," I try. "No?"

"Exactly," she says. "You have no idea. Because I actually know how to lie."

I groan. I mean, she's not wrong, but she's only so good because she's had help. While I was sparring in the yard and mastering Glyphs with Pavel, Sera was studying with Whispers, learning all the tricks of her trade: espionage, deception, strategy. I'm Whispers's secret weapon, but Sera is going to be her successor. "Fine. Teach me, oh, wise one."

"How I've longed to hear those words," she beams. "All right, listen closely. The secret to telling a lie is to find the truth in it. If you know you're lying, then other people will too. So the trick is to convince yourself in the moment that the words you're saying are true, by saying one thing and feeling another. If you're going to lie about liking jasmine tea, you can't think about jasmine tea. You need to think about something you do like, to picture that as vividly as you can, and convince yourself that's what you're talking about. Like those cream puffs we had at the market in Brisbane."

"Oh, those cream puffs..."

"Right. Think of them, feel how you feel about them. Tell the truth about them, even while you talk about jasmine tea."

I'm just thinking about the cream puffs now. "That seems hard."

"It's not." Sera shrugs. "Words are air, nothing more. Your mouth can say whatever it wants. What matters is what your body, your mind, what your heart, believes. " She pauses. "It's your heart that'll betray you."

I snort. "Are you a poet now?"

"Maybe I am," she says. "Maybe when you're asleep, I sneak out into the moonlight and write stanzas and stanzas of beautiful poetry."

I stare at her. "That's a lie. Right? That one's a lie?"

Now she laughs. "Try again. Do what I told you. Think of one thing, and say another. Find the truth behind the lie."

"All right." I take a deep breath and try it. I imagine, as clearly as I can, the face of a spider, its creepy twitchy legs, the way my skin crawls just imagining one running over me. I feel, as deeply as I can, that visceral, stomach-churning disgust. "I hate sharks. I love dancing. The day after we drank the sherry, I threw up six times."

Sera nods. "That was better. Genuinely. You improved a lot."

"But?"

"But it was obviously the sharks, right?"

I slam my face into my palms. "This shit is hopeless!"

"Don't swear," Sera says, and gently squeezes my shoulder. "You'll get it, Alka. I know you will. But you might not master it in a week."

"Well, that's when the mission is...."

I can actually feel Sera tense up, and when I look at her face she's biting her lip with apprehension. "What if... what if I went on the mission, then? I can pull it off, easily."

"What? No." I shake my head. "You don't go on missions. It's too dangerous, remember?"

"Oh, but it's not too dangerous for *you*?" She jerks back, and she actually looks angry, which is rare; Sera can be melancholy and distant, but she's rarely outright mad. "I'm twelve already. I'm never going to learn anything if I'm stuck back here while you're all out there in the field! It's not fair!"

"Sera..."

"No, I'm serious," she insists. Has she really felt this way all this time? Has she just been bottling this frustration and anger up, and I had no idea? She really *is* a good liar. "You're a better thief, fine. You're a better fighter, I accept that. You're a Wizard, nothing I can do there. But this is what I've trained for. This is my whole purpose here. Why can't it just be me?"

"You could get hurt."

"So could you!" She practically yells back. "But I live with that! Every time you go out, I sit here by myself, worrying, pacing, trembling, wondering if this is it, if this is the time you don't come home, if this is the day I lose you. It's awful, Alka. It's unbearable. But I've learned to live with it. And you and Whispers should, too."

A long silence lingers over us as I struggle to find words. I want to argue with her, but I can't. Every word she's said is absolutely true, and we both know it. And as badly as I want to just tell her no, to make sure she stays here safe and sound and alive, I know I can't. This is important. This means so much to her. I have to let her have it.

"Okay," I say at last. "I'll talk to Whispers. I'll tell her to take you. And if she says no, I'll put my foot down and insist I won't do it."

"You're serious?"

"Of course," I pull her in for a hug. "Sera, I love you, and this matters to you. I'm not going to stand in your way."

"You're the best sister ever," she says.

"Yeah, I know," I say with a laugh. "Just promise me you'll be safe, all right? Promise me you'll come back."

She grips me tight. "I promise I'll come back."

It's a lie.

CHAPTER 25

Now

Headmaster Aberdeen's office is in the main building, on the top floor, which means to get there I have to walk all the way across campus. The sun shines a hot white off the fresh, fluffy snow blanketing the campus, which makes the dull pounding in my temples so much worse. I'd hoped most of the campus would still be asleep, but a surprising number of people are out, enjoying the first snowfall of the year. Students lie on their backs, making Goddesses with their arms and legs, while others hurl snowballs or just sit on benches, admiring the view. Groundskeeper Tyms oversees some Humbles shoveling the path and snarls at me as I pass. At the center of the quad, Professor Hapsted holds court with a small group of gawkers. A snowball hovers in front of him as he weaves his gnarled wooden Loci through the air, creating a haze of silver strands of light that envelop it like a fly in a web.

I just want to quietly walk to Aberdeen's office and get whatever this is over with, but as I stroll through the quad, everyone turns to stare at me. *Everyone*, even Professor Hapsted, who looks away from his snowball long enough for it to crumble in the middle of the web. Some of the students, especially the Vanguards, glare at me with anger and hate. But a surprising amount stare without judgment, just awe, while a few even smile. A girl in Javellos colors gives me a wave. A boy in a Zartan cloak offers me a raised fist.

It seems I'm not the only one who wanted to see Vanguard defeated.

Aberdeen's office is up four flights of stairs, and every step I take feels heavy with dread. I've gotten confident in my ability to fool the other students and professors, but it's one thing to blend in with a crowd of Nethros and entirely another to sit alone in a tiny room with the headmaster and lie directly to his face. Sera could've done this effortlessly. But Sera's not here.

Aberdeen's office is behind a pair of heavy ornate doors, engraved with a detailed carving of the Gods. I stand outside awkwardly for a few minutes, and, when no one comes out to greet me, gently shove them open.

Aberdeen's office is massive. Bookshelves line every wall, reaching up nearly three stories to a domed ceiling painted to look like the night sky. A scarlet silk curtain blocks a wide window at the back wall, and instead the room is illuminated by dozens of magical lanterns built into the walls. A grandfather clock taller than I am stands against a corner, with a glass front so I can see hundreds of intricately clicking gears. Relics sit around the room behind displays: a pair of jagged black Loci, a six-eyed skull, a broadsword bigger than my head. The real prize is at the center of the room on a tall dais encased in glass. A massive tome, bound in chains, sealed with a crystal lock. The *Codex Transcendent*. I twitch a little just looking at it.

Aberdeen himself sits behind a desk at the back of the room. He gestures toward the chair opposite him. "Please. Have a seat."

I slide into the chair, just a desk away from the man who took it all away from me. "Headmaster. You wanted to meet with me."

"I wanted to congratulate you!" he beams, radiating paternal warmth. He's wearing a long robe, like always, this one a dark purple adorned with hundreds of tiny bright beads. His gray hair hangs down his back in a neat braid, a white eyepatch covers his eye, and a delicate silver circlet rests on his forehead. "Your victory yesterday, well, it was one for the history books."

"Thank you, Headmaster." I drop my head respectfully, sounding awed and a little proud. *Find the truth behind the lie*, I think, and the truth here is thinking of Whispers.

"If I may be so bold as to ask." He leans back in his chair. "It's not every day someone discovers an entirely new Balitesta strategy. It's not every decade. How did you come up with such a daring approach?"

This is a test, no doubt, but I'm not sure exactly what he's testing, which makes this delicate. "I knew I'd have to find some kind of unique strategy to win, so I spent weeks reading over accounts of the game and then…" I shrug. "It just came to me in a flash."

"How remarkable." Aberdeen's good eye shines with cunning. "So you did it all alone? No one helped you?"

My face doesn't crack, even as ice races down my spine. Is he asking about Marlena? How much does he know? "A Humble Nethro servant helped me. She—"

"I'm not asking about some Humble servant," Aberdeen cuts in, with a hint of annoyance. "I meant, did any of the other students help you? Perhaps those from other noble families?"

Oh. *Oh*. He doesn't think I could have come up with it on my own. He thinks I'm a patsy, a tool being wielded against him, some dumb girl manipulated by a powerful noble. I have to fight back a laugh. "No," I say confidently. "No one helped me."

"Remarkable. Truly remarkable." He leans back, smiling, and I almost think I'm off the hook when he abruptly stops, stroking his chin while staring me down. "All right then. Thank you for answering my questions, Lady Dewinter. I think at last I understand."

"Oh?"

"I'll admit, you've been something of an enigma to me," he says. "When I first met you, well, I can't say I was overly impressed. I thought you were just an ignorant new Mark, untrained and unprepared, spilling wine in the hall and nearly blowing yourself up with that ice Glyph. Then you pulled off the play of the century in the challenge, and I was just bewildered. Who is this girl? But now, now I get it." He leans forward, glaring right through me. "I know *exactly* who you are."

Do not blink. Do not sweat. Do not let my heart betray me. "And who is that?"

He rises from his chair, taller up close than I'd thought. "An outsider," he says. "You're the first in your family to get the Godsmark. A Wizard raised by Humbles on some dusty rock halfway across the world. Your father's a decorated general, a hero who proved himself through courage and strategy. A man who rose from nothing to greatness, all through his own cunning and conviction. And you're his daughter, fulfilling his legacy." I don't know how to answer that, how Alayne would have responded, but I don't have to, because he keeps talking. "You didn't come here to make friends or to learn magic, did you, Lady Dewinter? No, you came here to conquer. To make a name for yourself. To ensure that House Dewinter earns its place in our society. You came here ready to do whatever it took to come out on top. You're not a great Wizard, no, but you're smart, you're ambitious, and you're willing to do whatever it takes, break whatever rule you have to, in order to win. Is that right?"

"I haven't broken any rules," I say, to which he just laughs. "But yes. I am ambitious. I do want to win. I'll do whatever it takes."

"I respect that. I really do." He paces across the room, so I have to crane around in my seat just to follow him. "But as your headmaster, as the patriarch of this great institution, I feel a duty to caution you. In my long tenure here, I've seen a dozen students like you. And it has never ended well for them."

"Why not?"

Rather than answer my question, Aberdeen crosses over to the grandfather clock, resting his hand against its polished wood frame. "Byron Blackwater was the first headmaster of this school. He was a great man, a First Father, a visionary who helped create our beloved Republic. And do you know what his first act as headmaster was? Why, it was to commission this very clock." His hand runs down its surface, almost caressing it. "It's a beautiful machine made of hundreds of little parts, all working together in perfect balance and harmony. Every gear, every lever, every dial, knows its function. And combined, they create something truly great and wonderful, something that lasts across the centuries. Do you understand?"

"I'm afraid I don't."

"I see myself as a caretaker of intricate machines, Lady Dewinter. This clock... this school... this Republic. What matters most to me, the only thing that matters to me, is keeping it running smoothly." He steps away from the clock, pacing toward me. "I harbor my own beliefs, of course. I abhor rituals like the krova-yan, even as the Senate insists I permit it. I preach the wisdom of peace to Grandmaster Madison, even as he wages his endless wars. I wish for a world that is gentler, better, kinder... and yet when I must, I put my own beliefs aside. I stay neutral. Neutral and moderate, above all else. Why?" He takes another step. "Because I am just one gear. And if I placed myself first, if I let myself get too big, if I leaned in to my own ambitions, why, then the whole machine would fall apart."

Alayne would be angry here. I'm angry for her. "Are you telling me to know my place, Headmaster?"

Aberdeen presses a hand to his chest, a wounded look on his face. "I would never phrase it like that!" he says. "All I do is suggest caution. Systems, societies, exist to protect those within them... and to destroy those outside them. It's just nature." He takes another step, drawing closer. "If you can work within the system, if you can fit in and learn when to climb and when to sit, when to thrive and when to boost others, well, I see greatness in your future. I see glory for your family and for you...." He steps up close, too close, right behind me. I can smell his perfume, rose-water and lavender, can feel the heat radiating off him. I'm so tense I feel ready to shatter.

Then he reaches out and grabs my shoulders, and he's actually touching me, his horrible pallid hands resting on me, and my stomach lurches and my skin crawls and I have to use every ounce of strength not to whip out my Loci and stab one right through his neck. "Word of advice, Lady Dewinter." He leans in, so close I can feel his beard scrape the skin of my cheek, so close I can feel his breath on my neck, and his voice is a rumbling growl. "When the time comes for the Second Challenge? Lose."

Then he steps away and the mask is back on, a pleasant smile on his face, the kindly headmaster again. "Do we have an understanding?"

The cause. The cause. Always the cause. "Yes," I choke out, and I sound more scared than I want to, but maybe that's right for Alayne. "I understand."

"Good." He walks back around to his desk and slides into his chair opposite me. "Well. If that's all cleared up, I do believe we can move on with our day."

"Of course, Headmaster." My eyes drop, and I can still feel his hands on me, still feel his breath on my skin. "Thank you for the advice."

I rise from my chair and stride out the door and I'm halfway down the stairs before I actually let out my breath, before I release the tension built up within me like steam bursting from a kettle. I slump against a wall, gasping, shaking, and I lean there in the stairwell for a good ten minutes, eyes shut, just inhaling and exhaling, letting the air rush through me, letting myself become myself again. And as the tension melts away, as the fear of being caught dissolves, all that's left is the burning core of righteous rage.

This isn't the rage of my childhood trauma or the political fury that Whispers cultivated in me. No, this is something new, something personal and immediate. I'm angry on my own behalf, on behalf of Fyl and Zigmund and Desmond and Tish, on behalf of all the Nethros. None of us asked for this, to be put into this position. It's bad enough they shovel us all into the least-respected Order, bad enough we get mocked at every turn, bad enough we have to compete in a game stacked against us in every way. But when we actually win, when we give it all on the field and risk everything and actually pull through, now Aberdeen is going to try to threaten me into losing?

Screw that. Screw every last single part of that. Magnus Aberdeen wants me to know my place? He prizes his precious little clock, his systems, his order?

I'm going to take it from him. I'm going to wreck him. Absolutely utterly destroy him. I'm going to kill him, that's a promise, and I'm going to send everything he loves and values with him.

But first? I'm going to win House Nethro the Second godsdamned Challenge.

Chapter 26

Now

Founders' Day is the biggest holiday in the Republic, so of course, it's of utmost importance at Blackwater. According to Fyl, the Founders' Day Gala is the single most important social event of the school year, a grand ball for all students and faculty to celebrate the founding of the Republic. The patriotic framing is just pretense though; what matters is the party itself. Fancy gowns and expensive suits, the finest food and drink, dazzling decor and a performance by the Republic's premier band.

Fyl can't stop gushing. There's nothing I want less.

I've managed to avoid big social engagements through the fall and winter terms, sleeping through the Harvest Picnic and hiding in my room during the Night of Lights. After that disastrous trip to the village pub, it seemed like the safer bet. But there's no getting out of the Founders' Day Gala. It's mandatory, for one, and Fyl says she'd never forgive me if I missed it. So that's why I'm sitting in her room in a massive dress, wincing as she weaves my hair into a braid that encircles my head like a crown.

"I don't know, Fyl," I say, staring down at myself. Apparently, none of the dresses I'd come with were formal enough, so Fyl bought me one from the tailor in town. It's something else, the kind of dress I've seen in picture books about princesses. It's a lush, dark scarlet, the color of roses in winter, the color of blood on snow. The top half fits me like a second skin, hugging tight at my waist, trailing down with a low neckline that leaves me feeling exposed. Frills of black lace line the collar, and the back is a thin black mesh adorned with dozens of embroidered roses. Below the waist is an ornate floof of ruffles, a wide, round wedding cake of lavish red that flows around me when I walk and is impossible to resist twirling in. Long lace gloves cover my hands, stretching up to my elbows, and delicate black ribbons tie into bows along my sleeves. And of course, there's absolutely nowhere to put a Loci. "If Marius tries anything at the dance, I'll be useless in this dress."

"No one is going to try anything," Fyl replies, pulling a little too hard on a braid. "Founders' Day is about putting our differences aside and celebrating being Marovians. There's no Order competition at the dance. For one night, and one night only, we're all the same."

Except for all the Humble servants who make the night actually happen, I think. I haven't had a chance to practice with Marlena in more than a week, because she's been so involved in setting up the event, working through the nights to chop fruit and embroider decorations. I glance down at my beautiful dress and wonder how many blistered Humble hands sewed it together. "If you say so," I tell Fyl. "But I'm still watching my back."

"How can you be so visionary and so cynical at the same time?" Fyl laughs. "Come on, lighten up! This is going to be a blast. The dancing, the feasting, the wine, the music..." She pauses, leaning in close with a mischievous grin. "The romance."

"Kill me now."

Fyl playfully jerks the braid. "Everyone knows the Founders' Day Gala is *the* time to make a romantic gesture to whoever you've been smitten with all year. There's going to be so many dramatic declarations and long-awaited kisses. It's great."

I arch an eyebrow her way. "And I can't imagine there's anyone in particular you have in mind for a long-awaited kiss. Definitely not someone whose name starts with *D* and ends with *esmond*."

"It's not like that. I mean, it'd be nice if it was. I wish it was. But it's not. Also, shut up." Fyl's cheeks burn red. "Besides, I was thinking more about you and that prince…"

"Talyn?" I blink. "No. It's not like that."

"Sure," Fyl says. "I've seen you two on your walks. You're looking awfully cozy."

It's true, I've been spending a few of my evenings with Talyn. When we walk through the campus, the frost crunching so satisfyingly under our boots, he tells me about his home, about the great stone ziggurats and the crystal deserts. We commiserate over challenges in our classes, we laugh about the pompousness of the ceremonies, we fume together over the bullshit served up as history.

He makes me laugh. That counts for a lot. And when he takes my hand or I slide my arm into his, I feel my stomach flutter and my heart quicken. That counts even more.

Still, I'm not going to let Fyl know that. "We're just friends."

"Yeah, well, you won't be tonight. Not after he sees you." Fyl steps back proudly. "Take a look."

I rise from my chair and turn to the full-length mirror against Fyl's wall. I actually gasp. I've been many things in my life, but I don't think I've ever been beautiful, not like this. The girl in the mirror looking back at me, though? She's stunning. The lush scarlet dress perfectly frames my body, sparkling like a starscape in red every time I move. My hair sits in a regal crown of braids and runs down my back in delicate strands. And the makeup Fyl put on me, all those little powders and brushes… my eyelashes blink full, my lips shine a dark red, my eyelids a soft purple. Flakes of delicate gold dazzle on my cheeks, and tear-shaped diamond earrings catch the light like prisms.

"Come on. Admit it. I've done good," Fyl says.

"You have," I reply, but I'm transfixed, lost, like I'm in a dream. Looking in the mirror, I don't see myself at all. There's no trace left of the scrappy Revenant who slept in bales of hay, of the scrawny girl with the messy hair and the furious eyes. Looking in that mirror, I don't see a single trace of Alka Chelrazi. I just see Alayne Dewinter. And godsdamn, if she isn't beautiful.

"Are you all right?" Fyl asks, sensing something off. "Did I do something wrong?"

"No." I take a deep breath. "It's just beautiful. That's all." I take her hand and head to the door, away from that mirror. "Come on. Let's get to the gala."

I worried I'd stand out, but that fear is dispelled the second I get downstairs and see that everyone looks like this. Fyl, of course, has done herself up just as well as she did me, with a slim-fitting purple dress, its trim embroidered blue like sea-foam. Desmond is wearing a formal South Marovian suit, the kind with the ruffled collar and the high stockings and a silk coat with luminous pearl buttons. Tish wears a traditional Kindrali suit, a sheer sleeveless silver tunic that hangs over their torso like a veil, showing off all of their elegant tattoos. Zigmund looks like a Velkschen warlord of old, with a black leather cloak studded with metal, wrapped in a fur trim and trailed in a wolfskin. They all grin as they see me, Tish clapping me on the back, and Zigmund letting out a howl, which I think is acceptable up north. I grin back, maybe genuinely, and together we all make our way to the Main Hall.

I had thought it was fancy the first night when we got here, when the hall was set up for the feast. But as we stroll through the wide doors, my jaw drops, because the hall doesn't just look fancy, it looks *impossible.* It's already packed with dozens of students, a sea of trailing gowns and pristine suits. The air is thick with the pulse of magic, hours and hours of labor from the adjunct staff. The floor has been altered to look like the night sky, a vision of stars and comets and planets, twirling and shining beneath our feet. Hundreds of multicolored lanterns twirl on invisible string, casting the room in beams of red and violet and pink. Ribbons of emerald light twirl and dance through the air, like serpents chasing their tails. Tables are laid out against the far walls, offering mountains of spiced meat and creamy cakes and ripe, juicy fruits. Humbles in formal-wear stand by every pillar, holding bottles of sparkling wine that they pour for anyone who passes by. Music sounds around us, a beautiful orchestral waltz. Even with everything I know about how magic works, I can't make sense of this, can't figure out where the Glyphs end and the hard work of Humble labor begins.

Looking around, I can see all the usual faces: Marius Madison boasting away in a silk suit emblazoned with gold trim, Vyctoria Aberdeen quietly observing in a stark blue gown, even Professor Calfex reclining on a bench in the dark corner of the room, a goblet of wine in her hand.

"Well?" Fyl says. "You can say it. I was right. You're happy you came."

"Ask me at the end of the night," I say. "Now if you don't mind, I'm getting a drink."

Wine sounds nice, but I'm mostly interested in who's pouring it. Marlena stands at the far side of the room in a crisp white suit, her hair up in a high ponytail. I cross the room to her, weaving through the dancers, and her eyes light up as they see me, her lips crinkling into the faintest smile. "May I offer you some wine, my lady?" she asks, a touch too playfully, and I wonder if maybe she's had a little bit herself.

"Gods, yes," I reply, leaning back against the table next to her. "I think you can drop the formalities, by the way. No one can hear us over this music."

"Whatever you say." She hands me a goblet of wine, and I see her eyes roam over me, lingering for just a moment. "You look beautiful. Truly. Like a goddess made flesh."

"Everyone looks beautiful when they're wearing clothes this expensive."

"Maybe. But not as beautiful as you." She glances down, biting her lip, and I feel my cheeks burn. "I'm glad you're here," she says. "It's nice to talk to someone without plastering on a fake smile or worrying they're going to grope me." Marlena rolls her eyes. "If I may be honest, you Wizards may love Founders' Day . . . but we Humbles dread it."

"I can imagine," I say. Marlena's gotten much more casual when we talk, opening up more about what it's like being a Humble here, bringing me into that world with its secrets and fears and resentments. She's still holding a lot back, of course, but the veil is slipping. It makes me miss the Revenants, miss our motley mob, miss all my Humble friends.

"Attention, attention, beloved students and teachers!" A voice booms from the front of the room, and the music instantly stops, as if it had never been there. A bright white light illuminates a stage at the room's end. Headmaster Aberdeen wears a full-length robe, and as he paces forward, I realize it must be infused with Glyphs; its surface changes colors as he walks, a vivid turquoise, then a fiery red, then a soothing cream. His long gray beard hangs down to his waist in dozens of interwoven braids, and a circlet of silver, studded with gems of every color, adorns his brow. He looks like a Wizard out of the storybooks, like one of the First Fathers. "Welcome, welcome to the Founders' Day Gala!"

Everyone claps and cheers, even Marlena. I force myself to, even though I can still feel his hands on my shoulders, still feel his rank breath against my ear. "I know you all want to get to the dancing and the feasting and the merrymaking, but first, an order of business," Aberdeen says, and raises a hand. Behind him a banner unfurls, and on it are the sigils of the five Orders, alongside some numbers. Our scores from the First Challenge. "Here is where the Great Game stands."

Nethro—11

Javellos—7

Zartan—5

Selura—5

Vanguard—2

My gaze is on the board, but I can feel the eyes of the room light on me, can feel the stares and the whispers. Two months have passed since the First Challenge, and everyone still can't believe a world where Nethro sits at the top and Vanguard at the bottom. I relish that feeling, drink it up. Let them stare, let them whisper, let them gawk. I'm just getting started.

"But the game changes fast, as all games do," Aberdeen continues. "It is thus with great honor that I announce the Second Challenge here tonight! Two weeks hence, we shall all convene for a trial of wits and cunning, a test of magic and wisdom! The Second Challenge shall be... the Maze of Martyrs!"

A nervous titter runs through the room. I lean back to Marlena and whisper, "What the hell is the Maze of Martyrs?"

"It's one of the harder challenges," Marlena replies. "When we did it last, fourteen students were seriously injured and five died. One was never found."

Before I can ponder that, Aberdeen claps, and it somehow sounds like thunder. "But enough talk of competition!" he proclaims, and raises his hand high. Behind him the banner changes, rethreads itself before our eyes, the scorecard vanishing, replaced by an image of ten old-fashioned Wizards clad in long robes and pointed hats, holding hands in unity. "Let us come to the purpose of this great day. Five hundred years ago, ten great men came together, joined in vision. Where the world was all conflict, they saw a path to order. Where the continent was all chaos, they saw... a Republic. Today, we gather to celebrate these men! Today, we honor the First Fathers!"

Everyone cheers again, so loudly the room shakes, and the music mercifully drowns out any more speechifying. "I think I'm going to need more wine," I say through my forced smile.

"You might want to hold off," Marlena replies, looking just past me. "I think your night is about to get interesting."

I turn around and there he is. Prince Talyn Ravensgale IV, strolling through the crowd, his eyes locked firmly on mine. He's wearing a modern suit that clings tight to him like a shadow, its smooth silk the vivid burning red of a desert sunset. His jacket flows long after him like a cape, and the polished obsidian buttons on the top of his shirt are undone, exposing his taut chest and slim collarbones. Rings of onyx and ruby gleam on his fingers, and a ceremonial silver chain hangs across his chest, dangling tightly from each of his shoulders. His hair for once is unbraided, and his face is painted, lips gold, eyes framed by a horizontal band of vivid blue.

My breath catches in my throat. He looks good. Gods, does he look good.

"Lady Dewinter," he says, his voice smooth and low, as he extends a hand. "May I have this dance?"

I can feel the heat of people staring, and I see Marlena glance away. There's a pang of guilt there, the memory of her hand on my cheek still electric, but I push it aside. This is different. Talyn's a Wizard, hell, a prince. He holds the power here. I'm no danger to him.

I can do this. No. I *want* to do this.

I take his hand and let him pull me to him, onto the dance floor, as the music rises to a familiar upbeat tempo. The Martecisto. An old favorite.

We step toward each other, chest to chest, our hands raised and our palms touching, then we move as one to the side and back. "I see you know this one," Talyn says.

"Well, of course," I reply. "Everyone in the Republic does." Every Wizard and noble, anyway. I spent two years training with Whispers on all the things I'd need to know to fit in here, which included a month-long stretch on dances of the nobility. "The real question is, how do *you* know it? I can't imagine it's popular in your kingdom."

"Surprisingly, it is," Talyn replies. Our bodies move together perfectly, rotating in a delicate circle like two candles in a spinning chandelier. "One of the few Marovian imports that caught on. Your ambassador introduced it at one of my mother's garden parties, and it became all the rage among the court."

"And that's where you learned it? From our ambassador?"

"No, actually." We step away, just our fingertips touching, then draw in close again in a rush. "From his daughter."

I know exactly what game he's playing, but I play it anyway. "Now I understand. You dance the Martecisto with *all* Marovian girls."

His mischievous smile shines white in the light. "Just the ones I really like."

My heart leaps, just a little, and a flush burns my cheeks. Which is absolutely ridiculous because I *know* he's just an irredeemable royal flirt and also I'm supposed to be focusing on my mission. I force an eye roll, pushing away the tiniest bit and now we're hitting the fast part of the song, where the tempo rises, where we weave back and forth, my feet between his, hands releasing and clasping, circling and oscillating. All the couples around us speed up, too, a flurry of whirling skirts and crisp suits. We're two bodies in a sea of motion, two stars in a spiraling galaxy.

It ought to be beautiful.

It *is* beautiful.

That's the problem.

I always struggle with this part a little. The footwork is so damn precise, and there's so much happening with the hands. I slip up just the tiniest bit, my heel digging into Talyn's toe, but he doesn't even react, just slides gracefully aside like it hadn't even happened. He's dancing here just as much as he was dancing back in the tavern when we dodged Dean's punches, his movements graceful and effortless, like he's not even trying. "So let me get this straight," I say as we near the climax, moving faster and faster, and I've actually worked up a sweat. "You're a prince, a fighter, a dancer, and a flirt. Is there anything you aren't good at?"

"As a matter of fact, there is," he replies, and pulls my hand up high to twirl me around, once, twice, three times. The world spins, and my dress flares out wide and beautiful, and then I fall back into his firm arms in a low dip that leaves me staring up into his eyes. "I'm not great at making friends."

"That makes two of us," I reply, and pull myself back up, straightening my dress. Everyone applauds, whoops, and cheers, and the band, wherever it is, adjusts for the next song.

"The Martecisto is lovely but so brief," Talyn laments. "I don't suppose you'll permit me another?"

I shouldn't. I really, *really* shouldn't. And it's not just because I don't want everyone in the room to gossip about us, and it's not just because I know I ought to be planning with Marlena for this next challenge. It's because I actually *want* it. I want to stay and dance with him, I want to keep feeling his skin on mine, I want to press myself closer to him and soak him up. It's not something a Revenant on a mission should do, not something that serves the cause. But it's something *I* want, something I crave. I want to feel his touch, to savor his eyes on me, to have just another minute in his arms.

It's been so long since I've done something for myself. It's selfish. It's reckless. It's absolutely the wrong choice.

"Yes," I say. "Just one more."

The music strikes up, and now it's a slow song, a low melodic ballad sung by a woman with a haunting, smoky voice. I'd expected another waltz, but this is more intimate, more personal. The lights dim to a gentle pink. The couples around us either split apart or come closer together, a make-or-break decision I've already committed to. I feel Talyn's arm slide around my waist, his wide hand on the base of my back, as he pulls me in close, right up against him, my chest flush with his. I suck in my breath even as I lean forward, wrapping my arms around his shoulders, pressing my face into the crook of his neck, my cheek resting against the bare skin.

"I don't know this song," he whispers, because the mood in the room is too charged for talking.

I don't recognize it, either, but there's something deeply familiar about it, like a song that's been trapped on the tip of my mind. I close my eyes, trying to focus on the lyrics, even as I can feel Talyn's heart beating in his chest, feel his breath on my forehead. "It's an old Marovian love story, from the days of the First Fathers, about two Wizards from rival families who fall in love."

"How does it end?"

"Like all love stories," I reply. "In tragedy."

"You Marovians and your tragedies. What's so wrong with a happy ending?" The music is slowing down around us as the other couples come together. I can see Marius and Vyctoria, swaying gently, eyes shut, looking genuinely happy. Zigmund's with a brawny Zartan girl. And behind them are Fyl and Desmond, Gods bless them, dancing together, and Desmond leans in and kisses her, just once, timidly, and then she pulls him in and kisses him again and again and again.

Talyn slides one hand up, along my side, and my whole stomach tingles with a thousand tiny lightning bursts. "Gods," he says. "You're so beautiful it hurts."

My heart leaps into my throat. I should go. I should walk away now before this goes any further, chalk it up to a moment of weakness, get back on mission. But I love the way his eyes look, the way his hand feels on my back, the way his hips press into mine. "Talyn," I whisper, and then I lean forward and my lips brush against his and my whole body burns and I'm doing this, I'm really doing this, I—

Then the chorus of the song hits as the singer's voice rises to a mournful wail, and I suddenly remember exactly where I've heard it. It was from Sera. She was singing it to herself on that night, that last night, as we rode up to the manor, singing softly under her breath as we sat cramped in the back of the wagon. Whispers had hushed her, and she'd said it was just to keep herself calm, and then—

The image floods my mind, violent, invasive, the image that I spent so much effort forcing myself to forget, the image that's the absolute last thing I ever want to think about: Sera lying on the floor of Von Clair's study, blood bubbling out of her cracked lips, sobbing as the flames envelop her.

I jerk away like I've been stung, and I can feel my stomach drop and my heart slam against my ribs and the whole world throbs red at the edges, like it's pulsing with blood. My breath feels ragged, my knees weak. No no no. This can't happen. Not here.

"Alayne?" Talyn asks. "Are you all right?"

"I'm fine," I stammer, and just getting those words out feels like forcing hot coals through my throat. My entire body wants to collapse in a heap of panic. I can feel the faces all around me, feel the heat of their eyes, and the lights are spinning, and the music is getting louder and louder and louder, and I wobble on my feet and all I can see is Sera's face. "Fresh air," I choke out as I shove past a baffled Talyn. "Need fresh air."

It's a blur from there. I fly out of the hall, my dress flaring behind me like a cape, my body lost to me. I stagger into the night, but there are people outside, too, lovers walking hand in hand in the quad, so I rush aside, off campus, into the forests to the north. I keep running until the lights of the campus have faded to a faint glow, until the music and the chatter are just a distant murmur. Then and only then do I collapse onto my knees in the fresh snow, slumping against a tree's thick trunk.

"Keep it together," I whisper, "come on," but Gods, my heart is going to explode, and my breath is trapped in my lungs and I can't stop shaking, I can't stop shaking. I dig my bare hands into the snow, and it's cold, so cold it hurts, but that pain is something I can latch on to, something I can use to drag myself back into the world.

Let your thoughts go. Take in only what you feel.

The shivering wind against my face.

The smell of the trees, rich cedar, smoky and deep.

The freezing pain in my hands, sharp and real.

I anchor myself in that, and bit by bit, I'm able to get myself together, to still my heart, to find my breath. I push Sera back down, down into the depths, push the past into the past. I regroup and collect.

I'm a Revenant. I'm a girl on a mission. I'm Alayne Dewinter. I can do this. I can do this.

I stand up, exhaling sharply, my breath hanging in a white mist in front of me. Gods. Look at me. All alone in the woods, my beautiful dress caked in frost and dirt, my hands blue and raw from the cold, my cheeks streaked with tears. I look like a ghost from a horror story, a vengeful spirit who haunts the night. I actually laugh as I pull myself up to my feet.

That's when I realize I'm wrong. I might look like an absolute mess, but I'm not alone.

There are three of them. Three figures, boys, I think, wearing long black robes that turn them into dark silhouettes. They stand together in a line maybe thirty feet away, silent, eerie, just staring at me in the pale moonlight. A chill runs down my spine as I press myself back against the tree. I blink, trying to make out their faces, but then I realize I can't because they're wearing masks, pale faceless white, featureless save the eyeholes.

"Can I help you?" I call out, even as I steel myself.

The two boys on the side look to the one in the middle for guidance. He doesn't say anything. He just steps forward, drawing his hands from his robes, hands holding a pair of golden razor-sharp Loci. I suck in my breath. Marius might have his face hidden behind a mask, but I'd recognize those stags' heads anywhere. The other boys take note and draw their Loci, too.

Gritting my teeth, I reach down to my hips to grab my own.

And find only the smooth cloth of my dress.

Oh, *no.*

Chapter 27

Now

"Hold on, now. Don't do anything rash," I say, raising my hands, even as I know it's not going to work. If it were just him, I might try to rush him, a surprise attack, but there's no way I can take three of them, not without my Loci. I'm completely vulnerable, a good mile from anyone else. How could I have been so stupid? "Please, Marius. Let's talk this over."

The boy on Marius's right, the shortest of the three, turns to him with concern. "She knows your name," he whispers urgently through his mask. I can't recognize his voice, but I'm guessing he's one of Marius's Vanguard cronies. "I thought she wasn't supposed to know who we are!"

Marius shrugs. "Plans change." He raises one of his Loci, pointing its tip right at me. "Isn't that right, Dewinter?"

"I don't know what you mean, Marius," I reply, but all I'm doing is stalling for time, buying myself seconds to think. I scan around for anything I can use as a weapon, for anywhere to hide, anywhere to run.

Marius steps forward, closing the gap, and his shadows follow. "Well, for one thing, I *planned* to win the First Challenge," he growls. "I *planned* to make my father proud. I *planned* to graduate from Blackwater with my best friend Dean!" His hands go tight as he raises his Loci into a carving stance. "You took that from me. And now you're going to pay."

Even through the mask, I can see the second he enters the Null, as his eyes flicker into the purple-black starscape. If I had my Loci, I'd go with him, try to carve a counter, attack first, something. But all I can do is hurl myself to the side, and not a second too soon because his hand weaves in a blur and a concussive blast of force shoots out of him, a lance of wind that slams into the tree where I'd just been standing hard enough to shatter the trunk and send wood chips flying everywhere, hard enough that it would've crushed me to a pulp.

Oh, Gods. These boys aren't just here to hurt me. They're here to *kill.*

I scramble to my feet, panting, and try to run for it, but it's impossible in this godsdamned dress. I trip over my own feet, and I can hear the other boys laughing as they attack, like this is all just some big game. A pillar of crumbling earth shoots up in front of me like a sprouting tree, sending me tumbling onto my back, and vines of grass slither out from beneath the snow, lashing around my wrists and pinning me down. I struggle as hard as I can, kicking and flailing and tugging so hard it rips into my skin, but what can I even do? It's three Wizards against one, and without my Loci, I'm no stronger than a Humble.

I whip my head around to see them, the three of them, looming over me like giants. The tallest one has his Loci raised, twirling it slowly, controlling the vines binding me down with a smile of sadistic glee. I haven't felt like this since that night my parents died, so powerless and pathetic. It can't end like this. It can't.

The shorter boy looks to Marius, and even through his mask I can hear the breathless, gasping excitement in his voice. "Do it," he says. "Kill the bitch!" The third boy, the tall one, nods in agreement. Marius kneels over me, pressing the tip of his Loci to my throat. I feel the sting as it draws blood, and I can feel him breathing hard, even through his mask.

I can see his eyes through the slits, see the raw hatred in them, the total lack of empathy or fear. He's done this before. I'm sure of it.

"Marius," I whisper.

"I told you you'd regret crossing me," he says, and draws his Loci back.

But he never stabs it in, because right then, the sky erupts above us.

The boys fall back, hands over their eyes, and I wince and strain. Something's happened, something magical. There's an orb hanging overhead, maybe fifteen feet in the air, a whirling, writhing ball of fire like a miniature sun, bright enough to turn night into day, hot enough that it makes the snow around me sizzle and melt. "What is *that*?" one of the boys yells, and now I see something they don't, something coming from behind them. A figure racing through the woods with hands outstretched. A boy in a burnt-red suit, the jacket flaring out behind him like a cape, a boy with wild hair and wilder eyes, streaking toward us like a hurled blade.

Talyn.

"Get away from her!" he growls, his voice reverberating like a thunderclap. With every stride he takes, the ground rumbles beneath his feet, and the air around him wavers like a slick of oil on a lake's surface. His eyes burn with the dark fire of the Null starscape, but what really stands out are his arms. His jacket sleeves are rolled up and I can see those runic symbols he always has, the intricate painted bands that entwine his forearms and biceps. But they're not just painted bands anymore. They're glowing now, glowing hot and bright with an impossible colored light, dazzling blue and blinding gold and fiery red. It's like he has rivulets of energy surging along his arms, like he has raw power burning through his veins. It's like the Godsblood tattoo on my wrist but all over his body. It's like he's covered in magic itself.

The three Vanguard boys swivel around, raising their Loci, but they've been caught off guard. Talyn's left hand flares out, fingers weaving through the air like he's drawing with them, and his hand is enveloped in the rapid, dizzying blur of someone carving a Glyph. A whip of light streaks out, a searing horizontal lash like a slashing blade. The smaller boy hurls himself aside, but his tall friend isn't so lucky. He lets out a choked gurgle as it cuts through his throat, so deep his head lolls down his back like a puppet's, his gaping neck stump cauterized a sizzling black.

The vines binding me wither and vanish, and I scramble back as the boy's body crumples to the ground. Talyn swivels toward the short boy, but Marius is ready. He drops low in a roll, passing right under the whip, and his Loci cuts through the air as he hurls back a Glyph of his own.

A jagged disk of crystal, clear as glass and sharp as a dagger, hurtles out from Marius, spinning like a top as it shoots at Talyn. He tries to dodge, but he's too slow. The disk catches him right in the arm and rips it clean open, a deep cut that runs from his shoulder down to his elbow. Talyn falls to his knees with a pained hiss, and the light he's been emanating instantly fades, his eyes flickering back to their usual soft brown.

The shorter Vanguard boy leaps up, raising his Loci at the wounded Talyn, eager to finish him off, but before he can, I grab a heavy rock and smash it into the back of his head, a hit so hard I can actually hear the wet crack of his skull shattering. He falls forward, face-first into the snow, and lies still, his bright-red blood forming a halo around his head in the crisp white snow. He's not getting up again.

"Alayne!" Talyn shouts through gritted teeth. "Behind you!"

I swivel, expecting to see Marius geared up for another attack, but instead he's running, already vanishing off into the trees. Of course. His three-on-one ambush just turned into a one-on-two skirmish, and he has no interest in a fair fight. The angry animal within me wants to run him down, to smash him into the dirt and make him pay. But then I turn and see Talyn, breathing hard, clutching one hand over his wound as dark crimson streaks down between his fingers. His breath is ragged, his eyes bleary, the color fading from his face as he bleeds.

I rush over to him, hunkering by his side. I reach down, tear off a long scrap of my dress and wrap it around his arm, stemming the bleeding as best I can. He cranes his head toward me, chest rising and falling. "Was... was that...?"

"Marius Madison," I reply, and loop his arm around my shoulder. "Come on. We need to get you stitched up."

His nostrils flare, and I can see him want to argue and see the moment he decides not to. He nods instead, and I help him up to his feet. I can barely even process what happened out here. Questions race through my head faster than my heart thunders in my chest. But the one thing I know with certainty is that we need to get out of here before anyone else sees us. So with Talyn's arm draped around my shoulder, the two of us stagger back to campus, away from this forest grove, away from this bloody battlefield, away from the two bodies lying still in the snow.

CHAPTER 28

Then

I am nine when I learn to heal.

The injury's my fault, but so are most of my injuries. I was scampering around in one of the junk lots by our warehouse base when I tore my leg open on a long, rusty nail. Sera found me lying there screaming and brought me in, where Whispers, with some annoyance, had me lie down on a long wooden bench. It's hardly my first injury, so I know what to expect from the Revenant medic: the harsh sting of alcohol, the lingering ache of stitches, the scratch of the cloth bandages I have to wear for days.

But the medic doesn't come. Instead, Pavel lumbers over, flanked by a pair of soldiers, and wearily pulls up a chair alongside me. "Gods," he moans, "what have I done to deserve this?"

I crane my head up at him, and I'm curious enough that I forget, momentarily, how much my leg hurts. I've been studying with Pavel for about six months now, and my feelings about him are complicated. I appreciate having a mentor who can guide me safely in the Null, who can teach me how to hold a Loci and how to carve a Glyph. I'm less happy that this mentor is a surly, mean wreck who smells like the floor of a tavern. "What are you doing here?" I ask.

"Fixing your damn leg, you ungrateful brat," he grumbles. He holds out a hand behind his back, and one of the soldiers hands him his Loci, a pair of gnarled iron wands that we snagged when we rescued him from the labor camp. The other soldier draws his sword, pressing its point squarely at the base of Pavel's spine, to which Pavel just rolls his eyes. I understand his frustration. He's been with us long enough that it feels like he's part of our group, even if he is still technically a prisoner. But Whispers was clear that "a Wizard is always a Wizard," and so he's allowed his Loci only at sword point.

"What are you going to do?" I wince preemptively.

But there's no need. Pavel takes my shin with one broad, calloused hand, and raises a Loci with the other. His eyes flicker purple as he slips into the Null, and before I can think to join him, his hand blurs through the air. For someone so unkempt and bumbling, Pavel carves with exceptional grace, Loci flitting through the air like a hummingbird, and in seconds there's a soft green glow around his hand, the black hairs on the back sticking straight up. The air smells of freshly cut grass and morning dew. Pavel squeezes gently, and I feel a delicate tingling, like a thousand petals just barely grazing my skin.

And then before my eyes, my cut mends. It's like I'm watching days of healing happen in seconds. The skin knits back together like drops of quicksilver, the blood drying and fading, the wound scabbing and the scab fading away, just like that. Pavel slips back into the Real, the tiniest hint of a satisfied smile creasing his beard as the soldier takes the Loci back. "There," he says. "Don't put too much strain on it for a day, and it'll be fine."

I gape at my leg in disbelief. I haven't seen a healing Glyph in years, not since before my parents died. I've forgotten what healing magic looks like, what it feels like.

I've spent years thinking of magic as dangerous, destructive, a tool of war and oppression. I've forgotten all of the wonderful things it can do. I've forgotten magic can be *good*.

Pavel picks up on my reaction. "What is it, kid? Never seen a healing Glyph before?"

"Not for a very long time," I say, running my hand along the smooth skin where just minutes ago there was a long, nasty wound.

"Was it hard to do?"

"Not particularly." Pavel shrugs. "At least, not for cuts and scrapes."

I think about every injury I've ever had, every scratch and scrape and burn, about the itchy cast I had to wear for months when I broke my arm, about the burn scar on my leg that hurts to this day. All of those could have been healed just like that. It's not even *difficult*. "Why?" I demand. "Why don't Wizards heal everyone?"

Pavel snorts. "Why? Because they don't want to."

I shove his shoulder, hard, and I know it's not fair to take my anger out on him, but on the other hand, I'm *really* angry. "But that's bullshit! Think about how many people are hurt and sick and wounded out there!" I think of the Revenants brought in with their limbs blown off, with their eyes leaking out of their skulls, with their heads caved in. I think of the beggars in the streets with their ribs jutting out of their skin, of the children huddling in alleys with their bodies covered in boils. "If Wizards can do this, why don't they heal everyone? Why do so many people suffer?"

Pavel stares at me, surprised, and then shakes his head with a low, weary laugh. "Oh, kid. I don't even know where to begin. You're sitting here in a Revenant base, but you're still spouting the Wizard party line." He slides the chair closer, and when he talks, his voice is low, somber, sincere. "Look. It's like this. The Wizards want the Humbles to believe in scarcity, in limited resources, in a brutal world that's cold and harsh and mean. They need Humbles to believe that without their Wizardly gifts, they'd all die in chaos and poverty. They need Humbles to be dependent. But that means the Humbles have to suffer, and suffer constantly, because if they didn't suffer, well, they might not need the Wizards that much. They might start getting ideas in their heads like you lot here. They might start asking questions like, well, like the ones you just asked." He blinks, his eyes bloodshot and tired, the eyes of a man decades older. "The Wizards need you to believe that their cruelty is necessary, that their cruelty is inevitable, that their cruelty is just the way the world is."

"But it's a lie."

"It's a lie," Pavel repeats. "Their cruelty isn't a consequence. Their cruelty is the whole point."

I slump back against the bench, because, Gods, what a terrible, broken world, what a horrific time to just be alive. I blink, trying to fight off tears, and I expect Pavel to say something sarcastic or dismissive, but instead, he just reaches out and gently pats my shoulder. "You want to do something about it?" he asks, and his voice is the kindest I've ever heard it. "Fine. Scrap our lesson for tomorrow. No more learning cubes of light.

"Instead... I'll teach you to heal."

CHAPTER 29

Now

I've already decided I'm going to fix Talyn up by the time we stagger onto campus, but there's a bunch of Nethros on the steps of our dorm. So instead we shuffle to the Order of Zartan, to Talyn's room. Here we get my first lucky break of the night: everyone out in the quad is so caught up in their own festivities and dramas, they don't notice the two of us stumbling forward, arms around each other's shoulders, caked in dirt and blood and snow like we've just come from a battle.

The Order of Zartan is laid out exactly like the Order of Nethro but with a distinctly different aesthetic. Instead of moody blacks and crimson, this place is all lavish yellow and green, filigreed archways and jeweled doorknobs. Ornate statues of famous Zartans gaze at us from the alcoves, portly merchants and bushy-haired senators. Under their watchful emerald eyes, I help Talyn through the empty common area and up to his room, and only when his door is shut does he finally speak.

"Keshta za'n truk del mastor ne zanfas!" he growls, falling hard onto his bed, and I don't speak Xintari but I'm pretty certain he just said a whole lot of curse words. "What the *hell* was that?"

"Our famous Marovian hospitality," I reply, hunkering down to inspect his arm. My makeshift bandage stemmed the bleeding, at least a little, but the wound looks bad, a jagged rift dotted with dozens of little shards of crystal shrapnel. "I can heal this, I think. But I'm going to need you to take your shirt off."

Even like this, laid out bleeding, he can't help but laugh. "I'll be honest, Alayne, I'd hoped to hear you say those words tonight, but this wasn't really what I had in mind."

I roll my eyes. "Less flirting, more healing. Seriously. Shirt off."

He shrugs out of his jacket, but when the time comes to unbutton his shirt, he reaches up and then drops his hand with a wince. "I can't. Genuinely. Hurts too much."

"Right. Slide over." I take a seat on the bed next to him and lean over, undoing his fancy dress shirt. I feel his chest rise and fall under my touch, feel the heat radiating off him. With the last button undone, I pull it off him, and my fingers accidentally graze his bare chest, and I can see his whole body shudder, just a little, at the touch. "Sorry."

"Don't apologize," he says. His bare chest rises and falls with each breath, and mine stops in my throat. His body is like his arms, lean but taut, and I can make out the firm muscles of his stomach, the soft black hairs dotting his chest, the curve of his hip bones as they slip down into his pants.

Right. The wound. Talyn slides over, so I can clearly see his arm. "We're going to need to get all the little pieces of crystal out first. If I heal you now, it'll seal them in and, well, I don't think that'll be good."

"This is *exactly* how I wanted the night to end." He reaches around the side of his bed and pulls out a small glass bottle full of a delicate amber liquid. "Xintari liquor," he explains. "I was saving it for a special occasion."

"It'll make a good disinfectant," I nod. "Clever thinking."

He blinks at me. "No, I just wanted to drink it." He pops the cork with his teeth, takes a long swig, and then hands it to me. "But sure. Disinfectant sounds good."

"This might sting a little." I pour it onto the wound, and he hisses through gritted teeth, gripping the bed frame so hard I think it's going to shatter. With the cut cleaned, I can make out the shrapnel clearly, and I pull out the biggest piece of crystal. It's a brittle, clear blue, curved like a fishhook, jagged on the end and cold as ice. "Damn. That was a hell of a Glyph Marius hit you with. This wasn't just meant to hurt you, it was meant to kill."

Talyn stares up at the ceiling, nostrils flaring. "You're sure it was Marius?" I nod. "Good."

"Why's that good?"

"If it was just some random Vanguard stooge, I'd worry he'd rat us out for killing his two friends," he replies. I pull another shard out, this one sharp at both tips, and I can feel him struggling not to react. "But Marius? Marius'll keep his mouth shut."

"What makes you so sure?"

"The son of the Senate's Grandmaster trying to kill a prince of the Xintari Kingdom? That's the sort of thing wars are fought over. The sort of thing sons are disowned to rectify." He shrugs and then winces. "He'll keep it a secret because he can't risk the fallout."

"And we'll keep the secret, because, well, murder." Two more shards out, plinking gently into a little metal bowl. "So we all just keep acting like nothing ever happened. I suppose that's one less thing to worry about."

"Until he tries to kill us again," he says. "And next time, he'll be a lot more careful."

"A problem for another day." I pull out the last shard and use the scrap of my dress to mop up the thin trickle of blood running down to his wrist. "You didn't have to come for me, you know."

"Yes," he says, closing his eyes. "I did."

My breath feels heavy, my stomach fluttering. It's like there's something in the air, something hungry and desperate clinging to our skin, like it's sweltering hot on this midwinter night. I take his arm in mine, and that's when I realize I still don't have my Loci. "Shit."

"You can borrow mine," he says, one step ahead. "In the desk, bottom drawer."

I slide it open and take them out, a pair of daggers with golden blades and sapphire-studded handles. They're the fanciest Loci I've ever held, but right now, that's not what's on my mind. "You didn't have them," I say, which I'd suspected but still can't entirely believe. "Back there in the snow. You carved those Glyphs with your *bare hands.* How the hell did you—"

Talyn cuts me off with a weary sigh. "Not now. Please. Tonight's been hard enough."

"All right," I say, even though the curiosity is killing me. Instead, I settle back onto the bed next to him, gently placing one hand on the wound and raising his Loci with the other. With a deep breath, I slip into the Null and carve the circular Life Base and the intersecting diamonds of the Growth Form. It's a Glyph I've always struggled with, the form requiring a delicate weaving precision, but it works well enough now. My hand glows a warm green, and Talyn exhales with relief as his pain fades. When I pull it away, the wound looks much better. It's not all the way healed, because I'm nowhere near that good, but I've added at least a week of healing to it. That's something.

Talyn seems to agree, because he slides back up against the headrest, running his fingers along the freshly healed cut. "Well, that's a first," he says.

"You've never had someone heal you?"

His brown eyes meet mine, seeing right into me. "I've never been hurt enough to need it."

The moment is too intense, his gaze too intimate. I can't take it. I swallow deeply, rising to go. "I should get back to my room. We both need to r—"

His hand shoots out, grabbing my wrist. "You bashed that boy's skull in. Killed him like it was nothing."

His grip is tight, but I don't fight it. "You killed the other one."

"I've killed before."

"I have, too."

"Is that so?" he asks, eyebrow cocked. "Who *are* you?"

"I'm a girl who needs to win," I respond, and I know that I ought to go now but instead I stay, I let him keep his hand on my wrist, and when he pulls me closer, I let him, falling forward onto the bed, onto him. I'm wildly off the mission here, so far off the plan it might as well not exist. But I barely care. All I can think about is how his bare skin feels against me, the steady rising and falling of his chest under mine, the way our faces are so close I can practically taste him.

"Gods," he whispers. "I've studied diplomacy under the greatest scholars of the kingdom. I've matched wits with tacticians and philosophers. I've stared the most gifted liars in the world in the eye and called their bluff. And despite all that, you're the one person I've met who I just cannot figure out."

"Is that why you followed me tonight? Because you wanted to figure me out?"

"No," he says, his lips curling into the slightest hint of a smile. "I followed you because I was hoping to get that kiss."

And then I can't take it anymore, can't take being Alayne or a Revenant, can't hold back the burning inside me. I lean forward and kiss him, long and deep, a kiss that's desperate and powerful and vulnerable all at once. He kisses me back, his good hand on the base of my spine, pulling me down, my fingertips run along his side, grazing that taut muscle, savoring the slight shiver that runs through him, soaking in his smell of smoke and cardamom.

He pulls away, forehead pressed against mine. "Are you sure you want this?" he asks.

"Gods, yes," I reply, and kiss him again. His hands slide my dress down as he kisses my neck, my collarbone, the base of my throat, as I grasp along him and pull the sheet over us. As the snow gently frosts against the window, as the candles sway and burn, I kiss Talyn and he kisses me. For one night, for one night at least, I forget it all, forget the Revenants, forget the cause, forget my worries and fear and pain. For one night, I just feel.

It's more than I could have asked for.

CHAPTER 30

Now

I wake the next morning to the bright rays of the sun, the kind of waking where you just lie there for a good long minute as your brain realizes no, it wasn't a dream. It feels like it *should* have been a dream; the idea that I would sleep with anyone at Blackwater, much less a prince, is inconceivable. But no, it was definitely real. The sun is warm on my skin. The ceiling above me is a vibrant gold. And I'm lying naked under a soft fur blanket in Prince Talyn Ravensgale IV's bed.

I sit up slowly, even as a part of me just wants to burrow deep under the blanket and never come out. Talyn sits nude at his desk, his back to me, and I really wish he didn't look so good. He must hear me stir, because he cranes his head back. "Morning."

"Hi," I say, instinctively blushing and pulling the blanket up to cover myself, and I see the corner of his mouth twitch into a tiny smile.

"How're you feeling?"

"I'm good," I say, and as the words leave my lips, I realize it's the truth. I *do* feel good. Really good. My body feels more relaxed than it's been in years, like it's filled with light, the tips of my fingers and toes still tingling. Talyn isn't my first. That was Grenn back in the Revenants' camp.

But it had been different with Grenn, fumbling, quick, a union born more out of loneliness and desperation than real connection. It hadn't been bad, but it hadn't been like this. If I close my eyes, I can still feel Talyn's lips on my neck, his hands running along my side, his breath, his touch.

I clear my throat, pulling myself back into the moment. "How're you?"

"Your healing Glyph worked wonders." He raises his arm, showing me his bicep, where the wound has been replaced with a soft white stretch of scar. "No Enforcers have come smashing down my door. And the most fascinating girl I've ever met is lying naked in my bed. So all in all, I'd say I'm doing very well."

I snort. "You've already slept with me. You don't have to flirt anymore."

His eyes twinkle with mischief. "Oh, the flirting is just beginning."

"And here I thought I'd figured out a way to make you stop," I say, and then I blink because for the first time I notice that he's not *just* sitting naked at his desk. A half dozen jars rest on the desk's surface, ornate ceramic containers engraved with runic shapes, locked tight with thin silver chains. The jar closest to him is open, and I crane my head to look inside where I see... sand, I think? But the prettiest sand I've ever seen, a sand that's a rich dark purple flecked with thousands of points of sparkling gold, a sand that shines like the night sky. "What are you doing?"

The playfulness fades from his eyes, replaced by something else, something far harder to read. "Now that's a complicated question."

"Is it?"

With a heavy breath, he presses two fingers into the jar, just barely skimming the surface. When they come out, they glisten purple with that strange, beautiful sand, and he very delicately runs them down his arm, leaving a spiraled trail in their wake. So that's how he applies those runes.

"I could tell you that I'm just painting my arms in the traditional Xintari style. Or I could do something far more reckless." He trails his fingertips down to the inside of his wrist, weaving the trail around it like a bracelet. For just one second it glows bright, a soft pulse of power. "I could tell you the truth."

The air between us is charged again, a tension I can feel in my bones. We already crossed one threshold last night, but there's another still standing, the most guarded of all. I've still got my secrets from him. And he has his from me. "I suspect we've already crossed the point of recklessness," I say at last.

"That we have," he replies, finishing one arm and starting on the other. "I imagine you've already figured out that my magic is different from yours."

"You don't use Loci," I say, remembering the way he cut through the air with his hands. "The ones in your drawer, that you use in class..."

"A deception, to fool the Marovians." He closes the lid on the purple jar and opens another, this one filled with a dust that burns red like the hottest sunset. "I *can* use Loci. But I don't need them. And I don't have a Godsmark, either."

"Oh. Right." I hadn't thought to check his body because I was distracted by... his body... but he's right. There's not a tattoo on him. "So your magic comes from that dust?"

He nods, even as he delicately traces a spiral onto the back of his hand. "If you Marovian Wizards are to be believed, your Gods honor you with the gift of their blood, that it may run through your veins and grant you their power. But in the kingdom, things are different." His jaw tightens. When he speaks, his voice is low, guarded, barely above a whisper. "Our Gods live deep below the ground, in a vast palace at the heart of the earth. They whisper to us in our dreams, gift us with the flow of water, with the sprouting of trees, with sparkling gems and precious gold."

He finishes his hand and screws the jar's lid back on. "And they gift us with *this*."

"Magic dust."

"Gods' Ash," he corrects. "The most powerful element on earth, stronger than any blade, wilder than any hurricane." He slides the jar back along with the others. "At the center of the kingdom is Mount Xanrea, a great volcano that reaches into the depths of the world, down to the lands of the Gods themselves. Through that mountain, the Gods bless the people of the Kingdom with their offering of ash."

"So it's like Godsblood, but... on the outside?" I try to sound merely curious, even though my mind is reeling at the possibilities. "You put the ash on your skin, and then you can slip into the Null? And it just comes out of this mountain?"

"No." He shakes his head. "It doesn't just 'come out.' Gathering it requires a descent into the mountain's depths, a treacherous climb down a sheer wall of rock, over boiling pools and molten stone. Making that climb is a rite of passage for all royals when we turn sixteen. Some return in glory, with a bounty of ash, an offering for the kingdom. Others die." He swallows hard, staring down at his hands. "And some, well, some are too cowardly to even make the climb."

"Talyn... ?"

He looks back at me with a smile that radiates pain. "When my day came, when it was my turn to descend into Xanrea, I failed. I don't know why. I've fought, I've killed, I've stared death in the eye and laughed. But looking down into that darkness, into that smoke and ash and heat... I couldn't bring myself to do it. I couldn't will my body to move. I stood there for an hour, and then I gave up and fled. The shame in my father's eyes..." He turns back to the ash with a heavy sigh. "I lied to you, Alayne. The night we met. It's not an honor for me to be here. It's a punishment. A humiliation." He arches back in his seat, dropping his voice to make it old and brittle, his father's voice. *"If you can't honor our Gods, if you're not worthy of our ways, why don't you go live with the heathens, hmm? See how you like it there!"*

There's so much to take in here, I don't know where to begin. "I'm sorry, Talyn. . . ."

He clears his throat, and all at once he's back, the cocky, smiling prince I've seen all this time. "Don't be sorry. In every setback, there lies opportunity. And I've found it here. With you."

"Oh?"

"My father loathes the Marovians, but he hates Grandmaster Madison most of all. He thinks of Madison as a petty tyrant, a detestable brute who insulted him when they met, who dared to threaten our kingdom with war if we didn't open up to his trade deal. When I realized his son was here, among us, I antagonized him just on principle. But you . . . you've shown me the way." His teeth shine a dazzling white as he grins. "If Marius and his Vanguards lose the Great Game to a Xintari, it'll be a profound humiliation, both for him and Grandmaster Madison. They'll both be shamed publicly, their power and status undermined. And I'll be able to return home in glory."

"That's what this is about," I say with dawning realization. He's not just here as an observer or a diplomat. He's playing his own game, working his own mission. Everything he's done, every choice he's made, every word he's said, is in service of this, of regaining his status, of advancing in his own kingdom. Like everyone else here, he's climbing a ladder, even if it's an entirely different one.

I don't know how to process it. My mind is reeling with too many conflicting thoughts and emotions, a tempest of contradictions. There's too much to consider, too many layers of strategy and nuance. "Is that why you talked to me? Why you became my friend? Why you kissed me?" I ask, trying to get my bearings. "Because you knew I hated Madison, too?"

He rises and crosses over to sit next to me on the bed, gently taking my hand in his. "At first, yes," he says. "But then I got to know you, Alayne. I got to see the real you—fierce and brilliant and driven, full of fire and fury." He smiles now, a real smile. "I like you, Alayne. And I don't like most people."

"So what does that make us?" I ask, and I'm not even sure what I want the answer to be. "Allies? Friends?"

He raises my hand to his lips and kisses it. "Believe it or not, I don't normally do this with my allies." He laughs. "And only occasionally with my friends."

"Seriously," I say, even though I'm fighting back a smile.

He nods. "Look. I'm not going to claim this is simple, and I'm not going to make promises I can't keep. I'm here for myself, and I'm pretty sure you are, too. We're both ambitious, we've both got our own agendas, and we both badly need to win this game. Right now, we stand together, but there will come a day when we find ourselves in each other's paths. We both know how the world works."

The world *shouldn't* work that way, but now's not the time for that. "But until that day comes . . . ?"

"Until that day comes, I'd like to be your ally, and your friend." He runs a hand through my hair and leans forward, his lips almost touching mine, his breath soft against me. "And maybe just a bit more. If you'll have me, that is."

I feel like I should chafe at his honesty, that I should be wary of someone so willing to admit his agenda is purely his own. But the truth is, it's a relief. Because it's so much easier if our default is at a remove, if the walls are built in, if I can have his touch, his warmth, without having to bare who I really am, without having to worry about hurting him. We can just be allies, friends, occasional lovers, brought together by a fleeting shared cause. And that can be enough.

"I'll have you," I reply, and he leans in to kiss me for one long, intoxicating minute, and then he pulls away, forehead resting against mine.

"Now. It's almost time for morning classes, which means I need to get dressed. And as much as it pains me to say so, you do, too." He leans in again, kissing me just barely, an afterimage ghosting on my lips. "Will I see you again soon?"

Now it's my turn to kiss him. "It's a promise."

CHAPTER 31

Now

Classes are a blur. I try to focus, I do, but memories of last night keep racing through my mind. The way Talyn looked at me when we danced. The fury in his eyes as he saved me from the Vanguards. The way his hands slid down my side, the caress of his lips on my skin. Gods, what have I gotten myself into?

Finally, the afternoon rolls around, and I make my way to the library, because if there's one thing I can force myself to do it's research this Maze of Martyrs and how I'm going to beat the other Orders at it. I'd hoped to do it alone, because I'm still not quite myself, but a voice calls my name as I walk across the quad.

"Alayne. Alayne. *Alayne!*" I turn to see Fyl, bounding across the grass toward me with an enormous grin on her face. Right. There's no avoiding this.

"Fyl," I reply. "I'm guessing you had a good time at Founders' Day?"

"Oh, well, not a big deal, but Desmond and I are dating now. So, that happened." She bounces up and down, giddy with glee, and I have to admit it's infectious. "It was amazing, Alayne! Perfect! We danced and we kissed and then we took a long walk and he said I was beautiful and then we kissed again in the snow and ahhhhh! It was the best night ever!"

"I told you he liked you." I grin. "Good for you two."

"Thanks," she says, and then leans in close with a conspiratorial waggle of her eyebrows. "How about you, though? I couldn't help but notice that you and Prince Broody Eyes vanished at the same time...."

"What? No. That was a—we didn't—I mean—" I try, but my cheeks flush and that's all the confirmation she needs. She clasps a hand over her mouth to stifle a squeal, and I *shhh* her as intensely as I can. "Don't tell anyone! Seriously."

"All right. It's our secret. Our completely amazing secret." She shakes her head. "You're going to have to tell me all the details. You know that, right?"

"Maybe later," I say, even though there's no way I'm ever giving her even half the details. "Right now, I need to get in there and start preparing for this Maze of Martyrs."

"Right. Of course. Can't stop our winning streak. You do whatever you have to do." She turns to walk away, then stops, glancing back at me a little uncertainly. "And...you know. When you're choosing your team to go into the maze, if you want me to join you, I'd be honored. Not that you have to pick me, of course, pick whoever you think will be best. But, if you do want me then, I'll—"

"Fyl," I cut in. "Of course I'll pick you. There's no one I'd rather have by my side."

She claps her hands with glee. "Thank you. Seriously. To know that someone like you believes in me...I don't know. I'd never have expected it." She starts to go, then stops, and when she looks back, there's more on her face than just joy. There's something else, something serious, emotional. She bites her lip, hesitating, then finally speaks. "Alayne, can I tell you something? Something that might sound a little strange?"

"All right."

"When I saw you on the ferry, standing all by yourself, do you know the real reason I came up to you? It's because I had this…this feeling. Like you were important. Like my destiny was somehow tied up in yours. Like talking to you would change my life forever." Her eyes are down, unable to meet mine, and I've never seen her so humble. "I know that sounds delusional, but I think there really was something there. You're the best friend I've ever had, Alayne. I'm so glad I met you."

I feel a surge of conflicting emotions so strong I almost have to sit down. Because of course there's a part of me that warms at her words. I like Fyl, genuinely like her, and there is a part of me that wants her to be happy, that wants her to find the success and love and confidence she's been seeking. There's a part of me, a big part, that really sees her as a friend.

But she's not my friend, not really. She's *Alayne's* friend. She has no idea who I really am. She has no idea how much I've been manipulating her, no idea the web of deception I've spun, no idea that every step we take on this journey is to set me up to destroy her entire world. Fyl might be Alayne's friend, but she's Alka's enemy, and sooner or later I know the veil will fall and the truth will come out and then what? She'll be horrified. She'll be devastated. And this entire friendship will crumble to ash.

If anyone stands between you and our cause, cut them down.

No. Maybe it doesn't have to be like that. Maybe there's another way, a better way. Whispers would've had me kill Marlena, but I didn't and look where that got me. Maybe I can do something similar with Fyl, with Desmond, with Tish and Zigmund. They might be Wizards, but they're good people. Maybe this doesn't have to end in fire and blood. Maybe I could show them the way.

"Alayne?" she asks. "Are you all right?"

I clear my throat. "Sorry. Just got a little distracted. I'm so glad I met you, too." I shuffle to the library awkwardly. "I should go now. Crack the maze and all that. But you go have a good day." Then I smile. "Say hi to Desmond for me."

"Of course," she replies, and then walks off, still practically glowing.

It's decided, then. I'll find a way to save her, too. I'll have to.

Marlena is waiting for me at our usual table in the back. She glances up at me as I approach, and the sight of her feels sobering, clarifying. Nothing's felt real since I sank into Talyn's arms, but seeing her pulls me back to reality, to my mission, to who I really am.

She doesn't look any more well rested than she had last night. If anything, she looks even more tired. The dense tomes spread out before her explain why. I slide onto the bench opposite her with an apologetic shrug. "Marlena, have you been researching the maze all day? I'm sorry...."

"Don't apologize. I want us to win, and I'll do whatever it takes." Her amber eyes flit up to mine, thoughtful, scrutinizing. "Are *you* all right?"

"Me? Why wouldn't I be?"

"You ran out last night looking distressed," she says, and I can't tell if she's concerned or suspicious or...something else. "Right after you danced with the prince."

"Oh. That." I shift uncomfortably in my chair. I would really like to stop answering questions about my night. "That was nothing. I just needed some fresh air."

Her voice drops to a whisper. "And I suppose you had nothing to do with the two Vanguard boys who were found murdered in the woods?"

The room suddenly goes very cold. "I don't know what you're talking about," I say, and we both know it's a lie. Her gaze bores through mine, and I feel a deep uncertainty twist my stomach. Even after everything she shared with me, there are moments like these when I can't read her, when I can't tell what's really dancing behind those intelligent eyes. "Listen. I know this whole situation is very dangerous. If you want to pull out, to protect yourself, then you can. I won't tell anyone, I promise."

Her forehead crinkles with exasperation. "You misunderstand. I'm not worried about me. I'm worried about *you*." She leans across the table, her voice so low I can barely hear it. "I don't know what you're mixed up in or what happened last night. I just know things are moving fast. Aberdeen is watching you like a hawk, and the Vanguards are plotting something. You need to be careful, Alayne. You can't afford to slip up. Not now. Not when we're so close."

"I'm not going to slip up," I whisper back. In another context, I'd bristle at having to defend myself, but I can see the worry in her expression. "I mean it, Marlena. I know what I'm doing. We'll win this thing. I'll get you off this island."

"And the prince?" she asks, as something inscrutable dances across her face. Unease? Worry? Jealousy? "Can we trust him?"

"We can," I say, and I realize I genuinely mean it.

"All right, then." She pulls back, and it's like she's changed instantly, back in scholar mode, as if she hadn't just accused me of murder. She wears a mask incredibly well, and I know that should make me wary, but all it does is make me want to get closer. "So. The Maze of Martyrs."

"What do we know?"

"Upsettingly little." She gestures at the heaps of books around her. "Below the island, there's an ancient stone labyrinth, from back when the school was founded. It's a dark, dank nightmare of crypts and ruins, full of puzzles and magic. The professors place thirty gems throughout, and it's up to teams of five to find them." She spins one of the books around, revealing an illustration of a young man screaming in pain, a stone javelin skewering him to a wall. "There are also traps. Many, many traps."

"Gods," I mutter, and I can't help but wonder if Aberdeen is *trying* to kill me.

"The puzzles are all built to test deep knowledge of magical principles, history, and mathematics. The trial favors scholarly research." Her eyes flit across the room, and I see Vyctoria and a bunch of her fellow

Seluras gathered around a table overflowing with books, poring over research with military precision. "It favors Selura."

"So how can I win?"

"You could study intensely and actually learn the things they'll be testing?"

I glance back at the Seluras, where Vyctoria is shouting history questions at her fellow students who bark dates back. "Come on. Be realistic."

"Right." Marlena bites her lip. "I've been thinking, and there *is* another way, maybe. But it'll be incredibly dangerous and involve breaking many school rules. The kind of rules they'll expel you over. Are you all right with that?"

I almost laugh, because I literally killed someone last night. "Marlena. You know me. What do you think the answer is?"

I can see her fight back a smile, see the way her eyes sparkle. Because for all her worry and caution, she wants this, wants to break the rules, *wants* to get dangerous. She's spent her whole life being the perfect servant, the loyal Humble, but deep inside, there's a girl just desperate to let it all burn. "I think you're mad," she says, and her low purr makes it clear it's a compliment.

"Damn right." I lean forward, grinning right back. "Now let's be mad together."

Chapter 32

Then

I am ten when I learn Whispers's harshest lesson.

The moment is grim. Sera and I sit on a bench in the center of that ramshackle Laroc warehouse while Revenants scramble all around us, packing everything up. Crixus hurls pallets of supplies onto a wagon. A lean woman takes the weapons off the racks and lays them on a long cloth sheet. A clamor of shouts fills the air. I don't know what's happening, not exactly, but I can tell we're in trouble, that something bad happened last night. A half dozen Revenants lie on stretchers around the room, bloodied and battle scarred, while Pavel hustles between them, face red, chest heaving, healing what little he can. Three more lie at the back of the room, covered with sheets. Sera stares at them, her face so pale she's practically white. She's not taking this well.

"Girls." Whispers approaches us with purpose, her cane clacking loudly on the stone floor with each step. "Did you pack your things as I asked?"

"We did," I say, gesturing at the two heavy sacks lying in front of us. "Where are we going?"

"I'm not sure yet. Dunbar, maybe, or Midgar Bay." She glances down at her hand, then wipes a spot of blood off her shirt. "South, anyway."

I nod and nudge Sera, trying to sound chipper. "You wanted to go south, didn't you? Where it's warmer?"

But her eyes are trained on the bodies, her little mouth curled into a frown that seems decades older. "What happened?"

"A mission went wrong. We were ambushed. We fought. We lost. That's all you need to know," Whispers says.

For once, Sera doesn't accept it. "Who died?" she demands, and even though she's quiet, there's a hard determination behind her words.

I turn to stare at her. I've never seen her push back on Whispers, not like this. I'm the troublemaker who demands an explanation for everything; she's the good student who does whatever she's told. Whispers clearly notices, too, because she pauses, studying her closely. "Tasha. Baelyn. Valay. And I don't think Carlyle is going to make it," she says without a drop of emotion. "Now then. Are you satisfied?" Her eyes narrow. "Or is there something else you'd like to say?"

"I—I just—" Sera stammers, like she almost wants to be quiet but she can't stop the words bubbling out. I don't know whether to be proud of her for being assertive or horrified that she's choosing to do it *now*. "Why does it have to be like this? Why do we have to do *this*?"

"'This'?"

"This!" Sera almost yells, gesturing at the chaos, the wounded, the dead. "The running and the hiding and the fighting and the dying! Death, death, and more death!" A few heads turn to us, and Whispers gives them a glance so icy they quickly look away. "What if we could talk to the Wizards or make peace with them or help them understand? We know there are good Wizards out there like Pavel! If we got them on our side, if they stood up for us, if they were in charge..."

Now I'm firmly on the side of wishing she had kept quiet. Whispers stares at her for one endless, excruciating moment. "All right," she says. "I'll tell you." Then she turns and walks across the room, grabs a chair, drags it over, and sits down opposite us. "Let me tell you a story, girls. Twenty years ago, I was just a young Revenant, stationed at a little camp in Silvercreek. I had a very important job, though. See, our group had recently captured a Wizard, a young man named Gable Grimshaw. We were going to torture him for information and then kill him when he stopped being useful. That was the plan, anyway."

I look to Sera to see if she understands why we're suddenly having story time, but her attention is entirely on Whispers. "But?"

"But I was lonely and he was scared. So we started talking," Whispers says with a sad little smile, right then more human than I've ever seen her. "We became friends. More than that, really. I began to care for him deeply, to trust him. Maybe even love him a little. He assured me that he wasn't like the other Wizards, that his family supported Humbles. He promised me that if I let him go, we'd run away together, that we'd work with his parents to reform the system from within, that we'd fix the world without spilling another drop of blood. I believed him. So one night, when the coast was clear, I unlocked his cell and let him go."

I can guess where this story is going, but I'm riveted all the same. "What happened?"

"What happened was he drove six inches of steel into my side," Whispers says, and any trace of warmth melts away instantly. She lifts her shirt and shows us the jagged white scar running from her hip to her ribs. "What happened was he left me bleeding to death on the cold floor. What happened was that now I need *this*." She gestures at her cane. "That's what happened, Sera Chelrazi, when I tried to find another way."

"What happened to the Wizard?"

"He got away. We had to abandon the camp. I recovered, and I hardened, and I learned. I plotted and I planned. And ten years later, I captured him again, this time on a ship sailing to the Kindrali Isles."

Whispers smiles again, and this is her real smile, a shark's grin, terrifying. "I nailed his hands to the mast and set him aflame. And I stared into his eyes as he burned alive." She slides her chair forward, its legs scraping loudly against the floor. "Do you understand, Sera? Do you understand what happens when you show kindness, weakness, when you yearn for 'another way'?"

Sera stares at the floor. "You get betrayed."

"No. You get *stabbed*." Whispers rises from her chair, and I can't help but notice her subtle wince. "There can be no other way, Sera. No peace, no diplomacy, no understanding. Even the 'good Wizards' will turn on you eventually. Even the ones who'll listen will always choose protecting their own. Killing a king fixes nothing when the problem is the throne. Pleading with the captain doesn't save a ship in a storm." She turns away from us. "A broken world cannot be mended through kind words, through civility, through compassion. A broken world cannot be reformed or redeemed. A broken world only ends one way." She stares across the room where several Revenants are standing in silence, hands over their hearts, as Pavel drags a sheet across Carlyle's still form. "It ends in fire."

Chapter 33

Now

The Second Challenge happens in that odd half season between winter and spring, when the crisp snow gives way to muddy earth, when it's warm enough that you don't want to wear your coat but cold enough that you can't go without it. We gather at the entrance to the maze, an old stone amphitheater on the island's northern tip. Five doors are built into the structure's wall, each adorned with the crest of an Order. Even though the whole school is here, sitting on tiered benches around the entrances, this really isn't a spectator challenge like the Balitesta game; the other students will get to hear Aberdeen give his speech and watch the teams vanish below ground. The tunnels are designed so that all the teams start on different paths. We might meet up, or we might not; it depends on the choices we make and how fast we go. Meanwhile, out here, the other students will sit restlessly until the teams emerge, carrying however many gems we could find. It sounds miserable, especially in this gray, damp weather.

Luckily, I'm not up in the stands. I'm down on the ground by the door with the black sigil of the Order of Nethro, bouncing up and down on my feet as I await the signal to go. My teammates stand behind me:

Fyl, Desmond, Tish, and Zigmund. No one would call them the best scholars in the Order, but that doesn't matter. The only thing that matters now is that none of them raise any suspicions about what's going to happen next.

"So, do you have some great plan again, Alayne?" Fyl asks. We're all wearing matching black cloaks, but she has her hood pulled up high, framing her narrow face in shadow. "Because, I'm not going to lie, I don't think any of us have been doing our research."

"I have," Tish says quietly.

"Relax." I shoot Fyl the most comforting smile I can. "Just follow my lead."

Around us, the teams of five from the other Orders are gearing up. The Zartans look utterly miserable, bleary-eyed, and dour. The Seluras are still drilling, even here, Vyctoria barking last-minute questions at her squad. Behind them are the Vanguards, led by Marius. I've avoided him ever since the Founders' Day Gala, and I'm confident he's been avoiding me, too. Our eyes meet now, though, and his narrow with cold, seething hate.

I look the other way at the last team, the Javellos. Talyn's their leader, and he huddles with his teammates, whispering and strategizing. Even though we've spent a few more nights together, we've agreed that out here in the challenge, we're just two students competing for a prize. *May the best Order win*, he said last night, his lips brushing against mine. *Just do me a favor and let me take second place.*

He breaks from his huddle and for one tiny second sees me, his lips twitching into a crooked smile. I smile back, but mine's forced, because while I don't feel bad at all about doing whatever it takes to win, I do feel a pang of guilt. I don't feel bad cheating the system, but I do feel a little bad cheating *him*.

Aberdeen emerges, pacing down to stand by us, and he gives his big speech. I barely listen. There are only so many times I can hear the same platitudes. But I do notice how he looks at me, the way his gray eye flares. I can feel his breath on my neck and hear his whisper in my ear.

When the time comes for the Second Challenge? Lose.

Oh, I'm not losing today. I'm winning big, winning for all the Nethros who have put their faith and trust in me, for every student crushed by this island's twisted hierarchy. If Aberdeen's reputation hangs on me losing, he's about to be in for one hell of a shock.

The horn sounds. The doors on the stone wall swing open, exposing long stairs leading down into murky darkness. Next to me, Desmond swallows, and Zigmund lets out a whoop. Fyl reaches over and squeezes my hand. "Whatever happens next," she says, "we're in this together."

The underground maze is just as dark and unpleasant as I'd expected. The five of us hustle through a tight stone tunnel, barely wide enough for two to walk side by side. Dim orange lights flicker inside glass bricks, providing just enough light to get by. Cobwebs drape the ceiling, fluttering gently in a chill draft.

"So, not to make too big a deal out of this," Desmond says, glancing uneasily over his shoulder. "But you all do realize that if we win this, it's a *big* deal, right?"

"Of course," Tish replies. "If we win this, we could win the whole Great Game."

"No, I mean bigger than that. Bigger than this place. This will have real consequences," Desmond says, and that comment seems particularly directed at me. "My father wrote to me. Everyone in Arbormont, in the damn Republic, is buzzing about how we won the First Challenge. A bunch of no-name Nethros coming up with a strategy that totally breaks the game and humiliates Marius Madison in the process? That's the kind of story that spreads like wildfire... especially among Grandmaster Madison's enemies."

"Come on, you're exaggerating," I say, rounding a corner to find a forking path. Without skipping a beat, without even giving time for the others to ask, I guide us left.

"I'm not," he insists. "According to my father, it actually came up on the Senate floor. Grandmaster Madison was giving a speech about the unstoppable might of his army, and some Reformer made a joke about what would happen if they had to go up against a 'Nethro schoolgirl.' Madison got so mad, his allies had to drag him off the floor." Desmond shakes his head, and I struggle to wrap my mind around it. What I'm doing here is making ripples through the Republic, all the way to the Senate floor. That means Whispers has to know. Is she proud... or furious?

"So what if it's a big deal?" Zigmund says in his heavy Velkschen accent. "It's good if Madison is mad. He is a... as you say... shit-drinker?"

"Absolutely no one says that," Desmond replies. "My point is, one challenge could still be a fluke. But if we win *two*..."

"Then we'll have made names for ourselves." Fyl pats Desmond's shoulder, and he instantly relaxes. "And our parents will be proud. Sooner or later. Isn't that right, Alayne?"

"Of course," I say, and for once, it's not a lie. The path in front of us forks three ways, and I guide us left without even thinking. The others don't question it; that's why I picked them. Soon enough a stone slab looms in front of us, blocking our path. The first puzzle.

"What are we looking at here?" Desmond asks.

Five buttons jut out of the wall, each engraved with a letter. A carved slab at the top depicts a majestic hawk carrying a Loci in each claw, one an elegant sword, one a fine blackwood branch. "That's the symbol of the old Senate Grandmaster," Tish offers. "Drakovian era, I think? Around 321?"

I wait a second to see if they'll crack any more of it, but Tish falters. Still, a good start. "Senate Grandmasters of that era, then," I say, trying to sound like I'm actually piecing it together. "Maybe these are the first letters of their last names, and we pick them in order of tenure?" I step forward, pressing the buttons as I talk, and they slide in with a satisfying crunch. "Gabrus, Vorschak, Deranis, Ellarious, Volodya?"

There is a long, low rumble, the hum of infused magic. The slab rumbles, pulsing with energy, and then slides open. Behind it is a room where a single sparkling gem rests on a pedestal, framed by three doors leading deeper in.

The others all gape at me. "You... you are... smartest person... in world," Zigmund says, and Desmond nods. "What he said."

"I just got lucky," I say, and really hope they'll buy that. As they stare at me in incredulity, I walk to the pedestal, pick up the gem, and slide it into the bag at my hip. "Now come on. One down. Twenty-nine more to go."

Chapter 34

Then

I am seventeen when I cheat the Second Challenge.

The plan is all Marlena's, and it's equal measures brilliant and dangerous. The idea came to her in, of all things, an announcement to the Humble servants: for the week following the challenge, Groundskeeper Tyms would be busy resetting the maze to its initial state, so they would all have to work extra hours.

The other Humble servants groaned, but Marlena's mind whirled with possibilities. Tyms is a Wizard, but a mediocre one at best. There's no way he has the knowledge to reset this maze on his own. That means there are instructions for how to reset the puzzles written down somewhere. Instructions that could just as easily provide all the solutions. And there's just one place they could be.

We meet up a week before the Second Challenge, huddled in the bushes outside the library. It's the middle of the night and the lanterns are off, so the two of us sit quietly in total darkness, the air so cold our breath lingers around us. This is our third attempt at getting into the professors' wing. The first night Professor Calfex was there, working late; the second, Groundskeeper Tyms was doing rounds. But the third time's the charm, because the library is quiet and dark and empty, not a soul in sight.

We make our way through the dark to the building's side door, the one Humbles use. The library is eerie at night, the shelves looming over us like obelisks, casting long, grasping shadows in the pale moonlight. I have no idea where we're going, but Marlena does, so I follow her through the stacks, winding around the familiar tables, up a flight of stairs, and to an ominous towering door.

"What now?" I whisper. "Do we need to pick the lock?"

"Why would we do that?" She shoots me a sly smile and pulls a key out of her pocket. It blinks and pulses with magical energy, the metal trembling almost like it's fluid. I gape at it, which she must notice. "It's a skeleton key to the entire campus. I stole it off Groundskeeper Tyms while he was drunk. The best part is, he'll be too worried about getting in trouble to report that it's stolen."

"Marlena!" I gasp. What we did in the First Challenge had been risky, but that risk had fallen squarely on me. I can take it. She shouldn't have to. "That's so dangerous...if you'd been caught..." I shake my head. "You shouldn't have done that for me."

"I *didn't* do it for you. I did it for me," she answers, and as her eyes burn hot with intensity and determination, I realize she means it. If there had ever been a point of hesitation, of uncertainty, we've long crossed it. She's as committed to this as I am, as willing to risk it all, as willing to die. Part of me's impressed. Another part's terrified.

She jams the key into the lock. It trembles for one tense second, then with a hollow *click* springs open. The doors swing wide, revealing the forbidden room beyond: dozens and dozens and dozens of tall shelves overflowing with books and scrolls.

The professors' wing is one of the most forbidden areas of the whole campus, an entire half of the library dedicated solely to materials for the staff: personal research projects, high-level books to be taught with discretion, and procedural documents like the maze instructions. Any student caught inside would be instantly expelled, branded an apostate. Any Humble caught inside would be killed.

But Marlena doesn't hesitate as she leads the way with a tiny lantern that fits into the palm of her hand, a disk glowing with the faintest light. She moves with an expert's precision, consulting a heavy index tome at the front desk and then weaving through the stacks, trying to find the precise book we need. I have no idea what she's doing, and I don't need to. I just marvel at the wealth of forbidden knowledge around us, my mind racing at the possibilities of everything I could learn. I see heavy tomes wrapped in chains, scrolls that quiver like flesh, maps that flicker with inner light. The air is so thick with magic I can feel it vibrating in my bones.

"Here!" she says at last, stopping in front of a shelf stacked high with hundreds of little paper books, all labeled by number. "Give me a minute. I'll find the right one."

"Sure," I say, and turn around to keep a lookout. That's when I see it. The far wall of the library is adorned with paintings of the faculty, dozens and dozens of them. A particular year catches my eye though, 781, and in it, a particular face.

The school faculty stands on a set of risers wearing formal robes, smiles plastered across their faces. The year 781 was just sixteen years ago, so many of them are familiar. There's Professor Hapsted with a full head of hair, and Magnus Aberdeen standing tall, and Groundskeeper Tyms looking basically the same. Professor Calfex stands in front looking remarkably young, her hair black and wild and curly down to her waist, her eyes bright.

But it's the man next to her that I'm staring at. Pale skin. Messy red hair. A pair of delicate spectacles resting on his pointy nose.

My father.

The last time I saw him was ten years ago, but I remember his face perfectly, and there's no doubt, this is him. I'd known he was a powerful Wizard before he defected, but none of the Revenants knew what he did. It makes sense now, so much sense. The way he read, delicate and patient, just like a teacher. The massive chest of books we hauled wherever we went. The way Aberdeen spoke to him, etched into my memory like a carving in stone, the way he called him *old friend*.

I don't know how to process this. I don't know where to begin. My father had been a professor here. *Here*. He'd probably sat in this room, maybe stood in this very spot. What had he been like? Had he lectured with kindness and patience, read to classrooms of students the way he read to me? Had he argued with Aberdeen, pushed for reform? Or had he sat in the stadium during games of Balitesta, cheering as students bled and died? Had he and Aberdeen *actually* been friends?

I've never engaged with my father's past before he defected. I've never had to. But it lurks around me now, a great murky darkness, one I'm terrified to acknowledge lest it swallow me whole. How much harm had my father done in his life? How much blood was on *his* hands?

"Alayne?" Marlena asks quietly. "What are you looking at?"

"I—it's—this painting—" I stammer, my words interrupted as I let out the breath I've been holding, as I scramble to find a way to play this. "Amazing how young Calfex looks!" I try at last.

She stares at me quizzically, then shrugs. "She does look quite young, I suppose," she says, and then mercifully moves on. "But look! I found it! The guide to resetting the maze!"

"That's it?" I ask. It's a small book, maybe fifty pages long, as big as my hand. She flips through the pages under her lantern, and I can make out densely written instructions and even what looks like a map.

"Oh, this is it, all right. All the puzzle solutions. All the directions.

Everything. This is all you need to win the game," she says, her white grin shining in the soft light. "Give me a few days, and I'll have this copied over and we can put it back." Her hands are shaking with excitement as she tucks the book into her bag and she can't contain a laugh. "I can't believe it. It's all *right here*. And it's so simple! Any student could have done this, all this time!"

"No student would have thought of it," I say, and her joy is infectious. I forget the painting, forget my father, forget that murky darkness. Let the past stay the past. What matters is the present, the future. "No other *person* would've thought of it." The weight of this hits me even as I say it, even as I realize it's true. Marlena's been helping me for so long I've lost sight of just how remarkable she is, always ten steps ahead of everyone else while managing to act like she's ten steps behind. She's the smartest godsdamned person on this island, and no one knows it. "Only you."

She stares at me, and maybe it's just the shadows cast by the flickering light in the palm of her hand, but it feels almost like her face shifts as it runs an impossible gamut of emotions, at once happy and sad and worried and thrilled. Finally, she just looks down, cheeks flushed.

"Are you all right?"

"I am," she whispers. "I've just... never had someone believe in me before. Not like this. I hadn't known what that was like."

I want to say something to that, but I don't know where to begin. Even as I search for words, we hear footsteps approaching and hear the unmistakable phlegmatic wheezing of Groundskeeper Tyms. "Let's get the hell out of here," I whisper instead and we bolt out, streaking through the stacks, down the stairs, into the night.

"Huh?" Tyms's voice calls behind us. "Who's there?" But it's too late, because we're already gone. We run and run and run and when we're sure we're out of sight, we collapse into a snowbank, huddling together in that soft, cold white.

The night hangs dark around us, hiding us like a cloak. In that moment, it feels like everything's vanished except the two of us, lying there, pressed together, holding our breaths, just the warmth of our bodies shielding against the cold of the snow. "Are we safe?" I whisper at last.

"I think so," she replies. "There's no way Tyms has the stamina to chase us this far."

I let out a little laugh, but when I look up, she isn't laughing. She's looking at me, our faces just inches apart, her eyes wide and vulnerable. I can't read her expression, not entirely, but it feels open and tender. "Alayne," she whispers quietly, and I want to look away from her but I can't. "I want you to know something. Whatever happens in the challenge, whatever happens next, I'm just so happy I met you. You make me feel like...like no one ever has." She inhales sharply, nervously, and then edges just the tiniest bit closer, and now I feel my stomach flutter, feel that tingle of nerves in my palms. "When this is done, when we leave Blackwater...I'd like to stay with you. If you'll have me."

My breath is tight in my throat, "Stay with me...?"

"Wherever you go, whatever you do next," she says, and she can't quite bring herself to look at me, even though we're almost touching, even though I can feel the warmth of her breath on my skin. Her knee touches mine, and it's nothing and everything at the same time, and I lean forward, even though I don't really mean to, so I'm pressing my thigh against her, so close I can *feel* her whisper.

"I'll go with you," she says. "I'll help you. We'll do it together."

Wherever I go next. Oh, Gods. I haven't even begun thinking about that. Assuming this all works, assuming we make it off this island, I'd go back to the Revenants. And I could take her with me. She'd fit in well, and she'd be damn useful. With that cunning intellect, she'll be

Whispers's favorite in no time. If Marlena wants a cause to fight for, well, I've got that in spades.

But there's a part of me that balks at the idea because... because I don't want that for *her*. I don't want to subject her to that brutal life, to the endless bloodshed, to Whispers's cold cynicism. I don't want her to become just another hardened killer, or worse, another body under a sheet. Marlena's so vibrant, so brilliant, so alive and joyful; bringing her to the Revenants would be like putting a diamond in an abattoir.

She deserves better than that.

And so, I realize with a sudden clarity, do I.

It's a shock of a thought, one that hits me like a gasp, one I've never dared engage with, not seriously, not really. From the minute Whispers took me into her arms, I've defined myself as a Revenant. It's who I am. It's *what* I am.

But what if it wasn't? What if I never went back? What if I just *lived*?

I can't believe I'm thinking like this, can't believe I'm thinking of running, but I also can't believe Marlena's thigh pressed against me, can't believe her hand on my side, can't believe how full and soft her lips look, can't believe the way the starlight dances off her eyes. I, oh, Gods, I—

I pull away sharply, sharply enough that I see her eyes widen with surprise. I can't do this. I can't let myself go down that route, can't lose myself to fantasies and daydreams. I can't let myself go soft. And I can't bring her into my nightmare.

"Alayne?" she asks softly.

"I'm sorry," I say, rising up, brushing off my shirt. "But when this is done, when we're off the island, we have to go our separate ways." Her brow crinkles with disappointment, and I have to look away. "It's not personal. You're amazing. It's just... it's... I... it's just how it has to be. It's for the best. For both of us."

She sits there for one excruciating moment, then she exhales sharply.

"All right," she says, gazing out at the dark. "If you say so. If it's for the best."

There's so much hurt in her voice that I want to step forward and hug her, but I know that'll just make it worse, just chip away at this essential wall. So I clear my throat and turn away. "Come on," I say, striding away from her into the dark. "Let's head back."

CHAPTER 35

Now

I'm hardly a great scholar, but even I'm able to memorize the instructions Marlena prepared for me, the optimal route through the maze and the solutions to all the puzzles I'll encounter. So I make my way through with my team, solving one door after another, collecting gem after gem. It goes as smoothly as I could have hoped, with no surprises except for one moment where Zigmund wanders off a path and get his eyebrows singed by a flame trap. The hardest part is keeping up the facade for the rest of my team, acting like I'm actually solving the puzzles and not blatantly cheating. It works mostly, I think, especially the few times I act stumped long enough for Tish to come up with an idea; they don't say anything, and if they have their suspicions, they keep them to themselves.

An hour after we enter the maze, we come upon a pair of heavy-set double doors adorned with a dozen polished slabs, the frame covered with runic cyphers and mathematical formulas and Gods knows what else. We're at the center of the maze, the hardest challenge, and the room inside holds a whopping five gems. It's the last stop on my plan and sure to tip the Order of Nethro to victory. The actual puzzle is so complicated that I still don't understand the solution, even after Marlena explained it a dozen times, so I just act deep in thought and mumble the instructions and trust that the others will go along.

"You carve a Fire Base Glyph here." I guide Fyl in front of one slab, then hustle around positioning the others. "Tish, you go with wind. Zigmund, you're life, Desmond, you're earth, and I'll do ice. Elemental Base, Ornamentation Form. And we all have to carve at the same time. Understand?"

"Not even a little bit," Desmond says. "But if you say it'll work, I trust you."

"We're really going to do this. We're actually going to win the Second Challenge." Fyl bounces up and down on her heels. "Gods above. We're actually going to be the Order Triumphant. We're going to the Senate. My parents are going to lose their minds."

"Let's just take it one step at a time," I say, drawing my Loci. "Everyone ready? On three. One, two, three."

We slip into the Null together, all five of us, standing shoulder to shoulder in the gray. It's dark here, darker than usual, but our bodies exude a pulsing glow of warmth that cuts through the haze of ash, like five candles glowing through a heavy mist. I've never been in the Null with this many friends, and it feels different, safer somehow, less lonely. I could get used to it.

We all carve our Glyphs and pull back into the Real, where they glow bright and beautiful, each slab radiating with energy. A delicate melody resonates around us, the anthem of the Republic, and the doors slide open with a lumbering groan. Behind them is a wide rectangular room with a domed ceiling, every surface smooth stone. There's a dais in the middle with five grooves, each with a gem set inside, and a radiant light within shines out through the gems, bathing every surface of the room in dancing multicolored light, like the chandelier at the gala.

Zigmund pumps a fist in triumph and Tish clasps a hand over their mouth. We step into the room together, our faces lit up red and yellow and white and gold. "It's beautiful!" Fyl says, and I reach over to pluck one of the gems.

That's when it all goes to hell.

I feel the hum of gathering magic from my left, that electric crackle that sets my hair on end, the chill of a cold breath on the back of my neck. Tish makes a noise, a stifled scream, and I slip into the Null instinctively, swiveling just in time to see the melon-sized ball of earth before it smashes into my chest.

The world flashes red and black. I feel myself lift off the ground and fly backward into a wall, feel my chest flare with pain, feel my Loci fly out of my hands, feel myself gasp and wheeze for air that barely comes. I slam down onto the ground, hard, and I can't see what's happening but I can hear Fyl scream and Zigmund roar, hear the shriek of wind and the hammer of stone. My mouth floods with blood, and my knees become water. The room around me thunders and flares.

Get up, you weakling. Get up. *Get up.*

I force my head up, trying to make sense of what happened. There's five of them, five figures at the end of the room, pressed against the wall so we wouldn't have seen them when we came in. My vision is wavering, my eyes watering, but I can still make out their bright gold cloaks.

Vanguard.

Shit.

My Loci are lying just a few feet away. I move on instinct, lunging toward them, but there's another rush of magic and a crystal of ice bursts out of the ground, enveloping my grasping hands like a pair of gauntlets, trapping me in place. It's cold, the kind of cold that burns, but I barely even care because my body is screaming *fight*. "Get them!" I yell to the others, and it's only then that I realize the rest of my team is in even worse shape than me.

Zigmund lies facedown next to me, unconscious, outstretched hand twitching. Tish is slumped against the wall cradling their visibly dislocated arm, panting with pain. Desmond is on his back with a thick vine wrapped around his waist, and Fyl is upright against a wall, her hands frozen in ice crystals over her head. We're all disarmed, bound, trapped.

The battle's already over. It was over before it began.

"What is this?" Desmond chokes out, each word a struggle as the vine tightens around him. "What are you doing?"

"Winning," a voice hisses back. Marius Madison. He stands at the front of the group, his blue eyes bright beneath his hood, face lit up with the smuggest grin I've ever seen. I squirm, jerking my hands, but the ice around them holds tight, stockades of cold crystal. That just makes Marius's grin widen, and he strolls over to me, each step a flourish. I twist away from him, but I can't go far, so he kneels down, plucking the bag of gems off my hip. "Now, if you don't mind, I'll be taking this."

"Bastard," I growl.

He just laughs. "Oh, admit it, Dewinter. This is poetic. Winning the challenge by ambushing the leading team and stealing all their gems? Wherever could I have gotten that idea?" He tosses the bag back to a lanky girl with flaxen blond hair. "What goes around comes around. About time you Nethros learned that."

Fyl lets out a low moan, and Desmond's head falls with despair. I thrash about, trying desperately to break the ice even though it makes my hands hurts worse, even though it's futile. The world flares red. My chest is so tight it feels like it's going to burst. I'm so angry it hurts, so furious I'm trembling. And it's not just at Marius, though, Gods, what I would give to smash that smug smile in. I'm furious at myself. I walked right into this trap, got played at my own game. I got cocky, and look where it got me. All of Marlena's work, all our planning and scheming and risk. Undone because I couldn't check a room before strolling in.

"All right, Marius," Desmond's voice trembles. "You got the gems. You won. Can you let us go now?"

"I let you go when I godsdamn please!" Marius snarls, and it's clear this is about much more than just winning. "Now you shut your mouth, boy, or I will shut it for you. Understood?"

All the color drains from Desmond's face, and he swallows deeply, chest heaving. "U-u-understood."

"Good. Because I've got unfinished business." He kneels down, wraps his fingers through my hair, and jerks my head up, hard. "Don't I, Dewinter?"

Pain flares through my scalp, and I hate this, hate how powerless I am, hate the yawning chasm between how badly I want to fight and how little I can. "Let go of me!"

"I don't think I will." Marius crouches. "You thought you were so clever, didn't you? Making a fool of me? Killing my best friend? Well, where are you now, huh? Where are you now without your precious prince to protect you?" I can feel his hot breath on my face, feel his spittle on my skin as he talks. "I could kill you right now," he says, and presses his Loci right up against my throat. It's the second time he's done that. It'll be the last. "Cut your little throat open and let you bleed out. How would you like that, Dewinter? How would you like *that*?"

"You can't," Tish cries. "It's against the rules."

"The rules!" Marius laughs, jabbing the tip of the knife in hard enough to draw blood. "I'll tell everyone I did it in self-defense. Whose word do you think the judges will trust, hmm?" He turns back, jabbing his other Loci through the air. "What do you think, Desmond? Your father serves mine. Want to see if he'll put his son before his livelihood?" Desmond doesn't even reply. He just stares at the ground, utterly broken. "Exactly. I can do whatever I want down here." He tugs again at my hair, even harder, so hard it hurts more than the Loci poking into my throat. "How's it feel, Dewinter? How's it feel to be totally beaten? How's it feel to *know your place*?"

"If you're going to kill me, then shut up and do it," I growl at him, and his nostrils flare as he jerks his Loci back.

"No!" Fyl screams, and Marius freezes mid-strike. Tears streak down her cheeks, and her whole body trembles. "Please, Marius. Please. Don't hurt her. Please. We'll do anything you want, anything you say. Just please. Don't hurt her. *Please!*"

Marius glares at Fyl from the corner of his eye, like he's taking her in, and I see the moment something in him changes. He lets go of my hair and I fall back to the ground. Marius stands back up, dusting off his pants, and steps away from me. "All right," he says. "Fair enough." He takes a step away, and I don't know what's happening here, don't know what's changed, but I know I don't trust it. "I'm not going to kill you, Dewinter," he says. "I'm going to kill your friend."

It happens in a heartbeat. His hand flicks up, his Loci carving in the Null, an imperceptible golden blur. The air crackles with magical energy.

And a lance of cold stone plunges straight through Fyl's chest.

She twitches, stunned, as blood trickles from her lips. She stares at the spear skewering her with eyes wide and horrified and betrayed. She tries to talk, but all that comes bubbling out is a choked gasp. Desmond wails, writhing against his vines, and Tish is utterly silent, head cradled in their hands, unable to look. I let out a noise I forgot I was capable of, a scream so harsh it rips my throat. I thrash against the ice binding me so hard my hands start to bleed, staining the crystals from within. "You bastard!" I shriek. "You didn't have to do that!"

Marius just laughs. "You all saw what happened, right?" he asks his crew. "The Potts girl attacked me. I shot her lance back to defend myself. Everyone saw that, right?" They all nod, though the girl with the flaxen hair looks a little reluctant. "In that case, I think we're done here." He glances back down at me. "And there you have it, Dewinter. A friend for a friend. We're even now." Then he kicks me, smashing his boot across my face and sending me down into the cold stone, and I don't care because the hurt there is so much better than the hurt inside me, than the rage and the grief. "Let's get out of here," he says to his cronies, and just like that, they leave.

I force my head up, even though it all hurts so much. Desmond lies on the ground, moaning and sobbing. Tish weeps gently into their hands. And Fyl just hangs there, eyes still wide, mouth agape, that horrible lance in her chest. I look at her through my tears, and I want nothing more now than to be able to hold her, to cradle her in my arms, to let her know that in the moment, she's not alone. "Not for me," I whisper to her across that cold room. "Not for me."

But Fyl doesn't say anything.

She's already gone.

CHAPTER 36

Now

I don't leave my room for two days.

I can't. It was hard enough just getting back there, staggering out of the maze with Fyl's limp body in my arms, watching Aberdeen declare Vanguard the winner. It was hard enough sitting there while Marius spun his self-defense story, while the judges chastised me for not controlling my teammates. It was hard enough walking back through the quad in silence, every eye on me, every face clouded with judgment. It was hard enough to keep my head down and avoid Zigmund's haunted glare, Tish's grief, Desmond's wails of heartbreak. It was hard enough just to make it to my door.

When I'm in, when it's shut, I unleash. I drive my fist through my mirror and don't even flinch when my knuckles bleed. I shatter my chair against a wall. I scream and rage, loudly enough that I know everyone can hear me, loudly enough I don't care. And when it's all out of me, I collapse into a heap in the ruins of my room and I bury my head in my hands and grieve.

I messed up. I messed up so badly. I got cocky and I got careless and now Fyl's dead. Fyl, my first friend at Blackwater, the girl who was drawn to me because she thought I was her destiny, the girl who trusted me. She's dead and it's all my fault.

How am I supposed to go on from this? How am I supposed to face the others, face Calfex's judgment, face Desmond and Tish? How am I supposed to look Marlena in the eye and tell her I blew any chance we had of getting her off this island?

I don't know how to do it. So I don't.

A few people come by to check on me. Tish knocks just once, asking if I'm all right, and leaves when I don't respond. Talyn comes by and stays longer, long enough that I have to ask him to leave. Marlena's the most diligent, coming every morning and evening to leave a tray of food just outside. I barely eat.

On the morning of the third day, she stays. "Alayne," she says softly. "They're sending Fyl's body to the mainland. Your friends are down by the steps to see her off." I don't reply, and I can hear her sigh. "You might want to join them."

"I can't," I mutter. "I just can't."

I wait for her to go, but she doesn't, and I can see her feet shift uneasily through the crack under my doorframe. "Alayne," she says again, more firmly, as firm as she can allow herself to be. "The other Nethros need to know you're still with them. They need to know you can still lead them. They need to see you."

"Still lead them? Lead them to what?"

"The Great Game's not over," she says. "You lost the Second Challenge, but you're still tied with Vanguard overall. With a good showing, you can still win."

"How can you think about the Great Game?" I demand. "Fyl's dead, Marlena. Fyl's dead, just like… just like…" The words get stuck in my throat. "Please. Just go."

She lingers there another minute, choosing her words carefully. "If you're not going to go as their leader... at least go as their friend." Then she turns and leaves.

Damn it.

Damn her.

I throw on some clothes and make my way down. It's a miserable gray day outside, cold and windy, the earth muddy and damp. A small crowd has gathered on the steps of the Order of Nethro, a bunch of students clustered together in a half circle. They're all wearing black, more black than usual, somber cloaks and dark suits. Between them, on the cobblestone path, lies a coffin. Lies Fyl.

A few heads turn my way as I approach. Zigmund gives me a little nod, eyes downcast, the most somber I've ever seen him. Tish's face is painted, a hash of dark lines like a veil, and they whisper "thank you" as I walk by. The other Nethros stare at me, their Order Captain, their leader, and I can see their distrust, their disappointment, their suspicion. I'm supposed to be out here to reassure them. But how can I do that when I think they're right?

I place a hand on the coffin, breathing deeply. Fyl was a Wizard, but she was also a friend, a good person, a compassionate soul, and a victim in the end, as much as anyone else. I think in another life she would have listened to me and understood my cause. I think in another life we could have stayed friends. "I'm sorry," I say. "You deserved better."

"She did," a voice says from up the path. I glance up and see Desmond leaning against a tree, glaring at me through his dark bangs. The other Nethros look demoralized, but he looks furious. "Not that you ever really cared about her."

"Desmond." I walk over to him and speak low, out of earshot of the others. "I didn't want it to be like this. I never wanted her to get hurt."

"No. You just wanted to win, and you didn't care what it cost us." He shakes his head, angry, defiant. "You put us in harm's way, on Marius's bad side. And for what? For *what*? A chance to win their stupid, gods-damned game?"

"Desmond, I—"

"Tell me one thing, Alayne. Look me in the eye and don't you dare lie." His brow furrows deep as he scowls. "Did you cheat?"

I swallow hard. I'm too tired, too broken, too heartsick to think on my feet. "I... I didn't... I mean..."

It's answer enough. "That's what I thought," he says. "You lied to us, Alayne. You filled us with false hope, and you lied to us to gain our loyalty, pulling us into something we never would've signed up for. And you got her killed. You got Fyl killed." He shakes his head. "I thought you were different, Alayne. But you're not. You're just one of *them*."

It might be the most devastating thing anyone's ever said to me. "Desmond..." I say, and just getting the words out is impossible, like I've been punched in the gut.

"Spare me the pitch. I've already made up my mind. I'm leaving with her body, and I'm not coming back."

I blink. "What?"

"You heard me. I'm getting on the ferry with her and getting off this rock. I'm done with this place. Done with Wizards and magic and all of it. Done with you."

"What are you going to do?"

"Hell if I know. Maybe I'll wander the docks until I find work on a ship. One that'll take me to the Kindrali Isles or Sithar or out into the unknown." His voice trembles a little. "So long as I'm far from you lot, that's all that matters."

There's so much I want to say to him, so much I want to explain. Of everyone here, Desmond is the one who could most understand me, who could see the cruelty of the system, who could most understand my cause. And yet here he is, looking at me the way I look at *them.*

There's no way I can tell him. And even if I could, I don't think he'll listen. "All right." I say. "If you've decided..."

"I have." He turns to step away, then stops mid-stride. It's starting to rain, just a little bit, a drizzle that soaks through to my bones. "You know what I keep thinking about?" he asks, almost under his breath. "Back there in the maze. In that room. If Fyl hadn't said anything, if she'd just stayed quiet, do you think Marius would've killed her anyway?"

I don't answer. Which is answer enough.

"Yeah. Me, neither." He reaches up and brushes his cheek with the back of his hand. Behind us, a group of Humble men from the village arrive and lift the coffin solemnly, carrying it along the path to the docks. As the pallbearers pass us, Desmond joins them, sliding in between two to help carry the coffin. They seem surprised, but none of them say anything. He's still a Wizard, after all.

"Desmond..." I call out, though I don't know what I'm going to say.

"She believed in you, Alayne. She believed in you with all her heart." He shoots me one last glance over his shoulder. "I hope it was worth it."

He leaves. They all leave, Desmond and the Humbles and Fyl, gone forever, another person lost, another casualty in my wake. I turn away from them to get back to my room, but all the other Nethros are there, Tish and Zigmund and the rest, standing in the rain, staring at me, expectant and sad and scared. Marlena's words echo in my ears. *They need to know you're still with them. They need to know you can still lead.*

"I'm... I'm sorry," I say, and it feels like the words are shards of glass I'm forcing out of my throat. "I didn't want it to be like this. I didn't want... I just... I..." and I can't do it anymore, can't lie to them, can't drag anyone else down this path. "I'm sorry. I can't do this. I can't lead you," I say, and then I turn and run, away from the dormitory, away from the campus, into the forest. I hear Tish cry after me, but I keep going, sprinting into the trees. Every part of me knows this is a bad idea, that I forgot to wear shoes so my bare feet are already stinging with cold, that the rain is getting heavier and heavier, that this is how Marius ambushed me in the first place, but I don't care because right now I feel ready to make some bad decisions, ready to hurt and be hurt. I welcome the pain. I cherish it.

A root catches my ankle and I trip, slamming down hard into the dirt. The rain is heavy enough that I have to squint and blink to get it out of my eyes, soaking my hair down around my face, making me pant for breath. I scramble up under the tree and cradle my head in my hands and just sit there.

"Alayne."

I look up. Talyn. He's standing there, just a few feet away. He's dressed for the weather, at least, with long leather gloves and a black fur-lined coat that hangs low down his back. He's looking at me with his head cocked just the tiniest bit to the side, and it's not pity or disappointment I see in his eyes, but something else. Understanding, maybe. It's the only reason I don't bolt. "Talyn," I say, sliding back up against the tree. I look absolutely horrid, but nothing in his gaze suggests he sees it. "What are you doing out here?"

"I was coming to check on you when I saw you sprint off into the woods," he says, without a trace of judgment. "Gods, you look frozen. Here." He pulls his coat off and drapes it over my shoulders, and even though a part of me is screaming to tear it off and run, I don't.

"You didn't have to come," I say, and I don't know what it is but talking feels easier now, the words less forced. "Haven't you learned your lesson about chasing me into the woods?"

"I recall that night working out fairly well." He hunkers down next to me. I hesitate, and then I slide over to him, lean against him, just to stay warm. We sit in silence, the only sound around us the gentle patter of the rain. Finally, after a few peaceful minutes, he speaks. "Alayne... what happened down there in the maze?"

I close my eyes, leaning my head back against the tree. "Marius and his Vanguards were lying in wait at the heart of it. They ambushed us, captured us, took our gems. And then Marius killed Fyl, just to hurt me."

"Keshta za'n truk," he growls. "I worried he'd come for you, but not like that. The smug little shit..." He exhales sharply. "I'm sorry. Fyl deserved better."

"You barely even knew her."

"I knew her enough." He reaches over and squeezes my hand. "We'll avenge her. I promise."

"I wish it were that easy," I say, and my eyelids feel too heavy to open. "But I don't know what to do, Talyn. Marius completely outplayed me and I've lost the support of my Order and two of my allies are gone and... and..." My words choke up in my throat. "And it's my fault. I shouldn't have brought her in there. I shouldn't have put her in that position. She's dead because of me."

"She's dead because Marius Madison is a dog without honor," he says, and his hand is warm but his voice is ice. "You can't blame yourself. You couldn't have known." I open my eyes to look at him. His shirt clings to him like a skin in the rain, and his breath drifts out in the air, a soft heat against my cheek. "Listen... we'll avenge her together. We'll humiliate Marius Madison so badly he'll spend the rest of his life regretting what he did. We'll ruin him."

"I'm not going to ruin him," I say, putting words to the rage that's been smoldering inside. "I'm going to kill him."

He stares at me, and when he talks, every word is cautious, like he's taking the first steps onto a frozen lake. "I know where you're coming from. I hear you. But you know I can't let you do that."

Rational or not, the rage spikes toward him. "And why the hell not?"

"Because it's going too far. Shattering his reputation is one thing. But killing him? That would cause a problem between our nations. Hell, it might cause a war." He shakes his head. "My father wouldn't approve of that."

"And that's all you care about? Your father's approval? Your reputation? Your status?" I stammer. "I mean, Marius tried to kill *you*!"

"And he would've been in big trouble with his father if he'd succeeded," he says firmly. There is a tension here, an unease, a discomfort we haven't felt between us before. He doesn't pull away, but he tenses a little, swallowing hard. "Look. I'm here for one reason. To gain glory and to prove myself worthy to my father. Killing Marius won't help me achieve that. And I don't know what you're after, not really, but I can't see how killing him helps you. So let's just take a deep breath and remember why we're here. Let's remember what this is all about."

What this is all about? This is about injustice. This is about oppression. This is about vengeance for Fyl, for my parents, for Sera, for every last Humble who died on a Wizard's whim. It's about burning down a corrupt order, about righting so many wrongs, about ending centuries of bloodshed and cruelty. This is about the world.

I want to tell him that, but I can't.

Because he wouldn't understand.

My breath catches in my chest as a bolt of clarity hits me like a lance of ice. A chasm has always existed between us, a chasm I've willfully ignored, a chasm I've forgotten. But it's there, and it's real, and for the first time, it's insurmountable. Talyn is kind and generous and strong. But at the end of the day, he's still a Wizard.

I pull away instinctively, jerking my hand out of his. "Alayne?" he asks.

And there it is. One name, two syllables, that says it all. That's who he sees when he looks at me, who he kisses, who he holds in his arms at night. I relished my time with him, soaked up his affection, lost myself in his caresses. But it wasn't *me* he was interested in. It was Alayne Dewinter, noble Wizard, rebellious Nethro, the proud new Mark who dared to challenge the Order of Vanguard. He looks at me with admiration and desire, but what he's looking at, what he's so drawn to, isn't me. It's my mask.

Desmond was right. I lied to him, to Talyn, to Fyl, to all of them. I let them place their trust in a lie, let them bleed and suffer and die for it. But I won't do it. Not anymore.

I jerk back, away from his warmth. The cold welcomes me, embraces me. It feels like home. "I'm sorry," I tell him, with certainty growing inside me like a gathering storm. It was wrong of me to open up to him, wrong of me to let myself be vulnerable, wrong of me to bring him in. "What we had was good. Wonderful even." His brow creases, the corner of his mouth crinkling, and his soft eyes run the gamut of emotions: affection, uncertainty, confusion, then the sadness of understanding. "But…"

He stands up, takes a step to me, reaches out. "There doesn't have to be a but."

"Yes. There does," I say, and take another step back, and I know now he won't follow. "When we started this, you said there would come a day when we weren't on the same path anymore. That day is now, Talyn. Where I'm going, what I'm going to do, I can't bring you with me. So we have to part ways."

"Listen to me," he says, "I know you. I know you're hurting now. But I know you don't want to do anything stupid…."

"You *don't* know me, Talyn," I say. "That's the whole point. You don't know who I really am. And that's why we can't keep doing this."

"Alayne…"

"You're a prince, Talyn. You serve your kingdom, your father. That's who you are. And I'm…I'm…" I shake my head, struggling for words.

The walls are closing in, the boundaries dissolving. I need to get out. I need to be alone. "I'm someone else. Someone you don't know. Someone you wouldn't understand."

"You're making a mistake," he says.

"I'm making a choice," I reply, and walk off into the rain.

Chapter 37

Now

I don't know what I'm going to do next, just that I need to do something, to keep moving so I don't drown. Luckily, I suppose, I don't have to figure it out, because Professor Calfex is waiting for me outside my room. She takes one look at me, soaked through to my skin, and sighs. "Get yourself cleaned up," she says. "Headmaster Aberdeen wants to see you in my office."

Twenty minutes later, my hair still damp, I stroll into Calfex's office. I'm not nervous, though I probably ought to be. After this morning, I just feel numb.

Headmaster Aberdeen rests in Calfex's chair, perusing some random scroll, and his face lights up as I enter. "Ah! Lady Dewinter!" he beams. When we last spoke, he was cautious, analytical, but now he radiates a smug confidence, the cat grinning at the wounded mouse. It's infuriating, and I feel my hands twitch, tensing halfway into fists. Gods above, did he ever pick the wrong day. "Thank you so much for coming to meet me!"

"Of course, Headmaster," I reply, forcing a smile. Professor Calfex is in the room as well, standing by a bookshelf, and she glances over her shoulder as I enter. Our eyes meet, and hers narrow, intense, cautious. *Tread carefully*, they say. "To what do I owe the honor?"

"Why, to a headmaster's concern," he says, oozing patrician kindness. "I noticed your absence in our Glyphcraft class and I had to come check and make sure you were all right."

The idea that the headmaster personally checks on every student who misses a class is so patently absurd Calfex actually rolls her eyes, and I have to fight the urge to do the same. "Thank you," I say instead. "I'm all right. Fylmonela was a friend of mine. I needed a few days to mourn."

"Of course," Aberdeen replies, gently shaking his head. "It's always so tragic when we lose a student."

Is he trying to provoke me? Because it's working. And he picked the wrong godsdamned day, because I'm of half a mind to take him up on it, to draw the Loci at my hips and show him just how Fyl died. My hands slide to my side, but then I see Calfex's expression, the tiny shake of her head, and I remember how Aberdeen carves during class, his precision, his grace, the staggering complexity of his Glyphs. I'd be dead before I even finished.

So I let my hands fall and I lower my head. "I'm sorry I missed your class. It won't happen again." I take one long breath, hold it in, let it out. "Is that all?"

"Not exactly." He rises from his chair, his robe billowing out around him as he moves. He's wearing a thick black leather belt around his waist, and his Loci hang off it at his hips, neatly holstered. "Professor Calfex, would you mind if we had a word alone?"

"I would," she replies, and even though she doesn't look at him, her voice is iron. "You're in my office, Headmaster, and she's my ward. Anything you want to say to her, you can say in front of me."

Aberdeen's gray eye flits to Calfex, his brow furrowed. He's actually surprised; I can't imagine he hears no often. A long, tense moment passes as he considers his options, and then he just shrugs. "As you wish, Adjunct," he says, and turns back to me. "When we last spoke, Lady Dewinter, we had quite the philosophical conversation. We discussed clocks and gears, spoke of how every piece knows its place. I gave you some advice on the Second Challenge, if you'll recall?"

Lose doesn't exactly qualify as advice, but I nod all the same. "I do."

"If only you'd listened." He shakes his head sorrowfully, long gray beard swaying like the boughs of a willow tree. "How differently things might have turned out."

"Are you going somewhere with this?" Calfex growls. "Or have you just come to taunt my student in her moment of grief?"

"All things in time." He smiles, even as his eye narrows. "The truth is, Lady Dewinter, I'm not here out of cruelty but out of kindness. Because I believe that every student, no matter how stubborn or defiant, deserves a second chance. That's what I'm here to offer you."

"A second chance?"

"A chance to put the past behind you. A chance to start again. One last chance for the stray gear to find her place." He steps toward me, and I swear if he touches me I'm going to lose what's left of my calm. "It's clear to all of us on the faculty that you and Marius Madison have quite the feud going. While I do value the spirit of a heated rivalry, I worry this conflict may quickly escalate, particularly in light of what happened in the maze. I've seen feuds like this before, and they can spiral out of control, consuming whole Orders, distracting the entire student body, disrupting our learning environment. Competition is healthy, but in the end, we are all Wizards, after all. We're on the same side." He doesn't say who the other side is, and he doesn't have to. "I'm here to ask you to help put this feud to rest, Lady Dewinter. To resolve things with Lord Madison, and let us all move forward."

"You want me to make peace with Marius?" I can't help but growl. "After what he did to Fyl?"

"What he did to Fyl was defend himself from an illegal attack," Aberdeen says firmly. "Our judges all reviewed it and came to that conclusion. Yet despite this, I have heard rumors circulating through the student body, malevolent lies that claim Marius attacked her first." He has to know he's lying, he *has* to, but he says it so oily smooth it comes off like the truth. "I'm asking you to publicly put to rest any rumors of wrongdoing or foul play. To restore order. Do you understand?"

Oh, I understand, all right. That's what this is all about. He wants me to stand in front of everyone and tell them that Marius is innocent, that Fyl deserved to die. It's not enough that he did it, not enough that he got away with it. No, the final twist of the knife, the final degradation, is that I have to be the one to clear his name.

"It's your choice, of course," he says with the most genial of shrugs. "It was your choices, after all, that led you to where you are now. Friendless, humiliated, defeated. A girl on the cusp of ruin. I offer you now a chance to turn that around. Help me out, and I think you'll be surprised how quickly your fortunes will turn, how high your family will rise."

I dig my nails into my palm as hard as I can, focus on that pain, on the light glinting off the window, on anything but how furious I feel. "And if I don't?"

Aberdeen steps past me, resting a hand on my shoulder, and, oh, Gods, focus on the pain, focus on the hurt, drown out the rage. "Then you'll discover just how much more you have to lose."

"Headmaster," Calfex hisses.

He jerks his hand away with an apologetic shrug, a grandfather's kindly smile. "I'm done here, Adjunct. She's all yours. I do recommend you guide her to the right choice. Anything else, well, I'd have to consider a dereliction of your duties." His eye sparkles with malice.

He strolls out of the room, robe fluttering behind him. Calfex glares after him, her knuckles white in her clenched fists, and she mutters something in Izachi. "What the hell was that?" I say, letting out the breath that was tight in my chest.

"That was damage control," she says coldly. "The Potts family has rejected the official account of Fylmonela's death and is publicly denouncing Blackwater. Ordinarily, that wouldn't matter, and they'd be easily dismissed, but after the impact you all made during the First Challenge, well, it's not quite as simple as he'd like." She shrugs. "For the many Wizards out there who oppose the Traditionalists, you and Fyl were symbols of defiance. Her dying at Marius's hand doesn't sit well."

The idea of a bunch of Wizards *cheering* me as a symbol of defiance is so ironic, it makes my head hurt, but I don't dwell on that. "That's what this is about? Shutting up Fyl's family?"

"No, it's about restoring order," she says, venom dripping off the last word. "What Aberdeen cares about more than anything else is stability and civility, that his precious machine of a school, of a Republic, keeps on running smoothly. You've upended that order. You've caused chaos. And Fyl's death, well, it's oil on the fire." She pinches the bridge of her nose with a weary sigh. "You publicly absolving Marius would put that fire out. It would be understood by everyone as a declaration of surrender, of you bending the knee to them. It would take this nascent blaze you've started and smother it before it has a chance to grow." Her hand runs along the hilt of a dagger on her desk. "Nothing bolsters a tyrant more than crushing a rebellion."

"I won't do it. Not on my life."

"That's right. It'll be your life," she says. "If you don't do it, the next time you and Marius meet in the dark, it'll be *your* chest he puts the lance through. Unless he decides to kill a few more of your friends first."

My anger flares toward her. "So those are my options? To grovel or to die?"

"Or to grovel and *then* die. That might be the end game." She turns away, straightening a book on the shelf. "You played big and you lost. Now you're cornered, trapped, no good options. The only thing you can decide, the last thing you can control, is how you go out."

"I—" I start to reply, but the words freeze in my throat and no response comes. Because she's right. No matter how much it enrages me, she's absolutely right. I've lost. The mission's over. My friends are gone. Every second I spend on this island brings me closer to getting caught or killed or both. My grand plan is done.

Which means I'm free.

Oh, Gods.

I'm *free*.

"Thank you, Professor," I say, rising from my seat. "This has been deeply illuminating."

She cocks an eyebrow like that was very much not the reaction she expected, but she doesn't say anything as I turn and walk out the door. With every step I take away from that office, back to my room, I feel lighter, surer, more clearheaded. For the first time since Fyl died, I feel certain, confident even.

Calfex was right about what she'd said back there: I played the game and I lost. But there's a power in losing, a clarity that comes when you're out of options, when all doors are shut but one. I'm done pretending, done trying to win their game, done fighting the impossible.

I let myself lose sight of the mission. I became so invested in pretending to be Alayne that I became her, that I started to care about my status in the Wizards' hierarchy, that I lost sight of what really matters.

I flew too high and came crashing down to the earth. Fine. I always fought best in the dirt anyway.

I made friends, grew close, lost them. Fine. I was always better alone.

I was sent here to destroy the school from within, to plunder its knowledge and do as much damage as I can. I was sent here to burn the place down, not conquer it. It's time I remembered that. It's time I let go of

Alayne, of the noble girl who rallied the Nethros, of the good friend who cheered Fyl on, of the vulnerable girl who found safety in Talyn's arms.

It's time I became *myself.* A fighter. A killer. A Revenant.

The only thing I can control is how I go out. Fine, then.

I'm going out with one hell of a bang.

CHAPTER 38

Then

I am thirteen when I lose my sister.

Getting into the Von Clair manor turned out to be the easy part. Whispers and Sera played their parts perfectly, the visiting merchant and her sickly daughter, so convincing that even watching from afar, I forgot who they really were for a moment. Senator Reginald Von Clair welcomed them in with open arms. I don't know what happened next in the house because I was too busy scaling the mansion's high wall, too busy hiding in the brush, but an hour later, the servants' entrance cracks open and there's Sera, beaming at me with overwhelming pride.

"I did it!" she says through the doorway, as Whispers looms over her shoulder. "I got us in! Von Clair was so taken by my performance, he offered to let us stay until my illness passed!"

"Save the celebration for when the mission's done," I say, trying to sound serious, but her exuberance is contagious. My little sister's first mission in the field, her first real test, and she's passed with flying colors. She's finally a real Revenant. How can I not be proud?

I step into the manor, followed by the two other Revenants on the mission: hazel-eyed thief Edison and hulking bruiser Crixus. "What's the situation in there?" Edison asks.

"I drugged Von Clair and his bodyguards. They're unconscious down in the dining hall," Whispers replies. "The remaining servants should all be in their quarters. We make our way to his study, get into his safe, get the ledger, and get out without making a noise."

"Let's do it." I grin and take Sera's hand.

We creep through the wood-paneled halls, passing oil paintings of stately senators and majestic Wizards, our path lit by recessed candles. This house is so big I don't understand how you wouldn't get lost, but Whispers knows the way, rounding one corner, then another, before we come to a pair of thick wooden doors. "Von Clair's study is through there," she says. "It should be empty."

She pushes open the doors.

It isn't empty.

The study is a wide, rounded room, the walls lined with overflowing bookshelves that reach to the ceiling. An enormous iron safe sits at the room's far end, barred shut with an intricate lock. A heavyset, balding man sits at a long table in the middle of the room, a half dozen tomes laid out before him. A young girl sits alongside him, quill in hand, as she writes on long sheafs of paper.

There is a moment of silence.

Crixus is the first to move. He pushes forward in front of Whispers, whips a massive crossbow off his shoulder and levels it at the two of them. "Hands in the air!" he growls. "You make a noise, and I swear I'll end you all!"

The young girl jerks back, terrified. She's a Humble, a servant, barely older than me. Her dark hair hangs over her face as she slides back on her bench, hands raised, cowering.

The balding man raises his hands and slowly rises to his feet. The

Godsmark on his wrist tells me he's a Wizard, but he doesn't have his Loci on him, so he's powerless. Small blessings. "Listen here," he says in a crackly, phlegmatic voice, his beady eyes fixed on the point of Crixus's bolt. "I don't know who you are, but I assure you, there's no need for violence. My name is—"

"I don't care what your godsdamned name is!" Whispers growls. "Against the wall! Now!"

The two of them move against a bookshelf, hands still over their heads. The Humble girl is starting to cry, and the older man hushes her. Crixus follows, crossbow still leveled, and Whispers draws a knife.

"Whispers," Sera says, her voice low and urgent. "The girl is a Humble! We can't hurt her!"

Whispers shoots a glance back at Sera, her eyebrows arched into a hard, annoyed scowl. I don't know if she genuinely respects Sera's opinion or if she just wants to avoid a confrontation now. But with a sigh, she sheathes her knife. "Fine," she says. "Edison, find the safe. Alka, tie these hostages up. And if they try anything, kill them."

I grab some rope out of my pack and make my way toward the hostages as Edison paces to the safe. One at a time, I lower their hands and tie their wrists together behind their back. The balding man stammers something about paying me, which I ignore. The girl doesn't say anything, but she glances at me out of the corners of her eyes as I bind her hands, a look at once judgmental and pleading.

"I'm sorry," I whisper to her. "This isn't about you. Just play it cool, and you'll make it out of here just fine."

With the hostages secured, I make my way back to the entryway, joining Whispers, Crixus, and Sera. I lock eyes with my sister, and I see the apprehension there, the fear. She's never been on a mission before. She's never seen what we... what *I*... have had to do.

"Okay!" Edison cackles from the other end of the room. He's hunkered down by the safe, ear pressed against its lock, a tool set of picks laid out before him. "I think I've got it!" He raises a long, narrow pick and presses it against the lock.

I feel it first, a crackle in the air, a surge of power. The Wizard, the bald man, feels it, too, and swivels his head to Edison. My stomach plunges as the hairs on my neck stand on end, and I reflexively whip out my Loci, but it's too late. Something's appearing over the safe, something only Wizards can see. A Glyph on the wall, blazing into existence like the burn marks on a paper when you hold it over a candle, glowing a hot, terrible red.

A half dozen intersecting circles, connected like links in a chain, a snake eating its tail.

I know that Glyph. It's what I saw on the ceiling of my childhood home.

"Get down!" I scream, lunging to grab Sera, tackling her to the ground. I don't see the explosion, but I feel it, a thunderclap roar that shakes the floor, a blast of heat that scorches over us like a blazing wind. I hit the ground, hard, and for a few seconds, everything goes black.

When I come to, the room is chaos. Thick black smoke shrouds all of us, so I can only see faint silhouettes. Crixus stands over me, coughing hard; beside him, Whispers leans against a wall. My Loci are gone, tumbled out of my hands, lost in the smoke. Sera's still under me, thank the Gods, and she's okay, moaning faintly as she blinks awake. "You're okay," I choke out. "You're all right."

Then I turn and see the rest of the room.

The study has been completely blown apart. Bookshelves lie toppled, the table overturned, scraps of papers burning and fluttering all around us like blazing fireflies. Edison is completely gone, nothing left of him but a charred streak on the floor. The wall where the Glyph had been is gone, too, leaving just a gaping hole leading deeper into the mansion. And fire, fire is everywhere. It licks up the bookshelves like a ravenous serpent and streaks across the study's floor, hungry and hot and terrible. The whole room is burning, and burning fast.

"Gods*damnit*!" Whispers screams, and it's the most emotional I've ever seen her. She slams her fist against the wall, again and again. "No! *No!*"

The fire reaches the bookshelf on the side of the study and shoots up it, dozens of books swallowed in its ravenous reach. It's harder to see into the room now, to squint past the bright, licking flames. A shape lurches in the smoke, heavyset, bald-headed. The Wizard. He coughs, turns to see us, and then bolts the other way, vanishing through the hole. I can't see what's out there, but I hear a commotion, shouting voices, thundering footsteps.

Whispers breathes in sharply, nostrils flaring, and instantly makes the call. "We need to go. Now."

Crixus grunts and turns to go, but Sera stops him, grabbing his arm. "Wait!" she pleads. "What about the girl?"

The Humble. Oh, Gods. I squint through the smoke and now I can see her, a figure on the ground, trapped under a fallen bookshelf. She's still alive, I think, moving, and when I listen closely, I can hear her crying over the flame's roar, begging for help. "Please!" she shouts. "Help me! Help!"

"Leave her," Whispers says, without a moment's consideration. "We have to get out of here!"

"Please!" Sera begs, tearing up, at once afraid and determined. "We can't just let her *die*!"

"We can and we will!" Whispers swivels back to growl. Her hair is wild around her head, scorched black, and her eyes dance red with the flames swallowing the room. She looks terrifying, a demon made flesh. "I am not compromising our entire cause for some Humble!" she practically spits. "Now *go*!"

Sera looks at her, at that snarling visage, then she looks back at the room, at the trapped silhouette, writhing futilely as the flames close in around her. Then she looks at me. I shake my head. And I see that she's made her choice anyway.

No! I mouth, but it's too late. She takes off running, even as Whispers howls in fury, as Crixus snarls, as the flames roar higher. My sister, my baby sister, vanishes into the smoke.

And before I can stop to think, before I can even let myself consider, I take off after her.

It was hot out in the entryway, but it's so much hotter in here. The whole room around me blazes, dancing flames that lick up at the ceiling, so bright they hurt my eyes. And the smoke, scorching, miserable, burning my lungs with my every breath, blinding me so I can barely see. "Sera!" I shout, and I instinctively reach for my Loci but of course I lost them when the blast hit.

"Over here!" she shouts back. I see her now, hunkered down by the toppled bookshelf, straining to lift it. The girl is still alive, if barely, coughing hard as she strains against the shelf that's pinning her down at the waist, surrounded by flames that are drawing closer and closer. Sera has both arms under the shelf, and she strains hard to lift it, sweat streaking down her face, but it doesn't budge. "Please," the girl begs, clutching at Sera's side. "Help!"

There's a pile of burning books in my way so I kick it aside, and thankfully the hard leather of my boot doesn't catch flame. It's hot, Gods, so hot, like I'm in the heart of a crucible. The smoke is so thick around me I can't see out of the room anymore, can't see the room itself. My eyes sting shut, and my lungs hurt worse than anything I've ever felt.

"I'm here!" I tell Sera and slide up alongside her, grabbing the lip of the shelf as I strain with every bit of strength I have to lift it up. The Humble girl is lying next to me, and she pushes, too, jamming both hands under it. Together, with a collective grunt, we shove that bookshelf up, just enough so that she can scramble out. She pulls herself up and stands there, looking at me, eyes sparkling in the firelight. "Thank you," she says.

"Alka Chelrazi!" Whispers screams from somewhere out of sight, behind the curtains of black smoke. "Come *now*!"

The Humble girl takes off, and Sera grabs my wrist, jerking me forward. "We did it," she pants, her red hair hanging slick around her face, her breath hard and heavy. "We saved her."

She's awfully happy for someone who's about to be in huge trouble from Whispers, but I can't think about that yet. "Now let's save ourselves."

She nods and grabs my hand and tugs me forward, and the two of us rush toward the door. For one second, one last second that will be branded forever into my mind, the smoke parts, and I can see Sera in front of me, red hair billowing, looking back at me with love and fear and pride.

Then the beam hits her.

It comes smashing down like a great flaming club, crashing into Sera from above. She lets out a little shriek as it drives her down to the ground, throwing up a cascade of sparks that sting and blind. "Sera!" I scream, diving down beside her, and suddenly I don't care about the heat, don't care about the smoke. I don't care that I can barely keep my eyes open, don't care how weak my legs feel. I don't care that if I stay here a second longer, the flames will take me, too. All I care about is my little sister. My little sister who's trapped. My little sister who's sobbing. My little sister who's about to die.

"Alka..." she cries. The beam lies across her chest, pinning her down. It's heavy, but worse than that, it's on fire. I try to grab it and my hands jerk back, skin blistering and burned. I grab Sera's arm instead and try to pull her out, but the beam is too heavy and I'm too weak. The fire's spreading faster and faster. The edges of Sera's hair catches aflame, the bright red blazing terrifyingly. I pull again, as hard as I can, but her wrist slips out of mine and I fall onto my back, and no matter how hard I push, I can't find the strength to stand back up.

"Alka," she pleads again, and the fire is all around her, swallowing her like a storm, enveloping her like a grasping hand. Tears streak down her cheeks, and her voice is weak, wavering. "Run," she begs. "Please. Run."

"No!" I shriek, but my throat is so raw it's barely human, a desperate agonized croak. I force myself up, force myself forward, drag myself into the flame. I don't care that I'm in pain, don't care that I can't breathe, don't care that I can feel myself starting to burn. I'd rather die than abandon her. I'd rather die than live without her. I can't lose her. I can't.

Someone grabs me from behind, thick arms wrapped around my waist, a breath that smells of garlic. Crixus. "We have to run!" he bellows and drags me back. "We have to leave her!"

"No!" I scream as much as I can, biting into his arm, smashing my head against his chin, thrashing like a wild beast. I don't care that Crixus is my fellow Revenant, because right now, he's my enemy, the man trying to keep me from my sister, the body tearing us apart. "Let me go!" The flames rise behind me, and I can't see Sera at all anymore; she's lost in the blaze, her screams barely audible over the fire's roar.

I slip into the Null. I don't know why. Maybe it's a reflex, or desperation. Or maybe on some level I know this is the last time I'll see her, and I want to draw it out, to stretch this final second out as long as I can in that murky, slow-moving time of the Null. Either way, as Crixus drags me to the door, with the last of my strength, I close my eyes and slip into that gray.

There are moments in life when I feel like I'm out of my body, out of the moment, like I'm looking back on it as an old woman through the haze of time. There are moments that feel like memories, even as they happen. This is one of those moments, a moment that will haunt me for the rest of my life. This is a moment that matters.

It's peaceful here. The fire vanishes: the noise, the smoke, the heat, the light, all gone. The Null is cold and still, even in this terrible place, the air gray and heavy. A gentle rain of ash flutters down around me, and the world roars distantly, that haunting underwater howl. In the real world, Crixus is sprinting, but here, every one of his steps takes a minute, long enough that I can make out Sera. She lies prone at the far end of the room, as clearly as I can make out through the fog and the ash. I see her light, her spirit, pulsing, ever so faintly, like she's made of stars and they're all going out one by one, a galaxy plunging into endless night. I see her eyes, bright as suns, the last lights in the storm, and I see them vanish into the gray. And I hear her voice, somehow, in a way I'll never understand, echoing in my mind.

"Live, Alka," she says. "Please. Just live."

I reach out to her, and the darkness takes me.

Chapter 39

Now

As the clock strikes midnight, Blackwater goes to sleep. The lanterns in the quad go out, the doors to the Orders lock, and the students chattering in the common areas head to their rooms. The campus is still and quiet. In that silent darkness, I creep through the night into the main building, up the empty stairwells to the top floor. Then I break into Headmaster Aberdeen's office.

The door is locked, of course, but Marlena's skeleton key opens it right up, humming with a multicolored light. I stole it off her earlier in the day, while her back was turned. It felt wrong, but it was the only way; I don't know that she would have given it to me, and I couldn't risk not getting it. I hope she'll be all right. She'll have to be.

That guilt tightens my stomach, and I push it aside. I can't think like that. What matters now, what's *always* mattered, is the cause. Whispers's voice echoes in my ears: *You'll learn their secrets, rise within their ranks. And when you're done, you can burn that place to the ground.*

I'm sure as hell done here. Calfex made that clear. Which means there's just the last step to go.

In the daylight, Aberdeen's office had looked elegant, a well-curated museum of antiquities. At night, lit by scattered moonlight ghosting through the window, it seems far more sinister, haunted. The floorboards creak like moans under every step I take, the eyes of the Wizards in the paintings seem to follow me, and that six-eyed skull makes me so uneasy I can't even look at it. It doesn't matter though, because I'm after one item, the one sitting on a dais in the center of the room, enclosed in glass. The *Codex Transcendent*.

It's not the book I'm after though. It's just one Glyph in it, one last Glyph to learn. The Glyph that's haunted me my whole life, the Glyph that killed my father, the Glyph that killed Sera. *First-Degree Elemental Infusion, Fire Base.*

I'll do Aberdeen's little declaration, all right. I'll stand on a stage with him and Marius and whoever else he wants to drag along, get them all together in front of the school. I'll look them both in the eyes, both of those bastards, and I'll smile, and then I'll set it off, the Glyph I've carved into the floor. And then we'll all go up in flames together.

It's not that I want to die. But it's the only option I have left. I can't win. I can't run. So all I can do is burn.

There's a part of me, a small voice deep inside, that's screaming in protest. It's the voice that tells me I'm a coward, that I'm giving up too soon. It's the voice that tells me I'm letting down Tish and Zigmund and all the other Nethros, the voice that tells me I'm dishonoring Fyl. It's the voice that tells me I'm abandoning my promise to Marlena, that I'm letting down the one person who's counting on me most. It's the voice that tells me I'm just giving in to my anger, to my pain.

It's Sera's voice, telling me to live.

I silence that voice. It's a voice of weakness, a voice of loneliness, a voice of desperation. I'm a Revenant, a fighter, a killer. My mission comes first, and my mission is all that matters. If the price of that means dying, I'll do it. If the price of that means letting down my friends, I'll do it. If the price of that means betraying Marlena, I'll... I'll...

No. Can't think like that. Can't let myself get distracted. I've made up my mind, and there's no turning back.

But first, I'm going to have to find a way to open this glass case.

I run my hands along its smooth surface, and it's fixed in place. Of course. There's a small keyhole at the base of the dais, but the skeleton key doesn't work in it. I slip into the Null and don't see any Glyphs, but that doesn't mean there aren't some hidden. Breaking the glass is a last resort.

I go to Aberdeen's desk instead, hoping for a key. The drawers are locked, too, naturally. I shove aside some of the books on the surface, hoping to get lucky, but there's just a sheet of paper, a half-finished letter with the ink still fresh. I'm going to brush it aside, too, but then I see the words *Madison* and *Dewinter*, and I can't *not* read it.

Esteemed Senator Madison,

I trust that by now you have heard the results of the Second Challenge, and I write hoping that they are to your satisfaction. I have upheld my end of our bargain: your son Marius and his Vanguards stand victorious, soundly in the lead of the game once more. His choice to kill Lady Potts was his own and, if I may speak plainly, has put us both in a more difficult position. I certainly understand his rationale, but I do hope you can guide him from such excess in the future.

I expect the Dewinter girl to bend the knee, but should she not, similar precautions will be taken for the Third Challenge to ensure we have no surprises. The Order of Vanguard shall win the Great Game, and all shall talk of your son's glory. If anything, perhaps the narrative of him so soundly defeating the upstart Nethros will work to our advantage.

I shall be in Arbormont at the end of the month, and I hope that we can find time to meet.

The letter goes on and on, but I don't need to read it. My hands tremble, and my vision burns with a fire hotter than rage. Because of course. *Of course.* I'd been so rocked by Fyl's death, so overwhelmed with despair and guilt, I hadn't even thought to ask the most obvious question: how had Marius beaten me to the center of the maze, anyway? I'd been cheating, after all, breezing through every puzzle, but he'd still somehow gotten there first.

Turns out, he'd been cheating, too. But his cheating had come all the way from the top, from Headmaster Aberdeen himself, who'd made sure he'd win. All that talk of neutrality, all of the endless fixation on order and moderation...it was all bullshit. All of it. Aberdeen isn't some neutral arbiter who only cares about order. He's just as corrupt as the rest.

Corruption is the blood that runs through this school's veins, every brick, every stone, every vow and rite in place to ensure the preservation of the hierarchy. I'd thought my cheating was some bold transgression, but of course Marius and Aberdeen were cheating, too.

They're Wizards. It's what they do.

I tuck the letter into my pocket. I'm not sure what I'll do with it yet, but I know it's got value. Maybe I'll leave it for Marlena, something she can use to blackmail her way off this rock. Maybe I'll—

"Hey!" a harsh voice snarls from the doorway. "What the hell are you doing there?"

Even in the dark, I can recognize that growl, know the shape of that bald head. Groundskeeper Tyms. He jerks a lantern up my way, bathing me in its hot yellow light, and I freeze like a child caught with her hand in a cookie jar. "Dewinter!" Tyms growls. "I knew you were up to no good!"

My mind races. The world dulls. I cannot believe I let myself get caught by Tyms, of all people, but I am *not* going to let him be the one who ends me. My hand twitches for my Loci. "Not a move!" Tyms says, way too loud. "You touch those Loci, and I will end you, girl! I swear it!"

I curse inside. I could probably beat him in a duel, but I need to handle this quickly and quietly, which rules magic out; there's no use in dropping Tyms if it means bringing the rest of the building down on us. "Listen," I say, hands raised, stepping toward him. "This is a misunderstanding. Headmaster Aberdeen asked me to grab some papers for him."

He laughs, which is fair because it was a transparently bad lie. "Like hell! You're a little sneak is what you are! How did you get in here?" He pauses a moment, his beady eyes narrowing with realization. "Wait a moment. You're the one who stole my key, aren't you?"

"Groundskeeper, please..." I say, and I need him to just get a little closer, close enough that I can grab him. "We can work this out...."

He doesn't step toward me, doesn't give me the opening. Instead, his free hand pulls open his robe, and I see a whip hanging at his side, a cruel leather rope strung with jagged thorns. The whip he uses to punish servants. The whip he used on Marlena. "You devious little bitch," he growls. "I'm going to lash the flesh off your bones. I'm going to make you scream till you're raw. I'm going to—"

But I never find out what he was going to do, because right then someone steps up behind him and drives a knife into the side of his throat.

He lets out a horrible sound, a rasping, whistling wheeze, as blood sprays out in a hot crimson stream. Eyes wide and white, he stumbles back, his lantern falling and going dark, and I can see the person who stabbed him now, a silhouette in the shadow. It's small, slight, a girl, I think, with six inches of razor-sharp steel in her hand. He turns to her, gurgling, and now she stabs him in the chest, one, two, three times, each thrust sinking the blade deep into his flesh. Blood bubbling through his lips, he grasps for the girl's head and grabs only the hair on the side, tearing it out of its bun and sending it cascading down her shoulders, and she stabs him one final time, this time driving the knife up to the hilt in his chest. He lets out one last gasp and then collapses onto the floor and lies still.

It all happens in just a few seconds. I slump back against the wall, and now my Loci are drawn, points gleaming at the figure in the shadows. "Who are you?" I whisper.

The figure steps forward into the light. Pale skin. Black hair. A servant's uniform. "Marlena," I say, hands dropping with relief. "Oh, thank the Gods, it's you."

Her face is splattered with Tyms's blood, her hands trembling a little at her sides. "You stole *my* key," she says.

"I'm sorry. I can explain," I start, but then the words evaporate in my throat. Because as the moonlight hits her face, she looks different. Maybe it's the way her hair looks when it's down, hanging loose around her shoulders, the tips curling so slightly. But all at once, I see her, really see her, see her with clear eyes. When we'd first met on the docks, so many months ago, I'd felt like there was something about her, something familiar. Now I know what it was.

She breathes in deep, and her expression softens, just the slightest bit, with relief. "Alka Chelrazi," she says. "It's time we had a talk."

Chapter 40

Now

Hearing my name, my *own* name, is like a spell, one that freezes me, paralyzes me, reduces me to stone. I don't speak. I can't. The act of making words, of forming coherent thoughts, feels impossible, like weaving dust into gold. I just sit there in numb shock as Marlena drags Tyms's body to the side, as she tidies up the room. I just follow her distantly, silently, as she takes me by the hand and leads me out of the office, out of the building, across the dark campus and back to our dorm. I slump onto the floor of my room as she washes herself in my basin, soaking a wet cloth across her arms, her shoulders, her face.

And with each dab of the rag, I see her more and more clearly, the face I've blocked out because it's too painful to remember, the face that's so tied up with the memories I've repressed.

It's a face I saw just once before, in Von Clair's study on that terrible day. It's the face of the girl Sera died to save.

I don't know how much time has passed. Maybe five minutes. Maybe an hour. Finally I manage to come together enough to speak. "You knew...?" She nods, expressionless, her pale face still splattered with crimson. "That I was... that I was a..."

I can't quite form the word, so she does it for me. "A Revenant," she says, running the wet cloth along her arm, letting the droplets of Tyms's blood seep down into a basin. "Yes. I knew."

My mind reels at the idea, struggling to make sense of it, struggling to figure out what to feel. Relief? Excitement? Fear? After so much time building up this mask, so much time striving to hide who I really am, here I am, utterly exposed. And worse? I've been exposed all along. "Since when?" I manage to get out.

"When I saw you get off the ferry, that first night, I…I was struck by the resemblance," she says. She's not looking at me, can't look at me. Her hands are shaking just a little as she looks instead at herself in the mirror. When she speaks, every word is heavy, a footstep sinking deep into snow. "I thought perhaps I was going mad. Could this really be her? The girl who saved me from the fire, the girl to whom I owed my life? Could this really be the girl who I've been thinking about every night for the last four years?" She runs the cloth over her hands, and her lip twitches just the tiniest bit. "Then I saw you charge at Headmaster Aberdeen with a knife in your hand and murder in your eyes. And I *knew*."

"You ran into me on purpose," I say, as piece after piece slides together in my mind. "All this time—helping me study the *Codex*, get through classes, win the challenges—you did it because you *knew*." All this time with her, I'd struggled with what to tell her, how much to trust her, what I could do for her. I'd seen myself as the manipulator, her fate in my hands. But all this time, she'd been the more powerful player, the one with the knife to *my* throat. Ratting me out for cheating would be one thing. But exposing a Revenant spy in the midst of Blackwater? She would've been wildly rewarded, treated like a hero. She would've gotten everything she wanted and more.

But she didn't. "If you knew…why did you help me?"

She breathes deeply, her chest rising and falling as the drops of red fall off her cloth with a *drip-drip-drip*. "Because I believe in your cause," she says. "Because I hate Wizards. Because your sister died to save my life."

My heart freezes in my chest. "You... you saw...."

She nods again. "Yes. I saw what happened. I heard you screaming. I saw her burn." Her eyes water, just barely. "She gave her life for me. So that I'd have a chance to live, to be free."

It's like there's a lump in my chest the size of a fist, like I can barely breathe. My mind reels, trying to piece her story together, trying to make this all make sense. "You said you only left the island once, with..."

"With Professor Barclay. I was assisting him with transcription of Old Marovian texts. When Barclay was invited by Senator Von Clair to see his archives, he brought me along as his personal servant." She looks right at me. "Everything I told you was true. That was the one time I've ever left. And I've thought about it... about you... every day since."

I want to believe her. No. I *do* believe her. Because I've felt it all this time, felt, in a way I couldn't understand, a connection, a sense of something deeper and more powerful between us. This whole time, she hasn't been looking at my mask, hasn't been looking at Alayne. She's been looking at *me*, the real me. All of those moments together, studying side by side in the library, practicing night after night below the dorm, laughing as we ran through the snow... those weren't just part of the game, part of the deception, part of my cover. All of those were *real*.

It's been so long, I'd forgotten what it feels like. And now she's not the only one tearing up. My breath is coming in ragged gasps, and tears burn down my cheeks. She's seen me. She's seen *me*. All this time! "Gods, Marlena... why didn't you say anything? Why didn't you let me know?"

"Because I was scared," she says, her voice barely a whisper. "I was scared that maybe I was wrong, that maybe I was imagining things. I was scared that even if I wasn't, you'd see me as a threat or you'd be angry with me for lying." She swallows hard. "For the last four years, you've lingered in my mind, like... like a phantom. Like a guardian spirit. The girl who ran into the fire to save me, the girl who lost her sister, the girl who risked it all to give me a chance. I've thought about you so much, wondered where you were, prayed you were alive, dreamed of meeting again. It was a fantasy, a hope against hope. And then there you were, alive, real, back in my life again." A tear runs down her cheek, turning red as it strikes a spot of blood. "I was scared you'd reject me."

"No..." I say, and now I can move at last, now I *have* to move. I cross the room, taking a seat by her side. "I'd never reject you. Never." I take the wet cloth from her hand and without a word, raise it to her cheek, to that last splatter of Tyms's blood. The last barrier between us is gone now. She knows me, and I know her. I gently run the cloth along her soft skin, washing away the last of the blood, and she closes her eyes with a tremble, turning to lean into my touch. Her lips graze my skin for just the tiniest second, a shadow of a kiss that sends lightning through my veins, that makes my palms burn. "Alka," she whispers, leaning over to press her forehead to mine and, Gods, hearing my name, my real name, from her lips still feels so strange, so stunning, so powerful.

Then she kisses me.

There is one solitary second of surprise, one second when I can't quite believe it. But then I discover how she feels against me, her soft lips against mine, the warmth of her body pressed to me, and I kiss her back. Her arms are strong, surprisingly strong, and I let them envelop me, just as I envelop her. It's a kiss that's more than a kiss, a kiss that's a dam bursting, a kiss that shatters every wall I've built up, that shatters me. I kiss her and she kisses me and we sit there lost in each other, two souls adrift in a dark sea, clutching each other just to stay afloat.

She lets out a soft gasp as I kiss her neck, and I hold her so tightly it hurts, like I'm never going to let go. She feels like coming home, like belonging, like being held through the night. She feels like this is where

I was always meant to be. In her arms, I find myself at last. It's like all this time I've been in the Null, and I've finally, *finally*, pulled back into the Real.

"Oh, Gods," I whisper at last, when I'm finally able to catch a breath. "I've wanted to do that for so long."

She lets out a tiny laugh, playfully twirling a strand of my hair around her finger. "I guarantee you, I've wanted it longer."

I lean in for another kiss, but she stops me gently, two fingers to my lips. "Alka, wait," she says, not without a hint of nervousness. "Don't get me wrong. I want this—I want you—more than anything. But do you think—I mean, just, with everything going on—and the Great Game—and the thing is, I've never really—that is—" She takes a deep breath. "Do you think we could go slow?"

I almost laugh, not at her, but because kissing her has been so utterly exhilarating I could coast off it for months. "Yes. Of course," I say. "We'll go as slowly as you want."

She grins, beaming, more joyous than I'd ever thought possible, and she kisses me one more time, a peck that lingers long on my lips. "Now then," she says. "As badly as I want to keep kissing you, we probably have some practical matters to figure out."

"Right," I say, reality slowly bleeding back in around the edges, no matter how badly I want to keep it out. "You killed Tyms," I say. "That's probably going to be a problem."

She glances down at her hand. "He was going to hurt you."

"I know. Was he your first?"

"Yes." Her voice is cold, the kind of cold that means she's holding the feelings in. "I can't say I liked it."

"I'm sorry." I take her hand in mine, kiss it. "They're going to find the body soon."

"I know. That's why I wrote on the wall next to it, remember?" she asks, and I suppose I do. I was so caught up in the shock of the moment,

I hadn't even processed it, but she *had* written something with his blood. "I wrote *Frostwolves Reign*." She says that like it should mean something, then sees the look on my face. "They're a Velkschen separatist group."

"What do they have to do with this?"

"Nothing," she replies. "But hopefully it'll send Aberdeen down the wrong trail and keep him distracted." Then she turns to me, an eyebrow cocked suspiciously, as if suddenly remembering how we got here. "What exactly were you doing in Aberdeen's office? Why did you steal my key?"

"I—uh—I was—" I stammer, because I realize all at once how bad it's going to look. There's no way around it, though, and besides, I'm done lying. So I tell her the truth, the truth about what happened to Fyl, what happened with Desmond, what Aberdeen threatened. I tell her what I was going to do.

She glares at me, long and hard, in an endless silence. She's angry, angrier than I've ever seen her, her mouth curled into a hard scowl, her brow furrowed deep. "So that's it?" she demands. "You were just going to blow yourself up? Abandon your cause? Abandon *me*?"

"I... it just... it was all I could do...." I wince and look away. Other people have judged me here, but she's the first one to judge *me*, the real me, and it feels terrible. "I just couldn't think of another way. It seemed impossible."

"You're an idiot," she says with a weary sigh, and then she smiles just a little, and the relief I feel is like a cooling breeze on a scorching day. "Getting a spy into Blackwater was impossible, until you did it. Winning the First Challenge was impossible, until you did it. And turning this around? Winning the game, getting revenge on Marius and Aberdeen, taking all the Wizards down? It's only impossible until you do it."

"Until *we* do it," I say, and all at once I believe it. Marlena makes me feel changed, transformed, reborn. She makes me feel stronger than ever. "Will you join me?"

Her gaze bores into mine. "On one condition. That you never lie to me again, that you never just go off on your own. If we're in this, then we're in together."

I squeeze her hand. "It's a promise."

Then she smiles, radiant, and I find myself lost in the details. The way her hair falls over her shoulders. The way her skin glows softly in the light. The curve of her collarbone, the rising and falling of her breath, that thin scar on her cheek. "Let's do this, then," she says. "For the Revenants."

"No," I reply, because this isn't about them anymore. Whispers would've had me abandon Marlena to the fire. Whispers would've told me to kill her back in the basement. This is about something deeper. It's about two girls united by destiny. It's about two girls standing together against a system that would grind them down. It's about two girls who found each other, against all odds.

"We do this for us."

CHAPTER 41

Now

When I walk out of my room the next day, everything feels different. It's like I've been put through a fire that scorched away all my fear, all my doubt, all my cynical defeat. The world changed overnight, and I changed with it. The girl who strolls confidently through the Order of Nethro doors into the bright light of the sun isn't Alka Chelrazi, the angry Revenant, and she isn't Alayne Dewinter, the scheming noble who flew too close to the sun. She's someone else, someone new.

She's the girl who's going to win.

I start going to class again, where I shine brighter than ever (thanks to Marlena's help, of course). I talk to Tish and Zigmund, apologize for everything, mend those bridges. I promise I won't let them down again. I think they believe me. I speak to all the other Nethros as well, give a rallying address in the common room, the kind full of statements like "They knocked us down. Now we rise up." When I'm done, they all cheer, and even Calfex gives me a wry nod.

I keep things distant with Talyn. We pass each other in the halls, share a quick nod across the quad, maybe even a short walk after a class. There's a tension between us, not just the tension of what we had but the tension of our differences, of the chasm between who I am and who he sees.

Even though it physically pains me, I talk to Aberdeen about a public reconciliation with Marius. Marlena convinces me to do it, because it'll get my enemies off my back, if only for a little while, and give us time to prepare a strategy. I tell Aberdeen that I won't make any claims about Fyl's death and that I'm willing to publicly put an end to the feud with Marius, to join him in "friendship and solidarity," to make sure we Wizards are united above all. It's good enough for Aberdeen.

So we meet on the stage in the quad, surrounded by a half interested crowd of students and faculty, facing each other while Aberdeen presides. The sun bears down hot as he gives a speech about the nature of unity so unconvincing even he seems bored, and Marius and I both agree to put our feud aside. He holds out his hand, and I shake it, and I somehow muster the restraint to not squeeze hard.

When we're done, Aberdeen claps his hands. "And it is in that spirit of camaraderie, of friendly competition, that I announce the Third Challenge!" Everyone perks up at that, me included. Aberdeen waves a hand behind him, and that banner unfurls, the one with all our scores on it.

Vanguard—14

Selura—12

Javellos—11

Nethro—11

Zartan—7

Looking now, those scores seem close, the gap closable. "In two weeks, we shall gather to witness the culmination of everything you've learned!" Aberdeen says. "In two weeks, the Orders shall meet on the field of battle, to compete in the Fivefold War! In two weeks, we shall know who stands the Order Triumphant!"

There's an odd murmur through the crowd, at once excited and alarmed. Marius in particular seems delighted, his white teeth flashing bright. "I'll make you proud, Headmaster," he says, and it's amazing he can keep himself from physically licking Aberdeen's boot.

Later, I regroup with Marlena in the practice rooms, where we can be alone. We sit together on the floor with her in my lap, her back pressed to my chest as she gazes down at a book, my arms draped over her shoulders just right so I can gently kiss the back of her neck. It's been two weeks since we killed Tyms, two weeks of nights curled up together, two weeks of stolen kisses and tenderly held hands. And every single time has felt just as thrilling as the first.

"So what's the Fivefold War?" I ask.

"It's trouble." She exhales sharply. "The Fivefold War is one of the most celebrated challenges and also one of the most dangerous. It's a mock battle in which everyone participates, Order on Order, in a battlefield at the basin of a crater. At the center of the field, there's a tower, and at the top of the tower, through a maze of rooms and stairs, is a gem. The first student to make it to the top and claim the gem wins the challenge and receives five points. From then on, each team receives a point for every five students they still have in the fight."

"Still in the fight?"

"You know. Conscious. Able to move around. Free of any magical traps." She glances away. "Alive."

"Gods," I whisper. I still remember the sheer chaos of the Balitesta game, when it was just teams of five. Picturing that, but with every single student in the school... "It sounds like hell."

"It's meant to simulate war," she clarifies. "And it's certainly as bloody. There's a list of permitted Glyphs, as always, but even with it there are many injuries and usually several deaths."

"Is that why Aberdeen picked it? Because it's an opportunity for Marius to kill me without scrutiny?"

"Possibly," she says. "But more than that, the loose structure affords him infinite ways to ensure Vanguard's victory. He can have the judges look away when they perform illegal Glyphs. He can outfit them with all kinds of infused armaments and items. He could rig the tower with traps that only Marius knows to dodge. He could do all of that and more."

I hunker down opposite her. "So how do *we* win?"

She closes the book and looks up at me. "We need to win so decisively, so boldly, so unambiguously, that there's no way he can cheat his way out of it."

"And how do we do that?"

"Same way we always do," she says, eyes sparkling with cunning. "We break the game."

CHAPTER 42

Now

We fight the Fivefold War on one of the first days of spring. The snow has thawed at this point, fresh shoots of grass poking up underfoot, and the sun bears down warm under a clear blue sky. We gather at the base of a sunken crater on the western shore of the island. It's a massive field of battle, a rough circle probably twice the size of the Balitesta field, the ground lined with soft obsidian sand. I don't know if the Wizards made this crater or if it's geological, but it's certainly perfect for a game like this: the faculty stand on the crater's rocky rim, gazing down, while we take up positions along the inner circumference.

The Tower of Victory stands at the center of the crater, a winding stone spire maybe the size of a guard tower. Surrounding it are all kinds of obstacles meant to simulate a field of battle: fallen trees, crumbling trenches, an overturned wagon cart here and a stone parapet there. The field is big enough that I can only see the hazy silhouettes of the other teams, positioned at equidistant spots under tall, billowing banners. I squint at the Vanguards, trying to see if I can make out which little dot is Marius.

The rest of the Order of Nethro lines up behind me. We're looking quite formidable, if I may so, strapped up in black leather and armor, a squad of kraken helms and iron pauldrons, of thick bracers and Loci gleaming in the light. They all stare at me, waiting for my signal, ready to charge at my command. My two lieutenants flank me on either side, Tish at my left and Zigmund at my right. I nod to one, to the other, and they nod back.

"Listen," I say quietly, so just they can hear. "Whatever happens today…I'm so grateful to both of you. For standing by me. For rallying the others. For everything."

"We're your friends," Tish says, as if it were the most self-evident thing in the world. "We've got this."

Zigmund slams his chestpiece with the side of his fist, surprisingly hard. "Let's break some skulls!"

A horn blows, a warbling so loud it shakes the ground, sending tiny grains of black sand scattering up around our feet. A flare shoots up from the tower, streaking into the sky before exploding into a multicolored burst. The game's begun.

I jab my Loci forward like a sword and let out a furious howl, a battle cry of vengeance. The others roar behind me and we rush forward onto the field, a wild streaking charge. I see the others moving, too, from the corners of my eyes, rushing out with cries of their own, squads of green and red and blue, thundering onto the field and streaking across the crater. The earth shudders under our feet, and the world shakes with our cries.

I wonder at exactly what point the professors up on the crater's edge realize something's gone wrong. The Fivefold War is meant to be a mock battle and is usually fought with warfare tactics: flanking groups, slow advances, each Order trying to claim ground while risking as few of their number as they can. All five Orders battle one another for inches, an endless, fraught series of micro-battles that can last hours. But that's not what's happening now. Instead, four Orders are all charging forward together, every single student wild and reckless, totally indifferent to the goals of the game. And we're not attacking one another. We come together on the plain, Nethros and Javellos and Seluras and Zartans, join like a hand closing into a fist. And then we run together, side by side, Loci by Loci, howling wild as we charge down the crater toward that billowing gold banner, as we descend on the Order of Vanguard like a crashing wave.

Chapter 43

Then

I am seventeen when I create my army.

I meet with the Order of Zartan first, because that'll be the easiest conversation. Their captain is Terra, the girl who made the ice sphere with me in that first Glyphcraft class an eternity ago. She's a Velkschen, a full head taller than me with biceps bigger than my skull, her white-blond hair in the traditional Velkschen style: one side of her head is shaved and the other hangs long and low in interwoven braids. Zigmund's come with me, because the two of them are close and because she wouldn't meet with me otherwise.

We sit together in her room a week before the challenge, in tall wooden chairs resting on a wolf-pelt carpet. Her eyes dart back and forth as she reads Aberdeen's letter, the one I stole from his desk when I broke into his room, and I see her expression darken with growing fury. Finally, she shoves the paper back to me as if it were covered in poison. "This real?" she growls.

"It's real," I reply. "The game's rigged against all of us."

She shakes her head, the metal beads in her braids jangling. "You could be lying. Nethros lie."

"She's not lying," Zigmund says, then he leans over, and when he speaks, his voice is different, softer, more melodic. He's not speaking Marovian but Velx, the native language of his people in the north, and I'm a little surprised how much gentler he sounds. Terra nods as he speaks, and when he's done, she turns back to me. "If this is true, then what do we do?"

"We fight them in numbers so great they can't cheat," I reply. "All the other Orders standing together, attacking as one, making sure that at the end of the war, not one single, solitary Vanguard is left standing." I lean forward, whispering low and conspiratorially. "We hand them the most humiliating defeat in the history of Blackwater."

Terra stares at me, eyes dancing wild in the flickering candlelight, then she lets out a booming laugh. "You're a mad bitch," she says.

I extend my hand. "Let's be mad bitches together."

The Order of Javellos is next, and this one I have to work myself up to. I have no doubt Talyn's going to agree. That's not the issue. It's speaking to him one-on-one, asking him for help while sidestepping the awkwardness between us, talking while very much *not talking*. But I need him in this, so I force myself to march into his dorm, up his stairs, into the all-too-familiar room.

I don't say a word to him as he opens the door. I just hand him the letter and watch as his eyes skim it. Then he lets out a little snort and sets it down. "Well then," he says. "That answers that." His gaze flits to mine, and I look away. "I suppose you have a plan?"

I tell him. When I'm done, he nods, the tiniest hint of a smile. "I'm in," he says. "But I'm sure you already knew that."

"I did," I reply. "Thank you. Seriously."

"Wait," he says. "Has something changed? You seem... different."

I swallow hard. I don't know how I'd even begin telling him about Marlena. "Different how?"

"I don't know," he says, and takes a step closer. "More assured, or at ease? Like you're more... yourself."

"Something has changed," I say, because there's no point in lying. "And maybe someday, I'll tell you about it."

He nods, turning away, with a sense of resignation. "But not today."

Vyctoria in the Order of Selura is the last captain I talk to and the most risky. Marlena and I spent nearly a week debating if it was worth it. After all, she's the headmaster's niece and Marius's girlfriend. For all we know, she's already complicit in their cheating. And even if she isn't, there's a tremendous risk that she'll choose their side anyway, that she'll betray my plan and it'll all be for naught. Marlena insisted it wasn't worth it.

I saw her point. But I also saw how hard Vyctoria had trained for the Second Challenge, night after night, week after week, drilling in the library. I saw her look of hollow, stunned disappointment when Marius was declared the winner. I saw how much this mattered to her.

So, after a great deal of pleading, we meet in her room and I hand her the letter. She reads it over, and I see her brow furrow into an angry knot, see her narrow lips curl. When she's done, she crumples it involuntarily, crushing it in a tight fist. That answers one question. She definitely wasn't complicit.

"This could be a trick," she says at last, her voice even colder and flatter than usual. "You could have forged that letter."

"You know I didn't," I tell her. "Come on, Vyctoria. You know this is real. Deep inside, you know Marius couldn't have beaten you to the center of the maze."

"And how about you?" Her gray eyes blaze through me with so much anger I'm starting to worry Marlena was right. "How did *you* beat me to the center of the maze?"

If the truth is my weapon, I'll have to fall on its blade. "I cheated, too," I say, and her nostrils flare, her knuckles white. "But I'm just some lowborn nobody from a rock halfway across the world. I'm not your boyfriend. I'm not your family. I cheated, but I didn't betray you."

She breathes hard through gritted teeth. "What do you want from me, Dewinter?"

I tell her the plan. She doesn't move, doesn't even blink, as I talk, and when I'm done, she leans forward in her seat so her long black hair falls over her face. She's as unreadable as a statue. A lingering, uncomfortable silence hangs over us, until at last she speaks. "If everyone is attacking Vanguard... how do we determine who wins?"

That's just what I was hoping she'd ask. "We settle it between the four captains. You, me, Talyn, Terra. While our Orders rush the Vanguards, the four of us meet at the base of the tower and fight it out. No tricks, no cheating. An honest duel." I pause, letting her think it over, then say the magic words: "May the best Wizard win."

I can see the moment she makes her decision, the tiniest, subtlest hint of a smile. "May the best Wizard win," she repeats.

CHAPTER 44

Now

My one regret is that I don't actually get to see the Order of Vanguard destroyed. I would've loved to see the look in Marius's eyes when he realized what was happening, see the panic in their ranks as the mass of four combined Orders smashed down on them. But as gratifying as that would be, I still need to win this thing, so I tear away from the gathering mob and sprint for the tower instead.

We all arrive at the same time, Talyn, Terra, Vyctoria, and I, all converging on the tower from opposite sides. We don't speak as we pace forward, eyeing one another uneasily, trying to see if anyone decided to cheat. The thought crossed my mind, certainly. It would've been easy enough to bring a few Nethros with me to tip the scales. But it feels wrong, wrong on a level that I can't bring myself to stoop to. The others might be Wizards, rival Wizards, but by joining in on my plot they've crossed the line into rebels, however selfishly. They've chosen to back me over the school, to join the side of defiance. I know it's the most momentary of alliances, but we're allies all the same. And the least I owe my allies is a fair fight.

The four of us arrive at the foot of the tower at the same time. The sounds of combat wash over us, the great clash of our Orders on the far end of the field. The ground trembles with the roar of magic, with the thunder of explosions, the crashing of earth, and the crackling of ice. I ignore it, as much as I can, to focus on the three faces staring me down. None of us speak. None of us move. We just stand there, the four of us, hands on our Loci, waiting with bated breath.

"All right," Vyctoria says at last. "Let's do this."

We all draw at once, slipping into the Null as our hands whip our Loci out of our sheaths. The world vanishes around us, the thunder of the battle receding into a dull, distant roar. The ash flutters down, thicker than usual, and through that gray haze I see the flicker of life in the three others, see their Loci pulse as they draw them. There's no time left to think. All I can do is act.

Terra and Talyn are already carving, their Glyphs blazing in Vyctoria's direction. That makes sense. She's the strongest opponent, so they're aiming at her first. Terra's prioritizing speed, with a crude, hastily carved Blast of Earth that's almost done. Talyn's carving something more complex, an Ice Base, glowing a vivid blue. Vyctoria's also carving, though I can't begin to guess what she's doing: her first form is one I've never seen, an intricate web of crosshatched lines, shimmering gold.

I move on instinct. While the others focus on Vyctoria, I swivel on Terra and carve. Wind Base, Push Form. Simple but effective. It flares white as I finish my last stroke, bright enough to draw Terra's gaze my way. I see her face harden into a scowl, but it's too late. We're all locked in.

Terra's earth blast fires first, the ground underfoot rising in a wave that rushes at Vyctoria. It's barely left her Loci when my wind push hits her, a rapid current of force that sweeps her off her feet and sends her flying back across the battlefield. She hurtles excruciatingly slowly in the molasses time of the Null, and I see her howl in fury as she twirls through the air. Then she hits the ground hard, Loci flying out of her hands, and lies still. One down.

Talyn's attack fires off, too, and I see it clearly, four dull rods of ice, streaking toward Vyctoria like arrows, leaving trails of frost in the dirt underneath them in their wake. But Vyctoria's ready for it. She finishes her Glyph with a flourish, and a shape appears in front of her, no, no, *below* her, a spinning whirlwind of air, a hissing white cyclone under her feet. With the roar of a hurricane, it hurls her up into the air, like a leaf on a gust. Terra's wave of earth hurtles by harmlessly. Talyn's rods streak through the spot where she'd stood, crumbling into shards a dozen feet away. And Vyctoria rises up overhead, a full story above us, suspended on wind.

I know I ought to be carving my next attack, but I'm too distracted, stunned, staring. Every attack I've learned is predicated on fighting an opponent on my level, but now she has the higher ground. And she's already carving as she hangs there, her Loci slicing through the air with razor precision, her eyes trained on me, her next attack glowing into being. I'll never hit her in time. There's just one thing left to do, one last trick up my sleeve.

My gaze flits to Talyn. Our eyes meet, and I see in his the same bewilderment, the same uncertainty. We stare at each across the Null for that tense, endless second of deliberation.

Then Talyn begins to carve an attack.

At me.

My hand flits up. I'm not looking at Talyn anymore, not looking at Vyctoria. I don't even see what they're doing. There's just one Glyph I can carve, one Glyph that can save me. It's one of the Glyphs I learned from a page stolen from the *Codex*, the most complicated Glyph I've ever carved. A half dozen intersecting hashmarks for a base, three interlocking diamonds for a second form. I've spent weeks practicing it with Marlena in the basement, weeks of frustration and strain and exhaustion, weeks mastering it for a moment just like this.

I don't see their attacks fire off, but I hear them. A gust of wind bellows out of Talyn's outstretched hands, racing toward me. A blast of ice, shackles I think, rattle out of Vyctoria, hurtling at me from above. I feel the hissing wind and grasping cold, even as my heart thunders, as I beg my hands to hold steady, as I will them to carve the last stroke.

A crystal springs into existence in front of me, tall as I am and whirling like a top, glowing with a brilliant golden light. Its surfaces are smooth as glass and just as reflective, and I see my face in the closest surface, my sweat-streaked brow, my panic, my fear. Time moves at a crawl as I look up and see Talyn's and Vyctoria's attacks, wind and ice closing in on me. I see their eyes open wide with shock.

Their attacks hit my crystal. There's a thunderous bellow, a blast of energy that washes over us, at once freezing cold and scorching hot. The Null itself throbs, flickers, and there's a burst overhead like a lightning storm. My whirring crystal pulses with magic and shatters into thousands of golden shards that flutter on the air like leaves in the wind. And the two attacks come firing back, redirected toward the opposite caster, Talyn's wind at Vyctoria, Vyctoria's ice at Talyn.

The Crystal of Reflection. An advanced defensive Glyph requiring incredible precision that transposes and reflects two magical attacks. It's a rare Glyph, considered almost a novelty because it requires the caster to be hit by two attacks nearly simultaneously. The only time it was ever really used was in the Drakovian era, hundreds of years ago, when four-way krova-yans were common.

The other Wizards might have had years of training with the fanciest private tutors. But I had Marlena and a library full of history books.

Vyctoria scrambles to carve something else, but it's too late. Talyn's gust catches her from below and sends her flying backward off her cyclone. She lets out a little shriek as she plummets and then she hits the ground hard, face-first, her Loci tumbling out of her hands.

Talyn doesn't even try to carve. He lets out a laugh, amused and surprised, and then Vyctoria's ice shackles hit him with the force of a boulder, knocking him off his feet, slamming him back against the tower's wall. The blue ice wraps around him like a cocoon, pinning him up against the stone, entombing him in its frigid embrace.

It's done.

I jerk back into the Real, gasping like I've been underwater, staggering back. The other three are down. Terra lies unconscious where I threw her, Talyn hangs frozen to the tower's side, and Vyctoria moans weakly in the dirt, trying, and failing, to move.

"You knew," Talyn says. The shackles have enveloped his body but his face is still visible, poking over the lip of the blue ice. "You knew I'd attack you."

I cross over to him, panting, my breath burning in my chest. "I did," I reply. It was the right tactical move, after all. He expected me to attack Vyctoria and at least wound her, so he figured if he took me off the board, he'd then be able to finish her off. "I was counting on it."

Talyn laughs, a laugh that makes him wince. Then he glances down a little sheepishly and takes a deep breath. "I'm sorry, for what it's worth."

"It's all right," I reply, and I mean it. "We're both fighting for what matters to us. And besides"—I pat the ice enveloping his chest—"I did kind of do this to you."

"Gods, Alayne," he sighs. "In another life, we really could have had something."

"In another life," I reply, and gently kiss his cheek. It's a kiss of finality, a kiss of closure. It's a kiss good-bye. He nods a little, closing his eyes, and I see he understands. What we had was wonderful, but it couldn't last. We're both at peace with that.

I glance up the field, and it looks like the battle against the Order of Vanguard is all but settled. Through the billowing dust and howling wind, I can see shapes drawing closer and closer to us. The other Orders have all turned on one another. It's just a matter of time before someone else gets here.

No more time to chat. I need to move.

The doors to the tower shudder open as I push through them, revealing a flight of winding stone stairs that spirals up like a corkscrew. I'm running on pure adrenaline now, the goal so close in sight. I race up the tower, story after story, and soon hit a pair of heavy wooden doors that I slam through shoulder first out onto the tower's roof.

The wind howls around me, sharp and biting, as I lurch onto the round stone floor. I'm still low within the crater, but now, a dozen stories over the battlefield, I have a clear view. The Vanguard starting line looks like a war zone. The earth is blasted with magic: scorched black in one place, frozen solid in another, jagged crags of stone shooting out like obelisks. The battle is still raging, with explosions of flame and wind, bodies scattering and dodging, lattices of light streaking through the air like shooting stars. It's starting to move away from the Vanguard line, though, spreading out onto the field toward me, leaving dozens and dozens of students in its wake. Some are trapped, frozen in ice or bound with vines, suspended in the air, limbs flailing. Others lie cold and still in the dirt.

I hope Tish and Zigmund are okay.

I need to end this now. I turn back to the center of the roof, and there it is, a tall stone dais, and hovering over it is the single most amazing gem I've ever seen in my life. It's easily as big as Zigmund's fist, clear as glass, carved into a perfect pentagon. As it spins, the light bounces off it, glowing bright in a dazzling kaleidoscope of colors. I shoot out my hand and grab it.

The reaction is instantaneous. Horns, hidden within the tower's sides, bellow a victory call. The gem in my hand glows hot with a blinding light. The tower trembles and then the parapets around me blast open as fireworks shoot out, spiraling trails that race high into the sky and burst apart in dazzling cloudbursts of the richest, darkest Nethro black I've ever seen. On the lip of the crater, where the faculty is, I see frantic movement and shouting, the rising panic as they realize just what's happened.

I crane my head up to the sky and savor it, the feel of the wind, the rumble of the horns, the heat of the fireworks against my skin. I don't know what happens next. I don't know where this goes. All I know is that right then and there, I've won the game.

I've changed the world.

Chapter 45

Now

It takes forever for the actual winner to be declared.

With the challenge officially over, referees and medics rush the field, dozens and dozens of them, as students drop their Loci and collapse, exhausted, to their knees. The incapacitated students are freed, the wounded are rushed away in stretchers, and the rest of us are herded up out of the crater, led onto the grassy plain over the lip. There, we line up by Order, those of us still standing grouped together while the others are ushered into tents. By my count, there are at least two dozen Nethros still standing, and I quickly find the two faces I want to see most among them. Tish's nose is bloody, their smile missing a tooth, and Zigmund's arm is broken *again*, but they're both alive, and I let out a whoop of joy when I see them.

I scan the other Orders, too, just to see how they did. Javellos and Selura each look to have fifteen or so students standing, and the Zartans are looking better with twenty. Terra and Vyctoria stand in front of their respective Orders, gazing into the distance, while Talyn is hauled off into a medical tent, but not before shooting me a sly wink. The Vanguards, on the other hand, are totally wiped out. There are only five or so standing, and they're in bad shape, shivering wet or clutching arms still bruised from vines. No sign of Marius, though. Is he in one of the medical tents, having his wounds stitched together? Or was he one of the students carried away, cold and stiff? Did someone get to him before me?

The Humbles are there, too, all of them, scrambling to bring water and carry bandages and clean up in the crater below. I spot Marlena for one moment as she passes from one tent to another, and our eyes lock as I shoot her a wild grin. *We did it*, she mouths back, and my heart beats so hard it feels like it's going to shatter against my ribs.

We wait there. We wait and wait and wait, as the sun lazily drifts across the sky, as students gradually limp out of the medical tents and rejoin their Orders. The professors are all noticeably absent, gathered together in one big tent at the field's end. I don't know what's going on in there, but every now and again I can hear raised voices and fists pounding tables. I don't think they're happy with me.

At long last, maybe four hours after the game ended, the tent's flap parts and the professors emerge. They line up, grim faced, along the edges. I look at Calfex to try to get a sense of what's coming, but she doesn't react either way, cryptic as ever.

Headmaster Aberdeen, on the other hand, is an open book. He walks to the center of the camp, and everyone grows silent, every eye on him. Sweat streaks down his brow, and his face is bright red, nostrils flaring. He can't even bring himself to look at me. I don't think there's any way he can deny me this. But I'd love to see him try.

"We have now tallied all the points and come to a conclusion," he says, biting down his rage with every word. "By claiming the gem and having twenty-three students remaining in the fight, the Order of Nethro earns nine points. That makes them the winner of the Third Challenge. . . ." He swallows deeply, and it's like he's forcing shards of glass up through his throat. "And the winner of the Great Game."

There's no roar now, no great swelling cheer. Everyone's too stunned, too jaded, still reeling. We look around at one another, faces caked in dirt and blood and sweat, winners and losers, taking in the enormity of what he said.

Then the flap of a medical tent flies open, and a figure staggers out, a bandage around his arm soaked red and a look of unbridled rage on his face. Marius Madison. At last. "No!" he screams, his voice hoarse and raw. *"NO!"*

Every eye flits to him now, the shared nervous quiet of watching someone make a scene. Marius lurches forward, out into the central patch of grass where Headmaster Aberdeen is standing. "No!" he repeats. "This is bullshit! They don't get to win!" He spins toward me, and he's panting, snarling, eyes blazing with more hate than I'd ever thought possible. His perfect hair is a mess, and sweat streaks down his wild face. "*She* can't win!"

"She did win, Lord Madison, whether you like it or not," Aberdeen growls. "Now I'd recommend you settle down before you say something you'll regret."

But Marius is past the point of listening, past the point of even pretending to offer respect. "You can't just have everyone team up on one Order! That's not fair!" he howls, and he has never looked more small, more petulant, more insignificant. A few of the students even snicker, and that really sets him off. "You think you can do this to me? *To me?*" He turns around, directing it at all of us, flecks of spit spraying as he shouts. "I'll have you all ruined, you ingrates! My father will see to it!" Then his eyes light on Vyctoria, standing firm in front of her Seluras with her eyes on the ground, and he sucks in his breath. "And you! You! *You* were in on it, too?" He paces toward her, jabbing a finger in her face. "You sold me out?"

Vyctoria doesn't look up at him, but she doesn't back down, either. "You sold me out first," she says, cold as ice. "Turnabout is fair play."

"You little bitch," Marius snarls through gritted teeth. "You smug little bitch. You—"

"Watch your tongue," Aberdeen growls, voice rumbling with menace.

Marius doesn't heed the warning. He pivots back to Aberdeen, snarling with open fury. "You don't get to tell me that," he says, pacing toward him. "This is on you! I was made a promise! I was told I'd—"

"Watch your tongue!" Aberdeen screams at the top of his lungs, and we all jump back, startled, even Marius. The mask is fully off, any trace of composure gone, replaced by naked fury and desperation. Whatever pretense of nobility or authority either of them had is gone. In that moment, everyone sees both of them exactly as they are: frightened, pathetic, and weak.

I couldn't have planned a better outcome.

With a sharp inhale, Marius finally comes to his senses. He swallows his words and steps back, glowering, trembling, biting his tongue, clenching and unclenching his fists. A murmur runs through the crowd, whispers that slither like vipers, whispers that are going to spread like wildfire through the Republic. But when Marius looks up, he's not looking at the crowd. He's looking right at me, and I look right back. This time, I've got the blade to his throat, and he knows it.

But then he does something I didn't expect. He smiles. Not a frantic smile, not a crazed smile, but the vicious smile of someone who's about to twist a knife. The smile he had before he killed Fyl. My blood runs cold, and my hand dives for my Loci. What am I missing? What does he have up his sleeve?

"You think you're so clever," Marius growls. "You really think you've won this? You think this is just going to stop here? You don't think I'm going to make you pay for this every second of your miserable life?" He takes a step forward, and I think he might actually be making a move, but he doesn't go toward me. Instead, he jerks hard to the side, to the crowd of onlookers. . . .

And grabs Marlena by the arm.

My heart freezes in my chest. My stomach plunges. I don't make a conscious choice to grab my Loci, but they're in my hands all the same. Marius just keeps grinning that same cruel grin as he jerks Marlena out onto the green. "That's right," he says, shoving her forward. "I've had my Vanguards watching you, and I know all about your special Humble friend. All your late-night meetings in your room. Your endless study sessions. Your constant planning in the library. The way you giggle and laugh and act like the best of friends..."

"Lord Madison, please, you're hurting me," Marlena pleads, and Marius just jerks her arm harder. "Tell me, Dewinter," he says. "Are you some kind of Humble lover? Or is she just your little accomplice, helping you cheat your way to the top?"

Talyn steps forward, even though he must have no idea what's going on. "Cheating?" he growls. "That's mighty rich coming from you...."

"Oh, you wait your turn, Princeling. You'll get yours soon enough," Marius says, but his focus is still on me. My vision flares red. My hands are shaking. I can see his grip tighten on Marlena's arm, see her wince in pain, and it is taking everything I have to not murder him where he stands. "See, I don't exactly know what's going on with you two. But I don't need to. All I know is that you're close. Or at least, that you were."

"What are you talking about?" I demand, and I want it to sound firm but it comes out like a shout, because I can't keep this in, can't keep looking at him hurting her.

"I was going to wait until the end of the term for this, but I might as well do it early," Marius replies. "I've had my father buy her contract. She'll be working for the Madisons now. We're going to take her right off this island to my father's mansion." He twists her arm again, so hard she lets out a little gasp. "You're never going to see her again. She'll be *all mine*."

"Enough!" Professor Calfex finally speaks. "This is unacceptable behavior. You need to let go of that girl and—"

"Now, wait just a moment," Headmaster Aberdeen interrupts, and now his voice is calm, patrician. "If it's true that Lord Madison bought out the Humble girl's contract, then she's his servant. It's not our place to get involved in their private affairs." He glances back at me with a hapless shrug and the most infuriating of smiles. "If he wants to take her, well, that's his business."

I know what they're doing here. It couldn't be clearer. They're baiting me, trying to get under my skin, to provoke me into doing something rash and stupid, something that'll undercut my victory, something that'll shift the focus away from them. It's a trap, plain and simple, but it doesn't matter because even knowing it's a trap, I don't see anything I can do except barrel right into it.

Time slows down. There's one second of choice, one moment of agency, that stretches out across an eternity. I look around and see everyone's faces: the other students gawking in anticipation, Calfex's brow furrowed with tension, Aberdeen's condescending smile, and Marius's cruel grin. For all my planning, for all my scheming, everything's come down to what I choose here.

I can hear Whispers in my mind, clear as day. *Remember the cause*, she'd say. *If anything comes between you and the cause, you cut it down.* If she were here, if she could see this, I know she wouldn't hesitate for a second. I'm this close, *this close*, to the greatest victory the Revenants have ever had, to a devastating humiliation of the powers that be, to getting my foot into the door of the most powerful place in the Republic, to bringing the whole thing down. I'm closer to victory than any Revenant has ever come, and all it'll cost me is Marlena.

Then I look at her. Our eyes meet, just like they had earlier. There's no joy now, but there's also no fear. She stares at me with those amber eyes, and she looks determined, resolved, at peace even. She looks committed. *It's okay*, her eyes say. *Let me go.*

I know what Whispers would tell me to do.

And I know what would make Sera proud.

Just like that, my choice is made. I thunder across the green, wind up, and smash the butt of my Loci as hard as I can across Marius's face.

He goes down with a sputtering gasp. Marlena jerks away, stumbling back into the crowd. Marius hits the ground hard, and several professors rush forward to grab me, but they don't have time to because I'm already making my next move.

"Marius Madison!" I shout, jabbing the tip of my Loci his way. "You have insulted my honor and the honor of House Dewinter. I challenge you to a krova-yan!"

A shocked murmur runs through the crowd, this one so loud it almost becomes a roar. A krova-yan. A duel to the death. Everyone stops, even the professors about to grab me. On the ground, Marius blinks, surprised, and stares at me with a mixture of distrust, uncertainty, maybe even fear. He's smart enough to wonder if this is another trap, but there are too many eyes on him, too much hanging on this, too much at stake. "You're serious?" he says, pulling himself back onto his elbows. "Against me? All right." He stands up and steps back, and any attention he'd had toward Marlena is gone, utterly forgotten. She doesn't matter to him anymore. She was just a means to an end, and now I've jumped the line and given him that end. That's what matters here. "I accept your challenge, Lady Dewinter," he says, spitting a glob of blood to the side. "Tomorrow at noon?"

"Noon it is," I say.

And just like that, I seal my fate.

Chapter 46

Now

"You idiot!" Marlena yells at me the second I close the door to my room. "You absolute complete and utter idiot!"

I slump against a wall, muscles aching. "That's one way to thank me for saving your life."

"I wanted you to let me go!" She throws up her hands. "I *know* you could tell!"

"I couldn't do it," I tell her, and finding words feels nearly impossible now. I feel scared and exhilarated and anxious and proud and tired, so, so tired. "I just couldn't."

She isn't accepting it. "You were so close," she says, pacing around the room. "You did it. You won the Third Challenge, won the Great Game. You *had* it! And you're throwing it all away for what? For me?"

"You said it yourself," I reply. "We're in this together, or we're not in it at all."

"No. That's not fair. That's not what I meant." She shakes her head, her voice choking up. "I don't want you to die for me!"

"Who says I'm going to die?" I say back, maybe a little too argumentatively. "I could win."

She glares at me. "He's a better Wizard than you, Alka."

"I know."

"Much, much better."

"I know!" I yell back. "You think I'm not scared? You think I'm not panicking? I am! But I had a second to make a choice, and I made the choice that might keep you alive, that might keep you in my life!"

She paces toward me, breathing hard. Her gaze is like fire, like looking into the sun. The air between us is charged, electric, so tense I'd swear there was magic there. "I'm not worth it," she pleads. "Not worth your mission. Not worth everything you've done, everything you've built!"

"You're worth *everything*!" I shout back, and my voice is caught in my throat, and my eyes are burning. "Listen to me, Marlena. For the first time in I don't even know how long, I feel like I know who I am. I know what I want. I know what I'm really fighting for. It's us. It's this." I reach out and take her shoulder. "It's you."

It feels like everything in my life has been leading to this moment. It feels like a dam about to burst, like the well of feeling I've tamped down for so long thundering against me from within. "I don't want you to die," she whispers.

"I know. But I don't want to live without you," I say, and I hadn't realized how true it was until the words are out there. "I've lost everyone I've ever loved, Marlena. I don't want to lose you, too!"

Neither of us says anything for a moment. The weight of my words hangs in the air between us, hangs over us, a truth I hadn't dared to acknowledge even to myself.

I don't know if I kiss her or she kisses me. But one minute we're apart and the next we're together, tumbling back across the room, her lips against mine, our bodies pressed close. We collapse onto the bed, and neither of us is talking anymore, we're just kissing, caressing, tumbling together. There's a desperation now, a relentlessness, passion that can't be stopped, like rivers rushing, like fire consuming. My body burns as I kiss her lips, her neck, her collarbone, as her firm arms envelop me, as her hands pull off my shirt, caress my side, push me down. She lets out a little gasp as she presses her cheek against mine, as I gently nip at her ear, as the tips of her fingers run along my thigh.

Panting, we pause and stare at each other, our faces barely apart, our breath intertwined. There are no masks here, no lies, no layers of deception. She gazes down into my eyes and I gaze up into hers. All I want is *her.*

"Are you sure about this?" I whisper. "Is this what you want?"

"I want you more than I've ever wanted anything," she replies. "And if this might be our last night together . . . then I want all of you."

Then I kiss her again, and she kisses me, and I lose myself in the sensation, lose myself in her. As a gentle spring rain rattles against the window, as the sun slowly sets, our bodies come together, burning hotter than flame, scorching brighter than lightning. She feels so good, so good I can barely stop myself, so good that I forget all about tomorrow, about the duel, about the incredible danger I'm in. There's just her lips, her skin, her touch, her gasping breath. There's just her.

And as we lay together afterward, our bodies pressed together, staring into each other's eyes, she leans close and whispers, "I love you."

They're three words I haven't said in years, three words I never imagined myself saying again. But they flow out now as easily as water, effortlessly because they're my deepest truth. "I love you, too."

This is what I'd been so afraid of, why I built up so many walls, why I pushed her away for so long. But now the dam's burst, the walls demolished. There's no going back, and I wouldn't if I could. Marlena's more important to me than Whispers, more important than vengeance, more important than it all. There's only one thing that matters to me now, and that's living to have another day with her, another chance to kiss her, another chance to see her smile. She's my cause now, my fire, my fuel. And I'll burn the whole world down before I let it tear us apart.

Chapter 47

Then

I am seventeen the last time I see Pavel.

It's the night before I leave for my mission, my last night in the Revenant camp. A week from now, I'll be recruiting bandits in a New Finley tavern. Two weeks from now, I'll be on the ferry to Blackwater. But right now, I sit alone on the rocky shore of a lake a couple miles from our camp, gazing out at the darkening water as the setting sun turns the sky a vivid purple. Crickets hum in the woods around us, and a distant bird lets out a mourning caw.

"Hey, kid," a gruff voice says from behind me. It's Pavel. The years have changed him: he's about twenty pounds lighter, his hair's gone gray, and he walks with a pronounced limp, courtesy of a spear from an Enforcer. But when he sees me, his ruddy face crinkles into a smile. "Figured I'd find you out here."

"I just wanted to be away from everyone," I reply. "But it's okay. Not from you."

"I figured." He hunkers down next to me, wincing as he bends his knees. "So. Tomorrow's the big day." He scratches idly at his beard, which reaches halfway down his chest. "How're you feeling?"

"I don't know," I reply, because I'm feeling too many things, scared and excited all at once. "It's just hard to take in. I've been training for this for three years. And now it's finally happening."

"Yeah, well, I'll miss you," he says, then shoots me a sly look. "But don't tell anyone I said that."

"I won't." I grin back. "What are you going to do when I'm gone? Are you going to stay with the Revenants?"

"Oh, I doubt Whispers would let me leave if I wanted to. I know too much and all that." Pavel lets out a cynical chuckle, the kind that means he's not really joking. "No, I figure I'm stuck with you lot till the bitter end. You'll always need someone to heal you up, right?"

"Be safe," I tell him, struck by a sudden pang. I don't know quite what Pavel is to me... a teacher, a father figure, a friend? But I know he's the one person left in the Revenants that I care about. I know I don't want him to get hurt.

"You just worry about yourself," Pavel replies. "You're the one going deep undercover behind enemy lines." He scoops up a rock in one stocky hand and hurls it into the lake, where it sinks with a resounding splash. "Blackwater Academy. I ever tell you that I wanted to go there?"

I blink. "No."

"Well, I did," he says. "My parents were lesser Wizards. My father was a foreman, my mother a nurse. Both of them went to Highmorrow, which is a third-tier Wizard school in the west, the kind that just teaches you the Glyphs you'll need to do your job. But I had bigger dreams. I wanted to go to Blackwater, to study with the finest scholars, to become a professor myself."

"What happened?"

"They didn't accept me, of course," he replies, like it's the most obvious thing in the world. "So I went to Highmorrow instead. And that's where it all went wrong." He gazes out at the water, still rippling from where he tossed the stone. "When I was in the prison camp, I'd think about that all the time. I'd wonder how different my life would've been if I'd gotten into Blackwater, how much better things would've turned out." For once, there's nothing gruff about him, just a melancholy vulnerability that makes my heart ache. "Blackwater was always my lost fantasy, the promise of the life I could've had. And now you get to go there and live my dream."

"I'm not going there to become a professor," I say, maybe a little bluntly. "I'm going to burn the place down."

Pavel stares at me, one bushy gray eyebrow cocked, like he's impressed and alarmed all at once. "Can I give you one last piece of advice before you go?"

"All right."

"Whispers has filled your head with all kind of things. Her whole belief system, her whole worldview. And I'm not saying she's wrong. She's tough and she's strong and she gets shit done that no one else could." He reaches into his pocket, takes out a silver flask, then reconsiders and puts it back. "But there's more to life than what she sees."

"What are you talking about?"

Pavel sighs wearily, turning back to the lake. "Whispers is a creature of hate. She's got a core of fury inside her like a smoldering sun, red hot and forever burning. Anger's powerful, don't get me wrong. It gets you back up when you've been knocked down, keeps you fighting when everyone says you oughta give up, lets you push through the pain to do the impossible. When it comes to burning down the world, anger's all you need. But if you want to build something better, if you want to make a new world, you need more than anger. You need something to love, to guide you, to protect you. You need more than something to fight against." A gentle breeze passes over us, and Pavel closes his eyes. "You need something to fight for."

I'll think about his words many times in the months to come. But it's not until the night before the krova-yan, when I lie awake, staring at Marlena sleeping in the moonlight, that I'll really understand what he meant.

Chapter 48

Now

I nod off at some point, and when I wake up the first thing I see is Marlena's eyes. It's early morning, the bright light of dawn shining in through the blinds, sparkling bright against her dark hair. Her arms are wrapped around me, our legs entwined, and I linger in the feeling of her body, of her skin, of her warmth.

"Gods, you're beautiful," she whispers, and I somehow feel my cheeks burn. "I wish I could wake up to this every morning."

"Maybe you will," I reply. "Don't go counting me out yet."

She breathes deeply, and I can feel her heart beating through her chest, beating against mine. "I've dreamed about you for so long," she says. "And now we're together finally and... and I'm so afraid I'll lose you." She pulls me in tight, face buried in my shoulder. "Please don't die. I want so much more time with you."

"I won't," I reply, and I think I actually believe it. "I've never been one for the temple, but... if the Gods granted us this, if they let us be reunited after all this time, if they let us find each other, of all the people in the world, and let us be together... I can't believe they'd have it in their hearts to tear us apart."

She raises my hand and gently kisses my Godsmark tattoo, sending an electric tingle down the length of my arm. "I'll pray that you're right."

I rise. I get dressed, putting on my most practical clothes, comfortable pants and a loose shirt. I strap on my holsters, slide in my Loci, test their grips. I take in my room one last time. And we head out.

There's a crowd waiting for me outside. All of the Nethros are there, Tish and Zigmund and the rest, huddled together in a dense crowd, waiting for me, for their leader, for the captain who carried them to victory. Others are there, too, Javelloses and Zartans and even the odd Selura. Talyn watches me from the back, and when I emerge hand in hand with Marlena, he gives a little nod of understanding, like *Ah, I see.* He's not entirely right, of course, but it doesn't matter. Not anymore.

No one speaks as I make my way down the Order's steps. They don't have to. They part to let me through, patting my shoulders, bowing their heads, and when I set off to make the long walk to the Champion's Grounds, where the duel will be held, they follow me as one, a shadow, an army. We march together through the campus, and every step we take is a moment of solidarity, a rebuke to the order this school was founded on, a challenge to everything Blackwater, everything the Republic, is meant to represent.

Others watch silently from the sides as we walk by. Vanguards and their supporters scowl our way, ugly sneers and hateful glares. A few professors glance away, as if even acknowledging the defiance is somehow being complicit in it. But it's the Humbles that really catch my eye. Marlena is well liked in their village, and word must have spread about what happened. As I walk by them with Marlena, they stop working and watch me, watch us. Some look concerned. Others proud. An old gardener takes off his hat and presses it to his chest. A woman sweeping the path nods. A trio of children wave.

The Champion's Grounds are located maybe a mile away from the campus. We march there together, wordless, unified, a gathering storm, a rising wave. This moment feels significant, charged, heavy. Something is happening here, something bigger than me, bigger than the game, bigger than this school. Something that's going to matter.

Then we're there, at the grounds, and I feel a knot of anxiety tighten in my stomach, because this is really happening. Slowly, my crowd disperses, heads into the stands to take their seats.

Tish and Zigmund take their time. Tish hugs me tight and says, "Do it for Fyl." Zigmund claps me on the back, grinning wide. "Crush his ass," he booms, and I can't help but smile back.

Calfex is next. She approaches me, expression as unreadable as ever. "Do you have even the faintest idea what you've gotten yourself into?" she asks.

"Maybe the faintest?" I reply.

She lets out an exasperated sigh that reminds me more than anything else of Pavel. "Tell me you have some great cunning strategy to win this. Tell me this is all part of your plan."

"I wish I could," I say, and I feel Marlena's hand squeeze mine. "But I'm just winging it."

"You are alternately the most brilliant and the most infuriating student I've ever taught," Calfex says wearily. Then she leans in close and whispers in my ear, her voice so low I can barely even hear her. *"Ishmai vel pera, ishmai vel relos."*

An Izachi prayer. One my mother would say to me every night before bed. *May you find triumph*, it means. *May you find peace*.

Talyn comes up after she's gone. He glances at Marlena, then back at me. I wince a little at the awkwardness, but he dismisses it with a signature smirk. "Listen," he says. "You're going to win out there. You're going to show that prick he messed with the wrong person. You're going to get the justice Fyl deserves." He takes my other hand in his, squeezes it gently as he presses his thumb against my palm. "I know it."

There's a strangle tingle in my palm, and when I look at my hand, there's an imprint of dust on it, ash that sparkles a vivid gold in the shape of his thumbprint. His Gods' Ash. "Will that help me?" I ask.

Talyn shrugs. "It won't hurt."

"Thank you." I clench and unclench my fist, and my hand pulses with power. "You know, there's no glory for you if I'm the one who beats him."

"I have a whole lifetime to chase glory," he says, and gently pats my shoulder. "Today, I'm just here for my friend."

The last person to stay with me is Marlena. I know it's time to go into the grounds, to take my place, to finish this once and for all. But I don't want to let her go, don't want to be apart, not now, not ever. I turn to look at her, and she leans in and kisses me, long and deep. It's a kiss of longing, a kiss of desperation, but it's also a kiss of transgression, of defiance, of power. I can feel the other Wizards staring, hear murmured gasps and whispers, but I don't care. Let them stare, let them gossip. I might die today. I'm going to make it count.

When she pulls away, she stares into my eyes one final time. "Come back to me," she says.

"I promise," I reply, and then I head inside.

My krova-yan with Marius isn't some little duel to be played out on a strip of grassy lawn; even the professors who disapprove of the practice can't deny the significance. So we meet instead here, in the Champion's Grounds, an ancestral dueling field dating back to the school's founding. It's only meant to be used for special occasions, and the duel of the century certainly meets that criteria. A long stretch of flat, dry clay sits framed by tall stone stands of tiered seats on both sides, like a road cleaving between two mountains. Overhead, the sky is gray, overcast, and a cold wind rustles through. Not like that kept anyone away. It looks like the whole school is already there, packing the seats, ready to see one of us die.

Normally, today would be a big day of celebration, as the winning Order is honored for their victory. But the duel has stolen the focus from all of that, and I don't think even the Nethros have done much partying. Everyone seems to understand that, fair or not, this duel is the real culmination of the Great Game. If Marius defeats me, then even if Nethro is crowned the Order Triumphant, he'll have made it out of this with his dignity intact, with order restored. And if I defeat him... well, I don't think anyone's prepared themselves for that.

I take my spot at one end of the track, planting both feet firmly in the clay. My Loci sit in sheaths at my hips, and I rest my hands on their hilts, feeling the cold leather grips, comforting in their familiarity. The truth is, I've put barely any thought into what comes next, or any strategy into what I'm going to do. It doesn't really matter. Marius is a vastly better Wizard than I am, and there's no amount of preparation I could have done that would matter, not in a night. All I can do is hope to improvise and catch him off guard.

That made sense when I challenged him, and last night talking to Marlena, and this morning as I walked here. But standing there, on the dueling ground, I feel my knees start to tremble, my palms start to sweat, my heart hit my ribs. There's a nagging voice in my head I'd manage to ignore, but it's getting louder and louder, and it's asking the same question: *What the hell were you thinking?*

I breathe deeply, collect myself, and turn to the stands. They're all there, everyone. Zigmund and Tish sit in the front of the Nethro section and wave at me. Professor Calfex gives a slight nod. Talyn nods. And Marlena looks on with the most complicated expression of all, fear and pride and love all at once.

I can do this. I have to do this. For them. And for myself.

There's a commotion at the other end of the dueling grounds. It's Marius. He strides up, bold and smug, taking his position. He's dressed impeccably, resplendent in a gold and red suit, long leather gloves, tall boots with silver buttons. His stag-head Loci sit at his hips, and he shoots me a blinding smile, a smile I want to wipe off his face more badly than

I've ever wanted anything. The Vanguards cheer loudly at the sight of him, and I see a nervous titter run through the Nethros. That's not comforting.

"Duelists!" a voice cries, and everyone goes silent. Headmaster Aberdeen strolls onto the ground between us, his long black robe trailing after him. He's cleaned up since yesterday, and when he speaks now, it's firmly in his old voice, the gentle, wise patrician. Maybe he's had the time to recover after his outburst. Or maybe he's just confident I'm going to die here, and all his problems will go away. "I had hoped that the rivalry between Lady Dewinter and Lord Madison would be resolved peacefully, in the spirit of friendship," he says, and I have to wonder if a single person here believes what he's saying. "But it was not to be. So we settle it instead in the most ancient of ways, with a krova-yan. A duel to the death, here in these grounds where the First Fathers once stood. Here, with blood, this shall at last be resolved."

He turns to me, and I scan his face for a hint of emotion, but it's all hidden deep. "Alayne Valencia Dewinter! Do you relent, drawing the shame of the Gods unto your line?"

"I do not," I reply, and there goes the point of no return. This is happening. This is really happening.

"Marius Benedikt Madison!" Aberdeen booms. "Do you relent, drawing the shame of the Gods unto your line?"

"I do not," he says, loud and theatrical. "I shall fight for the Madison name, and I shall honor my ancestors!"

"Thus shall it be, in the eyes of Gods and men." Aberdeen steps away, out of the line of fire, to his position at the base of one of the stands. He claps his hands, a boom that sounds like thunder. "Let the krova-yan commence!"

I move first. I have to. My best shot is if I can somehow beat him to the draw, catch him right away while he tries something fancy. I slip into the Null, my Loci already drawn, breath tight in my chest. The Null here is quiet, still, the ash frozen in midair, like it's paused in anticipation. The fog hangs thick, blocking out the stands so that all I can see of the hundreds watching is the distant, barely visible beating of their hearts, like stars flaring out in a distant sky.

I jab my right Loci forward, carving the first strokes of an Earth Base, and my instinct's decided what I'm doing for me. A lance of stone, just like the one Marius threw at Fyl. Fast, deadly, and poetic. I just need to beat him to the draw.

But when I look up at him, he's not carving anything. He's just standing there across the Null, arms folded across his chest, a bemused smirk on his face. It's enough to stop me cold, to trap my breath in my throat. What is he thinking? What is this?

He sees me freeze, and that just make him smirk harder. He extends one hand, an endless motion in the expanse of the Null, and gestures at me. *Go ahead.*

The two lines of my Earth Base flare brown in front of me. Shit! I'm reconsidering everything now, trying to figure this out, but it's too late. I could try a different form, maybe, like a shield or an infusion, but I'm starting to panic and doubt myself and I'm not even sure which shield form works with earth. I don't have time to think. With a wince, I cut fast, the Lance Form, and let it fly.

My spear is far less elegant than Marius's had been, a jagged, crumbling shard of stone, but it should still hurt like hell. It flies forward, plunging over the clay with that lazy, molasses speed of the Null, its tip aimed perfectly at his heart.

Now he moves. He whips his Loci out with a flourish, twirling them midair, and then he carves with dazzling speed, a flurry of motion with both hands weaving like dancing birds, his wands slicing through the air with incredible precision. My lance is bearing down on him, inch by inch, but he doesn't seem to notice or care. The nervousness in my gut turns to full-blown panic. He's not just good, he's incredible.

A Glyph burns in front of him, one I can't recognize, an elegant interwoven purple star framed by a pulsing wavy line that flares white and yellow. The Glyph expands outward, a net that envelops my lance and burns clean through it, leaving deep red grooves in the black stone. Now a foot away, the spear crumbles and breaks apart, dozens of rocks falling to earth, and all that hits him is a gentle breeze.

The smug bastard takes a bow.

I suck in my teeth, falling back, as I realize exactly what he's doing. He's not worried about winning. No, he's certain he'll win. What he's trying to do is humiliate me, to win so boldly and cruelly that it's all anyone will remember, that it'll undo any damage to his reputation my victory yesterday did. This is going to be a duel for the history books, and that means making my loss as shameful as possible.

I need to get on the defense and buy myself time to think. I take one step back, and now he springs forward, waving his Loci with a flourish. I recognize the base this time, the long slash of fire, so without thinking I jerk my Loci up and start carving ice. But as fast as he was defending himself, he's somehow so much faster attacking. His Glyph is already carved, a perfect whirling ball of flame, and it's moving fast, faster than anything should in the Null, hurtling its way toward me like a tiny meteor. The fog swirls around it, a twisted spiral chasing its tail. I fall back, carving as fast as I can, the sloppiest shield I've ever done. It springs up in front of me, a pulsing blue hexagon, literally a second before the fireball hits it. The shield bursts apart in a frigid blast, shards of ice slashing my cheeks, the force knocking me over.

I hit the ground and snap into the Real for one awful moment. I'm sprawled out on the hard clay. I couldn't hear the crowd in the Null, but I hear them now, cheers and shouts and hollers. Marius stands at the other end, still in the Null, his eyes a pitch-black starscape, his hands moving in an impossible whirl. He's carving another Glyph. Shit!

I leap up to my feet and pull myself back into the Null, but it's too late.

His next attack hits me instantly, a sliding column of earth that slams into me like an avalanche and knocks me hard onto my back. Pain flares through me, my vision flaring with stars, and then something tangles tightly around my ankles, something that grasps hard and stabs with thorns. A vine. I look up just in time to see him grinning wider than ever, and then the vine whips me up, waving me through the air like I'm a rag doll and then smashing me face-first into the hard clay. I feel a tooth shatter, feel my nose break, feel blood rush into my mouth. I gasp for air, spitting crimson everywhere, pushing myself onto my hands. *Now* I can hear the crowd even through the Null, a distant shrieking and thundering, like a herd of gazelles.

Any capacity I have to think is gone, any strategy, any sense. I'm an animal just trying to survive, to fight her way out, to get away. My Loci are still in my hands somehow, my weapons, my lifeline. I just need to get one good attack in. One hit. I try to turn to him, to carve, but my hand is trembling, my fingers weak, my vision blurry. I don't see him. I just see the flash of light streaking my way.

It explodes in front of me, and I feel its heat scorch my face, and then I can't see at all anymore, can't see anything except hot, burning white. I have no idea what his next attack is, or the one after that, or the one after that. A burning lance stabs through my calf. A thousand needles tear open my side. Something hard and massive hits my chest, and I feel a rib shatter. My Loci fly out of my hands, skittering away across the fields. In that moment, I can't see, can't hear, can't scream. I'm just the rush of agony, the roar of blood, the taste of copper. And I'm a thought, a thought trapped in time like the ash in the Null, hovering in my head.

This is it, I think. *This is how I die.*

Then it stops. There are no more impacts, no fire, no ice. For one moment, everything is still. I'm still alive, I think, even if my entire body aches and burns, even if my breath is coming in ragged gasps. I strain to open my eyes and I'm still in the Null somehow, but the ash is thicker than it's ever been, a dense haze that coats me like a blanket. Everything hurts, hurts so much. I can barely see. I can barely move.

Something thunders toward me, pounding booms, louder and louder. Marius's footsteps. He's walking over to me. Of course. The cruel display has gone on long enough. Now he's going to finish the job.

My eyes burn and I feel something else, something worse than my body's agony, a sudden terrible burst of emotion and clarity. I lost, and I lost so badly. Everything I've built, everything I've done, gone. I got stupid and reckless and now I'm going to die here, all alone on the cold, hard clay, and Marius is going to laugh and smile and preen, and Aberdeen will keep on living his decadent life and my parents will be unavenged and the Wizards will stay in power, and it will all have been for nothing, all of it.

And the others... Tish and Zigmund... Talyn... Marlena... they're all going to watch me die. They're going to have to live with that forever, that pain, that defeat.

That thought, their faces, is like a bolt of adrenaline, a shot of lightning running through me. I'm not going to let it end. Not like this. Not without a fight. And even as his footsteps grow louder, even as his shadow looms over me, I feel a pulse of power in my right hand, where Talyn left his gift of Gods' Ash. In the Null, I see my hand glow bright and dazzling, filled with power, and I use my fingernail to scrape against the skin of the world, to carve what I can. It's a Glyph I know by memory, the simplest one I know, the only one I can carve without a Loci in my grip.

A weight presses down on my ribs, the toe of a boot, and the pain jolts me out of the Null at last, back into the Real. The world is impossibly bright and colorful, hurting my aching eyes even more. The clouds above have cleared, giving way to a blue sky, but it's blotted out by Marius's shape. He stares down at me, totally unharmed, his hair still perfectly brushed, his suit unblemished, his smile blinding white. He leans over me and grabs my hair, once again, jerking me up. The crowd is silent now, breath held tight, ready for the killing blow.

"You see, Dewinter?" he whispers, so low only I can hear it. "It was always going to end like this."

There's a tiny burst of magic from my right hand as I finish my Glyph, the smallest crackle. I feel something in my palm, something cold and hard. He sees it, and his eyebrow arches with curiosity. With an amused snort, he kicks my hand with his boot, turning it over so he can see what's in it.

A sphere of ice. Perfect and round, just big enough to fit into my fist.

"What are you going to do with that?" he laughs.

I smash it across his face.

The sphere is solid, hard as rock. It doesn't shatter, but his cheek does, cracking with a hard, wet spray. He lets out a gasp and staggers back, blood streaking down his face, but now there's something in me again, something burning with anger, with desperation, with pain. I leap up to my feet and I hit him again, this time in the forehead, as hard as I can. There's a brutal crack, loud enough that the crowd can hear it, and a collective scream cuts through the air. He whips toward me, trying to raise a Loci and slip into the Null, but it's too late, and I'm too close. I smash him across the face again, stunning him, and the Loci tumble out of his hands, those beautiful carved stags' heads hitting the dirt with dull thumps.

My vision pulses red, throbs at the edges. My heart thunders, my ears roar. In that moment, I am not a Wizard, nor a Revenant, not even really a person. I'm a beast of caged fury and pain, a lifetime of loss and fear. I'm every friend I've buried, every tear I've shed, every loss, every defeat, every fear. I am a force of nature, a hurricane of rage, a howl screamed into the ocean night. I am terrifying, and I am relentless, and I am unstoppable.

Marius Madison is the better Wizard. He effortlessly beat Alayne Dewinter.

But he's got nothing on Alka Chelrazi.

In the stands, the crowd is frantic, scrambling, shouting, pointing. I leap forward onto him, knocking him flat onto his back, and I hit him again and again and again, bringing that sphere of ice, now a bright ball of red, down onto his face. I shatter bone and break teeth, even as his hands grasp weakly at me, even as he kicks and flails.

"Wait..." he rasps, blood bubbling through his broken lips, and I do stop for just a moment, the sphere raised high. His face is a ruined mess, but I can still his eyes, puffy and swollen and terrified. "Wait!" he pleads, his voice desperate. In that moment, everything he has is gone. His privilege, his power, his wealth, his training. Every single advantage he has, taken away. In that moment, we're just two people, nothing more. And I'm stronger.

"Did you wait for Fyl?" I ask, and raise the ball for one last hit.

Then something hits me from the side, a forceful rush of air that hurls me off him, sends me flying back to where I'd been before. The ball of ice tumbles out of my hands. I slide back against the clay and crane my head up, and standing there, his Loci in his hands, is Headmaster Aberdeen.

"Enough!" he bellows at me, red-faced, livid, magic surging around him like a gathering storm. "This ends now!"

The crowd is in utter chaos, out of their seats, every last one of them shouting. The other professors stare at one another in bewilderment. Professor Calfex alone moves, lunging forward, her own Loci out and aimed his way. "Headmaster Aberdeen!" she demands, her voice booming over the dueling grounds. "You violate the laws of krova-yan! You disgrace these grounds!"

"To hell with these grounds!" Aberdeen turns back, roaring at her, at the crowd, at everyone. This is it then. I've fully forced his hand. Everyone backs away, pointing, whispering, and that just enrages him further. "Are you all out of your godsdamned minds?" he screams. "This is the son of the Grandmaster of the Senate! I'm not just going to sit back and let some lowborn bitch kill him!"

He pivots back to me, to where he thought I was, but I'm not there anymore. I'm up on my feet, right in front of him, and I drive my Loci up to the hilt into his chest.

Aberdeen's eye goes wide as he gasps, pulsing black as he pulls into the Null. I'm there with him. We hover together in that fog, in that gray, as the rest of the world melts away. The screaming crowd, the referees, the professors, all gone. Right now, it's just me and Magnus Aberdeen, the man who killed my parents, all alone at last.

We stare at each other as ash flutters in the air, as blood trickles down from his lip, as the fog swirls and dances around us. He tries to raise a Loci, but I grab his wrist, holding it tight with one hand, as I jerk and twist the bone knife with the other. He's trapped, powerless, dying, but even now he's still got his brow furrowed with rage and indignation.

"You..." he snarls. "You dare...?"

I jerk the knife up, to the side, down, cutting deep. In the Null, it's just us, so I lean in close and whisper. "My name is Alka Chelrazi," I tell him. "Daughter of Petyr and Kaelyn."

His jaw drops, and at last I see it, the dance of emotions. Confusion, surprise, and finally fear. "No..." he chokes, and I pull the knife up harder, up to his collarbone, even as terrified recognition dances in his eye, as he realizes these will be the last words he ever says. "It...can't be...."

"You killed my parents," I tell him. "And now I've killed you."

Then I jerk back into the Real and I shove him back, away from me, so he falls back onto Marius. Chaos rages in the stands as students jostle and shove. Professors rush toward me. I can see Talyn shoving his way down, see Marlena screaming. I stagger back, Loci tumbling out of my grip, and collapse onto my knees. The world grows hazy and gray, and I can feel the darkness coming for me, but I force myself to hold it together, to stay conscious just long enough to see this all the way through.

In front of me, Headmaster Aberdeen pulls himself up, trembling, gasping. A handful of professors sprint to him, but as he rises they jerk back, because they see it now, the Glyph I carved into his chest, flaring a terrifying, hungry red, the Glyph that's haunted me my whole life.

A half dozen intersecting circles, connected like links in a chain. A snake eating its tail.

Aberdeen reaches out to them in desperation, even as the Glyph glows bright and brighter, as his veins run hot with yellow rivulets of flame, as tongues of fire lick their way out through the chasms in his flesh. The headmaster lets out one last desperate scream.

Then the earth shakes with thunder and flame, and I fall back into the darkness.

CHAPTER 49

Now

For some time, I linger in that darkness. It's quiet there, and still, and oddly comforting. It's a bit like the Null, but without the ash and that feeling of heaviness and the shadows lurking in the fog. It's just dark and gentle and still. Peaceful, almost.

When I manage to open my eyes at last, the first thing I see is the bright white of a billowing canopy. There's a pillow under my head and a gentle breeze. The infirmary.

I try to sit up, but I can barely move. My body's wrapped tightly in bandages, my skin glowing that faint shimmering green. I ache, ache a lot, but it's a dull ache, bone deep. My head's foggy and my throat is parched, but I can feel the sheets under my fingers, the cool air on my skin, smell the distant scent of anesthetic. I'm alive. That's something.

"She finally wakes," a voice says. I crane my head to see Professor Calfex sitting in a chair beside my bed, hands folded neatly across her lap. She's looking more formal than I've ever seen her, in a neat black suit, her hair done up in a bun, a pendant of a kraken hanging on a chain across her neck. She's not the first person I'd want to see, but she's not the last, either.

"How long was I out?" I ask, still straining to process my last memories. It feels like it was just a minute ago that I was cutting into Aberdeen's chest, but also like it's been ten years.

"A week," Calfex replies. "You were injured very badly. Between the damage from the explosion and what Marius did to you, it's frankly a miracle that you're alive."

I swallow hard, my throat aching, and every word feels a bit like forcing out coals. "Headmaster Aberdeen . . . ?"

"Oh, he's dead," Calfex says, matter-of-factly. "Marius, too. You made sure of that."

I close my eyes, breathing deeply, feeling the cool comfort of darkness. It's over, then. After all this time, I got my revenge, for Fyl, for my parents, for Sera. I have no idea what happens next. But at least I've gotten that much. Calfex lets me linger there wordlessly, and when I look up again I notice for the first time the shapes just past the canopy. A pair of guards wearing armor, Loci at their hips. "Am I in trouble?" I ask.

"Legally?" Calfex asks. "No. Aberdeen violated the laws of the krova-yan in front of hundreds of witnesses. His life was forfeit and yours to claim."

I glance again at the guards. "Then . . . what about not legally?"

"Not legally, you are more in trouble than maybe any person in the Republic," Calfex replies. "You have absolutely no idea the chaos you've caused."

I look around uneasily for any sign of my friends, but it's just me and Calfex. "What do you mean?" I ask.

"The balance of power in Marovia hung on a delicate thread between Grandmaster Madison's Traditionalists and the disunification of his opposition. By killing his heir and exposing Aberdeen, the vaunted, neutral peacemaker, as a crony, you took that delicate balance and shattered it into a thousand pieces. When word spread of what Aberdeen had done, desecrating the krova-yan on the most sacred of grounds, it set off a firestorm, and reports that he'd been helping Marius cheat the whole time threw oil on the fire. Senator Madison's opposition, always disjointed, united for the first time against him, figured this was their moment, while he was still vulnerable. A vote to remove was called on the Senate floor for the first time in two centuries. Madison was voted out."

I exhale sharply, trying to take it all in. "So he's gone?"

"Oh, no, that would be far too simple," Calfex says. "Madison refused to resign. Perhaps his grief had driven him mad, or perhaps he simply couldn't let himself be beaten. He claimed this was an illegal coup and ordered his Enforcers to execute all the senators who'd voted against him. They marshaled their own forces and fought back and just like that we found ourselves embroiled in a civil war. Wizard fought Wizard in the streets of Arbormont, setting the city ablaze in a fire that's still burning. A half dozen different senators have all claimed their legitimacy to the title of Grandmaster, even as they gather their private armies to take it by force. In this chaos, every party has decided to take their stand. Sithar, the Kindrali Isles, even the Velkschen have declared sovereignty. The entire Republic is burning. All because of you."

I feel dizzy, light-headed, even though I'm lying down. It's hard to process, unimaginable, consequences begetting consequences on a scale I couldn't even conceive. "I take it the Order of Nethro won't be visiting the Senate," I say, mostly to say something.

"The Senate is gone," Calfex replies. "Burned to the ground. And a third of the senators with it."

I have to fight back the urge to laugh. Everything I'd done was to take down the Senate. And I've somehow destroyed it without ever setting foot inside. I wonder what Whispers is thinking, wherever she is out there. Is she proud, or horrified? I'm relieved by how little I care.

"Am I safe here?" I ask Calfex.

"For now," she says. "When the war broke out, the conflict hit here as well. A battle erupted between the professors loyal to Aberdeen and those of us who were against him. My side won." Her eyes twinkle with cunning. "By the remaining professors of Blackwater, I've been appointed temporary headmaster. This school was always meant to be a safe haven, a place outside of politics. I intend to keep it that way for as long as I can."

I'm still at a loss for words, but it feels like a situation where I need to say something. "I didn't... I didn't mean for this to happen."

"This Republic was always a pile of kindling," Calfex says. "You just sparked the flame."

I know I should maybe let her words sit there, but there's something about her manner I have to understand, if only to get my bearings. "You sound almost happy about it."

She pauses thoughtfully, choosing each word with utmost care. "When I spoke of the principles of the Order of Nethro, I meant every word I said," she explains. "I believe I was put on this earth to bring balance, to restore order, to bring justice to the corrupt and the cruel. For very long, I have sat and watched as the Aberdeens and the Madisons of the world have wielded their influence unfairly." She pauses again, a real moment of consideration, and when she speaks again, her voice is barely a whisper. "And I have seen for too long the cruelty of Wizards running unchecked and the world crying out under our tyranny." Then she rises, smoothing out her suit, and turns to leave. "I should go," she says. "There are many urgent matters I must attend to."

But as she reaches the canopy, I speak again, asking the one last question I need an answer to. "Is that why you chose me? Why you put me in the challenges, why you gave me advice? Because... you thought I might do something like this?"

She laughs, genuinely laughs, for the first time I can recall. "Never in my wildest imaginings would I have thought you could do something like *this*," she says. "No. I chose you because I like you." Then she looks at me, and in that moment she looks decades younger, decades more vulnerable, with the deep melancholy of an old wound. "And because you have your father's eyes."

The moment hangs over us, long and resonant, a moment beyond words. "Professor . . . ?" I ask at last.

But she's turned away. "Enough chatter," she says, pushing open the canopy. "I imagine there are a few other people you'd like to speak to."

She gestures across the room, and I see someone else, a girl with black hair and amber eyes, a girl whose smile instantly melts away my pain. "Marlena," I say, and she rushes over to me, to my side.

"You're alive." She clutches my hand and brings it up to her lips, kissing it again and again. "Thank the Gods. You made it."

"I made you a promise that I'd come back to you, didn't I?" I say. "I always keep my promises."

She leans over me, kissing me, and I run my hands through her hair and hold her tight, filling myself with the sensation, with her touch, with her love. "You did it," she says. "You really did it. Aberdeen, Marius, the Senate . . . you took down all of them."

"I couldn't have done it without you." I run the back of my hand along her cheek, and she leans into the touch. "We're in this together. Forever."

Then there are other footsteps pounding toward me, a bunch of them. More faces sprint into the room, surrounding my bedside. Tish. Zigmund. Talyn.

Calfex leaves, letting the curtain billow shut behind her. My whole body still hurts, but I force myself up because I need to see them, all of them. They're all smiling, and Tish is crying, and they huddle tight around me, hugging, laughing, beaming. Marlena squeezes my hand and Talyn pats my shoulder and Zigmund goes in for a hug so big that Tish has to hold him back.

"You were amazing out there," Talyn says, beaming with pride. "You beat that smug son of a bitch."

"You crushed his ass," Zigmund booms. "Hell yeah!"

Tish leans in, squeezing my shoulder, and I lean over to wrap them in a hug. "Have you heard what's happened? With the war? With the uprisings?" Tish leans forward. "My family is leading the fight on the islands. We are your allies in this war."

Zigmund proudly pounds a fist to his chest. "The Velkschen fight, too, once more to be free folk. The Frostwolves bite back. We can join our blades in the fight."

"The Xintari Kingdom officially remains neutral," Talyn adds. "But my father has written to express his deep admiration for my role in dismantling the Marovian Republic and boasts to all of how this was his dream for me all along."

"So you got your glory after all."

Talyn shrugs with a sly grin. "It's funny how things work out when you make the right choice."

"So that's it then," I say, still trying to wrap my mind around it. "The Republic's shattered."

"You did it," Marlena says, a tear running down her cheek, and I think I'm crying now, too, because I can't believe how happy I am that I get to see her again, to see her safe. "You changed the world."

"*We* did it. Together," I say. "And we did it our own way. For us."

"For us," she repeats, squeezing tightly against me. She leans down, kissing my forehead, running a hand along my cheek. I press against her, savoring her touch, the look in her eyes. "You had us all worried back there during the duel. I really thought... for a moment there... I thought I might not get to see you again."

Zigmund shakes his head dismissively. "I always knew she'd win. She has a wolf's heart."

Talyn grins. "No. A dragon's."

"All that matters right now is that we're alive," I tell the four of them, and now I'm definitely crying, even though I'm smiling and laughing. "We're alive and we're together. Let's treasure that."

There are moments in life when I feel like I'm out of my body, like I'm looking back on it as an old woman through the haze of time. There are moments that feel like memories, even as they happen. This is one of those moments, one I'll cherish deeply for the rest of my life, a moment of calm and love, a moment that matters.

The future is uncertain, stormy, inscrutable. There will be pain, and loss, and longing. There will be war and blood and death. But right now, in this moment, this forever moment, I have peace and I have safety and I have the people I love most by my side. I have loyal friends. I have a girl who looks at me with unconditional acceptance, a girl who sees me for exactly who I am and wants nothing more than to be by my side, a girl whose kisses feel like sunshine. I have this. I'll always have this.

I fought against the Aberdeens and the Madisons, against the institutions of Blackwater and the Senate. Now I'll fight for the people I love.

"All right," I say to them, to my love, to my friends, to my allies, to my family. "We burned the old world down. Now let's win ourselves a new one."

Acknowledgments

Every book takes a journey to publication, but this one felt more like an epic quest, forged in fire and blood and tears (and more than my fair share of whiskey). And like any wanderer on a quest, I never would've made it without a truly incredible network of people supporting me every step of the way.

Thank you, once again, to my amazing agent, Sara Crowe. You were with me every step of this journey, from that first excited "YES!" when I sent you the pitch through all the bumps and swerves along the way. As always, here's to this one and many more.

To the absolutely brilliant Laura Schreiber, who acquired this book and saw its potential, who helped me guide it through its messy drafts and find its beating heart. So much of this book comes from Laura's incredible guidance, her patience, her wisdom. Laura, you truly are one of the greatest editors in the industry. Thank you for everything.

To the team at Little, Brown Books for Young Readers who helped shape this book and get it out so beautifully into the world. Thank you to Hallie Tibbetts for the kindness and enthusiasm, and to T.S. Ferguson for shepherding it through the transition. Thank you as well to Cheryl Lew, Emilie Polster, and Stefanie Hoffman. And thank you to Mike Heath for a truly stunning cover!

To the wonderful friends who were there for me when I needed encouragement or feedback or someone to explain how to describe a dress: Owen Javellana, Chelsa Lauderdale, Cat Valman, Coral Nardandrea, and Jessica Yang. May the group chat always flourish.

To the writing peers without whom I never would've made it through 2020: Kelly Loy Gilbert, Jilly Gagnon, Tara Sim, Randy Ribay, Emily A. Duncan, Julia Dao, E. K. Johnston, Emma Berquist, and Linsey Miller.

And then there are all the friends I couldn't have done this without, who were always there with a drink or a laugh or a game of Jackbox: the Late Night PB D&D Crew, the Bullmoose Party, the Norcal Board Game Buds.

To my family: Anya and Simon and Pola, Yakov, Yulya, Marina and Daniel. I love you all.

And of course... to Sarah and Alex, my two greatest loves, my whole heart. For you. Always for you.

About the Author

ANDREW SHVARTS is the author of the Royal Bastards trilogy. He has a BA in English Literature and Russian from Vassar College. He works for Pixelberry Studios, making mobile games like High School Story, Choices, and more. Andrew lives in San Jose, California, with his wife, son, and two kittens. He can be found on Twitter @Shvartacus.